CHAPTER ONE – RUBY

You've never had a day, ...

"Happy six-year anniversary to you and Neil, baby sis," Amber says. I tuck the phone between my chin and shoulder as I shove the key in the door of my tiny rented house. "Are you doing anything nice for it?"

Music blares from the television, but there's no sign of the remote as usual. Bloody Neil.

"Oh, you know. The usual," I stutter. The five new Xbox games covering the floor distract me from asking if all couples stop celebrating their anniversaries early on, as Neil told me. I hold in my sigh. No present for me and I'll pay rent for both of us again this month.

I yank my hairband out of my ponytail and shake my blond hair free, cracking my neck as I do. "Yuck. Do you always smell of yeast after working in the cookery school, or is it just because I'm in a bakery?"

A cooperative bakery where I work all the hours I can to earn capital to make a success of my business, Naughty Treats. Fuck my life.

"No, I don't. Speaking of which, have you thought any more about my earlier message about coming home to run our family's cookery school?"

"Yes, but Amber—"

3

"You'd work with Chef Garett, your second favourite chef of all time and number one on your list of chefs you'd happily cook naked with... platonically, of course, with no sexual feelings."

I roll my eyes as I chuckle. "I said that one time."

"Just think what you could learn from him."

As Amber continues her sales pitch, huffing and puffing sounds from my kitchen. Maybe Neil decided to cook something special for our anniversary after all. I can't remember when he's cooked for me before.

"I'll think about it. But I have a life here with Neil." I force a smile so she can hear happiness down the phone. "And there's the business with Viv. They're important."

"But are you happy running Naughty Treats with her?"

"Sure," I lie.

I feel a pull to return home. As my relationship has soured, I've thought more about the little cookery school in the Cotswolds and the troublesome family I left to move with Neil.

"Although, I bet there's lots of things I could do at the school." Ideas of cooking events we could run, especially with a chef as experienced as Garett, bake in my head. Halloween is at the end of the month. We could cook—

Something clatters in the kitchen, but it barely registers over the music channel playing something I don't recognise.

"What about seasonal events? I've always wanted to do more of them, but I haven't got your creativity. You could make it your own." Amber's cajoling displays

GO COOK YOURSELF

Rebecca Chase

Copyright

To all the women who have been told their love of book boyfriends has made their expectations too high, I tell you to keep the bar where it is.

No one gets to tell you what you deserve.

the sales and organisational skills my younger brother, Jem, and I missed out on, but I can't go.

"But I'm not qualified to run a cookery school. I'd spend all day catastrophising and probably burn the place down in the first twenty-four hours."

Amber laughs. "You're not still the teenager who left her recipe on the gas hob and set it alight, causing all of us to scream and run around the kitchen like it was the end of days."

"Thank goodness Kath popped it in a metal bowl and ran it under a tap." I giggle. "Is she still as calm as ever?"

"Yes, and she's still the cookery school kitchen assistant. With her skills, you wouldn't need to worry about being unqualified."

"But—"

"Do you remember when I FaceTimed you with a tour of the place four years ago when we moved premises to a new barn?"

I drop to the berry loveseat sofa—the one I picked out with Neil during happier times—finding the remote shoved down the side. "Yes..."

"You loved it. You suggested things about décor that made the place even more special. You could make this work."

"I know—"

"So it's a maybe?" Amber presses.

I sigh even as I smile. I have to save face for deciding to move here in the first place. I must stick things out, and maybe I can make Naughty Treats a success so we can finally turn a profit.

My fingers tap the remote.

"I can't up and leave my life now. Neil wouldn't cope without me. And—" A smash drags me to the kitchen. It's going to be a mess. Cleaning up my kitchen and no present. *Happy anniversary to me*. I mute the music channel and toss the remote on the sofa. "I'll call you later. But think about finding someone else. Love you," I add before hanging up.

The huffing and puffing with added grunts are louder now that I've stopped the music.

"What is going—"

My phone nearly slips out of my sweaty palm at the sight of Neil and Viv banging on my kitchen counter, his blotchy pink bum bouncing in front of my eyes.

My prized handcrafted bowl, which Amber had gifted me on the day I started Naughty Treats, is in fragments on the kitchen floor.

"You pair of cheating, bowl-smashing bastards!"

Neil's pumping stops. He's still huffing and puffing as he does when I ask him to fix the front door so I don't have to throw myself at it to open it when it's damp outside.

"Ruby," he shouts. Viv falls to the floor because Neil's no longer pinning her to my worktop with his awkward thrusts.

"Amber offered me a job, but I wasn't going to take it because I cared too much about you and the business." I'm still talking. This must be shock. "But you both seem to be doing okay without me."

Neil's mouth gapes.

I stumble to the doorway.

"Ruby, it didn't mean anything," Neil whines. His voice used to make me lick my lips. Years ago, his moans would echo through me when he tasted my signature chocolate orange liqueur frosting, but those days are long gone.

"Ruby," Viv croaks from the sticky kitchen floor.

Ice snakes through my veins. She's nothing to me now.

"Babe!" Neil reaches for his trousers surprisingly quickly for a guy who can't get out of bed before lunchtime. His sorry excuse for an erection sinks before my eyes as a wide-eyed Viv pulls down her dress.

"Don't babe me. Don't talk to me."

I hide my eyes with my hands as if that will make me disappear. At least I don't need to plug away at this sexless, emotionless relationship that reached its sell-by date a couple of years ago.

"It was an accident," Viv stutters.

"Sure. Neil tripped, and his dick fell in you when he smashed my favourite bowl." My body shakes, and vomit climbs up my throat. "I'm done with everything. I'm leaving."

I swivel on my heel like I've practised the move a thousand times before, but remember I'm not done and turn and point at Neil. Thankfully he's not waggling his penis anymore but struggling with his zipper. Even at my five-foot-three height, I'm a force to be reckoned with. Projectile vomit threatens to destroy the surge of confidence this catastrophe has given me.

"You can deal with the rent, which you've never contributed to, alone. And I'm taking your Xbox."

"Wait," he bellows before a guttural scream explodes from his mouth. My mouth drops open, and I cover it quickly, swallowing down bile. Neil bursts into tears, not because of our dead relationship or because

7

I'm taking the game console that I'm fed up with tripping over every day. He's caught his dick in his zipper.

"Karma's a bitch," I mumble.

I freeze in the doorway. Should I stay and help? *No.* I'm not such a doormat that I'll rescue the man I caught cheating on me.

I throw the first aid box from the shelf at Viv. "He's your problem now."

I stumble to the bathroom in time to vomit into the toilet before hastily filling a bag. The things that matter—my cooking equipment—are still in the car. My family's cookery school owns the best stuff anyway.

The items significant to me have more than monetary value. In the boot of my car are the hand-carved spoons my grandad made for me and my grandma's favourite spatula, which she bought the month she set up the original Cloud Cookery School.

"Babe, don't leave me. Viv was just sex," Neil says as Viv dabs at his flaccid and bleeding penis. I modelled my first Naughty Treat cookies on that pathetic excuse for a penis.

I sigh, shove my hair into a bun before yanking the Xbox's cables from the wall, and tuck the game console under my arm.

"I don't care anymore. You don't deserve me." I don't know if I believe that, but I want to hurt him as he hurt me. I swipe at the tears that brim my eyes and snap, "The sex wasn't great when we met, and then it got worse. I'm done."

I stumble over Neil's five pairs of expensive trainers before losing my shit and throwing them out of the front door and onto the front lawn.

"You didn't even mow the lawn," I yell over my shoulder as if it matters.

I slam the door hard to make a dramatic exit, which is pointless, as my last words were about mowing the damn lawn. I speed-dial my sister as I throw my bag and the Xbox into my rusty tin bucket of a car.

I have no money, no partner, and no friends, and I'm about to make a ridiculous decision that will put me into the orbit of one of the sexiest chefs ever to hand-roll pasta.

Amber answers on the second ring. "I know you'll say you can't come, but please consider my offer again. The doctor told me I have to go on maternity leave early and—"

"I'm on my way. I'll be with you in about four hours," I announce loud enough for the nosey cow at number five to hear. I point at her net curtains, which suddenly flop down. She could've told me my boyfriend was sleeping with my business partner. She's mentioned the lawn often enough.

From the driver's seat, I close my eyes and fist and stretch my hands as if making biscuit dough. My pulse beats out of control.

I remember all the times Neil encouraged me to work late because we needed the money and the times Viv checked when I was coming home so we could "discuss the business." I flip down my visor and stare at my wild-eyed appearance. My bun is already a shaggy mess, and the dark circles under my eyes remind me that I've strained under the relationship and trying to make the business a success for too long.

"But you said your business and life were too important," Amber fumbles through her words. I bet she's rubbing her baby bump. This pregnancy and the fact that her naval officer husband is away on a submarine for some secret mission have got to her. Another reason why I must go home. I need to be with her and run that school.

But she's a confident and skilled cookery school manager, and you're not. I glare at myself. *Suck it up, buttercup. You're going home and learning cooking skills from a hot chef, which will help you develop a better dirty treats business.*

"I'm coming, and I have an Xbox for you to play on until the baby comes. So you can put your feet up and—"

"But what about Neil?" Amber crows.

"I don't have a boyfriend anymore." I grip the steering wheel as I run through all the reasons why staying would be a bigger mistake than going to the cookery school.

"Good. I hated that guy. He was lazy, selfish, and never supported your dreams."

"And he broke the bowl you gave me when I started Naughty Treats."

And he slept with my friend and business partner in my kitchen. But I'll wait until we're sharing cookie dough ice cream to tell her that.

"The bastard. I'll break him if I get the chance."

I laugh long and loud. It was what I needed my sister to say. Once the twins are born, Neil's a goner.

Pregnant with twins and without her husband, she must have been struggling for months. My true best friend and sister, who's always there for me, needed me.

"I'm sorry for not coming home sooner. I've wasted all this time in an ugly city with a crappy boyfriend—"

"Ruby, you can beat yourself up when you get here. Just come home so I can cuddle you."

"I am sorry, though. I'll do whatever it takes to make it up to you."

"I'll put you through the wringer, don't you worry," she jokes. "Can you start tomorrow?"

"Yep. I can't wait." My reflection tells me off for lying, and I stick my tongue out at my brown eyes and freckled nose. "I'll be at yours in four hours and then start tomorrow morning at the cookery school."

"Fantastic. See you soon, baby sister," Amber adds. "Love you to the sky and back."

"And even further," I say softly before hanging up.

I glance through the window of my former house, where a weeping Neil holds himself while Viv throws rolls of bandages at him. I start the car, which splutters.

"Come on, girl." Quickly, she starts revving like she's about to pass out. "It's now or never."

My tyres squeal my goodbye as I shout, "Go fuck yourself," to my old life.

CHAPTER TWO – GARETT

"**G**ive me my dog back, you piece of shit," I yell from the pavement outside the beautiful Regency apartment building in town. I hate this place, and not just because it belongs to Clive, my nemesis.

My phone rings as Cookie, my typically bouncy Cavapoo, stares at me from the window. His tail droops as he paces the windowsill with his lion paws. I love those paws. They're the ones I usually squeeze before Cookie tucks up to me in bed or that tap on the kitchen floor like he's doing his best Fred Astaire impression when I arrive home. I answer the call as I stare at Cookie. His brown eyes carry the sadness of an elderly widow at her sweetheart's funeral.

"You okay, mate? You're looking a bit red-faced. It's obvious behind that ugly beard of yours." Clive, the man I started a restaurant with before he stole our business and stopped every restaurant in the area from employing me, laughs down the phone.

There's nothing ugly about my trimmed beard. It lines my sharp jaw. Before I swore off women because nothing was more important than making the business successful, Clive and I spent every night partying in all the local pubs and clubs. Every woman wanted to be around me and stroke my rough dusting of stubble; many beautiful women came home with me, too. Clive was left trying to pick up whoever would have him. I stroke my jaw purposefully. I bet the prick is watching me from behind a curtain.

"You always were jealous of me. Is that why you told the judges it was your pasta and then kicked me out of our partnership? That award for the Best Cotswold Restaurant should be mine," I snap. "You duped those judges."

"But you don't have a restaurant, mate." He chuckles. "It's my restaurant and my pasta recipe, and you can't prove otherwise, or you wouldn't be working at some crappy cookery school in the countryside."

My limbs shake. Blood thunders through my head. "Give me back my fucking dog. He's not a gimmick for a restaurant." Clive thought the world's cutest dog would do wonders for our social media. The moment I saw those beautiful brown eyes, the teddy bear nose, and giant paws two years ago, I fell in love. It's the only time I've been in love, and it's with a dog who's been taken from me. I fist my hands. "Cookie was never a gimmick to me."

Suddenly, Clive looms from the window. Cookie doesn't glance at him. He only has eyes for me.

That's my boy. He knows who his daddy is.

"You can have Cookie back, but you have to announce that I'm a genius and you're a crap chef who wouldn't know what end of a spoon to use." My eyes are like pins as I take a deep breath and try to centre myself. Clive throws his head back and laughs like a drunken idiot. "Don't worry, Garett. I'd never make you say that. I'm never giving you back your dog—well, not until you tell me what ingredients are in your secret pasta recipe. Oh, and while you're at it, I want ten thousand pounds, too."

He doesn't need the money. He's a nepo baby with more money than sense, but he wants me to suffer. I don't have a penny to my name, and he knows. He ensured it.

I bare my teeth but regret it instantly as Cookie's face creases with a whimper.

"Aren't you late for work?" Clive chuckles. My heart rate climbs as I check my silver-plated watch. It was a gift to myself the day I got my first paycheck. I'm already five minutes late. I open my mouth in a silent scream. "Best get to your shitty job if you want to earn enough money to get your dog back."

I stick my middle finger up at him as I end the call.

Cookie won't hear or understand, but I still mouth to my fur baby, "I'm coming for you, beautiful. I won't let the bastard keep you for much longer."

Fuck Clive. I won't let him see that he's got to me. Besides, I'm already late. An extra twenty minutes won't make a difference. Amber will cover for me. I swagger to the bright blue van with "Cloud Cookery School" painted in white bubble writing. An older man in a pricey four-by-four beeps his horn, but I ignore him as I climb into the vehicle.

Sweat runs down my neck and beneath my crisp checked shirt. I'm grinding my teeth again. The dentist will kick my ass for this. I pop in the mouth guard I keep in the car and start the van.

I grip the guard between my teeth. I shouldn't be using it during the day, but when your best mate destroys your career, you need something to get through the days. I don't trust anyone enough to let them in, even for sex. It's not like I'm going to drink my pain away. I can't afford it. I resist the temptation to check my bank balance before I pull away from the curb. I looked this morning, and I had less than two hundred pounds to my name.

My pocket vibrates with a call.

"I'm coming, Amber," I grunt as I let the call go to voicemail. At least the cookery school pays me next week, although it won't put a dent in what I need to give Clive to get my baby back. I need to find extra work if I'm going to get through the next months.

The ten-mile drive to the cookery school gives me too much time to think. According to the recently "fancified" website, it's "nestled in the heart of the Cotswolds with stunning views that will make you fall in love with the beautiful countryside." I open the side windows. The smell of manure hasn't made this city boy fall in love with the countryside. The sight of autumnal harvests and the leaves turning from green to burning oranges and reds should fill me with excitement. But what if I haven't got my boy back by Christmas? He might forget who I am, or Clive could neglect him.

A tractor pulls out in front of me. I slam my palm on the horn, and the driver shakes his hand in a rude gesture and calls me a wanker. Fumes replace manure while the grind of gears fills my ears.

"Get out of my way," I snarl. The phone in my pocket rings again. The vibrations are the closest thing I've had to sex in a year. I shake my head. With thoughts like that, it's hard to believe I used to be a bit of a charmer.

I bang my fist on the steering wheel as the van climbs the hill. Fucking tractors. As if the driver hears me, he pulls into a field.

I should be excited about my first Halloween cooking classes at the school at the end of the month and planning what we'll cook. But then I remember dressing Cookie up as a spider last year with all these black legs hanging off him. He was hilarious, running around my flat with his extra legs flapping.

The phone rings again. I should have put it on hands-free. Amber left me a voicemail yesterday asking me to come in early today, but I needed to see Cookie.

I was so stupid when I let Clive put everything for the business in his name. My lying parents messed up my credit rating after taking out credit cards in my name, so all the contracts are under his name, and he'd registered Cookie at the restaurant's address. I grind my teeth again. He can get stuffed if he thinks he'll learn my secret pasta ingredients.

Expletives fly from my mouth as I pass the pub that hugs the cookery school's land. Its For Sale sign barely registers. It's been there the entire month I've worked at Clouds. It would make a fine Italian restaurant. The cookery school, essentially a barn with an extension, looms from behind the pub. The extension housing the reception and an office on the ground floor are all decorated impeccably, and I love how the mezzanine floor looks out over the cookery school. The whole place is beautiful, but it's not my place. I want to run a bustling restaurant again and be able to add new dishes while acting as the king of the business.

I yank the steering wheel to the side, relishing the flying gravel. I've lost everything, but I focus on Cookie's brown eyes begging me to get him back.

"What the hell?" My heart jumps into my throat as I slam on the brakes and stop inches from a crappy rust bucket of a car. Some idiot has parked in the restaurant's space, which is clearly marked in massive black letters.

My face flames as I throw open the door. The crunching of the gravel acts like a soundtrack to my wrath. I must be at least twenty minutes late but still stride like the boss.

Wicksy, the kitchen assistant, calls my name. He probably wants to tell me about his new conquest of the week. As if I care. I need to bellow at the person in my space. Grumbling voices come from the barn that adjoins the building.

I sidestep a box of seasonal decorations that should be in the back room. They need storing until the wine tasting and wreath making at the end of November. We can't risk being sued by a client.

I push my sleeves up, readying myself for an argument, but my phone vibrates with a message. I shouldn't look. Clive's done this each time I've stood outside his house to see my fluff ball.

I check it anyway. The video message breaks me. Cookie bounds after a ball. His tail wags, and his ears flap in the breeze. The words accompanying the message cut me deep: "Tick, tock, buddy. Cookie won't recognise you soon."

I aim the phone at the nearest wall, but a scream stops me. My kitchen should be revered. It would be if it were my restaurant kitchen. I roar around my mouth guard and shove open the double glass doors, storming into the kitchen ready to raise hell at whoever is screaming. I'm confronted by strangers running around the kitchen while blood drips from the hand of a curvy blonde stranger.

Kath, the school's original kitchen assistant, storms past me, first aid kit in hand, shouting, "Ruby thought she'd show the class how to bake cookies while we waited for you, but she tried to catch a falling knife."

"Who the hell is Ruby?" My yell is muffled, but Kath understands even with my nonsensical mouth guard–filled noise.

"She is," she huffs. That's when the blonde stares at me. Her perfect curves and big brown eyes transfix me even with carnage exploding around us. The blonde, aka Ruby, mouths, "Sorry" as Kath adds, "She's our new cookery school manager."

My mouth guard snaps in two.

CHAPTER THREE – GARETT

"**W**hat did she think she was doing?" My booming voice fills the reception area as Kath wraps a bandage around Ruby's hand. The scent of blood is in the air. Not even the sugary globs of marshmallow that had somehow stuck to my hands before I gave up trying to clean the counters could mask it. "What the hell is wrong with her?"

"You can ask me directly. I'm right here," Ruby snaps from her seat next to Kath.

I glance at her briefly and consider finding a spare mouth guard. Her blouse and jacket are so tight it's a wonder they're holding her boobs in. Her skirt grips her curvy ass like that's its only calling in life.

"I thought it was a children's party. That's what it says in the diary." She winces as Kath slowly bandages her. I can do a much better job, but I'm not going near our new useless manager.

"Didn't you think the grey perms and the layers of nylon and polyester were a giveaway? Bloody hell, what a mess." I fist my hands. "And you tried to catch a knife. Have you ever been in a kitchen before?"

"I was flustered. I know how to handle working in a kitchen."

"Are you sure?" I growl. "You know making a mediocre cup of tea doesn't count, right?"

"Garett, you need to cheer up. It was an accident. And those ladies will be back in five minutes after their early break. Homemade chocolate cookies will only keep them calm for so long," Kath replies, her voice soft. "You've got a session to run."

"And she has trashed my kitchen." I point at Ruby as if I still don't want to speak to her even though I just did. "There's marshmallow goop sticking to the demonstration counters and strands of dried spaghetti all over the floor."

I catch Wicksy staring at Ruby with big moon-like eyes. He usually reserves that stare for when we have a group of hot women in for a cookery class. I grind my teeth loudly.

"Why are you standing around, Wicksy? You need to tidy up. Get in the kitchen and sort it out before we lose these clients."

"Yes, Chef," Wicksy shouts before rushing out of the room.

"I'm going to have words with Amber about this." I pause, my brow furrowing. "I'm guessing Amber is fine."

When Kath nods, I add, "So why didn't anyone tell me we were getting a new manager? You'd think I deserve to know, or am I just inconsequential to all of you?"

"It would help if you turned up on time or answered your phone," Ruby grumbles.

"It would help if you didn't try and catch falling knives or—"

Ruby stands and faces me. "I checked the diary, and it said it was a children's party. I set out the room wrong. I thought I'd try baking with them. They were all asking for you, but you were late, which you could have warned us about. You're not perfect. Right now, you're far from it. You could try acting less like a petulant child."

"You shouldn't be working here," I retort. I'm being ridiculous. But I need this job to get Cookie back and to regain some self-respect. Pissed off clients mean bad reviews and no customers for our classes. "I am going to sort out this mess. I will put on my charm to keep everyone happy."

"That has to be seen to be believed. I'll have to run out to all the local villages to tell them how great your transformation can be," she mumbles.

"How about you do that and never return?" I snarl. "And don't let the door hit you in the ass on your way out."

As I leave the reception area, Kath says, "Ruby, do you need a moment? Maybe go and sit in your car for a second."

"Hopefully, space will help me forget that jerk."

I turn back and glare. I'll show her how much of a jerk I can be to her while I charm all the ladies to ensure we get their return business and keep our reputation. I give myself a shake, push my shoulders back, and force my fakest smile as I enter the kitchen.

"Ladies, it's time to get your cook on. Are you ready to make the best meal you've ever eaten?"

CHAPTER FOUR – RUBY

I grip my bandage tightly against my finger. My fingers flick at the corner of the plaster, keeping it secure. The cookery day with the retired businesswomen is into its second hour, and it's finally going well, but I can't stop peeling this thing.

Garett Kelsey, number one on my list of hot chefs, stares at me, but his wild eyes and snarling mouth don't dampen his sexiness one bit. It's impossible to look away from the hint of a beard that highlights the sharp cut of his jawline. His big brown eyes are mesmerising. None of that matters, though, because the guy is a grade-A arsehole.

The day has only improved for clients because of his charm and cooking skills. My day continues to get worse. I want to tell him that I'm not useless in the kitchen and that it was anxiety that caused my accident. I should have smoothed over our argument earlier, too, for Amber and the cookery school's sakes, but he won't talk to me.

He rolls his eyes before returning to his focaccia dough. That's the most attention I've had from him since he shouted at me.

"Keep folding it like this," he says to the ladies gathered around him. His smile is broad and welcoming. "Now, you want to really stretch the dough. Imagine you're on a date with a young suitor, and you're seducing him with your hands."

One of the women giggles.

"Marjorie over there knows what I'm talking about," he says with a wink.

I study his broad hands and thick forearms as he works the dough. His muscles are taut with each movement. My gaze travels up his arms to his swollen biceps. No chef should look like he does.

Ruby, all men are dicks, remember? Especially this one.

"Now, ladies, I want to let you into a secret," he says. "Come closer."

The ladies instantly do as he requests. His apron, displaying the cookery school's cloud logo, is wrapped around him in a way that highlights his frame. Mine makes me feel a bit more homely than it does sexy, but his clings to his washboard stomach.

"I had a lot of fun experiences when I worked in kitchens when I was younger," he reveals in a voice so seductive I have to stop myself from staring in shock.

He's as gorgeous as social media suggests. His eyelashes frame his big brown eyes, and his whole face lights up when he smiles. It's as if everyone in the room stops breathing to soak up his presence.

His voice drops to a rough timbre. "My favourite customers were ladies more mature than me. One night, after we closed the restaurant, a couple of infamous actors stayed for a lock-in."

Betty, one of the pensioners who's given him the eye for the last hour, gasps.

"One of the actors was stunning. So beautiful, the kind of woman who has wisdom and experience. It gave her that glow that was impossible to resist. She was absolute trouble, too. Within minutes of locking the doors, I was dancing on the bar with her."

"Who was it?" Betty asks.

He cocks his finger, and Betty shuffles closer. His eyes twinkle. "Surely, you know that a gentleman never tells."

The group giggles while jostling each other. One of them fans themselves as he pulls and stretches the dough. I lick my lips, my head tilting as I stare at the slow and gentle way he grips it.

"But I will tell you, ladies, that she tried to take me home with her. I nearly went, but I wouldn't have kept up. She was feral, like all sexy older women are."

Cue raucous laughter from his new fifteen fangirls. Fanladies?

I laugh along with them, although if Amber were here, she'd elbow me for the worst fake laugh in England. I've got to do something to make him talk to me and to hide my crushed confidence.

Garett's gaze snaps to me, and it's full of daggers. I choke on my breath. I splutter and cough, which makes his stare worse. I ease myself out of the room, bumping into Wicksy. The rosemary he's preparing for the group tickles my nose as I hide in a corner behind Kath.

"It's okay, Ruby, sweetheart," Kath murmurs as she rubs my back. The air conditioning whirs in the background, and I grip the edges of my suit jacket—well, Amber's suit jacket. It barely gives me room to breathe as it is. It's too big for her slight frame but fits like a straitjacket on me. Yet it still fits better than the pencil skirt my arse tests the seams of. "What you saw earlier was a blip. Garett isn't always this grumpy."

"Yes, he is," Wicksy replies. His wavy hair bounces as he carries the plates of rosemary to the ladies. He looks like the adored social media influencer and fitness coach Joe Wicks. I'm guessing that's the reason for the nickname. "The way he is with the clients, especially the female ones, is different from how he treats us."

"It wasn't all my fault," I say quietly in case Garett has impressive hearing to accompany his skills in seducing older women. "He wasn't answering his phone, and Amber couldn't help because her head was stuck in a toilet bowl. The diary said it was a children's party."

"I know. And the way you set up the room was so sweet." Kath moves around the table, effortlessly adding things to it for lunch. She's done this for so long that she could do it in her sleep. Sparkling cutlery and glasses of water turn the blue space into something suitable for a banquet.

The same space was laid out three hours earlier with party games and balloons. Amber never makes mistakes, but the children's party is next week, not today. "As soon as I saw that it wasn't a group of children coming through the door, I should have changed my plans."

I collapse into a chair.

"The huffs of the group this morning were like the noises the women who don't like my chat-up lines make," Wicksy adds before collecting the next batch of rosemary.

"I tried my best."

"Yes, you did. Amber will be proud of you," Kath coos.

"I shouldn't have let them fluster me."

"You shouldn't have demonstrated how to hold a knife if you weren't sure," Wicksy says with a shrug.

"I am sure." I press my lips together and breathe through my nose. There's no point explaining that my mobile was vibrating in my pocket the entire time because Neil was calling every five minutes. I know how to be professional, and I would have turned my phone off if not for Amber's sickness and Garett not returning my calls. "But I panicked when Betty asked who she could complain to, and then she knocked that knife. The most important rule of grandma's kitchen was never to catch a falling knife. She taught me that when I was a child, and I've never tried to catch one."

"We all make mistakes, Ruby, love," Kath replied. She was grandma's best friend until she died. Kath should have retired, but she's followed the cookery school from its former home in my parents' garden to here and has shown no signs of leaving. "I know you're a fantastic baker. This morning was first day nerves and a lot of anxiety."

"Garett doesn't see it that way. He's treating me like an unwanted guest at a family party, a feeling I'm not alien to after the last couple of years. I tried to start afresh and introduce myself to him properly. Instead, he looks at my hand and walks away without a word."

"Because he's a grumpy bastard." Wicksy stands beside me and gives me those damn puppy dog eyes again. "But I'm not."

"Can I have some help in here?" Garett yells.

"See," Wicksy adds, elbowing me before shouting, "Yes, Chef."

Garett sets the ladies to work on the bread with another quip and a wink.

I make fake dough with my hands to reduce my anxiety as he swaggers around the kitchen, giving the women tips and tricks to add flavour or stop the dough from sticking to their hands. I could pick up some techniques for my baking from the renowned chef, but I'm like a can of soda that has been dropped and people are too scared to open it because it will explode everywhere. "Stop picking at the edge of your plaster, or you'll undo your bandage," Kath whispers.

I pull myself up to my total, albeit short, height. "I'm going to make Garett like me," I announce. "Normally, everyone likes me, including animals. I'm going to make this day better, and I'm going to get him onside."

"Ruby," Kath tries to soothe me, but I won't listen.

Wicksy crosses his arms and shakes his head. "He's going to destroy you."

I squeeze my lips tightly and tap my hand against my thigh as I hover near the workstation where Garett presses the dough. He grabs at flour and flutters his fingers. It falls like a powdery white waterfall onto the counter. It's bad enough that he's not following the brief Amber gave me, which she warned me might happen before she hurled her breakfast, but to make it worse, he's sexy even when arrogant.

I roll my eyes, but as he turns to face me, I laugh as if his prowess enamours me. All that earns me is a glare.

"Let's try this again. Hi, Garett. I'm Ruby." He stares right through me, and I offer a glowing smile. "Could you tell me what I need to get prepped next?"

He blinks so slowly that I take a brief second to study his rosy lips. They're as kissable as his handful of TikTok videos suggest. I run my tongue along my bottom lip, imagining that he tastes like he smells, as if cinnamon has been mixed with honey and drizzled on my skin. These fantasies are just memories. The man in front of me is nothing like the one I used to crush on.

"Could you maybe give me a clue?" I stutter as I attempt to tuck my tongue back where it belongs.

He raises an eyebrow and glares. "Here's a clue—"

"Please, help me with the dough, lovely Chef Garett. I'd hate to have a soggy bottom," Betty says with a laugh.

Instantly, he walks around me as if I'm a post dropped rudely in his path, muttering, "Here's a clue. Knives are sharp. Don't try to catch them."

The scent of freshly baked bread is like an aura around him, but even as the smell fills my lungs, anger rips through my skin.

"There's no chance you'd have a soggy bottom, Betty."

His laughter rumbles through the room, and Betty joins in. I fight the temptation to stamp my feet. I want to do my job, make Amber proud, and rebuild the broken bridges with my family. That I wanted to improve my skills from watching his sessions was a mistake. I'm sure he knows techniques I've struggled with, but he'd be too arrogant to show me.

"I'm here today as a ringer. I'm not as old as the rest of them. I'm five years younger," Betty says with a click of her fingers.

He cocks an eyebrow, a smirk across his face. "So why are you here today?"

She pulls a piece of paper from her pocket. I busy myself clearing Garett's bowls at his demonstration counter. Usually, Kath would do it, but I can spy on how Garett works and maybe decipher what he's planning next.

Betty stretches a gold and blue printed flyer onto the worktop, smoothing the creases. "Chef Clive, a god among men, is running a competition on Christmas Eve. He's looking for an amateur who can bake the ultimate Christmas goodies."

Garett's face freezes, but Betty continues. Out of the corner of my eye, I study how he fixes his jaw and scowls at the dough that he's now pummelling like he's in a boxing ring. He lifts and smacks it down before stretching it. He does this again and again while Betty tells him about the competition. Flour flies into the air with every slam. It collects in his hair and sticks to his beard as the sound echoes through the kitchen.

"The best part is that the winner will be invited to work in his restaurant. Applications close tomorrow, so I want to perfect my skills."

Garett remains silent.

"You used to work for Clive," Betty says, confirming my thoughts. His eyes blaze as he thumps the dough. "You must have learnt so much from him."

He pulls and shoves at the dough. He doesn't deserve my rescue, yet I'm walking towards him. I whisper to my feet to stay still and mind their own business, but they don't listen. I'm drawn to the moment like my younger brother was drawn to fresh out-of-the-oven pizza, though the tomato would burn his mouth.

Betty's curls bounce. "And Clive has that special pasta recipe, too, right? His food is sublime. My friends treated me to a meal at his award-winning restaurant the other week. Sadly, they didn't serve the special pasta, but I still felt like a queen. What was he like as a boss and teacher? Did you learn a lot of your skills from him?"

I put on my most sunshine voice as I scoot closer. "Sorry to interrupt, but can I speak with Garett briefly?"

"If you must," Betty replies between pursed lips. Her beady eyes don't leave us as Garett follows me to the corner of the kitchen area.

"So?" Garett snaps.

"So..." I elongate the word, unsure what to add. I've helped him out of a conversation he didn't want to be in and stopped him from overworking Betty's focaccia. Garett fists his hands as if he's still working the dough. That's what I do, but I do it when I'm anxious. He looks more like the Incredible Hulk trying to beat up the air. "So was that story true, about the British television actor? Who was it?" I press on the smile I used with Neil's boring family.

His brown eyes pin me, and he grits his teeth. His dark beard highlights rather than hides his sharp jawline. I swallow loud enough to warn my sister to send reinforcements. I'm picking at my plaster again.

"The television actor?" I squeak. He presses his lips together and cocks his head to the side. "I was trying to help. Look, you'll have to talk to me sooner or later. I'm managing this school until Christmas in Amber's absence."

"Not if I have anything to do with it," he seethes. "Maybe you should spend less time gossiping and 'trying to help' and more time running this place. And you can start with the boxes of decorations in the foyer, which are a trip hazard. Are you trying to destroy the cookery school with accident after accident, or is that a happy coincidence?"

I cover my mouth, but a gasp still escapes. Garett's rugged lips are more like a wrinkly bum as he aims his wrath at me.

"Wicksy told me to leave them there and that he'd sort them out."

"Wicksy wants to get in your pants. He'll say a lot but do nothing. Have you run a cookery school before?" I shake my head and attempt to explain the cooperative bakery, but he cuts me off before I can utter a syllable. "I should have known. Bloody ridiculous. I won't continue to work here if you stay. Either you go, or I go. Now get out of my sight before you ruin this day any more."

He spins on his heel, dismissing me, and I run from the room.

CHAPTER FIVE – RUBY

"**I**'m leaving. I'm so sorry," I cry as soon as Amber picks up the phone. "You'll easily be able to find someone more qualified."

My low heels tap against the wooden floor as I speed through the reception area and out of the building. The burn of my humiliation fights against the chill in the air, and I fumble with Amber's suit jacket. I can't dress right.

"I'm such an embarrassment. I've made it a shitty day for the clients, and Garett said he's going to leave if I don't, and I've messed up. I'm so sorry." I shove the edge of my palm against my eye to stop any tears from falling, but it doesn't make a difference. Tears trickle down my cheeks.

"It's not your fault," Amber replies. That was what grandma said whenever Amber, Jem, or I messed up in the kitchen. But remembering Grandma and all she did for me makes it worse. I wanted to be close to my family today, and for a second in the cookery school, I felt the joy I used to get when I was with my grandma. I close my eyes and breathe deeply. "You're learning and can't beat yourself up for that. It's your first damn day."

"But I keep making all these mistakes, and I trusted Wicksy to move the boxes of Halloween and Christmas decorations that I brought in from your house because he saw I was struggling, but he didn't move them, and I cut myself because I tried to catch a falling knife! And I made the women angry. And Garett hates me and—"

"Take a breath. Firstly, Wicksy is easy to understand. Don't give him jobs that matter. Give those to Kath and let her delegate. He probably fancies you. Wicksy fancies all the women who enter the school, so he'd offer to do any job you asked."

My tears still. Amber is Wonder Woman when it comes to problem-solving. I'm more like Scrappy-Doo— small, useless, and annoying. She got her skills from our project-managing-cookery-school-running parents. I got grandma's cooking skills.

"Secondly, wasn't it supposed to be kids there today?"

"Ummmm..."

"Oh shit, I messed up." It sounds like she's palming her forehead. "The kids are next week. Of course, it's the retired women today. I'm sorry, Ruby. That's on me. But remember that older women love you. You can turn this day around. Pretend they're all as savvy as Grandma was, and you'll be fine. Thirdly, are you okay? How deep was the cut?"

The plaster still peels from my bandaged finger where I've picked it, and my palm throbs. "It's fine. Barely a scrape."

"Liar," Amber replies. "Get Garett to wrap it. He's a good first aider. And when it comes to Garett, there's only one way to deal with him. Listen up, baby sister."

That's it. I can do this.

I'm a strong, confident woman. I've worked with arsehole men before, and I need to get Garett off that pedestal I've had him on and treat him like any other kitchen guy. I stride back into the cookery school and toss Amber's uncomfortable jacket onto the coat stand. The jacket misses the stand and nearly drags a set of glasses off the shelf but stops in time. I shrug as if that was my plan all along.

Wafts of baking bread fill the space. It's like a warm cuddle on a cold day, yeasty yet cosy, and my belly rumbles as I'm reminded of my childhood running into the original cookery school that still sits in the giant shed in my parent's garden. I'd sit on my grandad's lap as my grandma buttered fluffy fresh bread for me. She'd make me close my eyes and guess what extra ingredients she might have added to each fresh batch. As I survey the scene, I long to visit my parents and the original cookery school, but with our fractured relationship, I won't.

Garett looks up, and a shadow crosses his eyes, but he quickly looks down. Is that guilt? Either way, I'm done with his shitty behaviour.

"Ladies," I shout at busy kitchen volume. They lift their gaze as one in my direction. I have Garett's attention, too, although I ignore him. "I have an exciting activity for this afternoon." Betty side-eyes me, but I don't let it dampen my resolve. I pull up my chest and yell, "In my possession are two Cloud Cookery School Best Baker trophies. This afternoon, I challenge you to make the best orange polenta cake. The renowned Chef Garett will judge both the taste and the decoration. We will put that fondant icing from earlier to good use, although I'm sure you can create something more exciting than dinosaurs."

There are murmurs of appreciation. I should have considered this before. All the ladies I've worked with or hung out with, even ones I didn't get on with at school, are competitive when baking, especially when pitted against each other.

"And you can learn icing skills that can help even the deadliest ringer," I add, winking at a suddenly smiling Betty.

Garett tracks me warily as I sashay towards him. I cock my head and shrug. His eyes widen, and I pretend I don't care, but it's nice to be giving the attitude rather than receiving it. "Chef Garett will tell you that it's impossible to cool the cakes in time to ice them and that fondant icing shouldn't go on polenta, but do you know what we say to that?"

The women stare at me expectantly, several of them clasping their hands.

"Do you know what we say?" I holler.

"No," the women reply in unison.

If I'm staying at this cookery school and sorting out my relationship with my family, I've got to manage the grumpy chef. "We say, 'Oh glorious Chef Garett, king of the cooking world and our guru, with your help, we can do anything.'"

Garett purses his lips and grits his teeth. His eyes tighten as he stares back at me.

"So what do you say, Chef Garett? Will you shove those sleeves up to reveal your muscley forearms and give us an afternoon we won't forget? Will you show us things that other chefs wouldn't dare attempt?" I drop my voice like Amber tells me I do so well. Amber explained that Garett responded best to compliments, cheekiness, and teasing. I can do that, although I need practice after never doing it at home. "Do you dare show this room full of excited women what you're capable of?"

He takes a deep breath and releases it. He shakes his head slowly, and I give him a wink.

"Ladies," he announces with his hands in the air, "we've got pasta needing our attention and bread moments away from burning in the oven. At lunch, we dine like queens for this afternoon—"

"You compete to be Cloud Cookery School champions," I cut in before he can argue.

CHAPTER SIX – GARETT

I squeeze the white fondant between my hands as I chat with Marjorie. It's nearly as sugary sweet as Ruby has been since she walked back into my kitchen. I grit my teeth.

"This has been a lot of fun, Garett. I'm glad you let us do it. I'm pretty sure I'm going to win, you know," Majorie says. She nods in the direction of Betty. "Although I think Betty might clinch it. She's very competitive."

Betty rolls out fondant as Ruby talks animatedly, pointing at the cake. Betty says something, and Ruby's melodic laugh carries across the counters, where Marjorie grumbles next to me.

"Maybe we should try something extra to help you win," I reply. And if it means getting one up on Ruby, that would be even better. My grumpiness struggles against her eternal sunshiny ways. Even when I ignored her over lunch, she gave me extra helpings of pasta and beamed at me. "We're going to smash this contest."

I squeeze the fondant ball, rubbing bits between my fingers as I stare at Ruby. She's been like a ball of joy since the argument where I told her I'd leave if she didn't. I can't believe I said that.

Ruby takes the elastic out of her hair. I hold my breath as she shakes her blond hair free before retying it. She's like a mirage in this kitchen. A smudge of icing sugar highlights one of her cheekbones, and I imagine brushing my thumb against it. Maybe I can make her face flush as I do. What is it about having a rival that gets me like this?

She starts walking closer, and I turn to Marjorie, shaking my head and dropping the ball of fondant, worried about what shapes I might create after staring at her. No one needs to see their rival making his idea of their boobs in icing.

"If you give me that white fondant, I can make a panda," Marjorie comments.

"I like pandas," I say absentmindedly as I side-eye Ruby's progress around the room. She's funny, clever, and has an ass that sways as she walks. I grit my teeth. "Especially GIFs of the angry panda chef. It reminds me of me."

You're a grumpy chef and you cannot be seduced by Ruby's loveliness. It's going to be three long months at this rate.

"Maybe I should make the actress you mentioned out of fondant. What was her name again?" Majorie presses.

"Nice try." I laugh as I bend slightly at the counter, my forearms flat against it. I'm exhausted from a day of charming these ladies while ignoring the other one who keeps demanding my attention.

"Do I hear grumpy chef Garett laughing? Surely, my ears deceive me," Ruby chimes as she stands beside me. She nudges me with her elbow to give herself space.

I grumble nonsensical words as she jostles me.

"Garett, you're going to have to get used to me, because I'm not going anywhere." Strands of her hair have fallen out of her bun already, and I'm tempted to tuck them behind her ear. "I'll make you like me soon."

I think she might be right. No one has been this nice to me for this long. Usually, I wear them down quickly.

"I shall leave you ladies to it." I rush back to my demonstration counter.

Ruby's smile falters briefly, and I curse myself. Like I said, I'm an arsehole. I'd be hard-pressed to find someone who would disagree with that label. Every person who's worked in one of my kitchens thinks so. No wonder Clive got me banned from working locally. The sooner Ruby realises she can't charm me, the better.

I lean against the counter, my arms folded as I survey the group, but my gaze returns to Ruby. She laughs with Marjorie as she offers her improvements for her cake decorating. Occasionally, she looks at me, and I hear the words angry panda.

I look away quickly and catch Wicksy's eye. Apparently, that's all he needs to bolt over.

"She's hot, isn't she?" he says louder than he realises. Ruby's eyes flick our way. "I reckon she likes me, too. She dropped that knife because she was staring at me."

I close my eyes and take a deep breath.

"I might ask her out later," he adds.

My passive-aggressive responses usually work on him, but Ruby has charmed everyone in the room within hours. Betty joins Marjorie and Ruby, and I swear someone says dick. Ruby side-eyes me again, only this time, her eyelashes flutter. Her eyes are big and brown and like liquid chocolate. I clear my dry throat noisily.

"What do you think?" Shit. I have no idea how long Wicksy has been talking. Goodness knows how many of his stupid ideas about Ruby he thinks I've agreed to because I've not said anything.

I glare at him and push my sleeves down. "I think you should get back to work. Tidy stuff up so we can leave on time. Yes?"

"Yes, Chef," he replies. Ruby looks over, her eyebrows furrowed, and walks to another bench.

I grab gum from my station to stop my teeth from breaking from all my grinding, but Kath sidles up to me before I can shove it in my mouth.

"She's doing well, don't you think?" Kath says, looking in Ruby's direction.

I shrug. "So no one is leaving me alone today, then."

"Don't be so surly," Kath replies, and a smile tickles my lips. "I know you're tired. I can see it in your eyes."

"Sorry." I drop my eyes and slide the gum into my back pocket. "Is Amber okay?"

"Yes, she's fine but won't return before Christmas. It's the twins. So you two should find a way to get along."

Together, we watch Ruby move from counter to counter, offering advice and bringing more smiles than when she arrived. Her fingers pick at the plaster that's keeping her bandage on. I could redress it for her as an apology.

"Ruby is a baker. She used to work in a cooperative bakery and run her own business, and I heard she was very good at it. You might learn something from her," Kath explains.

I snort, which draws Kath's glare.

"I meant learn something about how you treat people. You may have charmed the women here today, but you've upset someone who has the same goal as you—to make this cookery school work." Her hand rests on my shoulder. "And maybe take a moment to consider that you're not the only one having a bad week. She might be smiling, but a lot is going on in that head of hers."

Kath walks away, leaving me with a tight chest and a thickness in my throat. She's right. I don't know what's going on with Ruby, and ostracising my team and treating them like crap may have been the way I worked in the kitchen, but it's not going to work here.

I've acted today like Clive used to act. I drop my head, shaking it slowly.

CHAPTER SEVEN – GARETT

Ruby's laugh, as she stands at Betty's counter, is a tinkling melody, and I stop everything to listen as if it's my favourite song on the radio.

I should apologise for my earlier behaviour, but one of the rules of running a kitchen is that you never say sorry. Your staff shouldn't learn you're weak. It invites questions and uncertainty that don't fit a fraught kitchen environment. Boss it at all times. There's a reason why panicked people shout, "Yes, Chef."

I rub my sore jaw.

My career as a restaurant chef is still ruined, Clive is starting a baking competition, and I haven't got my dog, but if Ruby hadn't been here, seeing Cookie would have left me in agony for the entire day. She's made me smile even though I've tried to fight her happiness and kindness. That mixture of joy and beauty has excited me in ways I refuse to voice. I don't want to be another Wicksy.

As I watch her demonstrate fondant shapes to Betty, the flyer for Clive's competition lies on the counter. It churns my stomach. I bet it's an attempt to steal a contestant's recipes.

But there's nothing I can do about that.

I step towards the workstation where Ruby instructs Betty about an icing technique, fingering the packet of gum in my pocket, but then Ruby does that thing that makes me lick my lips as my body fires hotter. She pulls the elastic that keeps her bun in place. Her hair falls like flour blown across a countertop. It's like waves of spun sugar as it rests below her shoulders before her fingers twist and tease it into a simple yet elegant bun. She's missed a few strands each of the three times she's wrapped her hair, and this time is no different. It must be a nervous habit, but it's quickly becoming a highlight of my day.

I shouldn't butt in, and I certainly shouldn't go against one of my chef mantras and apologise.

A dusting of freckles cover her nose and cheeks, like icing sugar on a Victoria sponge. I steel myself and focus on unwrapping the gum, but I can't resist speaking to her as I do it. "So you're a baker rather than a cookery school manager?"

Betty replies for her, "Yes, she is. She was telling me about the business she ran before she moved here. It was called Naughty Bits."

"Treats," Ruby splutters. "Naughty Treats."

I pat her on the back. *Don't linger. You don't want to be creeping her out after you've already pissed her off.* The brief touch leaves my hand warm.

"And what does Naughty Treats involve? If you don't mind me asking."

Ruby's laugh is stilted, and pink tinges her ear lobes. "Oh, nothing in particular. Just fun shapes."

I slowly roll my shirt sleeves to reveal my forearms. She's staring at them like they're the secret to eternal youth. I flex my muscles like a peacock with a praise kink. "Why don't you show me the sorts of designs you did? I want to see what you're really capable of."

She smiles at Betty. "Keep doing what you're doing.

The fondant shapes look great."

Then she turns to me, and I prepare for a sassy comment.

"Maybe another time," she replies to me before walking away.

My face drops. I need to fix this for the benefit of the cookery school. At least, that's what I'm telling myself.

She moves towards the kitchen. I watch her go, making sure I don't look at that swaying ass.

I push my sleeves back down, and I follow her. Maybe I should ask what brought her to this cookery school in particular or show an interest in her old business.

"Fun shapes? Tell me more. I love fun things." I curse how awkward I sound, especially when her ears pink further. I slip gum into my mouth and chew slowly as I vow not to make more of a dick of myself. The mint bursts in my mouth, and my jaw works to relish the flavour.

"I bet you do," she whispers, forcing me to lean closer. The rest of the group focuses on their tasks. Ruby smells of buttercream and passion fruit. It overwhelms my mint, and I breathe her in slowly. "I bet you'd like nothing more than to wrap your lips around one of my breast-shaped cookies and lick the icing off slowly."

"I like cookies," I stutter. I want to palm my face, but instead, I lick my lips, imagining her sugary goodness coating my tongue.

She cocks her head to the side. "Shame you'll never get to taste them. I save my naughty treats for the best kind of people these days, which doesn't include angry chefs who say cruel things to new colleagues."

Sweat beads my neck, and I struggle to find a comeback. She wasn't flirting but getting me back for my behaviour, yet a brief flash of desire heats my skin. The same interest isn't reflected on her face. Instead, she smirks before striding to another workstation. I'm supposed to be in control of my kitchen, but with beauty, baking skills, and the cheek to bring me to my knees, Ruby's totally fucked me in seconds.

The ladies laugh and jeer the winners as they leave the cookery school.

"Thank you for such a brilliant day," Betty gushes. I look up, ready to shrug through the praise while secretly letting it fan my chef arrogance, but she's not looking at me. "I had so much fun, Ruby. I can't wait to tell everyone. I've gained lots of skills."

"It was my pleasure. It was a great day in the end, and you were an excellent student. I'm sure Chef Garett will be singing your praises for months."

Ruby looks at me, and I nod, although I'd rather roll my eyes.

"And maybe I'll see you at Clive's competition day," Betty replies, "if you're not doing your business anymore due to that awful boyfriend of yours."

I bristle at the mention of Clive, and her brows furrow as she catches my eye. Did she think I did that because of her boyfriend? Yes, I'm attracted to her, but I'd never get involved with anyone I work with, which is what I'd say to Wicksy if I thought he'd listen.

"Ex-boyfriend," Ruby rushes to correct. "It's still very raw, but he's definitely an ex."

She can't have said that for my benefit. *Get over*

45

yourself, Garett. I was someone before, but I'm nobody now. I catch her worrying the edge of her plaster, and her brows furrow again.

I clear my throat noisily, leaving the women to chat before throwing back, "I should redress that once we've tidied up."

There isn't much to tidy in the kitchen due to Kath's ninja cleaning skills. The place is pristine. If I ever run a restaurant again, I'm poaching her. Not that she'd leave. She adores it here, and she loves Amber. I should call Amber. I check my phone but quickly pocket it again. I've received another message from Clive.

"Okay," Ruby replies before helping the last of the group out to their cars with their bags. I pick up kitchen equipment before returning it to the same place. My gaze drifts towards Ruby's bum as she leaves the room. She's like liquid sensuality. The curves of her hips are the perfect size for my hands. But I'm too tall for her. If I wanted to kiss her, I'd have to lift her onto the counter.

I drag a hand down my face and storm around the kitchen. I need to get laid because it shouldn't take one beautiful baker giving me attitude to turn me into a horndog. Maybe it's all the tension from the situation with Clive and Cookie. The gold and blue flyer Betty showed me waits on one of the stations. Betty must have left it. I skim the swirly font announcing that Chef Clive's Best Cotswold Baker competition will be on Christmas Eve.

The winner will gain a spot in Clive's restaurant under the tutelage of the renowned pasta-making master and the prize of ten thousand pounds.

Bastard.

My fucking restaurant. My pasta recipe. My life.

I scrunch the flyer into a ball and toss it towards the bin. He has no idea what's in that pasta dish, and he hates that. I slide knives together to sharpen them. The metal-upon-metal sound fills the kitchen as I work them together. I need a plan to get my dog back, but I'm out of options.

An electric surge passes through my back.

"Sorry, did I make you jump?" Ruby asks, her hand lingering on my back.

"No," I grunt louder than intended. It echoes through the kitchen. I return the knives to their cases.

Ruby yanks her hand away and nibbles at her lip as she stares at me. She's raised her eyebrows with expectation. It's like a glimpse into a shyer, needier side of her, and it gives me ideas I can't allow to germinate. It's been months since I last kissed a woman, let alone slept with one, but that's not going to happen here. No way. I wish she'd stop staring at me like that.

"You said you'd redress my bandage?"

Shit. Am I really this arrogant to think this mysterious stranger is interested? One flyer has bruised my ego harder than if fifteen women rejected me. Ruby side-eyes me as she changes her hairstyle again, disarming me instantly. Kinked waves cascade from the tight elastic, and the nape of her neck is hidden, although I still imagine brushing kisses to her skin. I rub my stubble. Fans on the handful of TikToks I made before I got too busy told me the move made me appear wise, but I choke as I catch my reflection in one of the chrome ovens. I look like an ass.

I point to the chair in the dining area and grunt, "Yes. Sit."

I tug on my bottom lip as I stare at her hands. There's a couple of scars from kitchen incidents. Every chef or cook who's spent more than a month working in a kitchen has them. I've got several and one or two on my arms, too.

She spies me warily as she walks to the chair. *Do not stare at her bum.* But it's so damn curvy and draws me in like beef dripping on roast potatoes.

I shove several sticks of gum into my gob and release a groan of quiet exasperation before working the gum slowly. I need more mouth guards if I want my teeth to survive this winter. In fact, with Ruby in my kitchen until Christmas, I need to find a mouth guard wholesaler.

CHAPTER EIGHT – RUBY

I hold my breath as Garett slowly peels the plaster off and unwraps the bandage. His fingers are coarse, as expected. My grandma called it asbestos fingers—the effect of touching burning things so often that you burn off your fingertips. There's rarely anything glamorous about working in a kitchen, yet I've smiled more this afternoon than in months, even with Garett around.

"Kath did a good job on your bandage," Garett murmurs.

Our thighs are close but not touching as we perch on stools in the dining area. My pencil skirt stretches uncomfortably over my bottom, which is hidden from his view but still makes me feel more on show than I like. Amber is a curve-free size ten, but I'm nearer fourteen. We've always been jealous of each other's bodies. I can't keep wearing her clothes, but I can't find the time or money to go shopping while caring for my sister and running the cookery school.

The skirt stretches, but it can only do so much. Garett looks up as I pull the hem over my knees to my thighs to allow a little freedom.

"It's Amber's," I mutter, but he doesn't respond. He's not what I expected from his videos and the couple of articles I've read. He's got the sexy, brooding thing down, but his attitude goes from frosty to fake-friendly at a moment's notice.

He unravels the rest of the bandage. Should I talk to him as a colleague or as a guy who has treated me like crap for most of the day? My fangirling of him stopped the moment he was a dick to me, although I presume his redressing the bandage is his apology.

He eases the gauze away from my cut, and I hiss loudly.

"Sorry." His voice is deep and throbs nearly as much as my palm. Blood congeals around the cut like it had kept bleeding after Kath bandaged it. Wounds and blood don't freak me out, but my stomach rolls. "It needs cleaning and a new bandage."

He gets the items he needs and returns swiftly. Sweat trickles down my back. I'm so hot from hunger and seeing the blood that I take my chance to readjust my skirt again, but I can't do anything. I need to get it off. He turns as I fan myself between my legs. Fuck. His eyes are wide, and I mumble something about heat and hunger. He leaves again. This time, he returns with focaccia.

"Thanks." I shove a large piece of the bread straight into my mouth.

A moan nearly slips out. The bread is like heaven, with a little bit of salt and a tease of rosemary.

He shrugs. "It's just leftovers from my demonstration." He opens my hands and positions a warm, soapy cloth above the wound. "This is going to sting a little."

He draws the soapy, warm cloth across my wound. I jerk in his hand, but he squeezes my fingers reassuringly. "Keep eating the focaccia. It will help." His voice is gentle, and I lean closer, my stomach flopping.

His jaw moves up and down as he chews gum. The mint scent radiates from him, combining with the cinnamon that teased me every time he passed me that day. The movement adds to his brooding sexiness, and I kick myself. I'm here for work and have seen too much of his jerk side today. This misplaced attraction is from a lack of good sex and meeting a chef I've fantasised about before. Nothing more.

"I know you don't live here, as I know all the bakeries nearby. So what brought you to our little cookery school?" he asks as he dries the wound before adding antiseptic cream. I don't jerk this time. He blows on the antiseptic. It's just to dry it, but his breath on my skin makes my stomach coil, and I pull my lower lip between my teeth and suck it.

He glances up and catches my movement. His eyes lock with mine, and all the air is yanked out of the room. "I was surprised to see you running it today."

"I could tell from how you lost your shit," I reply, my lips quirking.

Garett harrumphs but doesn't say any more. A curl of brown hair falls across his forehead. It's a cute addition to his stern face. Hints of a tattoo peek out from under his right sleeve. His green checked shirt is on display now, and his cookery school apron hangs up on a hook at the side of the room. His shirt grips his muscles like a second skin, and he fills out his jeans in a way that necessitates the internal reminder that I've just broken up with Neil, and any crushes, especially on this jerk, would be dangerous.

A whirring dishwasher is the only sound as he covers the wound. He works delicately but efficiently. I wait for pain, but it doesn't come. His fingers are strokes of soft fur against my skin. My limbs tingle, and goosebumps cover my arms. A shiver hits the back of my neck as he secures the gauze. I manage to keep my body still, although I bite the flesh of my cheeks to do it.

I rush my words. "Amber wanted someone urgently because her doctors said she needed to rest. I was keen to get away, so here I am."

I shove more bread into my gob. His fingers brush my skin as he wraps a fresh bandage. The movement tightens the coil in my belly.

Stay away from men. That was the rule Amber and I decided on last night after I arrived and told her what Neil did. Since then, the twenty unanswered calls and fifteen messages he's left me have convinced me further. Garett is an expert chef, and if all I do is learn from him, then fantastic.

This is the result of eating his orgasm-worthy bread while having his hands on my skin. That, coupled with some horny rival bullshit and the buzz from turning around a crappy first day into an awesome one, has thrown me off-kilter.

"I'll be here until Christmas, probably, if not longer." I force colleague-like conversation.

"Is Amber okay?" His tone is brusque. "Kath said she'd gone off because of the twins."

"She's doing okay, all things considered. The pregnancy has taken its toll, but Mum and Dad will be on call until her husband, Kalen, returns."

"How did you get this scar?" Garett runs a fingertip across the silver slash on the back of my hand.

"I burnt my hand when I was baking. It was on the first batch of Naughty Treats cookies. It's like a fond memory now, but it hurt like a bitch."

I briefly smile at the memory, although I need a new focus now that the company and my friendship with Viv are dead. I can't buy her out. I don't have enough money for a new skirt, let alone a business. Maybe I should enter the competition Betty mentioned. It would show my family that I'm back and ready to rebuild our relationship, too.

"All the best chefs have scars." Garett holds out his hands. Where mine carry the odd freckle, his are tanned the colour of golden sugar. Kitchen work rarely involves tanning time, but he's probably earned enough to travel the world. Garett shows me his thumb. The skin pinches to form a marked line on the pad. He famously has an unexplained one on his face, although his beard mostly covers it. "I got this from the opening day of my restaurant. I'd never chopped so many onions, and my partner asked me a question, and bam, sharp knife into my finger."

"When did you run a restaurant?" I've read a little about Garett's career, although there's not enough online to get a complete timeline.

"A while back," he replies sternly. "But we live and learn."

I fight not to fill the silence, instead reaching for the last bits of the bread. He must have had reasons for leaving wherever he worked before, but it can't be because he had a burning need to work in a cookery school. He could be setting up his own place or leading at an exclusive restaurant.

"Kath said you'd worked in a cooperative bakery," he comments.

"Yeah, until…well, until yesterday, but that's the past."

"And your Naughty Treats? What's that about?" he presses, his fingers lingering on the secure bandage.

"A business I ran with a friend, but that's over now."

53

"Because?"

"I'd rather not talk about it," I say with a sigh. "It's been a difficult couple of days. Sorry."

He holds his hands up in surrender. "You don't need to apologise to me. I'm one of the reasons for your difficult day today, aren't I?"

I raise my eyebrows.

"Just so you know, you can talk to me if you need to. I know I'm an arsehole, but..." Surely, the great Garett Kelsey isn't about to apologise. "Hold on, did you say Mum and Dad?" he asks, referring to my earlier comment. "You're Amber's sister? You're a Cloud?"

I nod.

He rears back. "Is that the time?" He's not looking at a watch. "The bandage should hold at least another day, giving enough time for the cut to heal. But be careful in the shower." His jaw moves as fast as his hands as he tidies up the first aid kit.

My brows knit as he whirls around the room, collecting his belongings before rushing to the back room. I make a mental note to ask Amber about Garett's relationship with our parents. They're the most incredible people. They treated my ex with respect, and even with everything, they never stopped loving me.

Suddenly, a fluffball, the colour of freshly baked blondies, bounces through the dining room.

"Cookie," a woman calls across the kitchen. The pup barks and spins in circles like all its birthdays have come at once. It's a beaut of a dog with more energy than fifteen clowns on coke.

"Hello, lit—"

It makes a beeline for me. It jumps in the air, flies

towards me, and takes me down.

CHAPTER NINE – GARETT

The one rule you shouldn't ignore when working in a kitchen is don't shit where you eat. Not literally, of course.

And there's no way I should flirt with or have anything less than pure thoughts about someone from the Cloud family. They own the damn cookery school, and they're the only ones that haven't had a personal call from Clive warning them not to employ me.

Hookups and relationships are off the menu for kitchen workers, and my recent months with Clive have taught me that friendships aren't real, either. If I hadn't believed we were best friends and co-business owners, I'd still have a career and Cookie.

Barking echoes through the building. I rush to the doorway at the squealing accompanying it and a familiar voice shouting Cookie. Ruby giggles while lying on the floor, her skirt ripped down one side. Her blond hair splays around her as Cookie licks and kisses her.

Fucking hell.

"Cookie, heel," Flora hollers from goodness knows where, but my dog isn't heeding her. Instead, my fluffball bounces around a cackling Ruby, whose thigh-high hold ups are on show. An alabaster inch of skin shows above the lace top.

She's a Cloud, I remind myself. Yeah, but my dog loves her already. She's full of attitude and the sexiest woman I've seen in years. I bet her Naughty Treats taste like heaven.

I shake my head, divert my gaze, and command, "Cookie." He stops at my deep voice before turning and running to me. He nearly falls over his legs and can't keep up with his desperation to be with me.

He reaches me, bouncing on his back legs with his paws dancing in the air. His ears flap as he jumps, and I kneel to cuddle him. I bury my face in his fur, but I nearly end up on my ass due to his whirlwind of joy. It's been four weeks since I last held him. "God, I've missed you, boy."

"At least I'm not the only one without control over him." Flora's flame-red waves bounce as she enters the dining room. Her hand clenches at her hip, and she rolls her eyes to demonstrate how she regularly carries more attitude than accessories. "He got away from me in the car park. He must have smelt your everlasting cinnamon scent."

"Flora, honey, how did you manage this?"

I lift Cookie and hold him in my arms as he sniffs my stubble in the creepy way that makes me laugh. He nuzzles me, and my laughter turns to kissing noises until I sense Ruby staring at me. I'm supposed to be a grumpy chef, but I briefly have my boy. I hug Flora.

Flora's eyes narrow as she stares at Ruby, who's readjusting her skirt to hide the rip. "Can we chat in private?"

"Sure, do you want to come to mine or…"

"It's fine. I'll go." Ruby eases herself up. One hand grips the rip in her skirt, although there's still a hint of lace and skin. There's never been a better sight than my dog and this sexy woman happy together. She reveals a hint of cleavage as she bends over. Yep, that's a great view, too. *You are such a pig, Garett.*

"You don't have to," I reply, but she's already knocking over the stool.

I find Ruby's jacket, which she tossed earlier and nearly smashed the school's most expensive glasses, and give it to her as she rushes around the kitchen. As she passes me, I spot the gold-blue edge of a piece of paper on top of her bag, and my stomach churns. The flyer announcing Clive's competition still holds the creases from where I scrunched it before tossing it. So that's another reason to stay away from her. She has the power to betray me, and I'm not letting that happen.

She keeps her head down as she mutters goodbye, and her round bottom sways as she leaves the cookery school. A grunt vibrates my lips, but it sounds more like "never again" than "goodbye."

"So, big bro," Flora calls, bringing my attention back, "who was that?"

"If I told you, then you might tell your real brother," I cheek as I plop my gum into the bin. I shouldn't need it now that Ruby's gone. "How did you get Cookie away from Clive for a couple of hours?"

I lead Flora to the mezzanine floor. The kitchen will get a deep clean from Kath on the morning of the next scheduled cookery class, but the less dog hair she finds, the better. The area that Amber gave me a tour of when I first came to the school is like a cosy hideaway with a couple of sofas. Folded big blankets are in a box in the corner.

Maybe Clive thought the cookery school was so inconsequential that he didn't need to bother calling them to demand they don't employ me. I'd have taken any job, but there was something special about this place that didn't make the lack of choice as painful as it could have been. Amber suggested using the hideaway at Christmas for parties. It was a growing, lucrative business, and with the space and cosy feel, the school might venture into new business models.

I shake my head. This place isn't my future but a stopgap. I must find a restaurant where I can be the boss and regain self-respect.

I put one of the blankets down and settle onto a sofa. Cookie jumps straight up and cuddles up to me with a sigh. I avoid Cookie's scars from his beating at a puppy farm before the police saved him and gave him to the dog rescue centre where we found him.

"Clive's at the restaurant for a couple of hours," Flora replies, returning to our earlier conversation. Her hair is the same colour as her brother's, and her temperament can be as fiery as his, but there's often a kindness behind her actions. "So who was that?"

"Ruby is managing the cookery school. She's okay."

Flora rolls her eyes.

"Oi, Flora, I could go off you. Until thirty seconds ago, you were my favourite fake little sister."

She smirks. "I'm your only fake or real sibling."

"Which can only be a good thing," I reply, threading my fingers through Cookie's fur as he sleeps against me. If my parents had brought up Flora, she wouldn't have survived. I barely did and left home two weeks after my sixteenth birthday with less money than now.

"I need to get Cookie and leave this area," I mumble as Cookie's snores soothe the tension I've carried for a month. If I can get him back, I'll be gone by the end of the year.

Flora's eyes droop with sadness as she looks between Cookie and me. "I've tried to reason with Clive. I always knew he was selfish, but what he did to you makes me sick. You two were like brothers."

"Maybe he's always hated me, although that's difficult to hide for years. I don't know, Flora. I'll be okay, but I must find a way to keep my Cookie Bear."

"I have a plan for that." Flora tucks her feet underneath her and snuggles up to one of the blankets.

"You're not getting into trouble for me."

She chuckles, but then she fixes me with a stare that reminds me she's now an adult and wiser than her older brother. "Garett, you've been a better, sweeter brother than my own for the last seven years."

I shift uncomfortably.

"Don't deny it. We both know that Clive told me to deal with those bullies when I was fifteen, and if you hadn't spoken to the bully's parents and kept the girls at bay until I left school for college, I wouldn't have survived."

It's all true, but Flora and Cookie are usually the only ones who get to see the genuine, nice side of me. If I'm not charming people, I'm a grumpy bastard, and there's rarely anything in between.

"I'm going to get hold of the restaurant paperwork. I can't get you that place back, but I'm certain I can prove that Cookie isn't linked to anything but Clive and you, so you might be able to keep him."

I bolt upright, but the shift makes Cookie jump up, his eyes wide and his breathing rapid. If the puppy farmers hadn't gone to jail, I'd have left them in a state where they'd never touched a dog again.

"It's okay, boy. Lay back down." I stroke him gently, and soon, he calms. His head rests on my lap as he returns to dozing.

"You're not suggesting I keep him today?" As much as my heart soars, I can't put Flora in the middle of this. Besides, nothing will stop him from taking Cookie back.

"No, not today. But soon. I have a guy." I raise my brows. "Don't get all big brother on me. It's not like that. He understands contracts. Besides, you don't get to be protective when I've seen how you were with the newbie."

I feign ignorance and shut my mouth.

Flora laughs. "You weren't subtle. You were like Cookie when he wants a treat. Are you going to ask her out? Wine and dine her, do that thing where you offer to cook, and then blow her mind...with food."

I smile as I roll my eyes. "I'm not doing anything—Ruby's a Cloud and, therefore, off-limits."

"And you don't have a great history with hooking up with colleagues. Remember that sous-chef buddy you had when you worked in that French restaurant?" She makes bunny ears around the word buddy. "I guess it's hard to forget with that scar from the hot fat from that pan."

I rub the mark on my hand. "Your brother shouldn't have told you about that. I was a different guy then, and I learned my lesson from sleeping with co-workers. It didn't help the workings of the kitchen."

She gives me that smirk.

"Oi, Flora, I wasn't a pig. I always agreed with them that it was just a hookup, but they thought they could change my mind and that eventually we'd get into a relationship, hence the scar."

"Don't hate the player," she replies, shaking her head, but her smile proves she believes me.

"Anyway, I don't know how I got this job, but I need it if I'm going to get my feet back on the ground, pay my debts, and sort out my future. Besides, it's fun here."

Flora twists her lips to the side. "The job's fun, or being around Ruby is fun?"

"Ruby is a colleague. Although, I treated her badly today. I don't deserve her kindness. She thinks I'm a dickhead." Even with everything going on today, working in Ruby's presence made me smile for the first time in a long time. She knows baking, and as much as I'll never admit it, I've picked up a new technique for icing.

"Sounds like she worked you out pretty quickly then." I flip her the bird. "Always classy, Garett. You could apologise to Ruby. Even if you don't want to romance her because of kitchen worker rules—" I choke on the word romance. That was my last thought with Ruby. "You're such a dog. You know there's such a thing as romance, even if you only did it to get in women's pants."

"I don't like all the stories your brother may have shared about me. And how do you know about romance?" She never talks about boyfriends or girlfriends.

She shrugs. "Books. Anyway, back to you. You're just not a commitment guy. It's okay. But as I was saying, even if you don't want to be anything more than colleagues, you should still smooth over what I expect was you being a dick all day."

I rub the back of my neck and look anywhere but at her eyes. I let out a breath that vibrates my lips noisily. Cookie glares at me as if I'm threatening to blow a raspberry on his belly. "It doesn't matter, anyway. She's going to enter your brother's competition. What's his real angle with the competition?"

"I don't know, but I have a bad feeling." She sighs long and hard. "He'll probably screw someone over because he can't get your secret pasta ingredients. He was raging about that again before he left." She glances at the clock hanging off the wall. It's nestled between fairy lights. "Shit. I need to get Cookie back before he returns. I'm cutting it fine."

Cookie jumps up as we do. We rush down the stairs to Flora's jeep. Within seconds, I click Cookie into his doggy seatbelt. I give him one last kiss and cuddle and remind him how much I adore him. My throat feels thick with the sobs trying to rise to the surface. I don't know when I'll see him again. He might stop loving me.

"Stay safe, Flora," I stutter. "And don't get into trouble for me. We'll find a solution."

Flora swipes my worries away with her hand.

"Apologise to Ruby," she yells as she tears out of the car park.

Gravel flies, and I remember I blocked Ruby's car earlier. Plastic bits of a broken light cover reveal she must have knocked it on the sign while trying to leave. Did she do a fifty-point turn to get away without asking me to move my van?

The tears that brimmed my eyes after saying goodbye to Cookie disappear, and instead, I'm tempted to apologise to Ruby no matter what.

Or maybe I should avoid her and hope that will solve everything. I have rules I need to stick by.

But rules are made to be broken.

CHAPTER TEN – RUBY

"**A**nd then he had the audacity to flirt with me! After everything, he thought, yeah, I'll give her my sexy eyes and make her fancy me."

I'm storming back and forth across the living room floor. I told Amber about Flora, who Amber thinks is his friend, and then I filled her in about Cookie, and my skirt mishap. Well, technically, it's her skirt and my accident. I didn't tell her I broke my car light because I was too nervous to return to the cookery school and ask him to move the van. It took me ten minutes to move my car.

"You think his eyes are sexy?"

I freeze before glowering at Amber. She's in the cuddliest pyjamas. Her vomiting has subsided, and she's spent the rest of her day reading spicy romance under the comfort of a blanket.

"Not the point."

Her laugh is music to my ears. I've missed her so much. She beckons me closer, knowing what my look means. I tuck myself under the blanket and cuddle up to her. She smells of the cookie dough and marshmallow brownies I baked for her late last night. I rest my head against her shoulder and sigh. Garett's eyes are sexy, and this afternoon, I realised I'd missed laughing and teasing someone for years. And the time he took to redress my cut was full of care. The loving yet sexy alpha way he was with his dog also got me. But he was still an arsehole for nearly the entire day.

"How are you, really? You must be exhausted after vomiting all morning before devouring the brownies." She hums her non-reply. A sexy bodyguard fills the front cover of her book. "Have you heard from him?"

"No," she replies, instantly understanding that I mean Kalen, her husband. "His operations, especially secret ones like these, can go on longer than expected."

"I guess that's the life of the wife whose husband spends months on submarines." I've only seen Kalen a handful of times since their wedding, although I've spoken to him on the phone.

"Yeah, I know. He was a sexy stranger who saved me from an impossible situation when we met," she says with a sigh before her voice muffles. "I don't know how long he'll be away, and I'm scared he won't return before the babies come. I can't do this alone."

Tears slip down her cheeks. My sister is hard as nails, but the last months have taken their toll. She's struggled through a lot of sickness during the pregnancy. "I'm not the same as a strapping naval husband, but you've got me. Mum and Dad aren't far away and there are lots of people in this small town who could help." She cuddles me tighter.

"And you're okay with keeping the cookery school going until Christmas? Kalen is leaving the navy soon, hopefully. We're going to shut down the school in January when it's quieter, and with Garett's skills, Kath running the back room, one of the admin team I was training, and Kalen and me in the background, I should be able to make it work from February onwards. Mum and Dad will look after the twins on days I need to work, but the key thing is we won't need a full-time person at the cookery school. It's just to help us out right now."

I could stay longer and want to, but she'd say if she felt the same. I don't know what I'll do from January.

"We've got enough money to keep going until then. Kalen's health insurance means I can do this pregnancy privately, so he's not too worried while he's away."

I nod. "That reminds me. Clive Macdonald, the owner of Balencia, who Garett once worked with, is running a competition, and the closing date is tomorrow. I'm thinking of entering. The winner gets ten thousand pounds and a job developing a baked goods option at his restaurant. I probably won't even get shortlisted, but it would be fun to try out. The competition day is on Christmas Eve. Is that okay?"

Amber smiles. "Of course. Be wary of Clive, though. Mum said something about him when I last visited. She was the one who convinced me to take on Garett, not that I'd say no to a skilled chef like him. But she was adamant."

"She is the wisest person we know."

Amber nods. "Do you remember catching her talking to Dad about how Neil wasn't the guy for you in the first months of your relationship?"

"Yeah. It was partly what convinced me to leave to be with him." And because I was a fool and decided I needed to be independent.

I squeeze my hands, making fake dough, until Amber's cheekiness draws me out of overthinking. "Maybe Garett won Mum over with his sexy eyes."

I elbow her.

"Are you going to visit Mum and Dad soon?" she asks

tentatively. "They've missed you, and they know you love them even after everything."

I cuddle her harder, avoiding her question. "I still can't believe I chose Neil over them with the way he treated me, especially when Grandma and Grandad died. I've been the worst daughter, including where the cookery school is involved. I hate that I can't get the lost years back."

"You can't keep feeling guilty for grandma and grandad or about rejecting their gift of the cookery school," Amber replies. "Besides, Jem was a brat and rejected it, too, although we know his interest was only in eating food, not helping others discover the joys of it."

"Bloody Jem." Shame sits like a spiky ball in my belly. It's been there for the last couple of years, but I've ignored it by keeping busy. I will visit with my tail between my legs. But not yet. I need to prove myself first. "I'll think about seeing them."

We sit in silence. I need to win that ten thousand pounds for Amber. She never mentions money, but running the cookery school can't be cheap or easy, and she said she'll have enough money until the babies are born. She probably needs it more than she says. It will be a nice gift for her, as she's letting me live in her garden cabin, but more because she never gave up on me.

"I'm going to enter Clive's competition and win it." And be polite but not friendly to Chef Garett. "Maybe if I work under Clive for a year, I can start my own baking business again, but with much more knowledge and as the sole business owner." It would put my past to rest and help me with my self-worth.

"Okay, and I've got your back, remember."

I snuggle with Amber a little longer while working through my plans. The key is to not waste time with things that aren't moving my career forward and to ensure that Amber isn't alone or struggling with money.

"And I'm always happy to eat your practice bakes."

"Well, obviously." I chuckle before untucking myself and jumping up. "I need to complete the application within the next couple of hours. But grab me if you want anything, okay? You're not alone. I'm here for you, no matter what."

Amber's tears are gone, and a grin fills her face. "Thank you, sis. I'm so glad you're home."

"Me too."

"And promise me you'll visit Mum and Dad at some point?"

I nod. I walk out of the room, but her shout brings me running back.

"Is everything okay?"

"Why were you wearing hold ups at the cookery school, baby sis?" she asks while laughing.

I throw the flyer from the cookery competition at her.

"I wore them because I don't have tights. When I worked in a bakery, I wore jeans. My legs were cold today, and all I had were hold ups."

She raises her eyebrows and smirks.

"And I wanted to feel confident, okay? I didn't expect to end up flashing them at my number three chef."

"Number three? I thought he was second."

I huff. "Not after his behaviour today, even though I've seen his forearms up close now. They're the sexiest thing I've ever witnessed. I bet his dick tastes of magical cookie dough, too. But I won't fancy that grumpy bastard. He was such an arsehole today." Although, I need to get him onside if I'm going to have his help as I prepare for the competition.

Her laughter stops at the sound of the doorbell.

"You have to answer it. I am in no fit state to receive visitors," she says, faking a sad face.

"But what if it's mum and dad?" Already, my fingers are trembling.

"I'm pregnant and tired," she whines, although her eyes are twinkling.

"You can't use that for everything you don't want to do while I'm staying." I creep slowly to the door. A rattling exhaust suggests whoever the visitor is, they're already leaving. I ease open the door to find my favourite flowers—pink lilies—a foil-covered dish, and a note.

Whatever is under the foil smells like heaven, but I'm snapping my teeth to open the note. As I rip it open, I take in the moonlight hitting the stone-covered driveway and the leaves rustling on the slight breeze. There's no other movement, and the only vehicle in the driveway is mine. Maybe my mum and dad dropped it off because they're not ready to see me, either.

I unfold the note. The scrawly handwriting has more curves than I do.

To Ruby. I'm sorry for how I behaved today. I was a grumpy arsehole chef, and I shouldn't have taken my lousy morning out on you. I hope from now on we can make the cookery school a success because that's all I want. You and Amber have probably already eaten, but this lasagne should be good for a couple of days. Heat it in the oven with the foil on 180°C/160°C fan for 20-30 minutes and it will be perfect.

From Garett

It's hardly an emotion-filled message, but maybe I

should move him back to number two on my chef list. That's when I see the last sentence.

P.S. I never apologise, so don't get used to it and I'd prefer it if we didn't talk about this again, as I have a reputation as a grumpy chef to uphold.

Men!

CHAPTER ELEVEN – GARETT

Ruby's wearing jeans and a woolly jumper today. The weather has turned. It's a couple of weeks until Halloween, and a chill in the air makes me regret wearing the blue shirt that Flora once joked brings out my naturally tanned skin and brown hair. I'm not wearing it for anyone's benefit and certainly not for the woman who turns skinny jeans and a fitted pink jumper into the sexiest casual outfit ever.

"Everything going to plan?" I ask as she walks past me to the dining area.

She hasn't mentioned the note, flowers, or lasagne, and I'm totally okay with that because I asked her not to. But still, she could have said something.

I've noticed the dish from the cookery school has been returned, so I guess she ate it, unless she tossed it away. But even if she hated me, she wouldn't bin one of my specialities.

"Well done for keeping your cool earlier," Kath whispers as the children giggle at their freshly made cupcakes.

"Who brings ten children to a baking bread and cakes birthday session and only then mentions that one of the children is vegan and prone to vomit if they eat bread?" I huff. "They should have told us in advance because we want to make the sessions work for everyone."

"I know, but you behaved well. They'd have no idea that you were about to reprimand them."

"Only because you glared at me." And because I was distracted by Ruby and her pink jumper, which is the same colour as the lilies I gave her.

One of the children reaches for their fresh out of the oven rolls.

"Don't—"

"Hey, Cammie, leave it a little longer. They're going to taste so good," Ruby jumps in and smiles at the child. That's the fifth time that child has tried to burn herself today, but Ruby has been excellent at keeping her safe and happy. "You can all start decorating your vegan brownies now, like Chef Garett showed you. Let your creativity shine. You've got fifteen minutes."

I am useless around children, especially all these giggly, hazard-prone ones, but Ruby's party games and sunshine attitude have made today a smash.

"Ruby has shone today. She told me it took a while to get over her difficult first day." We both know that is a reference to my attitude. "But she's happier, partly because she ate the best lasagne she's ever tasted this week."

"Really? She said that?" I pull back my shoulders and puff my chest out. She liked it. I must remind myself that it doesn't mean she likes me, but maybe she doesn't hate me anymore.

"Yes," Kath replies. "She won't tell me where she got it from, though. Although it's all she talked about when we were setting up."

"Lucky Ruby."

"Indeed." Her lips quirk.

As the children decorate their cakes and Kath busies herself, I stroll over to Ruby, who is fiddling with something in the corner.

I want to swagger, but I also meant what I said in the note.

"Everything is going brilliantly. Well done for today," I whisper.

She blushes and I close my eyes briefly. Blushing Ruby is hot. "Yeah, it's all good. I'm getting the party bags ready, and the parents will be here to collect the children in about fifteen minutes. Are you finished with them?"

"Yes. Kath is packing their baking into boxes they can take home."

My gaze sweeps the kitchen. Every child beams as they ice their vegan brownies. I'm not sure Ruby needed me today. She's created a masterclass.

We've spoken a few times today, and it's purely professional, but I want to make her like me. "You said party bags? We've never done those before."

Her shoulders relax, and she moves so we're side by side at the counter. I'm aware of how much shorter she is than me. Again, I remember last week's thought of lifting her onto my counter. *Stop it, Garett. She's a human, not a sex object.*

"Yeah, party bags. I discussed it with Amber. A couple of treats like sprinkles, cupcake mix, and some Halloween bits to go with a flyer about our adult Halloween cookery class. We still have a few spaces to fill, and their parents might see the flyers and book with us."

"You must be knackered. How late were you up last night making these?" It explains the dark circles under her eyes. I was worried she was talking to her ex. Not that I

73

care. I don't date colleagues. I don't date anyone.

She's tricky to hear because she is shorter, but when I met one of Flora's friends, I learned that you don't bend down to talk to shorter people unless you want them to kick you in the nuts. "I've no idea. I was baking brownies for Amber, as it's one of the few things she can stomach now." She's too bloody kind and lovely and not a woman who'd want to spend too long chatting to me, but I can't walk away. She's like a breath of fresh air for my soul. "And I was doing other stuff."

"What other stuff?" I shove another piece of gum in my mouth and chew slowly as I recall her hold ups. "Doesn't matter."

"Hold on." She grabs one of the steps we get out for people who want to be a little higher to reach the various areas of the kitchen. She stands on it, and it brings her to my height. "That's better."

Her eyes meet mine, and I chew faster. At this height, I could kiss her. As if she'd ever be interested in kissing me, a washed-up grumpy chef.

"In terms of the other stuff... I was wondering if you'd help me with something. I've watched some of your videos, and your skills are amazing. I know you said not to talk about it so you don't lose your grumpy chef reputation, but"—her voice drops to a whisper, forcing me to lean in— "your lasagne was incredible."

"Yeah?" I grin and blush red. I'm needier than Cookie when he's told he's a good dog. "For sure?"

"It was the best thing I'd ever had in my mouth."

My eyes widen, and my jaw drops.

"Shit, I didn't mean... Like, I've had other things in my mouth and..."

I ready myself to tease her, but one of the children asks a question, and I put on my professional chef face and turn towards her bench while trying to wash my imagination out with soap and water.

I give Ruby one last brief look over my shoulder. Her face is in her hands, and she whispers in agony, "Oh God."

Even though the children have gone and I'm all packed up, I busy myself looking at menus for the next session. Maybe I can flirt a bit more with Ruby and find out what she wants my help with.

"You can go home, Garett. We're all done," Kath comments. "I'm about to lock up."

"I was just checking the menus."

"No, he wasn't," Wicksy replies as Ruby puts her coat on. She has a sparkly gift bag in her hand. "He's wondering if any of the single mums had left their numbers for him."

Ruby's eyebrows shoot up. "Does that happen often?"

"Hold on—" I stutter.

"Most weeks," Wicksy replies as Ruby cocks her head to stare at me. "There's at least one or two. There were loads after that hen party we had once."

"And does he call them?"

"Ask him yourself."

Ruby shakes her head. "Nah, I don't need to hear about his conquests."

"I'm standing right here," I grumble as Kath pushes us out the door.

"We know," Ruby cheeks. "With those seductive forearms and that little brown curl that falls on your

75

forehead when you cook. I've seen the videos on TikTok."

I turn and stare at her. "Are you a fan of mine? Were you the one who used to put filthy comments under them?"

Kath locks up, and Wicksy disappears into his car.

She giggles. "No, and I certainly didn't have your poster on my wall or kiss it the night before I went to sleep."

"I've never been famous enough to have posters."

"And I've never been creepy enough to print my own," she says with a laugh and a wink.

A weird flush of something grows in my belly. She's fucking funny, and although I should be going home, I just want to stand like this with her all night. I haven't laughed like this for months.

"Back to what I was saying before—"

"About things in your mouth?" She shoves me with her shoulder. "All I meant was your lasagne was tasty."

"Tasty like a chef's forearms or tasty like..."

Her laugh is like a squeal, and she quickly covers her mouth.

"What the hell was that?"

"Nothing. *Anyway,* I'd really like to get your expertise," Ruby adds with fluttering eyelashes.

I can't help that my mouth drops open at this point. I'm really without control of anything around her. "My expertise?" *Please mean my expertise with my hands.*

"Yes, but before I tell you with what, I want to thank you for the lasagne and flowers with some of my cupcakes."

"Do these have your boobs on?" Her brow furrows, and I have to backtrack. "Remember when you said that you made boob-shaped cookies the other week? I didn't mean your boobs." I close my eyes. I can't look at her chest right now. I'm not that guy. "I meant boobs you'd made..." I trail off before digging a bigger hole.

She throws her head back and laughs. "I do now. You know, you're blushing as pink as the beautiful lilies you left me. No, these are just normal cupcakes. I want to butter you up before I ask for your expertise properly. Once you've eaten them, I shall make my request."

She hands me the bag. Her fingers brush mine accidentally, but I still get a little jolt in my belly. Does she feel it, too?

"Catch you next time, Garett." She waves and walks off. I guess she didn't.

I'm left staring at her as she gets in her crappy car with the broken light and drives out of the car park.

"She's a whirlwind of joy, isn't she?" Kath calls out, catching me frozen in wonder. "At this rate, you'll be known as Garett, the formerly grumpy chef, by Christmas."

I nod, although it's more likely that I'll be known as Garett, the permanent blushing awkward chef.

CHAPTER TWELVE – GARETT

Another week has passed at the cookery school. We've had a couple of sessions, but they're not enough for me to raise funds to get Cookie back. I've swallowed my pride and emailed a college about teaching classes. I can do it around working at the cookery school, but it grates that I—an expert in my field—must work at a college rather than run a restaurant. It's another reminder that I have to leave this area. All I need is my boy, and I'll be gone.

Although I've seen Ruby at the school this week, I haven't learnt what expertise she needs me for, although I've imagined it most nights. She's a welcome distraction from my life. And those cupcakes were like spongey heaven. If my expertise means I get more of those, then I'm all in.

Today was another successful children's party, but now the kitchen is child-free. Everyone left smiling, and several parents signed up for next week's Halloween cookery class. We're full. Ruby is remarkable.

"What are you still doing here?" she asks, popping her head into the kitchen and catching me licking buttercream from my demonstration bowl. Only Kath knows I do this, and she's sworn to secrecy.

My face burns, and I throw the bowl into the sink. We've flirted during every session over the last week. Well,

I'm flirting. She's constant sunshine, so she's probably like this with everyone. It's become my favourite part about working here.

Ruby smirks. "Chill out, Garett. We all do it." She picks up the bowl and rubs her finger around the rim before popping it into her mouth.

Time slows as her cheeks hollow and she sucks that finger so damn hard. Her eyes flutter closed, and she moans in a way that would make me snap a mouth guard if I were grinding my teeth against one.

She shoves the bowl back at me, and I nearly drop it, so distracted by the pleasure I just witnessed.

"I thought you'd gone home," I stutter. I've forgotten how words work.

I slowly lick buttercream off the teaspoon to stop myself from saying anything stupid.

My stomach jumps as Ruby's eyes darken. Her chest flushes, but that could be the lighting or a rash or something. Please let it be me.

"I was going through the list for Tuesday's evening class."

We don't have loads of classes in the middle of the week, although Amber's business model involves getting additional work from evening classes, daytime team-building, and children's parties. Still, I can't afford to survive and build up savings on four day classes a week, even with the possibility of working at the local college.

Ruby adds, "We have a cookery class for a work team-building event on Tuesday, and we need to ensure we're all set with dietary requirements and accessibility issues." Her voice drops. "By the way, what are you wearing?"

"Right now? A shirt and—"

She facepalms, "No, for the Halloween session. It's

fancy dress, remember? I might dress as a naughty maid if I can find my costume and wash my hold ups in time."

She's killing me, and she knows it. My stomach is all over the place, and I'm tempted to shove all my gum in my mouth, but I don't want to ruin the taste of the buttercream. I pop the spoon in and suck on it.

Her laughter is a melody that I swear I'll hear in my dreams. "Keep up, Garett."

"I have to wear a costume? Maybe I could go as a grumpy chef," I utter around the spoon.

Her eyes twinkle, and that flush hits my stomach again.

"You'd wear that costume well, especially if you had those forearms showing."

"Would you be able to look away? I'd hate to be distracting you all Halloween."

"Sweetie," she says as she steps closer, pulls the spoon out of my mouth, and pops it in hers. She gives it a big suck. My eyes must be as big as saucers. She takes the spoon, puts it back in my mouth, and tips my chin to close it. "I'd be so busy readjusting my hold ups that I wouldn't notice you. You, on the other hand…"

She sashays away, and I'm frozen.

She has the measure of me, and the happiness bursting from my heart is disarming. Don't go there. *She's a Cloud, and you need this job.* But her giggles as she turns to me make my heart do that thing again. I stare back at her and roll my tongue around my mouth.

Will she finally ask for the favour I've been considering all week?

She comes over to me several minutes later as I check the stock. I don't need to, as Kath will have it sorted, but

80

I'm already looking for reasons to hang around on the off chance Ruby will speak to me again.

My old team used to call me the dictator, emphasising the *dick*, but her sunshine routine is wearing me down. I want to soak up her light and give some of it back.

She's back in front of me, and a tiny part of me hopes she can't get enough of me, even though that would be the worst thing. "I won't be a sexy maid next week, so don't get yourself all hot under the collar again." Her teases are relentless, and I'm all here for it. "I'll probably be a gnarled old witch with boils and bumps all over my skin."

"Will you need help applying those? Because I'm sure I could help with the hard-to-reach places."

She throws her head back and laughs. The pride hits my chest hard. I did that.

"I'm sure I'll be fine, but I appreciate the support."

"Always," I say with a smirk.

I get a waft of buttercream and remember tasting Ruby after she licked the spoon and popped it in my mouth. She was like strawberries and white chocolate, meaning she'd sneaked a blondie from somewhere or tastes of heaven. A kiss would confirm it. I glance briefly at her lips as she busies herself with the stock. They have a slight sheen, like she's licked them.

"How's Cookie? Based on how you two were the other week, I'm presuming the dog was yours." She's worrying that rosy lip now, nibbling at it.

"Cookie, yeah," I reply, relieved that she's giving me a reprieve from flirting. I don't know what's wrong with me. I'm usually an expert at banter. "It's nice that you remembered his name."

She shrugs like it means nothing, but it means the world to me. "What sort of dog is he? Apart from the cutest, liveliest ball of floof ever." She's tapping her foot now.

"He's a Cavapoo."

"And does he live with that lady that came? She's your..."

Her restless tapping and the little noises of her tongue clicking against the top of her mouth feed my devilish side. I study the bags of flour like they're the most important thing. I like making her wait.

"My...?" I smile briefly before wiping it off my face. I don't want her to know I'm enjoying it. "Oh, Flora. She's Clive Macdonald's sister." I nearly choke on his name. "Flora's like the little sister I never had, and she can be quite protective of me."

"Cool, cool," she says. It reminds me of Jake from *Brooklyn Nine-Nine* when he's super awkward. She's swallowing a lot. Maybe she thought that Flora and I were dating. I can only think of one reason why would she care. Again, I hide my grin while reminding myself she's a Cloud. But she tastes of strawberries and white chocolate.

"Did you—" I start.

"Could you—" she says at the same time. "Doesn't matter."

"No, you go." I wanted to ask if she'd eaten a blondie before she licked my spoon. It's probably wise to have a reprieve from asking that question.

"If you're sure." She raises her eyebrows, waiting for me to change my mind. "Okay, well, you mentioned Clive."

Joy leaves my body in one intense *whoosh*. I grit my teeth. "Yes."

"And the thing is..." She lets her hair out of the elastic and immediately starts tying it again. She should be nervous if she wants to talk to me about that bastard. "I entered his competition, and I've been struggling with my bake. Will you help me improve my skills with one of your techniques?"

I grind my teeth hard enough to snap the bastards. "No," I grunt.

"Sorry?" Her voice catches. "Oh, okay. I shouldn't have asked."

"No, you shouldn't."

The happiness that bounced between us has died. Tension fills its space.

"Well, thanks anyway." She's trying to be polite, but she doesn't know my history. I could make this easier for her, yet my shoulders stiffen and my throat burns.

"You shouldn't enter that competition."

"Why?" She's staring at me now and worrying her lip again. I can't say anything in case it gets back to Clive. I don't need slander added to my name. I can't prove what he did. Besides, I don't know if I trust her.

"Because," I grunt. Her eyes pinch as she stares at me. Way to make it worse. But I continue like Cookie in a china shop. "Anyway, you're a Cloud. You have a cookery school and everything you need. Why do you need to enter the competition?"

I'm deflecting, but if she enters that competition and wins, which I reckon she has a shot at doing after eating her cupcakes, Clive will steal her ideas. And if she works for him, he'll destroy her like he did me or try and seduce her.

"Maybe I don't want to only succeed in my family business. Maybe I want to be known for what I can do. What do your family do?"

They tell me I'm worthless, rack up debts in my name, and destroy my future. Oh, and my dad gave me my secret scar when he clipped me while wearing a sharp ring before I left home for good. But I don't talk about my manipulative family in interviews or with anyone for good reason. Clive knows some stuff and suspects more, but he doesn't have enough to use against me.

"Don't enter that competition if you know what's good for you. In fact, listen to me. I know what's good for you, so don't enter it." I scowl and walk away.

"Oh wow," she shouts. Suddenly, I'm confronted by the sunshine-free version of Ruby. "What makes you think I'd listen to you? You're a grumpy bastard with a hard-ass reputation, and now you're telling me what to do? You arrogant dick of a man."

I turn and raise my eyebrows. Ruby's correct, but it still hurts coming from her, although I've no idea why. She's not done with me, though.

"I refuse to be professional when you're acting like this. When I saw you with your dog and after how you've been over the last fortnight, I presumed I'd got you all wrong. But you're the same guy you were the first time I met you. You're such a wanker. Listen to you giving it the big I AM."

I puff my chest, ready to let rip, when suddenly Kath dives between us.

"I need you to make a wine run for the Halloween cookery evening." She's looking at me but then turns to Ruby. "Both of you."

"Hold on," I shout, but she puts her hands in the air.

"Both of you. You have the van and can help carry it. Ruby can't drive a manual car and can't carry it all on her own anyway." At least I know why she didn't move her van herself using the cookery school's spare keys that time.

"I can take my car and go on my own." Ruby's face resembles her name: bright red. Miss Sunshine is fucking livid with me. It might look sexy if I wasn't about to sit in a van with her.

"It won't fit, and your light is out. I'm not having you drive there at night. And before you say you can do it alone during the week, that's also impossible. The wine merchants are closing for a week." I open my mouth, but Kath silences me with a stare. "No, I don't know why, and no, we can't get it from anywhere else, because we're on account with them and Amber needs to pay for it after the party. Ruby must go because she needs to learn this part of the business, and you need to do it as it's one of the conditions of having the van."

Ruby and I stare at each other. Ruby's eyes are like little black beads. My jaw hurts from how hard I grit my teeth as I glare back.

Kath claps her hands like a teacher trying to harangue naughty kids. "Now that's agreed, I'll see you both soon. I'm going to finish the tidying and get away. Good luck."

"I'll be in the van," I grunt in Ruby's direction.

"I'll be there when I'm ready," Ruby snaps back.

The following two hours will be agony, and I won't do anything to make them more manageable.

"Don't keep me waiting all night. Some of us have lives."

Her guffaw winds me up further. Yes, my plans include sitting in my bedsit, eating whatever I can rustle up from my cupboards, while watching anything I can find on the television, but Ruby doesn't know that.

I hope she's not a mind reader either, because aside from that, I'd planned to think about Ruby in a maid's outfit tonight.

CHAPTER THIRTEEN – RUBY

I throw my bag into the footwell of the passenger seat.

"Do you need help getting in?" Garett asks. That had better not be a height dig. I grind my teeth together and scowl. "Because you're clumsy, not because of anything else."

"I can do it myself." I grab the handle and yank myself up, slipping on the step and nearly face-planting into the seat. At his chuckle, I give him my best death stare. He sucks his cheeks in and clears his throat. His gaze flicks to the windscreen. "Come on, then. Let's go. Neither of us wants to be together in this van."

"Not until you click your seatbelt in. We don't want to have an accident before we've left the car park."

I'm so close to getting out of the van and telling him he can go to the wine merchants alone. Amber doesn't need me after Christmas, so I don't need to learn this.

I count to ten slowly. Our argument isn't the only thing making me twitch. I suspect Chantelle, my childhood nemesis—well, the nemesis before Neil and Viv jumped to the top of the list—works there.

I click my belt loudly into its holder while staring at Garett, and he starts the van and drives us through the countryside to the wine merchants. It's nearly the end of British Summer Time when the clocks change. It heralds the coming of winter. It will be getting darker and colder soon. I usually love this time of year, the run-up to Christmas, when you wear your pyjamas as soon as you get home and make your house cosy with gingerbread wax melts and low lamps. And I'm addicted to Netflix Christmas romance movies. I don't care how many they make of someone moving to a small town and falling in love with the local Christmas tree farm owner. I'm here for every single one.

I already have plans for the cookery school this Christmas, too. We'll have wreath making nights, children's festive baking events, work team-building parties, and more.

Last Christmas, when I wasn't breaking my back preparing our special Naughty Treats Christmas treats— boob cookies with baubles on the nipples and Christmas tree cupcakes with dicks popping out of them—Viv, Neil, and I spent Christmas Day with Neil's family. My parents phoned and messaged me daily, asking if I wanted to join them, but I didn't return their calls. My relationship with Neil was flailing even then, but I was too invested to end it. I couldn't share that with Mum and Dad without them expecting action, so I avoided everyone, including my younger brother, Jem.

Garett side-eyes me. My pulse has slowed from its peak after Kath stopped me from ripping his head off, but I'm not ready to dignify his existence with conversation. How dare he tell me not to enter the competition? I presume he doesn't think I'm good enough, or maybe he thinks I will ask him to put in a good word for me, as he and Clive are former colleagues and he's still in contact with Flora.

I need to enter that competition. I can't spend the rest

of my life hoping that I'll succeed. I already forfeited my chance to be part of the cookery school long-term when I chose Neil above my family. I'm a failure now. This competition would be the chance to show my family that I'm back and can achieve something. I need it, and my sister needs the money.

I press my nails into my palms as I prepare to face Chantelle. Her bullying and snide digs from the other side of the classroom were relentless and one of the reasons why I was glad to move out of the area. And now I might be face-to-face with her the same month I caught my boyfriend cheating with my best friend and business partner.

Fuck.

"It's weird that Americans call a manual car a 'stick shift.'" Garett's words creep into the headspace that I'm reserving for self-flagellation. "So why can't you drive a manual? Is it the clutch you can't do?"

"What?" His gaze flicks between the road and my face, although when he glances at me, there's a wince in his stare. "Why are you talking to me? Don't you know 'what's good for you'?"

I tip my head and glare as I reference his comment earlier about me not entering Clive Macdonald's competition.

He puffs out his cheeks and releases a blast of air. "Never mind."

I pick at a fresh plaster from where I nicked my finger while chopping, remembering the bandage that Garett carefully redressed the other week.

I study him out of the corner of my eye. His shirt grips his muscles in a way I've secretly admired all day. His full lips are pressed in a tight line, and his short dark curls are a little messier than usual, probably from running his long fingers through them. He was number one on my sexiest chefs list for a reason, but I can't get past his attitude.

What should be a thirty-minute drive is over in twenty. Thank fuck.

Walking towards the shop attached to the warehouse, I glimpse Chantelle through the window.

"I'm going to stay here," I say.

Garett's hand is on the door handle to the merchant's reception. He turns to stare at me, his eyebrows raised. "Whatever. You do you."

As he yanks open the door, Chantelle spots me through the doorway. *Shit.* This day is the pits. She makes a beeline for me.

She smirks. "Look who it is. Dowdy Cloudy." She smirks, using a name she'd taunt me with at school.

"Hello, Chantelle." I don't fake a smile.

"I heard you were back. My grandma did a cookery course where you tried to catch a knife. How embarrassing."

I attempt to stare her down in a way I was too anxious to at school, but her mouth keeps flapping. "What brought you back, Dowdy? Did that shitty boyfriend that didn't even accompany you to your grandparents' funeral come back with you?"

"You're still a nosey bitch, then."

I can feel Garett's eyes on us as I feign ambivalence. Darkness falls, and I regret my thin jumper. I fold my arms tighter as I shrink under her gaze.

"And your business, how's that going? I'm guessing not well if you're back here." She challenges me with an ugly twist to her mouth that tells me she already knows the answer.

She's probably stalked me on social media. I've looked her up several times, but she must have visited mine regularly if she knows Naughty Treats closed.

Garett clears his throat. "I knew of her reputation as a baker, and I insisted she run the school in her sister's absence," he says with a raised voice, drawing Chantelle's attention. She hadn't noticed him even though he's a dark-haired, tattooed, six-foot sexy chef. He may be an arsehole, but he's a bloody gorgeous one. "She's already transformed our cookery school activities. Honestly, she's one of the best people I've ever worked with."

I try not to stare at him. God, he's good.

"Her reputation?" Chantelle mumbles until he pushes up his sleeves. I swear drool hangs from the corner of her mouth.

"Have you eaten her cupcakes? They're like baked bites of heaven. I ordered a box of them from her company earlier this year, and as soon as I tasted them, I proclaimed I'd never get enough of her baking."

That's a lie. Chantelle tips her head. If she spent time on my old website, she'll know we didn't do mail-order goods, although that's a great idea. I should've thought of that. But Chantelle doesn't argue with the great Chef Garett and his disarmingly sexy forearms.

"Obvs. Her cakes were great. I had some delivered." *Liar.* "I presume you're here for your wine order. Kath phoned and told me you were coming and not to close before you arrived. Why did you come this late when you could have picked it up during the week?"

"But—" I stop myself.

Kath. Of course. She set us up and stopped us nearly

killing each other at the cookery school. She used to sneakily mediate when Grandma and Grandad argued. Their relationship was fiery at times. She'd send them on a wild goose chase or make them do a stock run and insist it must be both of them.

I glance at a smiling, head-shaking Garett. He meets my gaze, and I shrug, returning his smile. Bloody Kath strikes again, and even worse, it's worked.

CHAPTER FOURTEEN – RUBY

Garett reverses out of the parking space. He's still got his sleeves pushed up to the elbow. He leans one of his panty-wetting forearms on the back of my seat as he twists his head to stare out of the car's rear window. It's like something from the cover of one of Amber's spicy romance books. His muscles flex, and I sit on my hands and tighten my jaw to resist touching them. He's still a dickhead.

I debate whether I'm tired or still carrying that end-of-shitty-relationship horniness that's dogged me over the last fortnight.

He drives us down country roads. The journey seems slower this time.

I glance at Garett as I consider something Chantelle whispered before we left: *"I don't like you, Ruby, but the cookery school is one of our best customers. You need to watch Garett. There was a big bust-up at his old place. Ask your parents why he's slumming it at the cookery school."*

I don't trust a word from her mouth, but it's another reminder that I must visit my parents. I want a bit of background on why Garett is at the cookery school, too, although I doubt it's as controversial as Chantelle suggests. Maybe I can get something out of him by opening up a little. I owe him for what he said to Chantelle.

"The stick shift manual car thing," I say, pulling Garett from wherever his head is.

"Yeah?" There's a softness to his gaze. I can't escape the niggle that there's more to him and especially more to why his dog, who he adores, isn't with him.

"I couldn't pass my test with a clutch, and I don't know why. I guess some things don't always click in my head. My grandad taught me to drive in the old cookery school van, but in the end, he gave up, and I drove grandma's funky automatic mini."

He gives one last bite of the mouth guard he sneaked into his mouth for a couple of minutes when we left the cookery school before slipping it into its case. A grinding teeth problem would explain the strip of gum he puts in his mouth every time he sees me.

"Were you close to your grandparents? Amber mentioned they helped your parents start the original school."

"Yeah, Grandad built it with help in Mum and Dad's garden. He was a carpenter. Grandma was the first chef."

"Was she a hard ass, too?" My eyes flicker as I stare at him. My heart jumps, my skin tingles, and I press my lips together to stop smiling. "I mean, like me. Chefs and all that," he stutters.

"Oh." I douse my belly fire. "She had her moments, but she wasn't anywhere near as bad as you." I offer a smile aiming for a joke between acquaintances rather than a tease. I don't need that flirty banter anymore, though I want it.

He smiles, too. "But Chantelle, who is a cow, by the way, said something about their funeral? When did they die? Is that okay to ask?"

"Yeah, it's fine. They died a couple of years ago." The funeral still leaves a sour taste in my mouth. It was the last time I came home. Neil was meant to join me, but as we were about to leave home, he started a fight and left me to go alone. It was probably better to be there without him, especially as there were always difficulties between him and my family, but I needed someone to be there for me that day. "Grandma died in the morning, and the next day, Grandad died in his sleep. The doctors said his heart just stopped."

"I'm sorry."

I pick at my plaster. "It's okay, but thanks. It was kind of for the best that they died at the same time. There's something called broken heart syndrome, and people do die from it. It's like his heart couldn't cope without her. That was my grandparents, though. They met in their early twenties and fell in love—the sort of epic love that most of us dream about. They were hilarious together, always cheeking each other, and my grandma had more sass than me."

"Surely not?" The corner of his lips turn up, and mine do the same.

"I know. Who would have thought that was possible? I get my attitude from her."

"I can't imagine having that level of love for anyone other than Cookie. I'm not sure if I'm capable of it."

"Me neither. I certainly didn't feel like that about my ex, Neil." I cover my mouth. I barely know Garett, but maybe that's why I said it. He doesn't know me, and he isn't a member of my family. It's not like I have anyone else in my world.

A silence settles in the car, and I don't like it. It's giving me too many thoughts about my revelation. It's the first time I've publicly admitted that my love for Neil was something painfully short of epic. It wasn't the sort of love I wanted.

"May I?" My fingers are on the heater dial. I need to erase the chill that's settled in my bones.

"Sure," he replies. Maybe he sees my hand tremble as I twist the dial because he keeps talking. "What happened with Neil? You don't have to answer, but I was curious what brought you home so quickly."

His jaw is so tight it could cut glass. I stare out the window. In the reflection of the glass, Garett slides a strip of gum in his mouth.

"He cheated on me with my business partner." Talk about the abridged version. I pull the elastic out of my hair and let it flow across my shoulders before using my fingers to work through the tangles from the day. "It's why I want to do Clive Macdonald's competition. I want to start my own business in a year. This will help me get my name out there. I don't want to go backwards. The cookery school isn't mine. It's Amber's name on it."

"But—"

"It's a long story. Ultimately, I need to give myself a future and prove to my family that I'm back and can be here for them. I think Amber could do with the money for the twins, too."

Garett is quiet. I can hear his gum chewing from here.

I must've made him angry by mentioning the competition again. I wasn't doing it to upset him, but I was trying to avoid more discussion about Neil and open up a bit. Garett can be relatively easy to talk to, and I miss having someone to chat to.

The For Sale sign on the pub near the school is tilted at an angle. The pub is a beautiful Cotswold building filled with low original beams and an original fireplace. I remember when Mum and Dad took us there for dinner when they first discussed opening a new cookery school. The owner was a family friend. It was a treat, and Grandma and Grandad laughed at Jem's jokes. I miss those days. I'll never get them back.

CHAPTER FIFTEEN – GARETT

My shoulders hunch. I grip the steering wheel and chew gum like it's my nemesis as I contemplate what Ruby has told me. I understand the need to be self-sufficient, but helping her is a considerable risk. I've learnt the hard way that Clive can't be trusted, but there are things I could put in place to offset risk.

Her family have given me a temporary future. I owe them for that. If they hadn't, then I hate to think where I'd be.

Thoughts swirl as I turn into the cookery school car park.

Ruby has a history that I'm curious about, and she deserves to have someone on her side. Maybe I can be that person between now and Christmas. It might be fun to teach someone as keen to learn and as skilful as she is.

"I'll help you," I say quietly. I swear she's holding her breath. "With the competition. I'll help you. I know what it's like to need someone to take a chance on you, and I owe your family a lot for gambling on me. So I'll help you."

"Are you sure? You need to want to do this without being guilted into it," she stutters. "You don't have to do it, and don't do it because you feel sorry for me or anything."

I park in my spot, cut the engine, and stare at her. I can feel her excitement bubbling, and I'm getting a buzz at giving her this opportunity. "Yes, completely. Your family have given me a lot, and if it can help raise the profile of the cookery school, too, then even better. We'll start next week once Halloween is out of the way."

She's not saying anything. Maybe she thinks she'll owe me or something. She couldn't even enjoy the lasagne without foisting orgasmic cupcakes on me. "Ruby, is that okay?"

"That's amazing. I can't believe it. Thank you so much." Her hands tremble. "This means everything."

Oh shit. Is she going to cry? I squeeze my lips into my mouth as she unclicks her seatbelt, reaches over the gear stick, and hugs me. I haven't had a hug from a beautiful woman in ages, especially not one laden with gratitude rather than a come-on. My heart beats wildly against her, and I breathe in that passion fruit scent that's still mixed with the buttercream from earlier. Everything about me warms up, especially when she kisses me on my cheek. I hope I'm not blushing. I cough and pull back.

Before I can explain it or justify it, she jumps out of the van and starts dancing what can only be described as the dance of a chicken after drinking too much wine.

I slip out of the van and lean against my vehicle to watch her, unsure if it's creepier to watch from inside or outside.

"Do you always dance like this when you're happy?" Her unyielding joy is infectious, and as she grins at me, her eyes twinkling, I already wish I'd agreed we start sooner, because then I would have been around her happiness for longer. "Don't make me regret this."

"One of us will." She waves her hands in the air. "You're a stern, grumpy chef with a reputation as a badass."

I chuckle at her excellent review of my persona.

"Promise you won't ride me too hard."

Her comment cuts my laugh dead. My eyes jump from my head, and a strangled sound leaves my mouth.

"I didn't mean…"

"I think you sniffed too much wine at the warehouse," I counter, trying to force out the images filling my head. "And on that note, I'd best be getting home."

Her smile is a bit of a wince, and I cuss myself for cutting her happiness short. "And I promise that if I have to ride you, I'll do it gently and not too hard."

She mumbles, *"That's a shame,"* as she heads back to her car. Shit. I tried to take the heat out of the situation, but her response has more comments teetering on my tongue.

I breathe a sigh of relief as she reverses out of the car park—or, at least, I do until I see her broken light. Great. Now I'll worry about her safety until the next cooking session. And if I have to buy a light to fix her car before the next cooking session, then so be it. It doesn't mean anything.

I drive home via Amber's, searching for Ruby's car in a ditch or smashed in the road. My heart only returns to average speed when I see it parked in Amber's driveway.

Deciding to help Ruby with the competition weighs on my mind. I need to discuss the decision with someone, but I haven't got anyone to share my worries with.

It's the right decision for all the reasons I said, and no matter what happens with the competition, she can gain skills to help her with a new version of her Naughty Treats company or whatever she wants to do in the future. It will also do wonders for the cookery school and raise their profile. I've heard a rumour from Flora that the competition will be streamed.

But then there's Clive.

Sick fills my throat, and I pull over to the side of the road to stretch my hands out from cramping.

Paramore plays from the van's speakers as I consider damage limitation. When we get closer to the contest, I can tell Ruby's family about Clive, and once the competition ends, I can tell Ruby what Clive did. I don't want to lie to her, but she said she needs the money for Amber, and she deserves to give a fuck you to her ex, who treated her like crap. I must keep her safe but let her make this decision, too. Once she has the money, I'll tell her everything even though I know she'll look at me like I'm not some great restaurant chef but a guy who fucked up. It will be worth it to keep her safe.

The last bars of "The Only Exception" play as I pull back onto the road.

Decision made. Ruby's success and happiness will be my priority, and I'll push down my anxiety, too.

This will end well.

Chapter Sixteen – Garett

I walk into the cookery class an hour early because I want to spend as much time as possible around Ruby. Proximity is dangerous, yet talking to her in the van last week and laughing with her at the classes this week have been the happiest moments I've had in months.

Or you fancy her and are making excuses for seeing those hold ups again. I grunt at my inner voice, which has a valid point. I want to see her costume. I hope she likes mine.

"Nice costume," Kath says with a smile. If she's surprised I'm here early, she doesn't let on. "I'm guessing it's for Ruby's benefit. If I'm not wrong, you're dressed as her favourite animal."

In the two months I've been here, I've learnt that Kath is never wrong, but I reply with a shrug. "I don't know what you mean."

I'm busy in the kitchen, so she can't see my grin. At the end of one class, Ruby mentioned that she loves pandas and wishes she could go on a panda cuddling trip.

When I first saw Ruby this week at our foraging and feasting class, I was suave and nonchalant, and I barely looked at her, though her hips called out for my touch. I was a badass chef until she made me laugh so hard at her impression of a baby chick that I spat out my tea.

I also fixed the cover on her car's light when she was busy tidying up after class. I don't think she knows it's me. I didn't do it for a thank you. I just want her safe.

"She knows you fixed her light, by the way," Kath comments, reading my thoughts. I smile to myself. "It's lovely that you care about her so much."

"I don't know what you mean," I repeat. "Besides, I only did it because the clocks have changed, and I want her to be safe driving in the dark. I'd do it for anyone else, even Wicksy."

I gaze at my lying reflection in the oven window. Big black ears peek out the top of my hood, and white patches of fur cover my body. I've barely got anything on under this costume, and I'm already overheating. I crank up the air con.

"Of course you would." I know Kath is smiling even without seeing her. "Could you get the wine out, Mr. Formerly Grumpy Chef?"

Kath has entered into the spirit of this adult Halloween party with a long purple witchy wig and black cobweb dress. Cookie would look fabulous as part of the group, running with his six waggling legs. He'd be chasing me if he saw me in this panda onesie. The pain in my chest at not having him with me hits hard as I rip open boxes and start pulling out bottles of wine. As much as I'm excited about the food we'll be preparing with the clients today, which will include a marshmallow cheesecake and mini spinach and feta pies, I would give it all up to have him by my side.

My phone buzzes with a reminder that Flora is popping by after class to get her onesie so she can lend it to another friend for their Halloween night. Maybe she's shown the contract to her friend and has ideas on how to make Cookie mine again, too.

We spoke the other night, and she told me Clive is barely walking him and not spending any time with him. He's cooped up in the apartment all day except for occasional walks with her.

I stare at the lock screen photo from last Christmas of Cookie wearing antlers. His beaming smile gives me a glow, and I sigh happily. I've no idea when I became the kind of guy who dresses up his dog. I used to be a lad who partied until morning and then dragged myself out of a stranger's bed to prepare lunch for a collection of upscale clients. Cookie has taught me that there's more to life. It's a shame I'll never be the kind of guy someone other than a dog could love.

Kath comes up behind me. "Are you done with that wine yet? Where is your head? I meant to add that I'm glad you and Ruby aren't fighting anymore. I wonder what brought on that change."

She smirks as I point at her. "I've got a bone to pick with you. I know why you avoided me at the cooking class this week. Apparently, the wine merchants were open all week. What was with making me and Ruby go there last weekend?"

Kath's eyes twinkle as she holds her hand to her mouth. "I must have made a mistake. I am getting so forgetful these days."

"The cheeky smile that you're badly hiding isn't fooling anyone. You're trouble."

Kath chuckles. "If only you knew. I have ways and means of making my work environment happy and ensuring that good people get good things. You're good people, Garett, even if you pretend you're not." The corners of my lips tease up in a wry smile. I've been told my whole life that I'm not a good person, and Kath barely knows me. "I was wondering if you could use your good side to help me with a surprise I'm planning for Amber."

This is significant. I try not to let my emotions get the better of me, but my grin gives me away. Kath trusts me! I nod and open my mouth, but she looks over my shoulder and puts her finger to her lips. "Later." And with that, she disappears into the back kitchen.

Big thumping boots hit the tiled floor behind me, and the scent of passion fruit envelops me.

"You forgot this, Mr. Angry Panda Chef Who Fixes Car Lights." Ruby's voice tickles my ear. "Bend a little, you bloody giant."

I bend. I'm too afraid to turn, and I can't understand why. A part of me doesn't want to see her face and realise she's embarrassed about dancing like a knob in front of me or doing chick impressions this week. What will she think about me fixing her light? I still remember that kiss on my cheek from last weekend, and I hope my kindness will earn me another. That kiss has made me smile as I've tried to sleep every night since.

Ruby pops something on my head. "We'll have to tape it on, or it will fall off."

I reach my hands to hold it. It's a chef's hat. I roll my eyes and turn. I stifle a gasp. I'm not prepared for Ruby or her costume.

"Do you like it?" She holds her hands out and twirls.

The cutest woman in the world stands in front of me, dressed in a checked green shirt, blue jeans, and an apron, with stubble drawn on her face.

"Please tell me you didn't." My accent comes out strong and booming.

"Please tell me you didn't," she repeats, husking her voice and adding the warmth to her words that my accent sometimes brings. She takes my chef's hat off my head and puts it back on hers, although she's cocked it to the side. "Are you sad because I'm not wearing the sexy maid costume?"

I won't admit that truth or that I love that she's dressed as me. I chose my costume for her, and maybe she decided on hers to get a reaction out of me.

"I've never been more attracted to myself," I reply, causing her to roll her eyes. "If you'd dressed as a maid, you would have looked hot, but now you're dressed as the sexiest person that ever lived."

She shoves me as Kath returns. Kath stares at Ruby, throws her head back, and laughs, causing her witchy nose to fly across the room. This starts Ruby off, and soon, the two of them are gasping for breath as they scrabble on the floor, looking for Kath's nose. I'm falling in love with this cookery school. I need to remember it's a stopgap, but as a very sexy version of me bends over with her curvy ass in the air, I'm not sure how easy it will be to leave when the time comes.

"Ruby was the best dressed," Wicksy comments after helping the rest of the clients out of the building with all their cooked goodies. They stayed an extra hour because we were having too much fun.

"We all know what you think," I grumble as I tidy up

the candy we used for Halloween cocktails. I yank one of the eyeball-shaped sweets stuck like glue to the countertop, nearly falling back. Sweat collects under my arms, and I curse my costume for the umpteenth time.

I reach for the air con, but Kath shouts, "Don't you dare. The rest of us have shivered most of the night because of you. Take off a layer."

"But—"

"Take off a layer," Ruby calls out. "You're amongst friends, Mr. Angry Panda."

I grumble loudly. I've been like a human radiator all night, but with only boxers under my costume, I don't want to undo it. "I'll get my change of clothes out of the van."

"I wouldn't," Ruby warns, "unless you're after a hookup."

I lock on her stare, and my forehead hurts from how hard my eyebrows furrow. "What do you mean?" My pulse races with hope.

"A woman out there wants to get in your panda pants." I offer my fakest grin. Shit. Of course Ruby isn't offering to spend sexy time with me. "Do you remember the woman dressed as a sexy nurse?"

I shake my head. She sounds like my perfect woman.

"Seriously? The beautiful blonde who was confused about the cheesecake base a lot."

"It's not ringing any bells."

Wicksy and Kath are silent, their heads moving back and forth like they're at a tennis match.

"She was slim, beautiful, legs up to here." Ruby points above her head. She's too bloody cute. "She laughed at your jokes all night." I cock my head to the side. "There were sixteen people here tonight. How can you not remember her? She was gorgeous."

Because I only had eyes for you. I grit my teeth, thankful that I didn't say that aloud. How am I this into Ruby already? Misplaced loneliness. That's all.

"She was the one who said my cocktail class was a silly idea."

"Oh, her. I didn't like her. She was mean about your strawberry cocktail idea." It was a great idea. All of Ruby's ideas are excellent. She made this evening what it was.

Ruby palms her face, but she's badly hiding a smile behind her hand. "Whatever. Anyway, she gave me your number as I walked her to the car park, and she hung around, hoping to see you."

I shrug. "I'm not going out there now."

Her smile broadens at my answer, although it quickly disappears. But I saw it. "You'd best take off a layer, then."

"But losing a layer means standing here in my boxers."

"Stop being such a prince. You're bright red, and I'm not giving you mouth-to-mouth if you faint." But the smirk she gives me suggests otherwise. *Rein it in, Garett.* "How about we all look away? Or you can go outside and hook up with the nurse."

"Fine." Ruby's face falls, and Wicksy and Kath stare at me until I add, "Look away, then. I'd rather be semi-naked in front of you three than hook up with the mean nurse."

Kath and Wicksy busy themselves, and Ruby turns around, but I swear she's looking at me in the oven's reflection as I undress. *Get over yourself. She thinks you're funny and nothing more. No woman who dresses up as you for Halloween fancies you. She thinks your grumpiness makes you the scariest thing in England.*

I unzip my onesie and then yank the whole thing off. I look again at the oven door, and Ruby's eyes widen before she suddenly looks down and back up. My boxers are tight enough to show what's typically hidden beneath my jeans. It's like the temperature drops suddenly by ten degrees, and I throw my head back and let my tension out with a loud sigh.

"Oh my," Kath says, staring at me as she tidies up.

Wicksy grumbles and throws an apron at me.

But none of the reactions compare to Ruby's. Her chest flushes beneath the V of the open checked shirt. She bites her lip, and her gaze travels down my body. She hums as her stare reaches my boxers. Suddenly, her wide eyes dart to mine. She's ruby red.

"I've suddenly remembered I've got to be somewhere." She stumbles through her words.

"Where? You can't get out of clearing up that easily," Wicksy says.

"Where have you got to be, Ruby?" I say her name slowly as I cover myself up with the apron. I want to pump a fist in the air. "I thought you were here until the climax of the evening. Surely, you can't go until you're satisfied. Do you need help finishing?" It's like my whole face twinkles.

Her chest rises and falls dramatically. "I'll tidy tomorrow."

"Don't worry. We've got this sorted," Kath adds with a smirk. "Some nights, we just need to get off."

I glance at Kath. She didn't just say that.

Ruby makes a choked noise. She's still staring at me as if all her Christmases have come at once.

"Yeah, you go and do whatever you need, Rubes." My eyes track her body. "And make sure you do it *exactly* how you need to."

I barely blink before she rushes to the door. She

crashes through it and is gone. Did I push the joke too far?

"Now, let's get this done," Kath says, not allowing my thoughts to linger on a flushed Ruby.

CHAPTER SEVENTEEN – RUBY

I haven't seen Garett since last weekend when he stood in just a pair of boxers in the kitchen and I ran for the door like a cross between a horny teenage lad needing a wank and a prim old lady who couldn't stand the sight of nakedness.

I wince as I unhook my seatbelt, I see the Cloud Cookery School van. The memory of his hard chest flashes to the front of my mind again. I knew he was hot. He was number one on my list of sexy chefs for a reason, but that body was like something else.

"And yet you panicked and ran away," I mumble, "when you should have climbed him like a fucking monkey scrabbling up a tree."

I push the door of the cookery school with my shoulder, my pulse out of control, but it's still locked. His van is in the car park. I fumble with my keys and after dropping them twice, I open the door, and walk into the cookery school. No one's around when I enter the building and most of the lights are off. Maybe he's doing something in the back office. I'm early to set up each station, as Kath is busy today.

I've hallucinated his god-like body all week. Whenever I attempted to plan my baking for Clive Macdonald's competition, I'd linger on the dark hair covering Garett's tanned chest. And I still can't believe I talked about him riding me hard the other week. I totally blame the way I am around him on my joy and not on his warmth from that time I hugged him or the scent of cinnamon that I can always smell or those damn arms that are like a beacon of sexiness or his chuckle that's the cutest sound in the whole damn world.

I retie my hair, holding my hairband in my teeth. I sound like one of his needy fangirls.

"Garett?" I call out, but there's no response except for my voice echoing around me.

I recall his hips with that perfect V I want to trace with my tongue. And his thighs are pure muscle. How does a man who spends his days in a windowless kitchen get a body like that?

I'd love to straddle those thighs. My horniness was a ten all week, but I only got my little bullet vibrator out a couple of times because it's nearly out of batteries and I haven't found time to get to the shop. Why do bullets take such tiny rare batteries? I need my powerful vibrator, but it's still at my old place. Although if I was using that one as much as I need to, Amber and her neighbours will be questioning why someone spends so long vacuuming a bedroom in a garden shed cabin or cleaning their teeth with an electric toothbrush.

So, instead, I've been needy with arousal and made a lot of dick-shaped strawberry and white chocolate cookies instead. They're based on what I imagine is hidden under his boxers, but I'd need to see his dick in the flesh to recreate him perfectly. I chuckle to myself. I'd probably combust the second I saw it. Based on his boxers, his cock is the sort that women would run marathons for.

My mobile rings, pulling me out of my Garett dick fantasies, and I cancel the call immediately. I've only had two missed calls from Neil today, which is an improvement. I've not answered them or any of the others, but I occasionally listen to some of the voicemail messages to torture myself.

The phone makes a *bing* as it receives a voice message. I creep around the school, but there are no noises or signs of people.

Paper ripped from a lined notebook sits on the demonstration counter.

Went for a run, be back soon. G

Wicksy said he occasionally drops his stuff off and goes for a run as he prefers the countryside and the local small town to where he lives. Maybe we should invest in a cookery school shower so he can wash that wet dream of a body rather than making him do some sort of sink shower where he throws water at himself. According to Wicksy, the men's bathroom is like Rihanna's Umbrella video after he's been in there after a run. I retie my hair for the umpteenth time that day, swallow loudly, and put my phone on speaker. If anything can erase the arousal from my body, it's Neil's whiny voice.

"Babes." I shudder at the sound of it. I've listened to a couple of messages on the off chance I might experience sadness, regret, or, God forbid, a longing to see him again. But there's nothing. Less than nothing. There's a hollowness in the pit of my stomach because, deep down, I know why I feel nothing. We were over way before six years. Maybe that's why I haven't blocked his number. I need to continue the self-flagellation. At some point, I'll build up the courage to tell him I want the rest of my clothes, too. "I miss you, Babes. My days aren't full without you. I wake up, and you're not there. I made a mistake, and I'm sorry. Like, really sorry."

Each message follows the same formula.   First, apologies and then—

"But it was your fault. You worked too hard on your business. You were never there for me. And don't get me started on the lack of sex."

I don't know why I'm not ending the message from the guy who was lazy, selfish, and shit in bed. Maybe I need to hurt myself for pushing my family away for this mistake of a man.

His voice cuts through the air con, the only noise in the kitchen. "You're not frigid. I remember the start of our relationship when you were a frisky madam." Neil pauses.

"And I remember that, even then, I rarely came because you weren't that bothered if I did," I rant at the message.

The clang of a metal water bottle hitting the floor above me echoes loudly, and I glance up at the mezzanine floor as Neil's message says, "But you changed. Like, you weren't sexy anymore, and to be honest, Viv took time to make me happy. Like really—" I switch the phone off, but it's too late. My number one chef, who's wearing more clothes than the last time I saw him, heard everything.

"Sorry. I wasn't listening." His gaze travels around the room as if he can't bear to look at me, but he suddenly meets my stare. My body flares with humiliation as sweat beads my forehead. "I returned from my run about ten minutes ago and needed somewhere to change. I didn't really hear."

"It doesn't matter." But it does. I pull my arms to my body in an attempt to hug myself and fist my hands, digging my nails into my palms.

"But–"

"Seriously, Garett," I snap at him, my stare boring into his soft brown eyes. "It doesn't matter. Just pretend you didn't hear about the frigid bitch who worked too hard at her failing business and whose boyfriend preferred to screw her best friend. Okay?"

He presses his lips tightly, winces, and nods.

"Great. Kath isn't in today, so I'm setting up. You'd best stay out of my way. In fact, everyone should stay out of my way today." I storm off without waiting for a reply.

The cookery class carries on in the same way, me in a foul mood and Garett avoiding me because that's what I told him to do. It's a successful pasta-making class despite my mood. To make it worse, my normal sunshine bug has bitten Garett. He's laughed with the clients, bent over backwards to give them a great day, and gone above and beyond with every request. It's paid off, too. We've had so much interest in Christmas cooking that we'll need to add midweek classes in December and work until Christmas Eve. Amber will be ecstatic, and it's all because of him.

"We don't have to cook tonight if you don't want to. I can help you with the competition another time," he says, sidling up to me as I fill the dishwasher.

I'd forgotten about that. I can't say no, even though I'm sweating at the idea of having to be kind to anyone when all I want to do is gorge myself on chocolate dick-shaped cookies and rewatch a true crime show where someone's ex-boyfriend gets murdered.

But this incredible chef is giving up his time to help me even though, for whatever reason, he won't tell me why he doesn't want me to do the competition.

"No, it's cool," I reply. "I'll finish tidying up, and then we'll get on with it unless you don't want to."

I wouldn't want to be around me when I'm grumpier than Gordon Ramsay mid-tantrum.

"No, I want to." His smile is tentative as he sticks a strip of gum into his mouth and chews in that slow way that transfixes me. "I've worked on the techniques I'd like to show you. I'll help you clean up, and we'll be able to start sooner. I've got a cinnamon idea you'll love."

My lousy mood fades quickly. He's willing to put all this effort into helping me.

Five minutes later, we meet at one of the counters.

"Are you okay?" he asks. He squeezes his lips together, his gaze attempting to penetrate my soul, before slipping another piece of gum into his mouth.

I shake my head. "No, but let's get on. I don't want to talk about it."

He nods but doesn't push. I like that, but it also makes my shoulders sag a little. I don't have anyone else to speak to. I still haven't built the courage to visit my parents, and I've avoided Amber's house when I know they're visiting. The pregnancy and absent husband are continuing to take their toll on Amber. She was green and asleep when I left this morning. My parents are caring for her, though. But I'm not pouring my heart out to Garett, either. I have to work with him, and I've already had enough humiliation to last a lifetime over the last month.

"Okay, let's begin. I want you to show me how you make cookies, and as you do this, I'll give you feedback and ways to improve, such as ideas on finesse or making things quicker."

"Quicker?"

"Speed means you have more time to add something to your creation at the end or perfect it. The key for these competitions isn't just making something the judges like; it's wowing them. You can do that with taste, decoration, finish, or something unique. What we want to do is to perfect all four. That's how you impress them."

I could listen to him talk in teacher mode all day. It's like he's doing one of his classes, and it's only for me.

I smile despite the day I've had.

"Can I have music on?" He raises his eyebrow at my request. "I'm used to cooking with music in the background."

"Something pop?" he says without inflexion, rolling up his sleeves and making my stomach flop.

"After the day I've had, I want nineties indie anthems. Do you know Jader?"

He throws his head back and laughs. He's so different from the guy I met nearly a month earlier. "I partied hard with them as a teenager and then spent a summer working in the restaurant on the drummer's cheese farm. They're good lads. But can we start with Oasis? I'm feeling their *Morning Glory* album, then maybe Kenickie and a bit of Republica."

His grin leaves me imagining what he was like in his partying days. The Garett I've met seems a bit broken, and every new side is a refreshing revelation that I want more insight into.

"Hard partier and restaurant worker on a cheese farm. Who are you?"

He shrugs, but his smile is wistful. As "She's Electric" blasts from the stereo, he watches me work. He gives me pointers on changing the taste and different methods to combine ingredients while sharing stories from his partying days.

My skills are on show, but instead of feeling uncomfortable and defensive, his smooth instructions and gentle advice make my limbs looser and my heart flush. As I knead the dough, it's like I'm kneading the kinks out of my shoulders or maybe the twists from my past.

"You know a lot about what the judges want. How come?" I press the dough with my hands, stretching it slightly before remembering I'm not meant to be making bread. His cinnamon scent is occasionally distracting.

"I worked under a famous television baker and judge for a while. People would stop and listen to her advice whenever she walked into the kitchen. She was the kindest woman unless you messed with her baking, and then she'd rip you a new one. I learnt a lot."

"We're talking about the baker who feigns innocence at every innuendo, and yet her necklaces resemble anal beads?"

He chuckled. "Maybe. Now stop distracting me and yourself and press that dough properly. Have you tried doing it slightly differently and moving your fingers like this?" He shoves his hands in the dough. His fingers brush mine, and electricity zips from my fingers to my scalp.

His eyelashes flutter as he side-eyes me.

I pull my lips into my mouth to prevent myself from beaming, but the excitement still needs somewhere to go, so I let out a tiny squeal before covering it with a cough.

"Anyway, you get the idea." He pulls his fingers back and walks to the sink. Oh shit. He knows I squealed with excitement because he touched me. I poke at the dough and grimace.

"I also know what judges want because I kind of entered a competition myself a while back." He's staring at the running water as he washes his hands.

"Yeah?" I keep my head down, but I glance at him occasionally. His shoulders are hunched, and he's scrubbing his hands repeatedly.

He clears his throat. "Yeah. It was with an old business partner."

Does he mean Clive?

I work the dough more, adding flour. He walks back to me, slower this time.

"Add a bit more here," he instructs, and I do.

"Did you win?" I ask, teasing information out of him.

He pauses. There's a lot about Garett I don't know, so that could mean any competition. There's no mention of Garett in the articles about Clive's Best Cotswold Restaurant win, but there's a niggling sensation in my stomach nonetheless.

"No, something happened. The business partner wasn't the person I thought or maybe wasn't the person I hoped. I should have known, but sometimes you trust the wrong people."

"I get that."

"And sometimes you make decisions, like to work exceptionally hard because that's important."

He reties his apron before he helps prepare the baking trays for my biscuits. Is this in reference to my voicemail from Neil or about his life?

I reach for the rolling pin, but he pushes it away.

"Not yet. One more press." It's a gentle command that

gives me weird, achy, yet pleasurable sensations in my limbs that I don't want to name. "That was my life. Work was the only thing that mattered to me. If I was managing a kitchen or a business and things weren't happening efficiently and people were wasting time on things that didn't make the business successful, they were wasting my life."

"And now?"

He adds a little flour to the counter. It's the fluttering thing he does. I attempt to copy it, but he chuckles. His laughter is like fingertips dancing across my skin.

"More like this." He holds my fingers and helps me make the fluttering shape. My belly does it, too.

"And now I see that there can be other things in life." His brown eyes track me, and sweat beads my neck. I push up the sleeves of my jumper.

"You could be a professional chef with that pushing sleeves action," he cheeks.

I shove him lightly, and he drops a flour dot onto my nose.

He stares at my lips, and I suck the lower one into my mouth. I'm so close to saying the wrong thing. He licks his lips slowly, and all the air leaves the room. He brushes the flour off my nose. I can't breathe. "Ruby, I—"

My phone vibrates, and we stare at where it sits on the counter.

Neil the Wanker is emblazoned on my screen.

"Video call?" Garett asks.

I press my hands to my temples while checking the clock. "He's probably drunk. He always video calls when he's drunk. I've not answered any of his calls since I left him."

Garett's expression is grave. "How many times has he

119

called?"

I nibble my lip. "This week, less than ten. The last weeks were more, and the first week was over fifty."

"Can I help?"

My mouth goes dry as an idea blasts me. I couldn't, and I really shouldn't, but it takes hold, and I can't stop my mouth from moving even as my conscience screams to stay quiet.

"Will you flirt with me?"

Garett doesn't miss a beat. His voice drops to a level that only horny women can hear. "Rubes, I thought you'd never ask."

CHAPTER EIGHTEEN – GARETT

The woman who's filled my fantasies since I met her and brought smiles to a difficult time in my life wants me to flirt with her. I'm on that like butter on a crumpet. I don't care that it's just to piss off her ex-boyfriend. I'm taking my chance to act out the fantasies I've had after every cookery class I've left the past month. The clothed ones, at least.

"Ready?" she asks. Her face flushes. I haven't even got started.

As much as I want to do this for my horny satisfaction, I also don't want her to have any more voicemails like earlier. How dare that jumped-up twat of an ex-boyfriend make comments about her frigidity and say she wasn't sexy. I've fantasised about her curvy bum for days. If I could grip it for a second, I'd die a happy man. Her hips wiggle when she's happy, yet make me want to douse myself in cold water. And I'm confident I must implore every artist to paint her, because she has the perfect hourglass figure.

"I was born ready for this," I say, and she blushes redder. She sucks that lip in again, and I try not to groan. "Flirting is a superpower I haven't used in a while."

She shakes out her hands.

Yeah, I sound cocky, but I was good at this once, and

she's about to find out exactly how good.

"Answer before it goes to voicemail," I growl.

She selects the answer button as she side-eyes me.

"Yes, Neil?" she snaps. I initially stay out of the camera. I want to get a measure of this guy, though my body demands that I get my flirt on.

"I miss you," he slurs. I'd be embarrassed for him if I hadn't heard his cruelty earlier. And with that number of calls and messages every week, I'm surprised she isn't continuously distracted by that harassing dickhead. "You left me."

"You fucked Viv, my friend and the person I ran a business with." Damn, I thought Clive was bad. If this co-worker also stole her dog, we'd be competing for the worst business partner and friend. "What do you want?"

He's holding the phone close to his face, and I do a double-take at the sight of him.

"I need you to say that you still want me and that I'm the best you ever had." I shudder at the gall of the man.

"You're the only one I ever had."

I gasp audibly and then grind my teeth. She looks at me, and I curse myself. It's not that shocking. I was a tart in my heyday, but not everyone is like me.

"Who are you with? Are you at work? Typical Ruby, always working and never having fun. I should have known."

That's my cue. I lick my lips as I stand behind her and grip her waist. Her curves are everything I imagined, and my whole body pulsates. I squeeze briefly, and she freezes. "It's okay," I whisper for only her to hear, although I doubt the drunk boy hears anything above his burps. "I'll be gentle."

"You don't have to be."

Blood rushes straight to my groin.

"Who are you talking to? Your lips are moving." He manages to get that out without a burp or a hiccup. Go Neil, you massive dickhead.

I'm barely a shadow on the screen because we're standing close together.

"It's none of your business," she replies. I run a finger across the nape of her neck, and she gasps quietly. So fucking sexy. I want to hear that noise again, although I'd prefer to have her do it as I kiss her properly. "So fuck off because I need to get to who—I mean, what—I was doing."

I hold in a chuckle. She's good. Why did I think she wouldn't be? The woman has had the measure of me since day one. As I reach for the elastic holding her bun, she shivers. Fuck, that's too hot. She's playing a perfect game.

"Who's that behind you? Is it a man?" I run my hands through her hair like I've wanted for weeks. It's soft and falls through my fingers like a dream. I find a knot and work it out like I've seen her do. She moans in a way that makes me instantly hard. I need to hear that moan again, but as she lies under me with my face between her thighs. *Chill, Garett. This is for Neil's benefit.* "He's playing with your hair."

"Don't be so silly, Neil." Her face is in the corner of her phone. It's a little image, but she's trying not to smile. "You need to stop calling me."

"You used to be sexier. You've let yourself go."

Her shoulders tighten, and the smile drops from her face.

The fucking bastard. She's a fighter. I've loved competing with her. How dare he say that and make her feel less than the incredible woman she is. I was tentative before, but now I'm all in.

I move the collar of her blouse to the side and brush her neck with my lips. She smells of strawberries, and I immerse myself in the scent.

She swallows loudly and bites her lip. I brush her neck again. I barely notice Neil's red toad face as he glares at us from the screen. I want to rid her of what he said and convince her how sexy she is, and I need to taste her.

Her skin burns beneath my lips as I kiss her neck. She leans her head to the side.

"That's my girl," I whisper as she undoes the top button of her blouse to give me more access. The barest hint of her dark green bra sends my pulse soaring.

"Who the fuck is that? Are you seeing someone? We just broke up."

"As if that matters, you fuckwit," she replies. But there's no anger, only acceptance. "Don't call again. I won't pick up. I'll be too busy." She whispers the last word.

My lips linger on her skin. She leans into me and moans a guttural sound that makes my body quake. She hasn't ended the call.

Suddenly, she turns.

His voice rattles through the speaker. "I'm not done. No one moves on from Wonder Neil that quickly."

I side-eye the phone as he hangs up, and it returns to the home screen. I step away, my performance for her ex over, but she shakes her head. "I didn't say stop," she says.

Oh shit. It's happening. She wants me.

She pushes her hands into my hair, and I grab her waist and pull her against me. We lock eyes, and for a moment, we stare at each other. Her eyes sparkle with more colours than in a rainbow birthday cake. She worries her lip. I cock my eyebrow, but her blossoming grin convinces me she wants this as much as I do.

I lick my lips, and she watches my tongue like it's her holy grail. My hands travel the length of her body until I'm cupping her face. I lean in to kiss her, and then her phone vibrates again.

"Fuck Neil," I moan against her plump lips.

"I'd rather not," she replies, and I glance at the phone. "I had someone else in mind."

My swallow echoes around the kitchen, and she giggles as she reaches for the phone. "I'll mute it," she says.

She stills, and her face loses its flush.

Before I can ask what's going on, she answers the phone. My hand is still on her hip, and I can't stop smelling those strawberries. Fuck, she's delicious.

"Amber?" Her voice shakes as she speaks into the phone.

The phone is so close that I can hear everything Amber says. "Before you freak, everything is fine."

"And yet you're calling and not texting. You never call without texting first." The warmth has left her now pallid cheeks, and her body trembles. "What is wrong?"

"You're freaking," Amber replies.

"What's that beeping in the background? There's a Tannoy, too. Where are you?"

"Chill out. It's nothing. Like really nothing, Ruby. I wasn't feeling great, so I made a GP appointment this afternoon—"

Ruby raises her voice. "And you didn't tell me? I'm supposed to be taking care of you while Kalen is away."

"Okay, if you're freaking out at that, then the next bit is really going to piss you off."

I pull away, but Ruby grabs my hand so tightly that I'm not sure I'll ever be able to knead bread again.

"Amber, I swear to God, if you don't tell me what's going on, I'll—"

"Rip off all my Barbie's heads?" Amber sounds pretty relaxed. It's not helping.

"That was one time, and if you remember, you'd broken my Easy Bake Oven."

"Accidentally, and you broke my bed by jumping on it." Ruby must have been a terror when she was younger. I love that.

"Amber," Ruby replies between gritted teeth. "Tell me right now where you are, or I'm going to lose it."

I can testify to that. She's still got that death grip on my hand, and her legs are shaking.

"I'm in the hospital, but I am fine. Absolutely one hundred per cent fine."

"Then why are you in the hospital?" Ruby screeches.

"Because they insisted on doing checks. Everything is fine. It was wind. Don't comment." Ruby opens and closes her mouth. "The nurse told me that there aren't any issues, but we have to wait for my gynaecologist to sign me off to go home, and she's trying to get down the country because she's stuck up north in an accident or something."

"Can't another doctor do it?"

"You'd think so, but Kalen, in all his wisdom, had it written into my private healthcare plan that if I come in with any issues, I must be seen by the gynaecologist *and* midwife. It's probably a guilt thing because he's not with me. After all, the insurance premiums to have this healthcare are ridiculous, but I don't dare argue with him. He cares so damn much."

"I'm coming over. I won't believe you're okay until I'm in front of you."

But she's not safe to drive. Amber can't see how her body shakes with adrenaline, but I can.

"I'll drive," I whisper.

She stares at me while Amber makes her swear she won't tell their parents. "Swear it, Ruby."

Ruby nods at me and mouths, *Thank you.*

"Swear you won't tell them."

"Fine. I swear it. I haven't had the guts to tell them I'm home or visit them, so I certainly won't be starting with this. But if anything happens, then I'm going to rip your head off next."

"I believe you, you little psycho. See you soon."

Ruby is avoiding her parents, her boyfriend cheated on her with a friend and business partner, she's got no business, and her ex is the only guy she's ever slept with. I've too many questions and emotions when it comes to this woman. She's going to be the life and death of me, and in a sick way, I'm excited about what's next.

CHAPTER NINETEEN – RUBY

I rush through the doors of the private hospital with Garett at my heels.

A man holds his bleeding head at the desk while his friend tells a slurring story to the receptionist. I can't keep still. My feet are trying to recreate a Dick Van Dyke tap dance as the stranger gets to the part of the story about a stripper and a cheese and pickle sandwich.

I avoid confrontation except with sexy chefs, but as my pulse spikes, I sense that ball of pressure sitting at the back of my throat.

Suddenly, Garett's warm, coarse hand slips into mine. His eyes are wide as he locks my gaze. I take a breath.

"Let's move this along. No one wants to hear about a pickle in a lady's frou-frou," Garett grunts.

I hold in a bubble of laughter at the words frou-frou as the two guys turn and stare.

"But the pickle is important. His head wouldn't be bleeding if there wasn't a pickle."

Luckily, my brother-in-law paid for private care for this pregnancy. At least we only have one drunk to deal with tonight and not a queue of carnage.

"My friend's sister was brought in. She's pregnant with twins. We want to see her and make sure she's okay," Garett explains as I attempt to regulate my breathing.

The receptionist catches the eye of a nurse who waits to direct us down a corridor while we sign in.

Abstract artwork reminiscent of an art gallery, not a hospital, adorns the cream walls. A water fountain bubbles as we pass it. Our footsteps tap across the linoleum floor, or whatever is beneath our feet, and although they've tried to create an atmosphere of a safe space, it's impossible to miss the clinical scent that's in every hospital. Garett holds my hand, and it's all that's keeping me grounded. I breathe in his cinnamon scent, and my pulse slows a little. I don't know how I would have managed tonight without him. I was buzzed after watching Neil get upset at seeing me with Garett. All that time, he thought I wasn't enough, and I'm starting to feel like I was and am. There was also the flirting and near kiss with Garett, but I refuse to linger on that, although it's burrowed in the back of my mind for later. Amber is all that matters.

A door opens, and suddenly, there's my beaming sister. At her smile, I well up. Garett hangs back in the doorway as I rush and hug her, careful not to squeeze her too tight. "You're okay," I pant, my panic exploding in a rush of breath.

"Of course I am. I told you I was. I've got snacks, my own super comfortable bed, and old episodes of *Columbo*."

"You're so weird," I reply as Garett moves a chair. It scrapes on the floor as he slides it behind me. "Only you'd be watching *Columbo* at a time like this."

I grab her hand, and it trembles a little. I tip my head as she forces a fake smile.

"What's really going on?"

That's when the tears flow.

"I'll leave you two be. Sister time," Garett murmurs. Maybe crying women freak him out. I appreciate his care. If not for him, I would have crashed my car or had a meltdown in the reception area. "I'll be in the waiting room."

"Sorry," Amber blubs.

"Don't apologise. It's more than okay to cry. But this is a moment for family," Garett says before slipping out the door. He doesn't want to embarrass her, and that realisation makes my heart flutter, even as cracks appear when I see my sister weep.

The vast width of the private bed means I have space to clamber up. I sneak under her blanket to hold her close. We used to do this as children when something scared us. Usually, it was one of the many crime drama shows we were too young to watch. She tucks her head against my chest, and I stroke her hair as she weeps.

"I miss Kalen so much," she says between sobs. "I thought he'd be home by now."

"Have you heard anything?"

"No. I'm sure he is safe, but when things like this happen, I get this terror that he'll die while on operations. That our babies will never meet him. I can't bear a life without him." She hiccups as she sobs. How long has she kept these fears to herself? "I can't do this alone."

I squeeze her tightly as sickness rises in my throat. "You're not alone. You're never alone. You've got Mum and Dad, who will do everything to ensure you're safe and cared for. I'm so sorry I've been selfish for years, but I'm home for as long as you'll have me. I got in my head that Neil was the only one that mattered, and I can't change that, but—"

She lifts her head and grabs mine between her hands, shutting me up instantly. Her sobs have slowed, and she glares at me with a fire that reminds me how amazing she will be as a mum. She's all love but can bring the force of a thousand dragons when she needs to.

"You weren't selfish. You had stuff to do. You're my baby sister and are allowed your own life." I brush tears from her eyes. "But I'm happy you're home and so glad I've got you. These kids will be lucky to have a caring auntie who will adore them and make them fantastic cakes, filling them with sugar so they can drive me mad."

I chuckle as her head flops back down. "So the tears aren't anything medical? Once the gynaecologist signs you off, I can take you home?"

"Yeah, she should be here in a couple of hours. The tears were all about Kalen."

"I bet he's doing everything he can to get to you. He adores you, and I'm sure he's hurting."

"I don't want him hurting. I wish he'd hurry up and get home."

"Me too, Ambs, me too."

She relaxes in my arms. Amber is my world, and I can't push away the guilt crawling over my body. If something happened to her and I wasn't close, I'd hate myself forever. I'm back and need to win that competition so I can stay and make sure she has extra money for the babies and be here for my family and future nieces or nephews. Nothing matters more than the competition and my family.

"Speaking of you and your life," she whispers.

"You're meant to be asleep."

"It's not far off," she replies with a long yawn that I can't help but copy. "So... what's my cookery school's grumpy chef doing with you at this late hour?"

"I needed a lift." I shrug.

"And he happened to be around to give you one." She

131

giggles.

"Are you laughing at the words 'give you one'?"

"Yeah."

I roll my eyes. "He's helping me with my baking techniques, nothing more."

"Well, if anyone can stop you from getting a soggy bottom, it's him." She giggles.

I smile broadly despite her teasing. "You need to stop watching *The Great British Bake Off* for the innuendos."

She sighs and slips farther down the bed. It's my cue to go and let her rest.

"I'll be right outside, okay? And you don't want me to mention this to Mum and Dad?"

"Definitely not. They've got enough on their plate dealing with something related to our baby brother and what he's up to at university. They haven't told me more, but one of us needs to have a word."

"He's twenty and old enough to stop stressing them out."

"Says you," she replies cheekily as her eyelids flutter.

"Touché."

"Now get out of here and ask Garett to help you with your buns."

I shake my head as I climb out of bed.

"No more *Bake Off* for you," I say as I pause at the door, but she doesn't hear. She's already snoozing, and I swear she's got a cheeky smile on her sleeping face.

CHAPTER TWENTY – GARETT

I scroll through my phone, but there's little there to keep me entertained. In the past, it was full of phone numbers and messages from women who sent texts and photos that made even me blush. I don't miss that, and I think a certain beautiful blonde with a huge heart, quick wit, and perfect lips is the reason.

I tap the back of the phone and click the case until the nurse at her desk glares at me.

Something claws at my insides. When Ruby comforted her sister, it stirred up something that Clive and Flora had brought to my life, before he destroyed everything. I squeeze my hands like I'm squeezing dough. I know the feeling, but I'm scared to voice it. I can't forget Ruby's pale face as her sister wept, her panicked verbal diarrhoea in the van on the way to the hospital, and the need to fix everything, including entering this competition. It all bunches together to remind me that I miss having a family.

It's stupid because I didn't grow up with much of a family. Mine didn't care about me, whether I was attempting my best in school or trying out hobbies. Cooking was originally an outlet and a way to keep myself fed, but my passion transformed into an obsession for success. I had to show them I wouldn't be a failure. And then I found Clive, who was like a brother to me until he ruined my life.

A grain of want is buried in my belly, telling me to find that family. As much as I should be considering my future and moving to a kitchen I can run, the family I've found at Cloud makes it harder to go.

But at the end of the year, I need to leave this place if I'm ever to find the success I've chased all these years.

A message flashes on my screen from Kath as if she heard my thoughts.

Kath: Thank you for helping Ruby with the competition. You two make a good team.

Me: No worries. It's nothing big.

The smile creeping onto my lips reminds me that this family thing isn't just the school and having someone like Kath caring about me. There's something special in Ruby, too, and with her, I'm tasting something I didn't know I wanted.

"What are you smiling about?" My face heats as I lock eyes with Ruby. She's all curves and curiosity as she stares at me. She's a force of nature that's too attractive for her own—and my own—good.

"Nothing, really. I was looking at old videos of Cookie." The lie slips out of my mouth. I can't tell her about my confusion about this cookery school without sharing my past, and I can't let her in because she'll hurt me, too.

Everyone does.

She sits in the soft chair beside me and looks over my shoulder. "Show me."

Another message appears from Kath as I fumble through the old videos on my phone.

Kath: We're lucky to have you.

"Are you having a secret affair with Kath?" Ruby asks as I swipe the message away. "I can imagine all the women falling at your feet. You're very good at seduction."

I remember the kiss we nearly had. For her, it was a fuck you to her ex-boyfriend, but I'll be thinking about it for weeks. But work is work, and after what happened with Clive, I need to be cautious. This isn't my future.

"As you must remember from the day we met, the older ladies can't get enough of me," I reply as I find a good video of Cookie. It's from his one-year birthday celebration that Flora and I gave him. He's barrelling around Clive's house, chasing the balloons I blew up for him. Ruby laughs as he barks and jumps at the balloons, pushing them higher. He jumps on sofas and bounces around like he's consumed more sugar than a five-year-old with their face in a chocolate birthday cake.

Suddenly, Clive appears in the background, his face red and his body shaking. The video comes to a quick stop, but I remember vividly how he snapped at Flora and me for letting Cookie jump on his overpriced furniture. Everything was a status symbol for him. We got carried away, but Clive and I fought that day because he shouted at Cookie until the dog shook. Cookie was scared of Clive hitting him and reminding him of his suffering at the puppy farm. Our

135

friendship had cracks before then, but I refused to see them.

"Is everything okay?" Ruby's hand rests on my arm as I stare at the screen, reliving parts of the past I've avoided. "Is it because you're missing Cookie? I'm sure Flora would bring him around again if you ask."

"Yeah, probably."

"Do you want to talk about it?"

I try to distract her from more questions with a smile as I shake my head. I want to tell her the truth about who Clive really is. I need to talk about him and process everything that's happened, but I can't ruin her passion for his competition. Instead, I do what I always do and change the subject, hoping everything will improve.

"Not right now. You've got enough going on. Is your sister okay?"

"Yeah. She misses Kalen. The nurse told me that the specialist is still three hours away, so they'll keep Amber in for rest and discharge her when the specialist arrives, which might be around seven in the morning."

I check my phone. It's already one.

"So you head off. I'll wait for her to be discharged and probably get us a taxi back."

"I can stay," I say with a shrug, even though I'm adamant I will   stay and ensure they're both okay.

I wait for an argument, but none comes.

"Okay. Thanks. You'll have to tell Kath you'll meet her another night so she can rock your world," she replies with a wink. The corners of my mouth turn up. Her brand of teasing is as addictive as chocolate fudge cake.

The waiting room sofa isn't the most comfortable, but the lack of arms means we can slide closer. I'm such an arsehole that I'm sitting in a hospital, wishing to get closer to Ruby, when her sister sleeps in a nearby hospital bed. The scent of strawberries and passion fruit has a Pied Piper effect on me.

"You can rest your head against my chest if you want," I say, as if I couldn't care less either way. Yep, I'm the biggest arsehole.

"Thank you." She pushes her boots off with the heels of her feet. They bang on the floor, drawing a cluck from the nurse at the desk. Ruby tucks her feet beneath her curvy bum. I open my arm so she can get closer, and she rests her head against my chest. My hand presses against her back to hold her steady, but the whole time, I can't get her fruity scent out of my mind.

"You're cosy and warm," she murmurs in a sleepy voice that makes my pulse climb. She's so sexy in this position but cute as hell, too.

I bite the inside of my mouth. *Be a proper friend, Garett, for fucks sake. You're a pillow to her.*

"And thanks for earlier," she says in a tired, sultry voice as she scoots closer. Her hand holds my hip as she snuggles against me. I count my breaths in and out to slow my heart rate.

"Earlier?" I ask before adding a forced sigh. There's no chance I'm going to sleep with her on my chest.

"With Neil. My ex-boyfriend."

"Oh yeah. No worries. He's an ass."

She chuckles, and it's like a vibration against my heart. Her laughter is so damn adorable. "He used to be my world, but he wasn't good enough to be my anything. You know?"

"Yeah." Although I don't. I've never had a partner, let alone one who I'd say is my world. My voice is possessed by a gruff beast when I say, "He was wrong about a lot of things, by the way. You're sexy as hell. I'm certain he said that because he can't deal with the fact that he lost someone as incredible as you."

She's silent. Hopefully, it's because she's asleep and not because I offended her. I hold my breath. I shouldn't have said she was sexy. This was a heart-to-heart, not me cracking on.

"I haven't felt sexy for a long time, and I don't consider myself anything close to incredible, more like painfully average. So thanks. I promise I won't tell Kath, though."

I hide my grin. "You said before that he cheated. You don't have to tell me, especially if you need to sleep."

I want to keep chatting to her all night.

"Yeah, that's why I'm back home and my business is over." I can relate to it, but this isn't about me. "The relationship was dead a long time ago. We were two eighteen-year-olds who got caught up in sex." I grit my teeth. I shouldn't be jealous of some prick who probably couldn't even make a cheese toastie. "But also in having someone for you that cares about you. I moved to where he went to university and gave up my dreams, which I was happy to do because I loved him."

"And you're not happy about that now?"

"It was that obvious?"

"I've had my regrets on past decisions." I kick myself for making her struggles about my life.

"I regret leaving my family and missing out on a lot, including the last years of my grandparents' life. I haven't spoken to my parents since I returned. I regret staying so long in a deteriorating relationship with Neil when I no longer loved him. We grew up, and what should have been our first relationship before learning about ourselves and moving on became this daily drudgery of existence."

"Shit."

Her laugh is empty. "It was. I stayed to save face. I didn't want to be proved wrong. Not that my parents are like that, but I guess my pride kept me there."

Maybe that was some of what happened between me and Clive. I didn't want all I'd put into the business to be a mistake.

"And now you're back."

"Yeah. I came home because Amber needed me and because I caught Neil screwing my business partner on my countertop. They smashed my favourite bowl, too."

"The bowl-smashing bastards."

She looks at me, smiling, but it's a sleepy smile that makes my heart echo with her name.

"Exactly." She drops her head against my chest again. "But catching them cheating was the best thing that could've happened. I'm glad I can be here for Amber, and I'm enjoying running the cookery school."

"I presume that's because you get to work with me. I am awesome."

She chuckles against my chest, and it takes all my control not to push it out with pride. "Obviously that."

"So now what?" I can't get my hopes up that she'll stay. I have no intention of still working there in a few months, but my breath catches in my mouth.

"I'll stay in the area for as long as I can. My family and the cookery school are here." I bite my lip to stop my grin. "And there's Clive's competition, too. If I can win that, I get to stay. I'll help at the cookery school and maybe one day start my own business again, but this time, it will just be me."

My heart drops, and I close my eyes. Of course. The competition. The one thing that gives her hope is the same thing that destroys mine.

"Yeah, cool. We'll do everything we can to get you that win," I reply, stumbling over my words.

"Team Grumpy Sunshine." I swear I can feel her smile against my chest.

She sighs softly, and eventually, she stills. Her silence turns to soft snores. As my eyes flutter closed, I pray for sleep so I can stop overthinking.

The vibration in my pocket wakes me. I struggle to open my eyes. *Where the hell am I?* The scent of strawberries fills me as a snoring, warm Ruby cuddles me tight. I hum my joy. Ruby is the reminder that I've missed out on something important for years. With one hand, I extract my vibrating phone from my pocket while holding her close. Her curves are soft against me, and I don't know if the need to kiss her can outweigh the one to keep her safe.

She stirs slightly at my jostling, and I freeze while looking at my phone screen. It's Flora. My watch reads six thirty in the morning. Since she graduated in the summer, Flora usually stays out until late, presumably partying, although I've never asked, and then sleeps for most of the day.

"Flora?" I whisper with a croak. Ruby continues to sleep. The hospital is busier, with staff moving around the waiting room and corridors. I can't believe we slept so soundly together on this poorly engineered sofa. "What are you doing up?"

My eyes strain against the lights that are slowly coming on.

"I have news," Flora exclaims as if the early hour means nothing to her. "And it's the best news."

"Can you say it a little quieter?" Ruby isn't snoring anymore, but her eyes are closed.

"Where are you? It doesn't matter. Me and Brine—"

"Who is Brine?"

"The law guy from university." What parent looks at a baby and thinks "Brine"? They must be fish fans. "We've worked on this all night... well, when we weren't doing other stuff."

"I don't want to know about my pseudo–baby sister doing anything besides studying hard."

"Oh, it was hard."

"Flora," I hiss as she laughs. I bloody love that girl and her dodgy sense of humour. Her brother doesn't deserve her.

"You know me. I'm not the kind of woman that men want in that way." I bite my tongue. Any guy would be lucky to have her, but I don't think me saying that will help. "Anyway, Brine's read the contract in detail. The only reference to a dog is that when one is purchased for the restaurant, it's legally owned by the person who owns the restaurant. Except you didn't purchase Cookie. You got him from a rescue centre, and although you gave them money, it was a donation. It wasn't payment of an invoice. You didn't purchase him, so there's a loophole."

I gasp, and the sudden blast of emotion overwhelms me, leaving me choked. "Are you serious?" I whisper.

"You can have your baby back, Garett. We need to

work out how to get him away from Shit Pants." This is her nickname for Clive when she's pissed off with him because he once got so drunk that he shit his pants. "But once we do, Cookie is coming home."

My lower lip trembles, and I close my eyes. Tears collect in my eyelashes. "Your friend Brine is a genius. But how can we bring Cookie home without being stopped? I want him with me as soon as possible, but if he stays at mine, Shit Pants will find him and take him."

"I need time to work it out, but we can do it."

"I can help, too," Ruby murmurs, and I nearly drop her.

"Is that Ruby? What are you doing with her at this hour? Are you returning to your bad boy ways?"

I fumble my response as Ruby looks up at me, smiling. She grabs my phone and tells Flora, "He was helping me with something."

"I bet he was," Flora jokes, and my face heats as Ruby laughs.

"Get back to Brine and let me devise a plan," Ruby replies, proving she heard enough. "I might have to get some details out of him, but I'm certain that Garett needs Cookie. I've never believed anything more."

"Yes, Ruby," Flora shouts down the phone. "Catch you both later."

The phone goes dead, and I prepare for questions, but instead, Ruby hands me back my phone and wipes my forgotten tears away from my eyes. "You should have told me someone took Cookie from you and that's why you didn't have him. We'll get him back and keep him somewhere safe so no one can take him from you again. I promise, Garett. Now tell me everything."

My heart bottoms out. *Oh fuck.* This woman has found the way to my heart, and there's nothing I can do about it except hide the fact forever. Now, I need to tell her everything while avoiding every mention of Clive. I can't ruin this competition for her.

"And who the hell calls their child Brine? Were they really into fishing?" she mumbles to herself.

And there goes another brick in my barrier wall. I'm falling hard.

CHAPTER TWENTY-ONE – RUBY

"**H**ow does that taste?" I ask Garett, holding a teaspoon of my freshly made salted caramel and chocolate buttercream to his lips.

His tongue pops out, and the tip touches the frosting as if he doesn't trust me. I raise one eyebrow and give him the sourest look I have in my arsenal.

His laughter hits my belly like I've eaten a batch of buttercream. It's like I'm filled with yummy goodness and want to bask in the endorphins it gives me.

Shit. I'm falling.

It's been a week since he stayed with me at the hospital and I slept against him. That doesn't happen. It took months before I could sleep in Neil's company, and even then, I always slept better when my bakery shifts meant I was sleeping in the bed without him.

But that doesn't mean anything. It can't.

Garett opens his mouth and sucks the spoon clean. It's not simple endorphins now. My belly lurches with something a lot more sensual, and I imagine those lips on something else.

I shake my head. It's just the after-break-up horniness that Amber tells me is inevitable. Yet, with the butterflies competing with the spicy thoughts in my head, I'm struggling to focus on anything but how he licks his lips and rolls them together.

He moans loudly. Oh God. "That tastes so good, Rubes." The way he shortens my name has heat building between my thighs. It's all I can do not to close my eyes and groan, but I need to think responsibly, not like a horny drunk woman on a night out.

A gruff Garett is oblivious to the impact his noises are having on me. "You should do something with that in the competition. How do you get it to taste so decadent but not heavy? I could eat that for hours."

I shrug, but his praise briefly calms my hormones and makes me beam instead. The great Chef Garett loves my frosting.

"Seriously," he replies, sticking his finger in the bowl. "You should cover lots of things in it. I would lick it off anything."

He pops his finger in his mouth and sucks it hard. His eyes lock with mine and widen like he's realised what he said.

"Anything?" I ask.

My voice is breathy. I want to dip my finger in the frosting and get him to lick that, too. How he cared about me at the hospital last week has replayed on a loop all week. Today is the first time we've seen each other since, and it's like our friendship is evolving into something I can't control.

His tired eyes darken, and he licks his lips slowly. "Anything, Rubes."

I swallow so loud that I swear it echoes around the kitchen. I should kiss those lips. The heat between my legs increases. I want to taste frosting off other parts of him. I briefly look down, and I'm sure he looks thicker down there. I smelt cinnamon when I slept on him, like his body was infused with it. Is that how his skin tastes?

Fire spikes my skin as I lean in to make my move, even though it's stupid. This is our workplace. Yet, as he licks his lips again, I tell myself it would be a kiss, and it would stop there.

Suddenly, he reaches into his pocket and steps back.

I stumble as I say, "I was reaching for…" But I can't think of anything to say to save face. I read the moment wrong. It doesn't matter, though, because he's distracted by his phone.

Shame creeps throughout my body, and I want to run, but I'm not a silly teenager, even if I act like one.

I return to the cake and busy myself adding the frosting. Curving the cream around the cake doesn't take me long, though my hands tremble. As I survey the cake, I plan the drip effect and lay out the delicate pink flowers I've created for the top. Garett wanted me to push the boundaries on my frosting. I'd never test my skills like this, but he's helped me with every step.

I sneak a look at Garett. He's engrossed in his mobile. His tongue darts out and grazes his lower lip. I miss my best vibrator, which I accidentally left at my old place. I only remembered my little bullet because it was hiding in my washbag, but it won't do the job especially if I'm going to keep imagining Garett's tongue trailing a line down my body. He taps a reply on his phone as I fantasise about his fingers between my thighs as his mouth pauses at my breasts and—

I grip the frosting bag tight, and buttercream flies across the table and onto Garett's arm.

Garett looks down before raising his eyebrow and

staring at me. "I know I said I'd lick it off anything, but I didn't mean my forearm."

I imagine licking those thick forearms and tasting the deliciousness of his skin mixed with the salted caramel chocolate. I shake my head and swallow slowly before busying myself with the cake—anything to avoid staring at his tongue sweeping across his skin as he cleans himself up.

"Ruby, what is the Cloud Burst?" he asks as I stare, dumbfounded, at the cake.

I stutter my reply. "It's our monthly family meal where we talk about how the cookery school is going and make plans for the next month. My grandparents named it that because we talk wild ideas for the future, like a cloud bursting full of them." His brow furrows, and I swallow loudly, grateful that some of my arousal has passed. "Why do you ask?"

"Kath invited me to it tonight."

I swear my stomach jumps to my throat and then back down again.

"Tonight?" I squeak. Shit, of course. We meet once a month. Then, on the twenty-third of December, we have an end-of-the-year cookery school Christmas Cloud Burst dinner. How could I forget? That also means I'll see my parents for the first time since my grandparent's funeral tonight.

Double shit.

"That's what she said."

"And she invited you? Okay, sure, yeah, that's fine," I reply, forcing an airy sound. "It will start in about an hour. Everyone will arrive soon, so you still have time to escape."

He cocks his head and holds his lower lip in his mouth, giving him a lost schoolboy look. "Don't you want me there?"

I scratch my forehead. No, I don't, but I don't know why. "Oh no, it can just be a bit much. It's my whole family, as well as Wicksy and Kath. But if you want to come, then sure."

"It's important, then." Maybe he doesn't want to come.

"It means they see you as part of the Cloud family. The temporary kitchen hands don't get invited. Amber told me that it took a year before Wicksy was invited. I guess you're privileged, as it's only a few months," I ramble.

"Yeah," he replies, and his voice wavers. His eyes wobble in his head, but suddenly, he slams his hand down. "I'm coming."

"Great."

Maybe having him there will distract me from worrying about my parents. My first monthly family meal since returning to the cookery school. Thank God I've made this fantastic cake. Maybe I can shove it at my parents and we can forget the last six years.

Garett licks my earlier projectile buttercream off his forearms again. My pussy whispers filth to me. Sweat beads the back of my neck, and my mouth goes dry. He's the last distraction I need while my family are around.

The next hour flies by, and soon, there's five of us instead of two in the cookery school dining room.

"Are my parents coming?" I ask Kath as my gaze flits repeatedly between the clock and the empty chairs. The dread that I've not spoken to them before now crept up on me over the last hour until it was all I thought about.

Kath shakes her head. "They tried to return in time, but their flight was delayed." I didn't know they were away. I need to visit. Fear pinches my heart. I was rude to them when I was with Neil, but avoiding them is rude now, too. "They messaged me a couple of minutes ago. They've just landed and will be home in two hours."

"Cool, cool," I reply. Garett squeezes his mouth to the side as he stares at me. Oh, great. Now I've got to worry about his pending questions about my parents, too.

A sound in the corridor makes us all turn. Jem rushes through the door, and the smile that covers my face is a mixture of nostalgia and surprise.

Jem gives me a side hug, the scent of cherry radiating from his clothes. "It's been a while, sis."

"Yeah, baby brother. I've missed your lazy ass." I ruffle his dark brown hair, and he slaps my hands away and ends the hug. I look up to him. "You've grown since I last saw you."

He shrugs. Shit, my baby brother has turned into a man. My heart pulls at the dark circles around his brown eyes. My hand hovers near his cheekbones, which are more obvious than I remember. "How's uni?"

"Oh, you know," he mumbles. He then sits as far away from me as possible as I try to introduce him to Garett.

Jem's broad shoulders hunch, and he avoids eye contact as Kath hands out the pasta dish she asked Garett to prepare when he agreed to come to the meal.

"This tastes like that one Clive Macdonald won the best restaurant competition with," Amber says, shoving penne in her mouth as if she's scared someone will steal her plate.

I raise my eyes at her, and she grunts, "Twins." She

points at her belly.

Kath takes a bite and chews it slowly. "You're right. I remember my friend sneaking us the leftovers after the competition."

Garett chews his pasta slowly before swiping a piece of garlic bread. It's like he can't hear the conversation.

"What's the secret ingredients, though?" I've read about that competition and that the pasta had a special secret ingredient, but Clive wouldn't reveal it. "I swear I can taste a bit of cinnamon, but what's the other thing?"

"No one would put cinnamon in pasta," Wicksy replies as he scoffs the garlic bread.

Garett locks eyes with me. He knows something. But why is he pretending he doesn't understand what we're discussing?

Throughout the meal, I linger on the ingredients I can't distinguish, nibbling bits or moving the pasta around my tongue. Garett doesn't answer any questions, eating something every time someone asks him a question—that's my technique—but everyone forgets the discussion as soon as they tuck into my cake. Everyone but me.

The discussion ranges from what events we have coming up at the cookery school to various contacts Amber can make from home to expand our client base. She's rallied since last week, although she hasn't stopped worrying about the twins and Kalen's return. After dinner, she announces she's exhausted and needs to get home. That's her excuse, but I reckon it's because she's desperate to watch *The Great British Bake Off* celebrity special. It's got a former naval officer turned actor on, and I imagine she'll fantasise about Kalen.

"Could someone give me a lift? This damn belly makes

it difficult to move the steering wheel."

"I can," Wicksy says.

"Out of the kindness of your heart and not because you can't be arsed to tidy up?" Jem shouts as Wicksy and Amber walk towards the door.

"Maybe I'll leave you to tell everyone about uni, Jem, especially as you haven't told your parents anything about what you're really doing," Wicksy counters, leaving us all to stare at Jem.

Jem's face instantly reddens as he snaps, "You dick."

"What's this about university?" I ask as the only official Cloud still in the room.

"It's nothing."

He avoids eye contact with all of us as Garett tidies up. I wait for more. The ticking clock highlights that we're not going anywhere, and he's not getting let off. I don't speak because I know my brother. He's changed since the funeral, but I'm confident he won't cope with the silence and my penetrating stare for long. It takes him less than a minute to break.

"Fine. I left university early into this term. But don't tell Mum and Dad."

I hold my hands up. As if I would. That would mean speaking to them.

"I don't mean you, Ruby. I mean Kath."

Kath shakes her head. "I'll keep your secret. But they'll find out eventually. It's better if you tell them than if they find out from someone else."

Jem shrugs, but I can tell Kath's wisdom is ruminating in that thick head of his. Not that I can talk. We're as bad as each other.

"Guys," Garett says, popping his head out of the room with the dishwasher in it. "Do any of you fancy doing something dodgy and possibly illegal?"

"Illegal?" I squeak.

"Always," Kath replies. "Count me into whatever it is. I need some excitement."

Jem's mouth drops open as he stares at Kath. I throw a piece of garlic bread at it.

"My pseudo-sister called me with a plan to get my dog back, and we can't do it alone. It's the sort of thing a Cloud Burst could help with." This must be what Flora and Garett discussed on the phone at the hospital. I've deliberated who Shit Pants is and why they have Garett's dog. I presume it's an ex-girlfriend and friend of Flora's.

I nearly asked while we were baking, but if he wanted me to know his relationship history, he'd tell me.

"The thing is, I need all of you for the first bit, except Ruby. Ruby, we'll get to you at the end of the dognap. Can you think of anywhere we can keep Cookie for a couple of months where he's looked after but can't be found? This won't work without that."

I open my mouth to argue and say I want to be part of the entire dognap, but Kath nods. "That's a good idea. Having Ruby come through at the end means we can still open the cookery school for classes if something goes wrong."

"Hold on." Surely, he's not serious about the potentially illegal part, but Garett nods as he clucks his tongue.

"Of course. Thanks, Kath. I need all three of you to be sure you want to be involved. This is a risk, and I don't even know you, Jem."

My brother grins. He always was the first to get in trouble when we were younger. And he loved it when my grandma chased him around the garden with a wooden spoon after he'd annoyed her chickens.

"I'm sure I can find a different way to get my dog back with more time. I adore Cookie, but I can't have you all get into trouble for him." He shakes his head. "It's a silly idea. Ignore I said anything." Sweat covers his forehead, and panic sits inside me.

"Whatever it is, we're going to do it, but we're not doing it just for Cookie," I say. I babble before anything, including my conscience, can shut me up. "We're doing it for you. For the guy who fixed my light, spent his spare time improving my baking, helped Amber, and made us dinner tonight without question. He's also the same guy who makes us laugh and happy and makes the cookery school a special place. The school is thriving because of you. So we'll do this reckless, risky, and potentially illegal mission for you. And Cookie, too."

Garett looks down at the floor.

"Garett," I snap, getting his attention. "We're getting your boy back tonight, no matter the consequences."

"But—"

"No buts, especially as I've realised the best place to hide him. Tell us what you need us to do. Mission: Cookie's Homecoming is all systems go."

CHAPTER TWENTY-TWO – GARETT

Kath looks at me with a steely gaze and offers an occasional smirk. We're in Clive's restaurant, which used to be our restaurant. All the additions I insisted on have gone. There's no wine bottles decorating the rustic walls or mini candelabras on the tables. He's replaced them with mirrors and hanging lamps. All the surfaces are white and stark instead of shabby chic wooden furnishings and a cosy ambience.

A waitress who could have fallen off a catwalk takes our order, but she doesn't check dietary requirements.

"Hi, sorry," I say. The waitress stares me dead. "My friend is allergic to peanuts. I'm sure you don't cook in peanut oil, but can I check?"

Kath smiles gratefully. She'll have her EpiPen, but she won't want to risk anaphylactic shock.

"I don't know," the waitress adds with a shrug. "Does it really matter?"

She walks towards the toilets. She's not going to find out for us. I wasn't planning to get in Clive's face yet—it doesn't fit Flora's plan—but already, my limbs are tight and demanding action.

Suddenly, one of my old team members waves me over to the kitchen door. Rumour must have spread that I'm here because familiar faces peek behind her.

Chrissy, who worked behind the bar, embraces me. "You're back." She has a glob of mascara stuck in her eyelashes and a patch of tomato sauce on her blouse, but her beaming smile hasn't changed. I shake myself. It's been three months since he kicked me out.

"Why do you look like you've been cooking?"

Although she's wearing one of the tight black skirts and breast-squeezing blouses that all the model-looking servers wear, she's also wearing a hairnet.

She worries her lip, but when one of the kitchen staff nudges her, she confesses, "Clive moved all of your staff to the kitchen and brought in younger waitresses. They're alright but don't care about serving and have no experience."

"But you were—are—brilliant at your job."

She shrugs. "But we're not attractive enough, and we were friends with you."

I grit my teeth. "I'm so sorry, Chrissy. I can't believe he's treated you all like this. You were with us from day one."

"That's what Flora said. But he treated you so much worse, and you were supposed to be his friend." Former servers, who also now wear hairnets and have splatters of food on their clothes, nod enthusiastically. "Everything's changed. Do you remember that you used to offer every diner a plate of tasters?" I nod. I was proud of that. "Not anymore. And he's reduced the number of desserts, too. He's trying to make the place stylish for the elite while cutting costs, too. It's all about money."

The pudding menu was my baby. Maybe I was foolish to want people to have an experience that sat with them for days. As much as I believe this is about cutting costs, it's also about wiping me from the place. I'd wanted to create a cosy Italian homely feel in the middle of the town, but he's obliterated that. This isn't my place anymore.

My face falls.

"We miss you, Chef."

"I miss you all, too."

I give each one a bear hug. I was as strict as hell when I was here, but I gave love, too. I lost that side for a while. Until Ruby.

I glance around the room. I had plans for this place, including offering an opportunity for people to take extra puddings home and order them when they weren't eating here. I wanted the experience to be more than a memory.

"Will you start another restaurant one day? We'd love to be part of it," Chrissy says.

"I haven't got the money. If I could, then I'd have you there in a heartbeat. You were the best bar manager I've ever worked with." Her smile is sad. "You were all the best," I add, nodding at the others. Their wincing smiles are another punch to my gut—so much talent and joy taken by one man's ego. "I hear he's running a competition. Why if he doesn't want puddings?"

Chrissy leans in, and my old team gathers around. "He's angry that you won't tell him your secret pasta ingredients. He's shouted at us for months, but none of us knew it." She laughs. "Not that we'd tell him if we did."

I give her another hug. My old team deserve better than what I left them with.

Another member of my old team adds conspiratorially, "We reckon he wants to steal recipes. We're not sure he'll give them a job after." *Shit.* I can't let Ruby have all her skills stolen, but this competition means so much to her and could elevate her. She needs a win after what she's been through. "But we can't prove that."

"You're thinking hard," Chrissy comments. I look her in the eye, my brow furrowed. "You're grinding your teeth. You did that a lot before you left."

I chuckle despite my worries. I haven't done that for a couple of weeks, in fact, since Ruby and I replaced our animosity with genuine friendship.

Suddenly, Clive's booming voice sounds from the corridors.

I whisper to Chrissy quickly before he catches her out of the kitchen, "Where's he been? Shouldn't he be out here chatting to the diners?"

Chrissy shrugs. "He's not you. He was probably chatting up one of the wait staff. Half of them walked out last week because of his letchy behaviour. He interviewed new ones this week. I bet he's working out which ones will most likely sleep with him."

Bile climbs my throat. I need to end this guy.

As if reading my thoughts, Chrissy asks, "Is there anything we can do to help your future?"

"I'm working on it," I lie. I can't crush them. Maybe if I keep their hope, I can find some of my own. "In the meantime, will you help me and Flora with something? I'm trying to get Cookie back."

Chrissy and the others gasp. "He kept Cookie from you? Clive told us that you didn't want him. I knew it was a lie. Whatever you need, we're here for you." Other kitchen staff behind her nod. "He doesn't deserve that gorgeous dog."

"You're the best. Flora will tell you what to do when she arrives."

I hug each one and scoot back to my seat as Clive enters the restaurant area. He's changed in the three months, too. He's got a rock-hard quiff that lava couldn't destroy. He's developed a golden tan since I glimpsed him a month ago when he taunted me about Cookie. He's also done something to his eyebrows, and he's wearing the tightest trousers I've ever seen. I can measure his cock from here.

He's become one of the Made in Chelsea men.

The scent of garlic and tomato fill the room as Clive laughs and chats with the guests. I adore the cookery school and everyone there, but there's nothing like running a busy restaurant. With the hustle and bustle and anxiety, you're within minutes of chaos every day, yet every night, you run your team like you're putting on the best performance of your lives showcasing every skill you've developed over your lifetime. Everyone wants to do their utmost and get that perfect reaction from a diner and nothing compares to the buzz when you change someone's life through a spoonful of your cooking. A pull in my stomach reminds me that I must start looking for a restaurant to work in. It won't happen in this area.

Kath nudges me, distracting me from my concerns. She side-eyes the window. Flora stands outside at an angle to hide from Clive, my Cookie by her side. She waves her phone, and mine vibrates with a message. The entire team knows their part in this plan and that we must keep the bulk of it hidden from Ruby because the competition is the most important thing for her. I can't have anything affecting her chances of winning, and I know her well enough already that if she suspected Clive had hurt me, she'd walk away without a future. That isn't happening, and Kath, Flora, and Jem have agreed to my terms. There's a lot of love for her.

I check my phone surreptitiously. There's messages from Ruby and Flora.

Ruby: You got this, Garett. We're bringing your baby home.

I try not to smile even though it's like popping candy bounces on my tongue before the same fizzing excitement fills my entire body.

Flora: Part one of Cookie's Homecoming is happening in five minutes.

I never wanted to see Clive again, let alone speak to him, but I'll do it for my boy. I nod as Clive spots me and strides over with an arrogant smirk.

Mission: Cookie's Homecoming has begun.

Chapter Twenty-Three – Garett

"What brings you to this fine establishment?" Clive's voice booms as he nears my table.

Kath rolls her eyes. She's here to keep me calm and raise hell when required.

"Keep him talking," Kath hisses under her breath.

According to the plan, Flora will come into the kitchen. Jem is near the back door, and Ruby remains at the Cloud Cookery School.

Kath forces a fake smile as Clive arrives. "So this is the great restaurant owner, Clive Macdonald."

"You know it." He winks at one of the waitresses who must be ten years younger than him. *Gross.* "And I presume you're Garett's date for the evening. He always sought a woman who would love him like his mother wouldn't."

I grit my teeth, running through all the insults I want to heave back. The guy stole my fucking restaurant and my dog, and he's throwing the things I shared with him in my face. Kath glances at me.

"This is Kath. She works with me at—"

"The only place that will take you—a crappy cookery school," he finishes smugly, not bothering to look at Kath.

I take a breath. As much as I want to rip his head off and pour scolding custard down his neck, I need to keep him talking, so I lean back in my chair and gaze around the stark restaurant. "The place is... different."

"It's better. When you worked here," he says as if I wasn't the co-owner, "we barely made any money, and yet now I'm raking it in."

"Because everyone wants to taste my pasta that you can't serve."

He throws his head back and laughs, but his hands fist, his knuckles turning white. I know his tells, unlike the people he schmoozes these days.

"This is my award-winning restaurant. You were a minion. I don't even care about the pasta. Besides, one of your old team told me about your special ingredients."

I stare him dead in the eyes and smirk. "Of course they did. They were always so loyal to you."

He glares back. "I'm surprised you're showing your face here. Look at the great Chef Garett Kelsey, everyone," he announces to the diners, who are watching our conversation. "You could get his autograph, but it's worth less than his tasteless focaccia loaves."

I hate that he gets under my skin. People stare, and my face heats. This is for Cookie.

"I presume Kath is paying for you. Or were you hoping to wash up because you can't afford my prices?"

Kath stares at him and says, "No, it's my birthday treat, or it would be if one of your servers could tell me if you cook with peanut oil. You need to train them better."

Clive's mouth waggles in shock.

Kath adds, "I'd like to see the oil you use. Take me to your kitchen."

Although this is part of the plan, I expect she's rushing through it because of the way he's treating me. I hope Flora's done what she needs to do.

Before Clive can disagree, Kath stands and walks towards the kitchen. "Come on, then. Maybe I can have a word with your waitresses, too, about their lacklustre skills."

Clive follows. His bum cheeks are restricted as he moves, giving him a stumbling walk. As they push through the kitchen doors, I message Flora with a progress update.

Kath's role is to pretend to feel faint in the kitchen and insist Clive opens the back door. It must be him so no one else can be blamed for opening it. Jem has hidden outside with Cookie's favourite meaty treats.

Within minutes, Kath walks back in and winks. I nod at Flora, who has returned to the front. While we were talking to Clive, she planned to walk around the back, chat with the kitchen staff, and instruct them to leave the back door open so that when Cookie runs into the kitchen, Jem can grab him and take him to his car. Kath and I are sitting in this bastard's restaurant because we can't be accused, nor can Flora. It will look like Cookie escaped.

The mission must work. I need my boy back.

"So tell me, Clive," I start. I have to know something before we go. The plan demands I anger him, but Ruby and the competition sit in the back of my head. "This competition you're doing, is it so you can steal someone else's skills and recipes?"

He glares at me and fists his hands again. The bastard. That's precisely what he's planning, but I can't prove it.

"Don't be a pathetic fool," he hisses. "And it's none of your business. This is my restaurant, and everyone loves it, including me."

His reaction is perfect. I guess it's time to rejoin the mission and make him angry.

"Really? Well, you can do whatever you want in this restaurant and town, but remember, you will never be a good chef," I goad him. "You will be a tight-trousered loser who will remain in my shadow, wanting women who don't want you, and in your heart, you know you're a failure because the thing everyone thinks you're the best at is actually my thing. And I've got so much more I can and will do, and you have nothing."

His face goes from tanned to bright red instantly, and he opens his mouth to rage as Flora walks through the door with an excitable Cookie. Right on cue. "Clive, look who I've brought to see you," she sings, drawing the attention of all staff and diners. "Shall I let you off the leash, Cookie?"

Clive's head turns, but Flora follows the plan and unhooks Cookie's lead before he can tell her not to. The briefest smile appears on Flora's face as Cookie runs around the restaurant. The smell of meat and cheese is too much for my pup, who jumps on all the patrons. Chairs fly, food falls off tables as Clive chases him around the restaurant, and Flora squeals as if it's all a big mistake. A lady screeches as her husband's wig flies off. Meanwhile, a family who's spent more time on their phones than speaking to each other crow as their electronics clatter to the ground.

And then I shout, "Cookie, come here, baby."

Cookie freezes, turns, and sees me for the first time in weeks. He runs at me from across the room. His tail is on full throttle as he bangs past tables. Clive can't stop him. I'm jumping up and down like it's the best day ever.

"Cookie, no," Clive yells, but Cookie doesn't listen because Clive wasn't the one who spent every day training him.

As Cookie is about to reach me, Kath screams. Cookie

halts.

"I'm so sorry," Flora cries as Clive comes alongside Cookie.

"You piece of shit," Clive shouts. This next bit is necessary, but I hate seeing Cookie told off. His head droops, and he whimpers. Clive pulls his hand back as if he's going to hit Cookie. That's too far. I'm jump up. Clive freezes. All the patrons are watching him. Phones are trained on us as people video for social media—further proof that I wasn't involved. Clive points to the kitchen door, which is handily open. Well done, Chrissy. "Get out of my sight."

Cookie looks at me longingly but then spies what only he and I can see—his favourite bone in the kitchen.

"I'm so sorry, big brother," Flora says between sobs.

"You go, too. I can't look at you,"

Flora continues her realistic yet completely fake crying as she pulls on his arm. She's amazing. She aims to buy time so that Jem can take Cookie and she can't be blamed. All those Saturday drama classes that I paid for when she needed an escape from the bullies at school were worth it. "Please, Clive, don't be angry with me. I can't bear it."

Clive's eyes burn with fire, but then one of the patrons videoing whispers, "I've never seen him like this." And suddenly, that mask comes down.

"I love you, little sister. I don't know what came over me. I've not felt well all day." Then he turns to those videoing him. "And, of course, your meals are all paid for tonight, and you must take an extra bottle of wine home with you. It's the least I can do."

"That's so kind of you. Do we get to pick our bottles from the cellar?" I ask, but he doesn't answer. No one's meant to know about that cellar he insisted on filling with the expensive bottles he only offers his most prominent guests.

"Please check on Cookie," he says to Flora. To the videoing audience, he adds, "I was mean to him and hate myself for it."

Flora barely enters the kitchen before she calls Clive to speak to her. Kath and I follow, feigning curiosity. "Clive, he must have escaped out of the back door. Did you leave it open?"

Kath is ready to say he did if he denies it, but he grunts a noise before adding, "We can't let anyone learn what's happened. If the people out there find out, I'll be cancelled."

"You've lost my dog," I cry out.

Clive rounds on me. "It's weird that you were here when all this happened. If I find out you had anything to do with it, I'll—"

"But I was in your sight the whole time." I widen my eyes and fake innocence, but it's hard not to smile.

This is why Cookie goes to the safe house where Clive can't find him. He won't be there forever, but he'll be secure until I decide what to do next.

He gives me one last glare before pointing at each of us in the kitchen. "If anyone dares to speak about this, I'll take you all down. You've seen how I destroyed Garett."

I must stay in front of Clive for another ten minutes to appear utterly innocent, although I'm desperate to be reunited with my boy.

"I'm going to find him. Are you coming, Clive?" Flora says.

Clive's blank look has my blood boiling. "Why would I? He wasn't my dog anyway. I've got a restaurant to run and damage limitation to sort out." And with that, he strides back into the restaurant, announcing to the patrons that Cookie is heading home after a rest.

I check my phone.

Jem: Cookie is safe with me. I'll message you when I give him to Ruby. You've got the address where to meet her.

Garett: Thank you.

My boy is mine again.

CHAPTER TWENTY-FOUR – RUBY

Cookie snores in my passenger seat. The curl of hair over his eyes reminds me of Garett.

I don't understand who kept the dog from him or why Garett wouldn't tell me who it was.

Jem dropped Cookie off to me in a quiet lane in case he was followed. We've taken to this plan like secret agents. Maybe Garett doesn't want me to meet his ex. He said it was best I wasn't too involved because he didn't want me in trouble, yet it was okay for Jem, Kath, and Flora to be in trouble. None of it makes sense.

But the ultimate goal is worth most of the secrets.

Garett's joy that he might get his dog back nearly broke me, and I'm glad I'm part of it. I don't want to fall for him, yet I spend most of my time daydreaming about him.

I shake myself. There's something else I should be thinking about. My car crunches on the gravel as I drive through a gateway and pull up to the house that carries memories that make me bite the inside of my cheeks.

It's a typical bricked house in the Cotswolds. Plant plots sit outside the front door. Even in the dark, they appear like they've battled a hedge trimmer and lost. My parents were never good at gardening and weren't house-proud either.

The cookery school was their proudest achievement. Guilt ripples through my body. It was a proud achievement I didn't want a part of until now.

Jem found out that Cookie could stay. I still haven't spoken to them. My fingers tremble as I stare at the wooden door. Grandma and Grandad lived here until they died. Grandad made the door during his retirement. Not that it was much of a retirement, as they were all running the cookery school from the back garden building as it was then.

Tears stream down my face as I remember my grandparents. I missed out on so much, and it was all my fault. I can't bring their last years back, and I can't replace the time I've missed with my parents.

Cookie paws my arm. I bury my face, now stained with sadness, into his fur as I cuddle him. I won't choose a man above my family and future again.

Suddenly, my door opens, and delight rumbles through the car.

"My little girl," my mum's voice cries out. "You're home."

I turn, and instead of anger or wariness, her eyes sparkle with delight. Her smile is the same as the one she'd have when we opened Christmas presents as kids.

I'm aware of a van pulling behind me as I unclip my seatbelt. I expect it's Garett, but for whatever reason, his door remains closed as I jump out, and my mum embraces me in a hug that wipes away all the fear and guilt I've carried for years. My dad joins us, and soon, it's a three-person hug that smells of honey and orange gin—my mum—and whiskey—my dad. It's the scent of family parties, accompanied by all the other scents of my childhood: apple crumbles and rosemary handwash.

"I've missed you, Ruby Red," my dad says, and I swear there are tears behind his words. I'm crying harder now. My mum's sobs carry through the wind as Cookie's paws tap behind me signalling he's jumped out of the car. He nuzzles my leg like he wants to be part of the reunion.

"Are you back for good?" The hope in my mum's voice warms my heart instead of cutting it like it would have done a few months ago.

"Yes."

"Every cloud."

I roll my eyes at my dad's use of our family saying. Every cloud has a silver lining. It's a Cloud family favourite, but as I roll my eyes, the tears continue and my heart soars.

This carries on for ages. Soon, Cookie jumps at us like a circus poodle. His arms are in the air, and he bounces on his back feet. My parents step back as Cookie dances. Belly-shaking laughs burst from my dad, who, under the moonlight, resembles a Father Christmas wannabe with his salt-and-pepper beard and hair. My mum's aged, too, but she still looks like a viper who'd kick your ass and hug you at the same time.

"Garett," my mum exclaims. "Come and join the love in."

I turn. Garett stands against his van with a sheepish smile. It's the same one he wore for most of the family dinner earlier that evening. But either Mum can't see it or she doesn't care. She beckons him into a hug that suggests she could squeeze the life out of him even though she'd struggle with his height.

My dad hugs Garett as soon as my mum is done with him. No stiff upper lip back tapping from my parents. When they want you to feel love, you know it. I've missed that.

"Dad," I call out, "put him down. He should spend time with Cookie."

"It's okay," Garett replies gruffly as Dad puts him down, but the pop of his eyebrows suggests relief.

"Shall we all go to the house and discuss what's happening? Jem said we're dog-sitting for a couple of months."

"If that's okay," Garett says.

This was my part of the plan. My parents didn't have time for a dog when they ran the cookery school, and it was their dream to have one. This will allow them to try one out until Garett's ex-girlfriend, or whoever we've taken Cookie from, gets bored of looking for him.

"Of course. You're part of the Cloud family now," my mum replies.

My parents turn to walk into the house, so they miss the wince on Garett's face and the hunch of his shoulders. I don't know why family is a bad word for him. I'm going to find out, though, because whether he likes it or not, with the dognapping and caring for my sister and me, my family has no intention of letting go of him.

CHAPTER TWENTY-FIVE – RUBY

My parents and Cookie are safe in their house.

Cookie sniffed every bush and flower in their garden before falling asleep on Garett's lap. It took a bit of cajoling, but soon, he was in the bed that Garett had brought. He didn't want to leave the garden, which Garett said was understandable after months trapped in a flat. My parent's garden is big enough for the old cookery school and a whole host of equipment to entertain three kids and their friends. I wanted to stay out there, too, and reminisce over the swingset that Jem and I would fight over while Amber rolled her eyes and the monkey bars that I spent my summers building my strength to cross while Grandma and Grandad cheered me on.

"We did it. I can't believe we got him safely away and that he's happy and mine again," Garett exclaims. His grin is unrelenting.

We're at the pub down the road from my parent's house. Garett wanted to stay nearby for a couple of hours in case Cookie needed him. His worry that we might have been followed is ludicrous, but maybe his ex is like that.

"He loved seeing his toys again," I reply, deep in thought, as I stare at the curl falling onto Garett's forehead. His leg bounces against mine and jostles the table.

"He did. He loved chasing that squeaky egg around your parents' house." Garett wriggles in his seat like he's drunk fifteen espressos. "When I was forced to leave him, I took a couple of cuddly toys and his special squeaky egg. He still had some, but I wanted something to remind me of him."

"You're not the person I thought you were the day I met you."

"I was an arsehole. You can say it. I was having an awful day, and I took it out on you," he confesses. "But I owe you big. I owe all your family."

I shrug, but he grabs my hand.

"Seriously, Rubes. I won't forget this." Warmth spreads from his skin to mine, and tingles move up my limbs. "But while I decide how to repay you, I need you to say that I was a dick."

"You were a dick," I repeat half-heartedly.

"Not like that. I need you to say it like you mean it. Repeat after me: Garett Kelsey, you were a dick."

I smile even as I stare him dead in the eyes and say clearly, "You, Garett Kelsey, were the biggest dick I've ever met, and you're lucky I still talk to you, let alone helped you tonight."

He chuckles in a way that fills my belly with sparkles of joy. "You enjoyed that too much."

I tip my head and wink. "I don't know what you mean, but I have forgiven you for that day, not that you deserve my forgiveness."

"Whoa." His face is animated as his mouth drops, and his thumb rubs my palm like I'm a bit of dough for him to

172

play with. "I've worked really hard to get you to like me. Remember that lasagne and the baking and how I helped you out with your ex?"

I don't know if it's the way he's stroking my hand or the reminder of how he helped me out with his lips on my skin. Maybe the guilt I've carried for years for mistreating my family is ebbing. I'm a little dizzy, but that could be from the rescue. I suck on my lower lip before answering. "No. I don't. You're going to have to remind me about that."

His chest rises and falls, and his voice lowers as he teases, "You don't remember?"

The pub is quiet, and we're in two chairs next to each other in the corner. A lamp accentuates the change from delight to burning heat across his face. I rasp my reply, "No, not at all."

"Do you want me to remind you?"

More than I want a strawberry and white chocolate cupcake, and I'd love one of those right now. Instead, I reply, "Maybe."

The adrenaline fuelling my body from the anxiety of the mission to the fear of seeing my family has turned into something electric.

Garett's finger grazing my hand escalates the charge. "But if it wasn't that memorable before, maybe I'm just not good at helping people taunt their exes."

"Practice might help." I swallow as he fixes me with his stare.

"It's helping with your baking. Your hands are nearly as good as mine." I shiver as one of his hands cups my face. The pads of his fingers are rough against my skin. My tongue peeks out to lick my lips, and he tracks my movements. Although we're sitting, he crowds me with his body.

Cinnamon combines with the smoke from the burning logs in the nearby fireplace. His thumb traces my lip, leaving his ownership on it. I close my eyes, imagining his stubble against my skin as he leans in.

His lips are soft. At his gentle touch, I press closer for more. His hands reach into my hair as we make out. His eyelashes flutter against my skin like little butterflies. I tease his lips apart with my tongue and kiss him with the pent-up energy I've carried all evening. It's passionate yet careful. My tongue explores his mouth as he massages mine. I moan into him. He kisses me harder. There's some kind of rush in my belly, like need and hope combining to drive me further into his embrace.

I run my hands across his arms and then to his lap. His body is rigid. My fingers dance across his thighs. I want to trace his entire body, and I would if we weren't in public. I'm grinding my body into the chair as if it's him beneath me. Electricity flows through my limbs, and there's no expectation to push it further, although if we were anywhere else, I'd be straddling him. I'm revelling in his brief touches and the taste of the hot chocolate he's drinking in this pub. Heat pools between my thighs, and I battle against the desire coursing through me that demands more. I moan again, louder this time.

A crash of the chair against the table brings me back down to earth, and we quickly pull apart. My body still tingles, and there's a ball of need inside me telling me to kiss him again, but it's the person standing beside me that demands my attention.

"Jem, what are you doing here?"

"I saw the work van outside, and I wondered how the end of the rescue went," he explains as he rearranges the furniture. His sullen attitude surprises me. "But I guess you two are busy. I'm heading off."

"We were just—"

"Don't lie. You've caused enough problems over the years." I gasp at Jem's cutting comment. "All it took was one night back with Mum and Dad, and you're willing to make things difficult for them again. I was the one left at home when you hurt them before. Screwing the chef at their cookery school isn't wise, so don't, yeah?"

His words turn my joy cold. "We're not screwing."

He rolls his eyes, but his jaw is tight, his shoulders hunch, and he shoves his hands in his pockets. "Sure. That's totally believable."

"Hold on," Garett says, but I rest a hand on his arm to stop him.

I was gone a long time and missed my baby brother growing into whatever this is. My behaviour was a mistake, but I didn't realise it ruined Jem's teenage years.

Before I can say anything, Jem walks out of the pub, leaving Garett and me with goldfish mouths, staring after him.

"I've got to go, Garett. I need to sort this out." I rush out the door as gravel flies from Jem's squealing wheels as he tears out of the car park.

CHAPTER TWENTY-SIX – RUBY

I bang on the door of one of Jem's old school friends. It's taken an hour of calling and messaging all his contacts to find out where he's living now. When he said during the Cloud Burst that he'd left university, I knew we'd need to have a conversation about his living situation eventually. Still, I didn't think it would be so soon.

"He's in the garden," the sullen-toned guy says, barely leaving me enough space to get through the open door. "Do you want a drink or anything?"

I take in the slug trails on the floor and the faint smell of damp and decline.

The guy points in the direction of the back door. I think he's called Pete, but I haven't seen him since he was fourteen, so I avoid saying his name. I slip out to the unkempt patio, a collection of weeds and missing concrete slabs, and sit on the plastic patio chair next to my brother.

The scent of a cherry vape surrounds him.

"I don't know much about you anymore," I say after a few minutes of silence. "How long have you been vaping?"

He lets out a burst of air. "A while."

"And how long have you lived here?"

The cold air sneaks under my jacket, and I resist a shiver.

"About a fortnight."

"And when did you start just giving short answers to questions?" I huff.

He turns to me, and I can see his glare from the light streaming from the kitchen window behind us. It gives him an eerie glow, highlighting his red face and squinting eyes. "About the same time you left the family to be with your arse of a boyfriend. It may have been after that, but you wouldn't know, because you weren't here."

I flinch. Score one for Jem. He's not lying, and while others may sugarcoat their words, I can rely on my brother to tell it how it is.

"No, I wasn't here. But I should have been. I've realised that more and more over the last month," I concede as the corners of my mouth droop.

He takes another drag of his vape, turning his head to release it before fixing me with his stare. "Too right you should have been. You should have visited and spent time with Grandma and Grandad. You broke their hearts. And you should have helped me with my homework or hung out with me in town on a Saturday afternoon like you used to, and you should have cared about us rather than just yourself and that prick you were dating."

Memories I'd forced myself to forget flood my consciousness. Saturday afternoons at McDonald's with a twelve-year-old Jem, laughing at stupid shit before heading to the skate park where he'd perform tricks with his friends. Amber usually joined us after she'd finished working at a café. Not many twelve-year-olds wanted to hang out with their big sisters, but Jem did.

"I'm sorry. I should have thought more about you and your life."

"Did you even miss me? I got the occasional text and saw your social media posts. But when you were busy shacking up with Neil, did you wonder how I was doing or how my exams might be going? Did you ever think about me?" he asks as he shoves his free hand into his hoody pocket. His face drops to the ground, and I'm selfishly relieved I don't have to meet his penetrating stare.

"Yes, I missed you. I got busy and thought I had to make a success of my life and make Neil happy, but of course I missed you," I stutter. It's only since talking with Amber that I've realised how toxic my relationship was with Neil. He didn't force me to go with him or say I couldn't see my family, but there was hostility if I tried to. I'm still trying to unpack that and build my confidence. Seeing my parents tonight, and now faced with Jem's truths, I fight unwarranted embarrassment for how easily I gave up everything for Neil. I deserve to be happy, loved, and respected. Maybe with more time, I can admit this, but not yet and not with a hostile Jem.

Another waft of cherry cuts through the cold November air. I take a breath. "I thought about you a lot and wondered how you were doing, if you were going on dates or stressing out your teachers. I thought about all of you."

I stare into the garden, where a ginger cat prowls closer to a bird minding its own business in a tree.

"Did you know what it was like back home without you? Mum and Dad were always stressed. They used to have you to chat with and to make them laugh, but without you, they had nothing." He drags his vape again.

My voice shakes. "They had you and Amber."

"Amber was trying her best, but she was busy helping with the cookery school. That was how she tried to relieve their stress. But I had to pick up the pieces. There were days when they were tearing their hair out, trying to sort things you used to help with. There were a lot more arguments, too."

"I had no idea. Amber never said any of this."

"And they were worried about Neil because they knew he wasn't good enough for you. They wanted you to go to culinary school or develop your cooking skills because you were meant to take over the family business, but you just left. And that put more pressure on me to do better, too. You left all of us. And if you date Garett, you'll mess things up again."

Jem digs the front of his trainers into the mud beneath his chair, adding, "I know I got angry in the pub, but you can't fuck it up again. Garett is alright, I guess, but if you get into a relationship with him, it will cause problems at the cookery school. It's the last thing Mum and Dad need, and then they'll be on my back again."

"Okay," I reply in resignation. My family come first, and I can't mess up again. I vow silently to keep my distance from Garett and remain professional when I'm at the cookery school. There's an attraction between us that I can't deny, but if I work on the competition on my own, then I can avoid him.

Jem is shivering. No wonder the chill is creeping through us. It will be Christmas soon, and I'll need to decide my future. I don't want to be in my sister's cabin forever, especially not getting under her and Kalen's feet while they're trying to bring up their babies.

"Do you want to go inside?" I ask, my hand resting on his shoulder.

"I can't. I've been sleeping on the sofa since I left university, so I have to wait until everyone goes to bed. It will probably be another hour yet. I've got a job at a local café but can't find anywhere to rent."

"And you can't go back to Mum and Dad's?"

"They don't know I left university, and I don't want them to yet. I want to show them I'm not a fuck-up," he replies, shaking against the cold.

"You and me both."

That gets a laugh out of him. I've missed that sound.

"Why did you leave university?"

"Because I don't want to be a bloody accountant. I'm not good at academic stuff. I scraped through my first year and knew I'd fail my second within weeks of starting back."

"Amber got the business brain in our family."

"Lucky cow," he replies grumpily, making me laugh.

"Is that the only reason you left uni?"

"It's the only reason I'm sharing with you."

I shrug. "That's fair. Now, come over here. I'll keep us both warm until you can go in," I say, opening my arm so my baby brother can snuggle in. "And we'll work on finding you somewhere to live, okay?"

Maybe if I win the competition, there will be enough money left over for Jem and me to get a place for both of us.

I have to win it now, but alone. That will mean more late nights trying to learn new things without Garett's help, but it will be worth it. It has to be.

CHAPTER TWENTY-SEVEN – GARETT

I haven't spoken more than a hello to Ruby since she bolted from the pub last week. I've led a few classes, but she only stayed long enough to ensure they ran smoothly. The rest of the week, I was at the local college, showing them a range of skills. It was something Ruby organised and gave me a bit more money.

I nearly texted her a load of times, but we don't text. We never have. And the regret covering her face both at the pub and the times she looked at me since suggests there's nothing to talk about.

I've seen her parents a lot, though. They said to visit whenever I wanted. I've visited Cookie most days this week after the community college. The third time, they insisted I stay for dinner and talked to me about my dreams.

I can't do anything to destroy the family who've taken the time to give me a chance, which means Ruby and I are a no-go. Not that she's interested.

I've considered my future in other ways, too. Cookie and I have had several long, muddy walks. The fresh air and endless throws of the ball have filled me with the space I've missed. I need to find a job and somewhere I can move to, but instead, on those walks, I've deliberated recipes and designs for a restaurant.

I want to run a restaurant, but I can't do it without

earning head chef money for a while. I've put some feelers out with old contacts around the country and as far as Scotland and Ireland. There's one possibility: the owner of a Michelin Star restaurant in Ireland said there might be a job after Christmas. She can't tell me more for a few weeks, though.

As I walk into the school, music plays. My gaze darts right and left before air escapes my lungs.

"Hey, champ," Kath says, making me smile. I've not had a nickname since I worked as a minion in the kitchens. "How is Cookie?"

I give Kath a bear hug that knocks her off her feet, and she does the same to me, although mine is an emotional knocking. This place has seeped beneath my skin, and as much as I need to pull back, I can't. "Thank you again for everything. You were amazing."

Kath squeezes me back. "Anything for family."

I recognise Ruby's clumping heels behind me. She has unusually stompy feet sometimes, but I don't turn. I've thought about that kiss all week. The warmth of her skin against my hands and the moans she made when she took the kiss deeper. I can't give her any promises for the future or be the reason for her family's trouble. They've given me the world.

But eventually, I turn, and she's staring at me like she wants to talk. The change from barely noticing my existence this week causes a tightness in my chest.

"Is there anything I need to know about today's class?" I ask Kath.

She looks from Ruby to me, squinting. "No. It's a normal Italian class, but please push the wine and wreath making on Monday night."

There's been a chill in the air all week, and as much as it reflects the mood I'm trying to instill in myself, it's more from the change in seasons. Winter is here. In less than a week, it will be the first of December and the run-up to Christmas.

"Are we still baking later?" I ask Ruby. "I've got some ideas."

She's worrying her hands, and I pop a stick of gum into my mouth so I don't grind my teeth. I want to make things better and hug her, but I've sat through a meal and several coffees where her parents talked enthusiastically about her return.

"No. I'm going to do the whole baking thing on my own," she replies flatly, her stare focused on the floor. "I don't need your help."

I stand back. A pain hits my chest, and air whooshes from my mouth.

Her eyes meet mine. They're wide as she stutters, "I didn't mean—"

"It's fine," I say, cutting her dead. Did I do something wrong, or is this about her family? She could just talk to me. The peppermint bursts in my mouth as I chew slowly. I miss the taste of strawberry that lingered after my kiss with Ruby, but from the brusque way she's rejected my help, I guess we're done. Maybe she doesn't even want me as a friend. "I have plans."

Ruby's brow furrows. "Like what?"

Kath continues to stare at us with her lips squeezed to the side.

I shrug. I'm being pigheaded, but her rejection is triggering some stuff from Clive and my parents. I should walk away or smile and be kind, but my grumpy chef persona is rearing its head. "It's just stuff."

183

Her face falls briefly. Shit, I did that. I'm an arsehole. I need to apologise.

"Right," she says.

I clear my throat, readying myself to tell her that if she ever changes her mind, I can help, but she's forcing a fake smile and turning to Kath. She says breezily, "Let's get through today. I've had a late night, and the sooner I can get home, the better."

"That's probably for the best. It's going to snow tonight," Kath replies. Her beady eyes monitor me.

I chew the gum harder. Ruby dismissed me. I cancelled extra work to help her tonight, and although I don't need money for Cookie anymore, I'm still nowhere near earning enough to get out of my present situation. Did she have a late night because she was on a date?

"But it's November," I say grumpily. I shouldn't take things out on her, but the rejection still stings. I didn't realise I was so easy to dismiss, at least not so easy for her.

"But it's going to snow. I've got one of my snow headaches," Kath replies.

"And we're less than a week away from December," Wicksy adds as he walks in the door. "We've been known to get a flurry every so often, and based on how my chickens are acting, it's going to be more than a flurry."

Ruby yawns as she side-eyes Wicksy.

"Your chickens?" Ruby asks.

"Yes, Princess Pickle Pants and Lord Fairmont of Londinium."

"Fucking hell," I reply.

Wicksy pushes his waves out of his face and throws aprons at us.

"There's no one like you, Wicksy." Kath shakes her

head with smile.

"Thank fuck for that," I add as Ruby yawns again. I'm returning to who I used to be because of one little rejection. I shake my head. I need to get it together. I walk towards my demonstration counter. Maybe if I prep, I can reset and bring back the version of myself I was starting to like, and then maybe I can talk to Ruby like a friend. She understands me better than anyone else. Maybe if I apologise and—

"Oh great. Garett is being his grumpy bastard self. It's going to be a long day," Ruby snaps.

I stare at her, my mouth wide as she puts her apron over her head. It hurts more coming from her. "Maybe you shouldn't have stayed up doing whatever you were doing. Was it fun?"

"More fun than you can imagine." She sucks her lower lip into her mouth in the way that she does when she's turned on. She must be remembering a date.

I chew my gum harder. I should walk away and get on with the day, but my voice lowers as I reply, "I've imagined you can have a lot of fun. I've imagined it all week."

The desperation to have the last word and to get a reaction out of her is like chilli flakes under my skin.

"Shame," she replies. I tip my head as she sidles past me. The scent of passion fruit causes my body to respond instantly. "Because you'll never have more than imagination when it comes to me."

And then she walks away, leaving me huffing as I push up my sleeves.

The day continues like that. We push each other's buttons

or back-chat whenever people are out of earshot.

When I was bent over checking the oven, she leaned in and whispered, "Shame that your personality is ninety-five per cent arsehole and five per cent chef." And then she hit me on the bum.

I took my opportunity for payback when I caught her sorting ingredients in the pantry. "At least my arse isn't the most interesting thing about me," I grunted in her ear before tapping her butt. The whoosh of air out of her mouth was satisfying as hell as I swaggered away.

She got me later, though, as I led a section on how to season focaccia. "Your shirt isn't tucked right. Let me get that for you." She yanked the shirt so tight that I braced myself against the countertop. Her nails scraped the hint of my naked back when she tucked the shirt in. Arousal zipped through my body. I gripped that countertop so hard my hands hurt.

What started as trying to piss each other off was quickly becoming ways to turn each other on. She would prowl around the kitchen, sliding between me and the counter, her bum across my groin. I'd stroke her neck with the tip of my finger every time I was close when she retied her hair.

But later, when we were alone in the dining area, I stood close to her. "Your apron isn't tied. Let me get that for you."

I flipped her around quickly and held her hands up against the wall. I slowly tied a bow in the strings of her apron as she pushed her butt against me. My hands paused at her hips as she moved against me. Goodness knows where it would have gone next if I hadn't heard Wicksy telling one of the students about his chickens outside the room.

The whole day was unprofessional. As I was teaching the class, she stood at the back and slowly began to undo the buttons on her blouse. Sweat dripped down my back as she bit her lips and gradually revealed the pink flowers edging the top of her black bra. Maybe she didn't like that I shrugged and continued explaining pasta preparation, because then she stood in my eyeline and slowly lifted her skirt. Inch by inch, she pulled the hem higher until I was gifted the image that had played in a loop since the moment Cookie floored her. Lace black hold ups highlighted the white skin of her upper thigh.

Suddenly, I was choking on my words. The class rushed to check on me and get me water. Ruby dropped her hem, winked, and then sashayed past me with a smirk.

As the class finishes for the day, we wave the happy and oblivious clients goodbye. I growl in her ear, "I'm going to get you back for earlier."

The sky is darker now, but it doesn't have that glowing grey look that it often has before a heavy snowfall. Besides, it's November. Snow is rare at this time of year, especially in the Cotswolds. It's Kath's old wives' tales.

"Of course you are," she replies with a teasing smile. "It's a shame you must get home for your fun night of activities."

I glare at her. She shivers in time with me as a gust of cold wind lifts the hem of her skirt. "Nice hold ups, by the way."

"I thought you'd like them."

"You wore them for my benefit?"

She grumbles, "If that keeps you hard at night, then sure, you can believe it."

Her eyes travel down my body and back up. She's eye fucking me as she lets her hair out of its bun before securing it into a ponytail. I grit my teeth and imagine lightly winding that ponytail around my fist as she's bent over in front of me.

I need a cold shower. My blood has boiled all day, and the sooner I'm away from her, the better.

A second stronger gust of wind draws us quickly inside.

Wicksy and Kath are finishing up. We're all leaving soon, which means no more time with Ruby until tomorrow when we're decorating the school in preparation for the cooking and wreath making classes. That has to be a good thing, as she hasn't contacted me, her brother doesn't want us near each other, and she doesn't want my help with baking ever again.

"Anyone fancy going for a drink?" Why did I say that?

"I will," Wicksy replies quickly.

I fold my arms across my chest and look at Ruby.

"We all need to get home. It's going to snow," Kath states. "My headache is worse. It's a sign."

"And you have somewhere to be, remember? Isn't that what you said this morning?" Ruby snaps.

I curse my earlier petulance. "Oh yeah."

"Date, is it?" Wicksy leans against the countertop. "I need to learn your moves. All the women in the course love you. Another one left me a number for you."

Ruby slams her handbag down.

"Enough of this chat. We need to go before it snows."

Kath practically shoves us out the door. I grab my stuff as we're turfed into the car park.

"I'll lock up," Ruby shouts.

"Thank you," Kath replies as she strides away. "I'll see you all on Monday to decorate the school. I'll be in early."

"Aren't we doing it tomorrow?" I fumble with my words. I want to see Ruby tomorrow.

"It's going to snow heavily. You need to listen to me. We won't be going anywhere tomorrow morning." She's in her car and reversing before we can argue. "Now get home while it's safe."

Wicksy leaves just as quickly. He's more scared of Kath than he lets on. We all are.

I turn to speak to Ruby, but she's already waving me off. "Best get to your date before you're snowed in and away from her. They don't grit these roads, and I'd hate for you to be late."

I get into the van, huffing. I need to tell her that I'm not going on a date, but she isn't bothered, and if she were, it wouldn't matter. She's not available, and soon, she could be working with Clive.

I recheck the weather forecast because Kath has panicked me, but it says light rain. Ruby sits in her car, looking away from me.

As I depart the car park, something niggles me. I run through all the things I saw before I left, but I can't put my finger on what's wrong. The sky has a weird grey glow, but it's not going to snow.

That's when a couple of flakes fall. But as soon as they've fallen, it stops again—Kath's panic was for that?

I'm halfway home when I facepalm. Before Ruby leaves for the day, she always pulls her hair out of the elastic that's held it up and leaves it fully down. She also didn't lock the door or change out of her apron. Kath shoved us out the door, but Ruby said she'd stay to lock up.

She's still intending to bake!

I roll my tongue around my mouth. I should leave her be. She's already told me she doesn't need my help. Besides, I can't be around her and embarrass myself with how horny she makes me, especially after a day of teasing, but if it snows more, she won't get out.

I want to chat with her and laugh with her. I need some joy today but can't see Cookie because I've bothered her parents enough this week.

I yank my steering wheel and turn in the middle of the road. Drivers that I didn't know were behind me beep their horns loudly.

I can't resist the pull of her.

Her car sits in the car park, and the lights on in the cookery school glow from the windows. I should leave. She must make her own decisions. Yet I still park beside her car.

CHAPTER TWENTY-EIGHT – GARETT

I tiptoe as I walk into the cookery school. She's going to be pissed off with me.

Her curses sound into the corridor. "Why won't this fucking work? You piece of shit."

I stand in the doorway and take in the scene before me. There's buttercream splattered across the countertop and the floor. Her back is to me, and her ponytail swishes as she shouts more expletives at the icing bag she grips tightly in her hand. She's trying a piping technique on paper that I haven't seen anywhere but on YouTube videos of the most advanced professionals. There are master patisserie chefs who don't bother with it. The thing is, I know how to do it. A particular celebrity chef judge with anal bead necklaces taught me it.

Again, I debate helping or walking away.

"I know you're there, Garett," she yells, although she doesn't look up. "Either get off the pot or fuck off."

"I don't think that's the phrase." I remove my coat and put on the apron hanging by the door before I walk to the counter. I use a cloth to wipe the frosting from the floor. Strands of blonde hair stick to Ruby's forehead. "What are you trying to do?"

"Isn't it obvious?" She slams the piping bag onto the

counter. A glob of frosting squirts from the bag, but it doesn't reach the freshly cleaned floor. Still, she refuses to look at me. Maybe it's stupid, but I slowly roll my shirt sleeves. They're in her eyeline, and she loves staring at them. "Is this the time to be a dick?"

"It's as good a time as any." She lifts her head, and her eyes lock with mine. I wasn't trying to turn her on but to break her from the anxiety that owned her. She's a ball of stress and won't achieve anything if she can't recentre herself. My forearms can help, although I usually listen to Taylor Swift when I need to regroup. "Do you want me to go?"

She shakes her head. There are tears in the corners of her eyes. I resist the temptation to pull her into my arms. "Music?" I ask.

She shrugs. That's enough. I select a pop playlist and take the piping bag off her. "Your buttercream isn't thick enough. If you want to do the Faringdon technique, it must be robust enough to hold its shape."

"I know that, but I've added powdered sugar, and it's still not holding." She slumps against the countertop, her head in her hands.

"You overmixed it, and it's too warm in here. Let's make it again."

"I know all this. I'm better than this." There's marks on her hands where she's pinched her skin, and those tears are threatening to flow from the corners of her eyes.

"Because you're too in your head. Are you panicking about the competition?"

"Yeah, kind of. I guess. You could be less annoying."

"Noted, Chef," I bark, hoping it makes her laugh. She sighs loudly and glares at me, but there's a twist on her lips as if she's trying not to smile.

We mix the buttercream to a Hailee Steinfeld song I recognise as one of Flora's favourites. It doesn't take long before Ruby moves her hips to the tune. Her shoulders bob as some of the stress eases.

"When I've fucked up in the restaurants where I've worked, it's not due to my techniques but because I'm wound up about something. You can learn and practice techniques for days, but you'll struggle and fail if you're anxious. How did you relax when you got stressed before?"

She raises her eyebrows quickly, and I shake my head.

"Not that," I warn.

She laughs. "Don't worry, I won't make you do that." I long to ask precisely what *that* is and if she'll explain it to me slowly before acting it out with me. I squeeze my lips together to stop asking anything that can get me into trouble. "I also tried mindfulness, but it's not for me. My mind never stops."

"Same."

We spend the next half an hour practising the Faringdon technique. She was correct; she knew how to do it. I've never baked with people before Ruby. I've taught plenty of times, but my cooking was always high pressure and about showcasing what I could do like an overperforming teenager.

I like creating without pressure more than I realised.

"Have you ever baked while wearing headphones? It always grounds me, which is why I'm playing this. I used to have a playlist for energising me and one for calming me. I also add a scent to my shirt to give me a different focus."

"Cinnamon," she exclaims with a grin.

"Yes, and something else."

We start tidying up, but I don't want the evening to

end. She might not let me bake with her again. I check the clock. It's already getting late. We've been here for three hours.

She licks her lips and breathes me in. She's so damn sexy. I avert my eyes. This isn't what I'm here for.

"I can't work out what the other smell is."

"You will," I reply covertly.

"I'll get it out of you eventually," she says, popping a bit of frosting on my nose from our practised biscuits.

"I don't doubt it." I dip my finger in it and lick it off. Her eyes are tight with frustration that she can't get to me, and soon, she's picking up icing sugar between her fingers and tossing it at me.

"It's like that, is it?" I grab some and chase her around the kitchen.

She squeals in delight. Suddenly, we're on either side of the demonstration bench. Her eyes light up as she swishes her fingers under the tap, ready to flick water at me, but instead, I reach forward and fling icing sugar down her blouse.

"That's for earlier when you teased me."

"You were a dick," she says between laughter as she throws water at me. Droplets collect in my curls.

"It's what I'm good at."

"Ain't that the truth?" She's walking back around the demonstration counter.

I throw my hands in the air. "Hey."

She grabs an iced biscuit and shoves it in my face like a cream pie.

"You cheeky cow."

Frosting covers my nose as I peel off the biscuit and wipe it across her lips before popping it in my mouth.

"You bastard. Maybe you should help me reach all the icing you've got on me." She runs her finger through the icing on my face and slides her finger against her neck. Arousal rushes me as I lean down to suck on her neck. She braces herself, her hands wrapping around my biceps.

The desire that's toyed with me all day overwhelms me. I brush my lips against her skin. The taste of vanilla frosting mixed with her scent of passion fruit makes every part of my body ache with need.

But then her brother's reaction in the pub and her response pushes through my consciousness.

"Ruby, we shouldn't. I don't want to cause problems in your family, and I can't give you a relationship."

Ruby sighs and leans against the counter. "I know. I like you, Garett, but you're right. Sorry for getting carried away. And sorry for saying I didn't need your help with baking. I was rude. It's the family stuff." She gives me a tight smile, and I nod. "Shall we tidy up and head off separately?"

As much as I'll do the right thing, the hardest part of me tells me to head to her little cabin in Amber's back garden and share everything I've imagined doing with her.

But I can't.

Instead, I nod.

I owe Ruby's family more than I can repay. This isn't how to thank them. And I can't offer her a relationship or a future. We must stay away from each other, or we'll be ripping each other's clothes off. Our inability to resist each other is in her lingering gaze as we tidy, and it's in mine every time she bends over or reaches for something that I should help with.

Tidying up takes less time than expected, and soon, we're ready to leave. We step outside, and Ruby yelps.

"Kath was right," I stutter.

Inches of snow blanket the car park. It's not powdery stuff like icing sugar. It's more like thick buttercream. It must have started minutes after I entered the cookery school and continued heavily since.

There's no way we're going anywhere tonight.

CHAPTER TWENTY-NINE – RUBY

I look at Garett. "Shit."

He gazes at the car park. His dark-eyed stare takes in every lump and bump of snow. "I couldn't agree more, Rubes. What do you want to do?"

Cold settles in my bones. I'm not warm enough to be out here in my skirt and heels, especially in the hold ups I wore for him, even though he wasn't meant to see them. It was like I was my own worst enemy when I put them on this morning—wearing something sexy for a man I can't be with. "My parents might know someone who can get us out."

"But…" He senses my hesitation. It will take more than a local guy with a Land Rover to get us home.

"But no one can get us out right now, and if they could, their time would be better spent off the roads. I don't need anyone to get into an accident to help us." I don't know if I'm only making an excuse so I can spend more time with Garett. "We could stay in the cosy mezzanine area. There's lots of blankets and cushions as well as the sofa."

Garett's stare lingers on the van. He lets out a puff of air. "Okay."

"I'll let my sister know I'm safe and that I'll be staying

here," I reply as if the prospect of one night in his company won't destroy me. We walk back inside. "Can you sort out the heating while I contact her? We should keep the heating low to not waste money but to stop pipes freezing. The blankets should be enough to keep us warm."

"Cool, cool." Garett clenches his jaw, his eyes dart all over the place.

The call to my sister is brief. Everyone is safe. I manage to allay her fears yet fail to mention that I'm not alone. She doesn't need to know, and from what she says, the snow should be gone by lunchtime tomorrow due to the rain and rising temperatures first thing.

I shake my head as I reach the hideaway. The last thing she said won't leave my consciousness. The sofa is a sofa bed. I don't know how to tell Garett that without sounding like I'm propositioning him, because that's exactly what I want to do.

Again, I remember what my brother said as we sat on plastic garden chairs.

I second-guess every decision as I turn on the fairy lights and prepare the space for sleeping. I unfold the blankets before pushing them to one side.

"No, we need blankets," I grumble before laying them out. But it's the sofa that holds my attention. If Garett comes up in the next minute, I won't mention anything. I take off my shoes before putting them back on again. I can't look like I'm seducing him.

Don't be stupid, Ruby. You can't sleep with your shoes on.

I remember how I teased Garett today. It wasn't about annoying him. It was about turning him on. I want him. I need my Garett itch scratched, and whenever I'm around him, I need to know if he fancies me. Even if we can't be together.

I look down the stairs, but he's not there. I tap my foot restlessly against the floor and clatter my teeth together. Maybe I should test the bed. It's probably too old to fold out, anyway. We can sleep on the sofas, but they aren't big enough for us both. What if we end up cuddling on one, and I'm grinding on his—*stop, Ruby! You've read too many of Amber's spicy books. All one-bed tropes and hard cocks.*

I test the bed, attempting to yank at the bottom even though it's a bad idea.

It comes out quickly.

"Fuck," I grumble. I pull at my eyebrows.

It looks like a proposition. I can't leave it like this. Garett's footsteps hit the stairs. I flap around, pushing and pulling different parts of it, but where it came out quickly, it won't go back. He's getting closer. I yank one of the sides and trip over it.

I land face first on the sofa, my ass in the air, a chill on my thighs as my skirt rides up.

"And I thought I was preparing dinner," Garett says. He sounds cocky, but the choked way his words come out suggests this situation has unnerved him too.

I jump up, unable to make eye contact, yet my betraying gaze flicks to his face. One of his hands covers his eyes, and his cheeks are redder than a sunset on a frosty evening.

"You averted your eyes?"

"Eventually," he grunts. "I've brought a snack."

He's balancing a cheese board precariously on his free hand. I yank my skirt back into place.

"I'm all decent," I announce.

"Are you sure? Because I'd hate to see that again," he

replies, peeking between his fingers. His cheeky grin makes me want to smack him on the shoulder, but I resist.

"You're such an arsehole," I grumble, eventually testing my wobbly legs and taking the cheese board from him. I gasp. "It's beautiful. I've never seen anything like it."

Brie, fondue, Wensleydale, cheddar, and loads more cheeses cover the board. He's added grapes and different types of crackers, olives, pepper, hummus, and cherry tomatoes and made roses from slices of cured meats. He's even decorated the board with nuts, berries, small orange segments, and more meats.

His smile spreads as I pop a grape in my mouth. I sink my teeth into it, and the taste explodes against my tongue. "How did you do this so quickly, and where did you get all the food?" I eventually ask.

"I rustled it up from the things for the wreath making workshop. I'll replace it all before the first one on Monday." He says it like it doesn't mean anything, but it does. Even on my lowest days, Neil wouldn't make me a crisp sandwich. "I found a bottle of red that will go well with it. Are you up for it?"

I nod eagerly, too nervous to share my thoughts. I can't date Garett, but as he runs down the stairs to fetch the wine and glasses, I press my fingers to my lips, remembering our pub kiss.

His footsteps hit the stairs. I bite the inside of my mouth.

Nothing can happen tonight.

We spend the next hour laughing as we share the cheese

board. We stick to the one bottle of wine. I don't want my inhibitions lowered any more than necessary. But being with him is fun and a little like an evening with a great friend. A friend you want naked, but I'm pretending I'm not fantasising about him even though I remember how hard his thighs were beneath my fingertips. I wish he wouldn't waggle those forearms when he talks.

He tells me stories of growing up in a family that knew nothing about cooking, and I share moments of the trouble I used to get into at the old Cloud Cookery School and some of the clients my family put up with.

"My mum once burnt our ready meal pasta dinner," he explained. "It wasn't a bad smell. A bit like roasted fennel."

"Weird. But sometimes people get distracted when cooking, so—"

"She was heating it in the microwave. She decided that less than a couple of minutes wouldn't kill the fridge germs." I raise my eyebrows. "Don't ask. Anyway, she put it in the microwave for twenty minutes. That's not the worst one. She once tried to cook raw chicken in the microwave in a foil tray."

My eyes are going to pop out of my head.

"I know. It was lucky I saw it because we'd have needed the fire brigade. I did all the cooking from about eight years old, so as soon as I heard the microwave go, I was on high alert."

"You were so young."

Maybe he senses I have more questions because he diverts me with a request. "Tell me more stories about your grandparents and their wars."

"One day, Grandad convinced Grandma that there was a new spice he'd learnt about called tamagotchi. He explained that it was electrifying. She asked everyone about it and how to add it to her cooking. When one of the participants in the school explained it was a toy from the nineties, it kicked off."

"What happened?" He sits close to me on the sofa bed as we grab the last bits from the cheese board.

"They went to war." I giggled. "Initially, it was salt in his tea rather than sugar, but it escalated to things like bread dough in his hair until Kath stepped in and stopped their fight."

"Kath is wise."

"We should have listened to her today, and I shouldn't have stayed to bake." Our hands linger on the last cracker. "You have it."

"No, you," he replies quickly.

"Share?"

He nods as I break the cracker. His fingertips brush mine, bringing tingles all the way to my neck.

"So why did you stay? I thought you were going home."

"I wanted to learn this new technique and needed time out. Amber is at Mum and Dad's tonight, and I didn't want to be sat in her house on my own after a difficult week. She's secretly crying about Kalen. She doesn't want me to know. Last night, I stayed up until the early hours to make her some treats."

"You're a good sister." I shrug and lower my eyes, but he brushes his fingertips across my cheek, and I look back at him. "Rubes, you're a good sister."

"I wasn't always. That's why this thing between us can't happen."

He pulls his fingers back quickly and sits on them. I

hold back a sigh. "Is that what Jem was talking about in the pub?"

I sigh loudly. "Yes. When I got with Neil, I became a different person. I went from being completely invested in my family and the cookery school to acting like a stranger. I moved away, immersed myself in my relationship with Neil, and kept that life going. It wasn't always a healthy relationship. He didn't want to spend time with my family, and it got weird if I went to visit. He also didn't pay for anything."

I pause for way too long.

"But you stuck with him anyway." There's no judgment in his voice.

"Yep," I confirm. Garett tips his head to the side, and for once, I'm genuinely listened to about Neil. No one understood why I distanced myself. "He made me feel loved. I was searching for what my parents and grandparents had even from such a young age, and I thought I could have that from this random guy who said all the right things and gave me these emotions I'd never experienced before. I couldn't think straight when it came to decisions. I was into him."

"I get that." Maybe it was the same with his dog-stealing ex.

"But over time, I realised he was an arsehole. He wasn't the devil or anything, but he was a bit of a shit, and I didn't like him that much. The relationship got toxic," I admit. "But I'd given up everything to be with him, and I couldn't go back on that, or rather, I was too ashamed to go back on it."

"And then he cheated on you."

I nod as we turn to sit facing each other. He's got his legs crossed, and mine are to the side. Due to my tight pencil skirt, it's like I'm at a sleepover with my best friend, although the temptation to kiss him never goes away. His hands lightly tap his thighs.

"I ignored my parents when they offered me a third of the cookery school. I wasn't there when my grandparents died and only came home briefly for the funeral, alone," I add. "I regret it all, and if something happens with us and it affects the cookery school, they'll be devastated. Jem said that I nearly ruined the family before, including breaking my grandparents' hearts. I can't do that again."

I share a little more of what Jem said, and Garett sighs his understanding. "I've never had a family like yours. My parents were the type to ignore me or clip me around the ear when they were angry about something and I got in the way. They didn't hit me often." He points to the scar on his chin, and I touch the famous, never explained mark. He shivers slightly. "This was on my sixteenth birthday when I shouted at them. They'd forgotten my birthday, so caught up in their arguments."

"You've never mentioned them in your interviews."

"There's nothing to talk about." He shrugs. "They never contact me except when they want money, which I won't give them. I gave them an agreed-upon one-off payment a couple of years ago."

He talks like a robot, and against my better judgment, I take his hands. They're cold to the touch, so I wrap them between mine to warm them. "That's it? No other contact?"

"No. I did offer them a chance to visit me last year, but they asked if it came with spending money. I cut ties that day. I nearly got them arrested a while back for some of their fraudulent behaviour, but I couldn't do it." He squeezes his lips tight as if resigned to pain. Then, he quickly shakes his head. "But that's enough about me. We're supposed to be talking about you."

Surrounded by thick snow, the cookery school is cut off from everyone. It's like we're in another country where no one can get close. The fairy lights highlight his dark eyes, and it's getting cold with the heating on low.

I don't know I'm shivering until he drags one of the blankets closer and drapes me in it. "Your family, and by that I mean everyone at the cookery school, have done more than anyone has for me in years, except Flora. I owe them so much, and I don't want to do anything that hurts them. I can't promise how long I'll be around, probably not more than a couple of months. I want to run a kitchen again. I love this place, but it's not my forever kitchen." He laughs half-heartedly, but it's not enough to make me forget our impossible situation.

It's my turn to squeeze my lips together and nod my head.

"But more than all of this," he adds, scooting closer. My tight blouse and pencil skirt with hold ups underneath aren't suitable for a sleepover with a bestie, but I can't remove them, especially not in front of Garett, the man who makes my heart thunder and the space between my thighs burn. His voice drops, and I lean in as he takes my hands. "More than anything, I don't want to hurt you. I can't give you a relationship or a future. I can't promise that anything between us won't cause problems for the cookery school or your next steps. We can't date."

I take a breath. I'm about to say something stupid. Maybe it's the wine or that, here, nothing can be said because we're stuck in this place together, but I fix his eyes with mine and say, "But we could have no-strings sex."

And that's when he starts choking.

CHAPTER THIRTY – GARETT

She didn't just offer me sex.

She. Did. Not. Just. Offer. Me. Sex.

But as I rasp through the breath I sucked in so hard I choked on it, I replay Ruby's words.

No-strings sex.

She thrusts a glass of water into my hand and pats me on the back three times.

I'm still trying to breathe when she stands.

"Joking!" she shouts as if there's a tsunami outside. "Right, I'd best clear up."

Before I can stop her, she grabs the empty glasses and bottle and rushes downstairs. Her feet slap her retreat.

I finally get enough air in my lungs to speak, although my voice rasps, and I can't get enough volume to call her back. The deep brown of her eyes as she stared at me and the way she licked her lips suggested she wasn't joking. I can blame the moment—telling her about my family and showing care for hers—but that's not it either.

There's something between us. This attraction and heat that doesn't disappear even when we're not near each other. I love cooking with her and laughing with her, and I've fantasised about her more than anyone ever. But no-strings sex with someone I spend this much time with isn't possible. I set my mind to telling her that, but I can't get the words out when she returns.

She won't look at me.

There's still the empty cheese board, so I take that downstairs while she busies herself, getting out more blankets. By the time I return, she's covered the sofa bed with them.

I stare out the window. The snow has stopped, but white covers everything. We can't go home.

"I need to take my clothes off," she says so quietly I barely hear her.

"What?" I turn to find Ruby with her head down and fiddling with the cuff of her blouse.

"I need to take my clothes off," she repeats slower.

Did we agree to no-strings sex without me realising? My body wants it. It's all I can do to keep my cock still when I look at her.

"I can't sleep in this skirt and blouse. When I was younger, I went through a phase where I slept on the bedroom floor." Her cheeks pink as she rambles. "Anyway, one morning, I woke up with the cable from a charger wrapped a little around my neck. I presumed Jem was trying to kill me. We had a fiery relationship growing up, but he was away on camp."

She says all of this so quickly that I can barely keep up. Her head is down, but she lifts her eyes occasionally, her eyelashes fluttering. She's so beautiful that I grind my teeth to stop all the thoughts running through my head. It doesn't work. I want whatever she's willing to give me.

"I can't sleep with anything around my neck, including blouses with collars. I have underwear on that I'll sleep in, although I will lose the hold ups."

I groan inwardly at the mention of the hold ups, but the way she looks at me, all wide eyes and biting lips, I suspect it wasn't as inwardly as I'd hoped.

"Which side of the bed do you want?" she asks softly.

"We're sleeping together?"

"We're sleeping in the same bed. If you're okay with that." My cock jumps. "There's enough blankets that we can be human sausage rolls. We'll never have to touch each other's skin or anything."

I groan again. I want her to touch me. I fantasise about her fingers skimming my body approximately a billion times a day. I rub a hand down my face.

"I'm sorry for suggesting no-strings sex. I really am." Her forehead wrinkles as she breaks eye contact. Her light is gone. "Can you look away so I can get ready for bed?"

I nod and turn. A rustle of material has me digging my teeth into my lips. I imagine her fingers pulling those hold ups away from her thighs before sliding them down her legs. A metal taste touches my tongue. I try closing my eyes, but that's when all my fantasies of her undressing for me distract me. I shake my head and run through all the implements I might find in the cookery school drawers to ease my desire.

"Finished," she says minutes later. Thank fuck for that. She's already under the blankets. "I picked the left side. I hope that's okay."

I nod again. This is the right thing to do. There's nowhere else to sleep, and I'm cold, so I need a blanket. She's consented to sharing, and we're both adults who are able to control our urges. That's when I see her clothes bunched up at the side, her hold ups sitting on top.

Oh shit.

"I'm going to sleep in my underwear, too, if that's

okay? I don't have any history with charging cables, just cable ties." I meant to be lighthearted, but I wince after I say the words because her eyes are so wide. "*Joking.* I can joke, too."

"Oh, right. Yeah."

This couldn't be more awkward.

"I usually sleep naked. Dick out and everything." *Oh, it could be more awkward.* I made that happen. "Anyway, enough about my dick. Please look the other way."

"Sorry, of course."

Her bra strap slides down, and I watch it, my mouth dry. She yanks it back up before scratching her forehead. Ruby ducks her head under the blanket, but it's like her stare is still on me. I've tasted her need all night.

She said no-strings sex, but she decided that was the wrong decision, and it is. It doesn't matter how much I want her because I can't have her. I just need to get through tonight without saying anything else stupid, and then we will return to being colleagues and nothing more.

In record time, I'm diving under the blanket. "Goodnight then, Ruby."

"Goodnight, Garett," she says breathlessly, causing my cock to jolt.

Stay strong. You can't let her get hurt.

"I'm not fragile, you know."

Shit, did I say the hurt thing out loud?

"I know you're not."

"Good. I wanted to check," she adds. Her voice is low enough to thrum through my body.

"Good."

I turn away from her, but I can tell by how she's breathing—practically panting, unless that's me—that she's not asleep. I grind my teeth. I want to be between her legs. Make her really pant. I grind my teeth harder.

"Do you normally sleep with a mouth guard?"

"Yes. How did you know?"

I turn to face her, and sensing my movement, she turns to face me. Her eyes are dulled.

"You had one in the van when you drove me to the wine warehouse that time. And you grind your teeth."

"Do I?"

I can smell passion fruit and the wine. She smells like heaven.

"You do. A lot. I'm surprised you have any teeth left."

"I stopped doing it for a while, but now I only do it around you," I stutter. In the last week, it's come back in force. I don't want her to think I'm some teeth-grinding serial killer.

Her brow furrows, and she worries her lip. I want to be licking and biting that lip. "Why me? I thought we got on."

My senses are heightened. I can't stop the words that flee from my mouth, even though I know once they're out, I won't be able to drag them back in. "Because I want you. I've wanted you from the first moment I saw you."

"But you were angry with me."

"I was angry, full stop. But my wants haven't stopped, and getting to know you has made it worse."

"Worse?"

I blame the snow and the silence and the bed and the alcohol and her soft skin for what I say next, even though I know it's me. It's all me.

"Worse, better, either way, it's always there. I fantasise about what will make you moan. I long to bury myself between your thighs and see your head thrown back as I slide my fingers inside you. I want you to ride me with that black lace bra with the pretty pink flowers. I—"

Her mouth against mine silences me. The scent of passion fruit swirls around my head as she sucks on my lower lip. Her hands burrow into my hair. We're a tangle of blankets and frenzy as she tries to climb on me, but the material keeps getting in the way.

Weeks of passion explode as she moans into my mouth. It's frantic and messy, and I love every second. She teases my lips apart with her tongue and explores mine with an unexpected tenderness.

I could kiss this woman for hours, but one-off sex prohibits longing kisses for me. Not that we've agreed to anything. I push her hair to the side, the blond waves splayed around her head, and brush my lips against her neck. She gasps before growling, "Garett."

I need her to say my name precisely like that again. My cock presses against my boxer briefs as she writhes above me, but with all these blankets surrounding us, it's like we're trapped.

"Wait," I finally say as she bucks against me. She bites that lip in a way that shows her worry, but it makes me want to soothe it with my tongue. "Wait."

CHAPTER THIRTY-ONE – RUBY

I wait as Garett instructed me, but he's not saying anything. He's staring into my eyes. It's hard to see their colour as the eerie glow from the white snow outside fills the room. After hearing everything he'd wanted to do with me since we met—me, the woman ditched by her boyfriend for her business partner and told she wasn't sexy anymore—my body fires for him.

I bite my lip, but suddenly, he replaces it with his thumb.

It teeters on the edge of my mouth.

I want to suck it.

I want to suck his cock more. It's pressing against me even in this sea of blankets I regret insisting on. Who says sausage roll when they're looking at the man they want to have inside them?

"Ruby," he finally says, "are you sure you can do no-strings sex?"

I nod because, with the arousal coursing through my body, I'm not sure I can do anything else.

"Use your words."

"I can do no-strings," I croak. "I want you, Garett. I don't care if it's just for one night. I *need* you. You turn me on more than anyone has, and if I don't have you inside me in the next five minutes, then I'm going to explode."

"Then I best call the fire brigade because the things I want to do with you aren't going to include me inside you for at least an hour."

Aren't?

I can't help but giggle from the cheesiness, but then he flicks on the fairy lights and gives me the *I'm about to devour every part of you* look. *I'm the fireball that will ignite every inch of skin, and you won't survive it.* I'm drowning in that look.

We clumsily unwrap ourselves from the blankets. There's giggling and awkwardness, but then I'm underneath him. His hands slide onto the sides of my head. The hairs on his chest tickle my skin.

"It's a shame you took off the hold ups. I wanted to see you in them properly before I ripped them off you."

I go to move. "I can—"

But his growl freezes me to the bed. It's a primal growl that makes me feel owned and worshipped. Garett is an animal coming out of his cage because he wants me.

His mouth presses against my neck as he pins my wrists above my head. A throaty moan leaves my lips.

"Anytime you want to stop or you want me to do something different, you tell me, Ruby." His voice is so deep, and my body throbs with need for him. "Promise me, Rubes."

"I promise," I gasp.

"Good girl," he grunts, and my body quivers beneath it. "Oh, you like that, do you? You like being my good girl."

I whimper.

Garett kisses me hard on the mouth, and I forget all my typical smart-arsed responses. I wasn't expecting to be in bed with this cooking sex god. He's barely touched me, and already, my body sears for him.

"Maybe save up those whimpers because I'd hate it if you lost your voice. I'm only just getting started."

His voice is gravelly. I knew this man of pure sex was under the guise of a chef all this time, but he still takes me by surprise. His kisses rain down on my skin as he rubs my pussy through my knickers with the palm of his hand.

I'm grinding against his casual touch.

When I said no-strings sex, I thought it would be a quick bang that would remove the tension, and then we'd be sorted. But this is like a masterclass in sexual prowess. I thought his cooking was good, but he should teach this instead.

"Hmmmm, you're already wet for me, Ruby." He slides his fingers into my knickers briefly before holding them up to his lips. Our stares are locked on each other as he opens his mouth and presses his glistening fingers between his lips and sucks hard. I nearly come right there. "So fucking good."

I buck against him, and he chuckles a laugh that rumbles against my body. "Not yet. I've got so much I want to do."

His other fingers dance across the flowers on my bra. "You showed me this bra when I was trying to teach. You teased me with it, and I wanted nothing more than to rip it off you."

I deliberate whether I'm happy that he's about to yank off my favourite bra. My pussy says yes, it practically pulsates the word, but my bank balance says a very definite no. He doesn't hurt the bra at all. Instead, he pulls down a cup, and with his fingers, still wet from me, he runs the tips across my hardened nipples.

"I know you shouldn't mix business with pleasure, but

I'd love to cover these nipples with melted chocolate before licking it off."

"I could find you some." My voice is barely a rasp. I'm so fucking needy, and it's all because of him.

He chuckles again. "Another time."

And with every fibre of my being, I hope to all the presenters of *Bake Off* and *MasterChef*, current and legends, that there will be a next time, and it will involve every sugary sweet morsel ever created. And maybe ice, too.

His tongue replaces his fingers, and before I can consider which I prefer more, his fingers slide into my knickers and run in circles around my clit.

"Mary Berry," I gasp before squeezing my eyes tightly closed. Shit, I cried out the name of a former baking show judge. Is that my way of blaspheming? It's never happened before.

"Mary Berry?" At his laughter, I open one eye, then the other. His grin is broad, and a zip of joy explodes in my chest. I love that even pleasure with him is filled with fun. "Please don't tell me you shout Gordon Ramsay when you come, or I'll have to edge you all night."

I glare at him, but the beginning of a smile and wrinkly nose give away my true emotions. "There's one way to find out what I shout when I come. I hoped it would be Garett Kelsey, but I can't promise."

"We'd best find out, then." And that's when his whole body moves down. He kisses my inner thighs, and I swear he's trying to leave love bites as he sucks and nibbles at my flesh.

His fingers go to my knickers, and I lift my bum so he can pull them down my legs. I'm rewarded with another "good girl" in a voice so deep it caresses my soul.

He slides the knickers down my legs with his kisses trailing behind them. I want to pull his head back to my pussy. I want him to lick it or finger it or do whatever else he can. But maybe he senses this because he does everything to avoid it.

"Garett," I growl.

"Yes, Ruby." There's amusement behind his words. "What do you want?"

I grind my teeth, which I'm sure amuses him, too. It's just no-strings. There's no pressure, and I can say what I want without consequences.

"Lick my pussy now." I close my eyes in preparation for his teasing, but instead, stars pulsate across my vision from one swipe of his tongue.

My moan elicits more of the same. One hand continues to play with my nipples while the other slides a finger inside me. Maybe it's because he's a chef, but he's fantastic at multitasking. He's licking and sucking as I ride his fingers. He's pinching and circling, and fuck knows what because every bit of pleasure I never knew existed fills my body.

I grip and squeeze the blankets, desperate to hold onto something as I swear my body tries to levitate off the bed. I don't know if it goes on for minutes or hours. It's like I'm on the highest sugar hit as he swirls his tongue around my clit while pressing his fingers deeper and deeper inside me. He hits that G-spot that even I thought was a myth.

I jerk off the bed before wrapping my thighs around Garett's head. I'm moving my body in time with his fingers, crying out in pleasure as my climax nears. His fingers drag me closer to it with each press. He sucks my clit between his lips and thrusts a second finger inside me.

I come so hard that I would have fallen off the bed if I hadn't been anchored to his face. Stars, fireworks, and even giant fairy lights fill my head as I scream his name. I ride out the orgasm like it's something I've always done.

I pant nonsensical words and come off the highest high.

He murmurs, "That should help you sleep."

"I'm not done yet."

"I haven't got a condom, Rubes." My mind is a mess, and his thick cock that I'm absentmindedly stroking isn't helping either. It looks massive in my tiny hands. I want it inside me. Suddenly, I remember what Amber told me a couple of weeks before.

"My sister keeps condoms here. She and Kalen were going to have sex in here, but they didn't make it beyond the car park. Hence why there are twins on the way."

Garett's laughter amps up my arousal. I run across the mezzanine floor naked, feeling his eyes track me.

"Turn around slowly," he demands, but instead, I throw the condom at him and cock my hip, shoving my fist on it. "Everything about you is sexy, especially your attitude."

I'm practically glowing. Surely, your first time with someone new is meant to be an awkward fumble and embarrassing in places. This is like a perfect dream.

"Whatever." I roll my eyes, but I can't tear the grin from my face. He fists his cock as he watches me.

"Please spin slowly, Rubes. I want to see every inch of you. I never want to forget this image." That's not something you say to a hookup, but I throw my hands in the air, and I comply. I can't get enough of how he worships my body. "Now get over here and ride me."

I prowl closer as if he's not the boss of me, although he totally is. I straddle him, positioning my entrance at his now sheathed cock. "What do you want, Garett? Say the words."

"I want you to slide—"

But I don't give him a chance to finish. Instead, I drop down onto him, filling myself instantly. I knew it'd hurt—he's bigger than all my toys—but I don't care. It was worth it to watch his eyes roll back in his head and hear his gasps of desperation.

"Even when you're torturing me, you're the sexiest woman that ever existed."

I grin and begin to ride him slowly. I'm grinding against him, using my thighs to ease myself onto him again.

His fingers grip my hips before moving to my bum and then back to my hips. It's like he doesn't know what he wants to touch more. I put my hands on either side of his head, desperate for that scent of cinnamon that never leaves him. It's embossed on my heart, just like this moment.

"You're fucking beautiful, Rubes. I want your perfect thighs to wear the imprint of my fingers. I will dream about you soaking me for the rest of my life. Does my dick feel good, baby?"

I nod, my forehead tight with desperation for more as words refuse to fall from my mouth.

"You're stunning. You're the sexiest woman I've ever met," he murmurs, and I feel it because of him.

His lips caress my neck like he already knows I love it, and his hands move into my hair, slightly pulling it before breathing me in.

"I've longed to be close enough to touch you and caress you, and I'm so fucking lucky that I get to be inside you and watch how beautiful you are when you're aroused. Because you are beautiful, baby, you're fucking stunning."

I can't believe that this guy whose tongue is like licks of fire against my skin is my friend who fixes my car light and cares about my family. He has more skills in this room than in the kitchen, and that's saying something.

He holds my body against him with his mouth-wateringly sexy forearms. I can't see them, but they feel amazing. He pushes up, penetrating me faster and faster. I'm like jelly as my body can no longer sustain all the pleasure he's offering me.

"Your pussy is perfect." He bites my neck, and I cry out. I'm going to wear so many of his marks tomorrow. His stubble when he was between my thighs must have left a scratch that I can't wait to admire in the mirror tomorrow. "You're perfect."

I can barely moan as my second orgasm hits. I need to predict these better so I have some control over them. But who am I kidding? I'm not in control of anything when Garett is inside me.

"Good girl," he says as my body jerks against him. "Ride me, you fucking sexy woman."

His thrusts are more feral as waves of orgasm wash over me repeatedly. "I'm coming," he says between gritted teeth. He growls in my ear as he thrusts one last time. It's like every ache leaves him as his body shakes and he collapses underneath me, but throughout everything, his kisses don't stop.

I know he's finally back to some form of normality when he whispers in my ear, "You didn't even shout Martha Stewart when you came."

I start giggling, but then he adds, "I hope there's

another condom, because once I've got my breath back, we need to go again."

My laughter is caught short by the burn between my thighs. I want him a million times before the sun rises.

I lie down on his chest, giving his nipple a quick bite before he disposes of the condom. Even horny, I need a nap. I start to drift off, naked, with his forearms holding me close, his back rippling against my hands, and his kisses brushing my forehead.

CHAPTER THIRTY-TWO – GARETT

The rain beating the windows wakes me. Passion fruit kisses filled my dreams and some of my awake hours, too. Multiple times in the night, Ruby gave me glimpses of her technicolour orgasms. I didn't know they would be the greatest thing I've ever witnessed.

I stare at her fluttering eyelashes as she sleeps softly. Her blond hair is more-sexy-night-in-a-hotel than soft, gentle waves. A mixture between a smile and a wince crosses my face. I promised her no-strings sex, and yet my thoughts are anything but. I imagine what she'd wear on a date, the gourmet restaurants I'd take her to when I can afford it, and the kisses I'd steal between spoonfuls of chilli chocolate ganache. This woman reached into years of grumpiness and obliterated it with the sweetness and sass that streams from her. I've become someone I only thought I could be when it was just me and Cookie.

The moment I told her about my family, I knew I liked her more than I can admit out loud, but I've promised her this moment and no future, and I can't go back on my word. She still doesn't know about Clive, and I must protect her. I must hide my feelings so that her family isn't affected.

Yet my hand cups her face, and she murmurs her happiness even while she sleeps. In our secret hideaway, we can be whoever we want, but after we leave, we must return to acting like two colleagues and nothing more.

As her eyes open, I say something that isn't a typical conversation between platonic colleagues or the woman you have a one-night stand with, but I can't stop myself. "Can I make you breakfast?"

"Yes," she replies with a smile that hits my heart. This reaction is because of the sex. The incredible, mind-bending, life-changing, unforgettable sex. I let go in a way I was too scared to before, and she was with me every step. For now, I'm pretending it's just the sex making me like this. I will return to being a grumpy arsehole in minutes. "I need whatever you can rustle up, and I want it stat."

Her cheeky face has the most kissable smile I've seen, and I cover her with those kisses. Maybe I'll be a grumpy arsehole tomorrow instead.

"Kisses don't mean I'm eating bread. Hurry up, Garett," she says, but she's climbing on me and straddling my lap.

"Neither does fisting my dick." Her cheeks redden as if she didn't know she was stroking my length. "Out of curiosity, have we got any condoms left?"

She screws her mouth to the side as if she's pretending to think before she reaches under my pillow. So that's where she moved them to in the night. "We've got one, so you'd better make this moment last."

"You're so demanding." But the cockiness is yanked out of me as she rips the foil and rolls the condom down my length.

"You have no idea." She lifts her eyebrows twice quickly. I pick her up and roll her beneath me. She squeals but then grins in a way that pulls at my heart and makes me harder than I thought possible all at once. "Shame we only have one, as I wanted to see those forearms as you fucked me."

I flip her so that she's bent over in front of me. I plant my arms on either side of her as I enter her quickly. If the middle of the night was gentle, then this is anything but. She nips at my forearms as I fill her quickly. I never want this moment to end.

"**B**reakfast is served," I announce as we meet in the dining area. She's wearing my shirt over her knickers and... "Oh, fuck. Ruby. You've got the hold ups on."

They grace her upper thighs, and I kneel in front of her. My fingers tease the lace tops until she slaps my hands away. She tucks a finger under my chin, and our eyes meet. "Garett, we're out of condoms, and we both need to eat."

My growl makes her laugh long and hard.

"Let me clarify," she replies, wiping away tears of laughter. "We need to eat food, and you've prepared this incredible meal for us, so first, we eat."

"First?" My belly rumbles, but it's hungry for her.

Her grin as she shakes her head at my lunacy is everything. I want that smile featuring in every one of my memories.

"Breakfast, Garett," she says, telling me off.

This woman.

I sit on one of the benches, and she slides onto my lap to eat. Her skin is warm against mine, and I hold her against my bare chest as she massacres the eggy bread and pancakes I prepared for her.

"So is this your guilty pleasure food to cook?" she asks

as she shoves a piece of pancake in her mouth. There are no delicate-sized pieces. It's like she's possessed, and it's all I can do to eat and not watch her while puffing out my chest with pride.

"Guilty pleasure cooking?"

She moans around a piece of pancake. "Yeah, people have guilty pleasure movies and music. I reckon all incredible chefs have something a bit easy that they like to cook. Maybe something that reminds them of their childhood or a comfort they like to prepare, but it's something they don't admit often, and they'd never add it to a menu."

I chuckle. "The eggy bread is my guilty pleasure, but not because of my childhood. In my early twenties, I'd make this and serve it with fizzy orange pop for Flora when she was bullied at school. It was only eggy bread, but it helped."

"You really care about her."

"Yeah. She gave me value. When I had a bad day in the restaurant, fired incompetent staff, or was shouted at by managers or clients, this person would like me for me. I was a dick at times in those restaurants, ruling with an iron thumb, but Flora saw this brilliant big brother type who could cook her favourite comfort foods or make her smile with bad impressions of her actual big brother."

"Is that how you met Flora, through her brother?"

"Um, yeah."

Ruby finishes the last bite of her pancake, drops her cutlery like a mic drop, and leans back. Her hold ups brush my skin, but instead of ravaging her, I enjoy the closeness. She puts her hand on mine, the one holding her against me. I brush kisses to her neck, and she tips her head to the side, gifting me more access.

Again, I remind myself this is no-strings sex.

"Was your childhood hideous?" she asks, surprising me.

Even that question is a reprieve from discussing Clive. "Yeah. I counted down the days until I'd leave and then got as far away from my parents as quickly as possible." Where this topic used to make me grind my teeth, it no longer does.

Weird.

"You suggested last night that they did something fraudulent." I swallow slowly. I have to tread carefully so I don't reveal the truth about Clive. I sigh louder than expected, and she stutters, "Sorry, I'm nosey. I like this extra side of you. I like knowing something about my second favourite chef."

"Second?" I ask, tickling her hips. She squirms and giggles against me as I hold her close. "Did your first make eggy bread for you?"

"No, she hasn't, but then Mary Berry is a very busy woman. She's the best baker in the world, after all."

I continue to tickle her as she cackles. "How can anyone this delicate make such awful noises? My ears, my ears!"

She turns her head and covers me with kisses. "You're my top chef now, although, with your comments about my laughter, I might have to change that."

I cup her face. My voice drops. "I guess I'll have to find a way to stop your cackles." I kiss her hard, and her laughter turns to moans that vibrate through my body.

"You're a seductive bastard," she murmurs against my lips.

"Mary Berry doesn't compare," I add with a wink, slide

a hand underneath her shirt, and thumb her nipples. She grinds against me and opens her legs as my nails scratch between her thighs, travelling higher with each kiss.

We make out like that until we start shivering. Kissing her is my new passion.

Eventually, she pulls away. I stroke the strands of her hair, unable to let her go completely. She worries her lip and looks down at the floor. "The thing we did last night…"

"And again this morning?"

"Yes," she replies before hesitating.

My body trembles. I shouldn't be anything but blasé. It was meant to be no-strings, probably a one-time deal, yet my stomach rolls in anticipation of what she'll say.

"Use your words, Ruby." She huffs, and I'm rewarded with that smile again. I want it against my lips.

"We didn't say how many times we'd do it, and we already did it four times."

"So we're not counting when you rode my face before you fell asleep the second time?"

She grins at the memory I've purposely made her relive. "That wasn't sex."

"I'm pretty sure you came harder than an earthquake, so you'd better count it. Not all sex is penetrative."

Her brow furrows like I've given her a revelation that she needs to process. "Fine. We did it many times, but we never put a limit on our no-strings sex. We didn't say it would be once or only one night or…"

"Words," I growl because my body thrums at the prospect of being inside her again. "What are you saying?"

"I frequently have an itch that my bullet vibrator won't scratch, and I hoped you might scratch it."

"Still no strings?"

Although impossible, I want her to say we're adding

227

strings. "Of course."

I smile, trying to hide the slight deflation. It's still sex with Ruby, and that is near perfect.

"So, like fuck buddies?" I ask.

She nods.

"Do we need ground rules? Like not seeing other people." I try and say that last part casually, even though I'm not sure if exclusive fuck buddies is a thing. "And… shit, I don't know the rules. I've never done this."

"But—"

"I've only had one-night stands," I reveal, though I hate that she knows that about me. I'm not ashamed of my past, but I want her to view me as boyfriend material. "Let's Google fuck buddy rules." Anything to end that cocked head, knitted eyebrow look she's giving me.

She reaches for her phone and then yelps.

"What?"

But a flustered Ruby jumps off my lap, falling and nearly faceplanting until I catch her.

"Amber is on her way," she screams before running to the window, staring out as if Amber will be glaring at her from the car park like a deranged nineties serial killer. "The snow has gone." I should have realised the heavy rain would melt it, but I was cocooned in our perfect hideaway. "You need to go."

"You wouldn't speak to Mary Berry like that," I say with a wink.

"Garett," she warns. With her hands on her hips, she appears livid. To me, she looks cute and fuckable.

"Will she be more angry that we slept together or that we used her secret condom stash?"

"Garett!" She scowls. "Get upstairs."

We can't let anyone see, especially Ruby's family, but she's captured me with her sensuality and kindness.

I pick her up and throw her over my shoulder. She squeals but doesn't struggle. "Fine, but you're coming, too."

"But—"

"Sweet cheeks," I say with a quick spank of her arse. My cock judders. I'm going to do that again, especially now that we're fuck buddies. "I'll need my shirt, as all I'm wearing are my boxers, so you're coming with me."

I catch her reflection in the window. Her body is glorious, and I know exactly which parts of it can elicit noises and which parts make her writhe. I can't wait to find out how we seal our fuck buddies deal. I'm hoping it involves me inside her or her on my face.

I spank her again.

"Garett," she shouts as my laughter echoes around the cookery school.

.

Chapter Thirty-Three – Ruby

Garett and I haven't spoken since I chucked him out of the cookery school yesterday in case my sister found us. I snicker to myself as I remember how he Googled rules for fuck buddies while face-planting on the sofa bed, his jeans around his ankles, all while I shouted, "We haven't got time!"

While dressing, we disagreed with most of the ones we found online and decided on five for us.

1) To remain professional at work no matter how horny we are

2) No dates, just hookups

3) Not to tell anyone about what we're doing

4) Never text unless it's to do with work or arranging a hookup

5) No staying overnight at each other's houses

This is why we haven't spoken. Now it's Monday early evening, and we're baking mince pies and doing the last bits of preparation for the cookery school before the mulled wine and wreath making workshop.

I catch sight of Garett in the glass of the cookery school door. He's wearing a Christmas shirt, as per instructions. I'm in thigh-high boots and a red woolly dress with white reindeer silhouettes. It clings to every curve. It's not full-on Mrs. Christmas, but it's much sexier than I'd typically wear. His eyes nearly jump out of his head when he sees me, but then he nods with his furrowed brow. He doesn't offer me a hello. His body is stiff and his face blank. I manage not to stomp my feet in annoyance.

"Where do you want me?" he asks Kath brusquely, although his wincing gaze keeps drifting my way as I struggle with the streamers.

I climb on the chair to hang the decorations above the dining table. This is a job for Wicksy, but he's too busy flirting with Flora, who's leading the wreath making session. It's like she's taken courses in every skill, including flower arranging.

"Please help Ruby with the streamers. She's going to hurt herself," Kath replies as she gets the trays out for the mince pies.

"Ruby?" Garett looks around the room with his arms in the air, moving his head from side to side as if he doesn't know where I am. "Oh, there you are," he announces loudly. "I didn't realise you were already here."

"It's not like I'm hiding," I reply with a roll of my eyes. "And you've already nodded to me."

He clears his throat noisily. "I don't know what you mean. It's nice to see you again after the last cookery day." He clears his throat again and grinds his teeth. "Did you get home okay before it snowed on Saturday?"

I stare at him, wide-eyed. It's like he's a robot trying to pretend to be human. Kath shakes her head before continuing to set up.

"Get over here and stop being so weird."

Garett stands in front of me as I try to attach the streamers.

"Are you going to help or just watch?"

There's no one around us, but he whispers between gritted teeth like he's a ventriloquist, "I'm trying to be professional. I'm following the rules."

"By acting like a massive knob?"

He grunts his annoyance. Even at this distance, I can smell the cinnamon and that mystery scent I still can't place. I want to kneel on the table, grab his head, and pull him to me for a kiss. His professional demeanour wanes as his stare licks like flames up my boots before raking up my body. Heat pools between my thighs as I remember the way I sat on his lap, writhing, on Sunday morning. I swear he's thinking the same as he runs his knuckles across his stubble.

I wobble under his hungry glare, and immediately, his hands grip me around the waist. His fingers pinch my hips, and my chest moves up and down with the depths of my breaths. We remain like this until a clattering tray sounds from the demonstration counters.

"You look very nice," I say as he helps me off the table. I breathe him in again, a moan escaping from between my lips.

"You resemble every sexy Christmas dream I've ever had." He pops me onto the ground, practically pushing me away, shaking his head and grunting an expletive. He pulls his hand away. "I'll get on with the streamers. You do something else."

I cock my eyebrow, but he busies himself as I hang baubles onto the tree. At least he's not regretful about Sunday. I've overplayed what we said to each other and everything else. My bullet vibrator is barely surviving, but in the mix of horniness, there are moments of panic and struggle. I can't do hookups. I want to be able to, but I already like him a lot. Not that he needs to know that. I want to continue having sexual experiences that give me life, so I'll continue pretending I'm cool as a fucking cucumber about our arrangement. I want him to want more, but I can't forget the reasons I gave. My family is too important to be hurt again, and us being in a relationship or trying to do anything more than a short-term hookup agreement will cause problems.

Ideally, we should talk it out before the class starts, but it's nearly time for the punters to arrive.

"Hey, Ruby, did you lose one of your marshmallow earrings? Flora found it in the hideaway upstairs while setting up. It was under the sofa."

Garett freezes.

"I slept here when it snowed. I stayed to bake but got snowed in, so I slept on the sofa," I reply breezily.

"It sounds like the start of a winter horror movie. Were you safe all alone?" Wicksy asks.

"Of course she was all alone," Garett grumbles, and everyone turns to stare at him, including Flora, who just walked into the room.

Should I fall into the tree to distract everyone? Thankfully, vehicles in the car park do the job. We move to greet the people who'll be coming through the doors as I say loud enough for my team to hear, "Yes, I was safe. It was nice. It was the best sleep I'd ever had. Like ever."

Garett stands by me, and when everyone is distracted by the first clients, he whispers in my ear, "The best ever?"

"Yes, by a mile. Like a perfect lemon drizzle cake that you want to eat again and again. Did you enjoy your sleep on Saturday?"

"I've never had one like it. It was the best sleep I've ever had, too."

We beam at each other. I'm desperate to kiss his smiling face. His arm brushes mine, and then, as I lick my lips, he tracks my tongue. I can't wait to get him alone after we're done tonight. What with the sex god next to me and a fully booked class, nothing could be better.

But then a voice ices my veins and sets my teeth on edge. "Ruby, we hoped you'd be leading this tonight."

I turn to find Neil and Viv, and they're holding hands.

CHAPTER THIRTY-FOUR – GARETT

I recognise Ruby's ex-boyfriend's piggy face from the video call several weeks ago. He's wearing a red tracksuit that could be described as retro, but it doesn't fit the Christmas vibe unless he's come as Santa's thieving little brother.

And the mystery woman beside him wears a PVC green elf dress. It'd look okay if she were heading for a night out, but that isn't cooking attire.

Both of the in-your-face outfits pale in comparison when my secret lover and friend trembles beside me. I don't know if she's shaking because she's upset, anxious, angry, or all the above. I lean in to touch her as a friend, and she flinches as if she doesn't recognise me.

Her reaction is like food stuck in my throat. Kath looks warily over, not at Ruby, but at me. I don't know why because I'm sure I'm hiding my reaction well. We're just friends, after all.

"Best get to the demonstration counter," Kath says. "We'll get started."

My feet hesitate.

"You weren't on the list of attendees," Ruby stutters. "Neither of you."

"We didn't think you'd be here if we signed up as ourselves," the woman states. Her PVC dress makes the sound of little farts as she nears Ruby. "And when you ignored my calls, we decided this would be the best way to apologise. And ask for your consent."

She practically gags at the word. "My consent?"

I'm at my demonstration counter as per Kath's instruction. All of the action continues in the doorway. Kath directs the rest of the students to aprons, but everyone looks warily at the reality television–style conversation.

Ruby's shoulders are stiff. From my angle, her eyes blaze as the woman waves her hand.

"Viv and I are getting married," Neil says.

I wait for tears or shouts. Instead, Ruby turns to the counters and the other students and says, "Right. Are you all ready for a fun evening? The great Chef Garett will start by making mince pies. We've got Christmas music, wreath making, mulled wine, and massive smiles. Let's get our jingle bells on!"

I recognise the strain on her face, but spying the excited faces of the other students, it's clear they're oblivious.

Viv and Neil stare dumbfounded at each other. They may not have devil horns, but they're the epitome of villains to me. They hurt the woman I care about.

"Get your aprons on, then," Ruby hisses to them before walking around the room.

"Are you okay?" I ask as she nears me, but she dismisses my question with a wave of her hand.

"Neil thinks we're together, remember?" Her eyes flicker up to mine. "Screw our rules. Play along with me, please?"

I lock eyes with her. She nibbles her lip, and her hand trembles as she pushes back the strands of hair that have escaped her bun. I grip her waist and dip her as I plant a kiss on her lips that's like something from forties Hollywood. It's chaste but with promise.

She's breathless as I let her go.

"Sorry, everyone." I point up at the mistletoe that Kath added earlier. "When your girlfriend looks like this and makes demands, you have to comply, especially when there's mistletoe. Who's ready to make mince pies and find love this Christmas?"

A cheer fills the room, led by Kath. The only quiet ones are Flora and Wicksy, whose mouths are practically on the floor, and Neil and Viv, who glare at us.

If Ruby thought the flirting would be subtle, then tonight's a revelation for her. I enjoyed myself once I'd confirmed with Kath, Wicksy, and Flora that we were faking our relationship because of Neil and Viv. She'll never be my girlfriend, so I've made the most of it and given her the whole Garett boyfriend experience.

During the cooking, I'd find ways to touch and tease her. When I told the class that the pastry needed to be soft like butter, I compared it to Ruby's lips on a warm day. There were sighs from all the ladies, especially when I added that I wrote a message when I first asked Ruby on a date and placed it in Ruby's favourite pie in a heart-shaped crust.

It was fun to cook with her, getting her to demonstrate how to roll the pastry and then telling the group that Ruby was a fantastic baker who'd taught me a lot of skills, too. I was talking about baking, but when one of the ladies giggled, I may have winked and added, "Lots of skills there, too. The person who let her go must be the biggest idiot."

That earned me a grunt from Neil, much to my delight.

I've called her nicknames like sweet cheeks and floury buns and threw in the odd cutie pie.

But now it's time to excel and join the wreath making. The sofa bed is decorated with tartan Christmas blankets, but all I see is Ruby and me chatting and kissing on it.

"Old Garett never would have done wreath making, you know," Flora whispers as I reach the top of the stairs.

When the teams in my restaurants enjoyed Christmas activities or Easter egg hunts or went out for Halloween, I'd continue working or go home early to focus on menu planning.

I shush Flora, whispering, "It's all an act."

Flora tips her head. "I'm calling you Timothée Chalamet from now on."

I let her comment roll off my shoulders. I'm here to make Neil feel like crap for how he hurt Ruby. There's something irresistible about spending time with Ruby, especially making her do that unimpressed laugh or grumpy face when no one's looking because I've pushed it too far. It doesn't mean anything more than that.

"What did Flora say?" she hisses when I join her at the craft station. It's nice to be the sunshine to her grumpy for a change.

Neil watches us, his eyes pinched with suspicion. I cup Ruby's face and peck her on the lips. Her eyes widen as I say loudly, "Don't be cross with me, sugar plum. I know I shouldn't tease you so much. When we get home, I'll make it up to you just how you like." I press my lips to hers again, struggling not to laugh when she bites my lip. "And we can make one wreath so that when we move in together, it will be the first thing people see, an expression of our love."

One of the older ladies coos while another grumbles to her husband, "Why don't you ever say nice things like that to me?"

Behind me, Neil grunts again, but I've stopped caring. What would it be like to come home to Ruby? It's a dream I can't realise, but it still fills me with a cosy swirl.

"You're enjoying this too much," Ruby whispers with a scowl.

I twirl loose strands of her hair around my finger before running my fingertips across the nape of her neck. No one sees us except Neil, who's baring his teeth. "Aren't you enjoying yourself, Rubes?"

She licks her lips and huffs, but she doesn't deny it. I beam. I'm falling so hard for this off-limits woman.

Once Flora finishes her instructions, we make wreaths in our pairs. As expected, Ruby and I have different ideas about what makes a good wreath.

"But, baby, we need more colour," she says, certain I won't argue in front of everyone.

"Nope. It's got to stay all brown and green, like Christmas should be. It needs cones," I announce.

She licks her lips and stares me down, even though she's much shorter than me. "But what about red berries or dark pink flowers? Browns and greens are dull. I thought you weren't boring. I hoped my favourite chef was more exciting than this. You're more exciting in other places." I raise my eyebrows. "In the kitchen, I mean."

"I thought he was your number two chef," Neil shouts from across the room, causing everyone to stare. Viv side-eyes his challenge.

Ruby's mouth drops open, and she stutters to

respond, but I've got this.

"It's true. When she first told me, it nearly broke my heart." The group is pretending to continue with their wreaths, but their pupils are ball bearings rolling back and forth, as they're desperate to witness the exchange. "But I agree with her first choice. I, too, am in love with Mary Berry, although I'd say she's more a baker than a chef."

Ruby elbows me in my ribs, causing everyone to laugh, but Neil hasn't finished with us. "If you're such a great couple, tell me about your first date. I bet she's had better."

Ruby trembles and stares at me.

I'm unsure what Neil did for Ruby on their first date, and I don't care.

"I'll never forget my first date with my Rubes. I considered something flashy and overpriced, but that's not what matters to her." Neil glares and bares his teeth. I guess that's what he did. "Family and food matter more to Ruby than anything, so I started the date at the kitchen of her favourite restaurant. I decorated it with colourful flowers and sweets because even though she's sweet enough," I say with a kiss on her cheek, "I know how sweet her tooth is. It was like a mini version of Hansel and Gretal but with no witches."

Everyone gawks at me now, waiting for what's next. Ruby stares at me with an intensity that feeds the story.

"Together, we baked something neither of us had tried before under the tutelage of one of my favourite bakers. I'm not saying it was Mary Berry, but I'm not saying it wasn't." Everyone laughs, and the energy in the room goes to my head. "Once we baked our baumkuchen with a kind of croquembouche hat, the only way I can describe the monster we made, we gave Mary—I mean, the baker—our thanks, and we met up at Ruby's family's old cookery school for a special meal. I'd secretly asked her family for ideas of her favourite courses."

"Oh, that's lovely," one of the older women says.

Neil continues to scowl. Before he can poison the dream date, I add, "And at the end of the night, we went for a walk in the moonlight, where I pretended to name stars and made up ludicrous names for them, which made her laugh. And then we had a chaste kiss."

"It wasn't chaste," Ruby says, and I can't focus on anything else. "I'm pretty sure it was like this."

I hold my breath as she stands on tiptoes and pulls my head down to meet hers. It's as hot and heavy as it can be in a room full of older people and someone's ex-boyfriend, but it hints at the night we spent together, her mouth against mine, the scent of passion fruit enrapturing me. Her hand is against the back of my neck, and mine presses into her hips. As I come up for air, I say breathlessly, "I was trying not to sully your reputation."

Her eyes are sparkling, and there is a pink spot on each of her cheeks. "Oh, it's a bit late for that, Chef Garett."

A chorus of *ooohs* and *aaaahs* fill the room as Flora says, "If you two don't mind, this is a wreath making class, not an Amsterdam show."

Ruby throws her head back and laughs. There's a lightness to her whole being, whereas, for me, it's like someone punching me repeatedly in the belly. I like her too much for what we're doing.

"You heard the woman. Let's get back to it," I say as my stomach quivers. "I need to grab something."

Ruby laughs with one of the ladies at the next table as

I walk down the stairs. I barely make it because my whole body shakes. My legs are jelly, and I wait to get sick. I said I could do no strings, and I will because I want her with a fire in my belly and a wobble to my heart, but I can't sleep with her tonight. The boyfriend experience unleashed too many things in me that I didn't know I was capable of. I have to let go of these emotions before we do anything.

I want to make love to her.

Even as I debate this, I pick up little candy canes and sparkling foil–covered truffles that I brought for Ruby for another evening. The items will make the wreath pop with colour, which will make Ruby happy.

All I want is her smile.

CHAPTER THIRTY-FIVE – RUBY

Neil takes me to the side as everyone packs up. "You just have to say the word, Ruby, and I'll take you back."

I suck in my cheeks. "You're engaged to Viv, or have you already forgotten her?" I snap. I should have known that engagement meant nothing to him and his wandering eye.

He dismisses my comment with the flap of his hand. "I don't know what that chef arsehole thinks he knows about you, but I know the real you. We were together for years, and I saw you change and helped you develop into the woman you are now." I hold back both my laughter and the fist I want to hit him with. "No one knows you like I do."

The irony is that Neil was with me all those years but never knew me. The story about the fake first date shows Garett understands me better than Neil ever could. The kiss I gave him was to hide my shock of emotion.

Garett watches as he tidies up the remnants of the mince pies from his demonstration counter. I give him a wink, not to annoy Neil, but because I want to. This is what I'd do if my boyfriend were here, and for one glorious night, I was lucky enough to learn how it felt to be Garett's girlfriend.

"So what do you say?" Neil asks.

"Go fuck yourself, Neil," I reply with no anger or

bitterness. "And never come near me again. I'm happy without you, happier than I thought possible."

"Car, Neil. Right now," Viv yells from the doorway.

Neil stares at me longingly. "Bye then."

I turn away, which seems to be the hint that Neil needs. I talk to the stragglers, who tell me their first date stories and ask more about Garett. He's their new romance hero.

"And have you seen his forearms?" one of the pensioners asks. I have seen them, kissed them, been held by them as he does the filthiest things to me.

I wave them off ten minutes later. Should I suggest a hookup tonight with Garett? All those kisses and the care have made me hornier than a frat boy during rush.

But Garett has gone.

"Have you got a second to help, Ruby?" Kath asks. "We need to set up for tomorrow. We're fully booked with wreath making and Christmas classes for the next three weeks."

"It's great, isn't it? Amber's hard work over the last few years has made a difference. There's so many return customers." I glance around the cookery school. "Is everyone staying on to help?"

"Everyone except Garett. He said there was somewhere he had to be. All that fake boyfriend work must have exhausted him." She chuckles.

Did he run off because of something I did? I can't message him to check if he's okay, because that's against the rules. I know he's not seeing anyone, but that doesn't explain his disappearing act.

I'll check in tomorrow night, all casual. I don't know how because I don't do hookups, and it's not like I can speak to anyone about it because that's against the rules, too.

I grimace as I walk up the stairs to the mezzanine.

"You doing okay, Ruby, love? I couldn't believe it when Amber told me you were caught here in the snow on Saturday," Kath says as we tidy the hideaway. "How is Amber?"

The scents of oranges and firs from the wreath making fill my lungs. Christmas will be good this year. I catch a whiff of cinnamon. My gaze is drawn to the sofa bed, but I shake my head.

"She's been better. The pregnancy is going according to plan, but she's frustrated that she had to go on maternity. She's missing being involved. She knows it's not safe for her or the babies, but it was so sudden."

Kath clucks in agreement. "I do miss her. I bet your grandma would have loved to have seen her pregnant and blooming."

"She adored Amber and wanted a good future for her. It's nice she got to meet Kalen before, well, you know."

Kath perches on one of the chairs brought up to make wreath making accessible for those who struggle to stand. "She was ecstatic to meet him. It's a shame we don't know when he'll return."

I nod, unsure what else to say. With Kath, you can never be sure what her angle is.

"And your grandma would've been delighted to have you back here, too."

I smile as I busy myself making a pile of wreath bits that can be used for tomorrow. I don't want to return to the regrets of not being around my grandparents in their last months, although it's motivating several of my life decisions.

"But she'd want different for you, too."

I catch Kath's eye. She's staring at me with the raised eyebrow stare that used to annoy Jem and me when we were younger. She always knew when we'd pilfered grandma's silver cake sprinkles. "What do you mean?"

"You're amazing for this cookery school and carrying on your sister's work amiably, but it's not what you want. I've tasted your practice bakes for Clive's competition and seen the skills you teach the groups here. You need to start your own business again. When baking, you're individual, creative, and in your own world. You're a lone wolf, and your future should reflect that."

I stutter to respond. It was often what I thought with Naughty Treats. I want to go it alone, but I don't have the capital to start something like that again. I don't want to do the competition with Clive. With the skills Garett taught me, I want to start my own business, but I can't without the finances.

Kath jumps up. "Let's get on because we've got busy weeks coming up." She reels off the following days at the cookery school, ticking them off with her fingers as she does. "Wreath making the next three nights, then Friday we've got a ladies group in the day. On Saturday, we're hosting a children's party during the day, followed by more wreath making in the evening. Sunday is that Christmas meal cookery session for beginners. That was such a good idea of Garett's. Of course people hosting for the first time want help."

I nod absentmindedly. This competition with Clive could limit me rather than benefit me. But Amber and the babies need the money.

"Garett really seems to care." Her words grab my

attention.

"About me?" I squeak.

"About the school." Her eyes soften, and some of the wrinkles around them disappear. "But he cares about you, too. Tonight was enlightening."

I recall the teasing and the laughter. It pulls at my heart like the old wives' tale of tying a string around a wobbly tooth and shutting a door to pull it out. "But it was fake."

"It's not how it looked to me, but then I'm an old lady with no knowledge of people." I cock my head at her, and she laughs. She's not fooling anyone. "But is anyone that good at faking feelings, especially a formerly grumpy chef who's changed since you joined us? It appeared real."

I shrug and turn away to hide the myriad of emotions reflected on my face. There were the public moments, but there was also his extra care when no one was watching, like when he slipped me a dark red flower to add to the wreath or ensured I had a glass of wine and sat comfortably before he sipped his. The glances and the occasional touch of hands were just for me.

A shiver crosses my shoulders as Flora stomps up to the hideaway. She eyeballs me suspiciously, and I recall how she glared at me the night we met.

"It was all for show," I counter to Kath, my face flaming under Flora's stare. "We're friends, and he's very good at doing the right thing. That's all. He probably employed all his skills with his dog-stealing ex-girlfriend." I laugh in an attempt to lighten the moment, but no one joins in. When we were together, he said he'd only had one-night stands, but I'm sure that meant in addition to his ex-girlfriend. I shake my head. I don't like thinking about that awful woman who stole his dog. "But let's talk more about Amber. I want your advice on how I can help her mood."

CHAPTER THIRTY-SIX – GARETT

Cookie jumps up at me as Ruby's parents, Iain and Liz, welcome me into the house.

"You have a key that you can use at any time," Iain says as I cuddle Cookie. "Not that we mind opening the door, as it's always lovely to see Cookie's excitement with you."

I smile and say the same thing every time he or Liz opens the door. "I don't want to be rude. You've been so kind, and I can't thank you enough for this."

"But think of my weary body every time I have to get up," he jokes.

"Don't listen to him," Liz adds. "It's good for him to get his lazy bum out of the chair. He spends too much time watching *Columbo* and eating Ruby's baking."

We have this conversation almost daily, and I lap it up like the needy-for-family man I am. It's the real reason I still knock. I live for it.

"There's nothing lazy about my bum," Iain replies as he proceeds to chase Liz around the open plan kitchen that looks like something out of a Cotswold Homes brochure. Cookie joins in and starts chasing them.

It's a thump to my chest. For years, I've tried to prove myself and create a business that shows that my childhood didn't define me. I've always chosen work above a potential relationship. And yet, when Liz whips Iain with a teatowel as he wiggles his bum at her, there's this deep pull in me. I want a partner to chase me around our kitchen as Cookie jumps around us. I hold my breath. When I imagine it, it's Ruby chasing me.

But I can't want her.

There's a knock at the door.

"I'll get it, if that's okay. It's my little sister, Flora. We're going to walk Cookie together."

"Of course," Liz says with a smile.

"Now be on your best, woman. Garett is used to your towel-whipping ninja skills, but Flora is a guest," Iain says with a waggle of his eyebrows, which earns him a slap around the arse.

I chuckle as I open the door, but that pull for a future grips me like a vice. Even if Ruby could be mine, I haven't got the money to make it happen. If I still owned the restaurant, I'd sell my half to Clive, but he ended that dream like he tried to destroy me. There's one other way I could earn money, but it means saying goodbye to the life I have now.

"Stop worrying," Flora says as soon as I open the door. "It's like you're trying to plan a coup."

It's her turn for the Cookie experience. He barks and bounds up to her.

I grumble but check myself in the mirror by the door. Worry lines cover my face. It's been two weeks since I acted like Ruby's boyfriend, and the experience has warmed my heart and panicked me every moment, as has my new secret.

We've been rushed off our feet at the cookery school,

and after each session, I've stayed behind and helped her with her baking skills. It fills me with this unending joy and painful anguish. We've not mentioned hooking up again, but we're both thinking about it. There's been tentative kisses and touches. I love teasing her and the warmth that fills my body when she smiles because she's conquered a new skill.

"Let's go for that walk," Flora says, pulling me out of my internal debates. She's been speaking to Iain and Liz the entire time, and I have no idea what they were saying. "Hopefully, the fresh air will help, or you're going to end up like one of those chefs with permanent forehead wrinkles."

"You're not too old for me to ground you." She rolls her eyes. "Right. Let's get Cookie on a lead. Come on, boy."

Flora waggles the leash that's already clipped into Cookie's harness.

"What's going on in your head, Garett?" Liz comments.

"I have an idea," Flora replies, pushing me out the door. "It was lovely to see you both. I shall work on what we talked about."

I cock my eyebrow as she shoves me out the door. "Secrets?"

"I'll tell you all about it in a minute, but first, I want to know what's causing that storm in your head. Is it a certain red jewel?"

I speed up my steps.

"Cookie, do you want your ball?"

Cookie spins, his tongue lolling and his tail wagging.

His big brown eyes fix on the ball. He looks like I feel when I'm with Ruby: all desperate and focused.

"What's going on?"

I shrug before throwing Cookie's ball relatively close. He's back in seconds, the perfect distraction for getting out of Flora's interrogation.

She glares at me and elbows me out of the way as I try to grab it. She throws it farther than I ever could.

"I forgot you were on the local rounders team. Is there anything you can't do?"

"Decide where to focus my efforts rather than picking up everything and dropping it." I forgot what she might be going through, as I've been caught up in my problems. "But this isn't about me. Is Ruby the reason you're jumping between every emotion these days? I've seen you with her, and you're happier than ever."

"It's not that," I reply, still avoiding the topic of Ruby. "The owner of a Michelin Star restaurant in Ireland, Ciara Kelly, is considering me for a job. Did you ever meet her?"

Flora smiles broadly. "She worked with you and Clive a couple of times. She was the best."

I nod. "She was. If I get the job and accept it, I'll be gone for a long time. I'm not sure if I'd see you for months." Or if I'd see Ruby.

Flora stares at me like I've grown another head. "But you love the cookery school."

I sigh and lower my gaze. "I know, but I miss working in a restaurant, and I need money to run my own business in the future." I look up. Her eyes are wide. She's sucked her lower lip into her mouth, and it reminds me of when she was bullied and she'd come home but refuse to cry. "I don't want to leave you, Flora. You're the best little sister

I've ever had."

She punches me. "Stop using that line."

I laugh, but it's not my usual chuckle. "But you are, and I wouldn't want any others." Cookie returns and Flora flings the ball again. She is fantastic at so many things. All I've got is being a chef. "I want to stay, but no restaurants locally will take me because they're all scared of your brother. Clive never had influence over Ciara. She knows I can do great things and wants me to create menus and make the place my own."

Flora's sigh is like that of a dejected warrior who knows the battle is lost. "How will you tell the staff at the cookery school?"

"They'll understand. The business is growing, and there's enough skill there as it is. They'll be able to get different chefs for different types of classes. Having me there as their regular chef limits them."

Flora guffaws. "Sure, tell yourself that if it makes you feel better. It's not only about the school, though. They've all welcomed you in as part of their family."

"It's just a job," I lie. My forehead wrinkles again. Kath checking in on me every morning, Wicksy coming to me for relationship advice, the window to Iain and Liz's life—it's like the family I never knew I needed.

"And Ruby? Is she another co-worker?"

I focus on Cookie's ears flapping as he sprints back.

"She likes you," Flora adds, gripping my shoulders and turning me to face her. "Don't play games with her if it doesn't mean anything."

I toy with the idea of telling Flora about my arrangement with Ruby, but I promised I wouldn't. "She's a friend. That's how we both see it," I reply brusquely, gritting my teeth.

253

"I'm not sure that's how she sees it. Based on something she said to Kath."

My heart jumps with hope, but it's like a firework, and as it hits a high, it quickly turns and crashes back down. In a month, she'll be deciding whether she works with Clive because I'll have told her the truth. I'll be away, and that's precisely how it should be. It's for the best. Yet it feels like I'm destroying myself from the inside out.

"It doesn't matter. I don't want to know what she said." Yet curiosity controls every fibre of my being. "Tell me about the plans you're making with Iain and Liz. What's happening?"

As she talks, I bury my face in Cookie's fur and attempt to control my feelings before I hurt anyone else or send myself into a spiralling pain I can't escape.

CHAPTER THIRTY-SEVEN – RUBY

Another day at the cookery school is another opportunity to get as close to Garett as I can.

A group of women have chatted him up all day. It was a hen do cocktail-making and cake-baking class, and they arrived drunk and moaning about how cold it was. What did they expect in mid-December? They heckled me through my cocktail demonstrations, and now they're finding ways to touch Garett as he walks around their benches. He stifles a yawn. He's done that throughout this class. His hair is messy from how many times he's shoved his hand through it.

One lady sips her cocktail while staring at Garett over her glass. She flutters her eyelashes. I've put up with it all day, and this is the last ten minutes of the class while they decorate their cakes. "So tell me, Chef Garett, do you give instructions in other places, too?"

Garett furrows his brows. "I often tell my dog what to do."

"Is your dog a good girl for you, Garett?"

I let out my hair before retying it. He likes it when I do that but is too busy to notice. My blood boils as I rip into the chocolate bar he left for me when he came in this morning. He keeps bringing me treats. He probably got it because he was late today. He hasn't explained why he was late or tired, and not knowing kills me.

"Well, he's a boy, so no."

"I have a dog, too. If she's well-behaved, what would you say?"

"I'd tell her she was a good girl for me." His head wrinkles because his eyebrows are so knotted. I know he's not flirting back, but the fucking jealousy monster is jabbing at me.

Within seconds, I've destroyed the chocolate bar. It's given me no comfort. Garett and the woman continue chatting. I huff loudly. I'm being unfair, as he's not into whatever that woman is doing.

My knuckles are white where I grip the countertop. Since he pretended to be my fake boyfriend, he's been distracted when we're together. We've laughed and baked, but he's hiding something. We haven't had sex since that last night, and as much I know it was incredible for both of us, a voice still niggles me that maybe he doesn't want to repeat it because I was terrible. Spending time with him has lessened my anxiety about Clive Macdonald's competition, even though there are ten days to go, but I'm anxious about Garett instead.

"Say good girl again."

Now she's stroking his forearms. They're my forearms.

I storm over. Everyone's staring at me, including Wicksy and Kath. I yank Garett down to my level by grabbing his shirt collar. "You only use those words on me," I grunt before kissing him with every ounce of neediness that's brewed in me since our night together.

At first, his hands falter, but then one hand presses against my back while the other thrusts into my hair, pulling the elastic out. His tongue presses my lips open, and I taste the spiced orange from the mocktail I gave him. Orange and cinnamon with a rosemary fizz. He tastes of all the best Christmases, and I take the kiss deeper. His hand on my back presses me closer, and it's all I can do not to grind against him.

The woman flirting with him huffs and moans about unprofessionalism, making me pull back. "That's my good girl," he growls in my ear as I push away from his chest.

"I've got to go." I rush to the exit, shoving my hair back into a messy bun. That woman was right. I was unprofessional. "Don't say a word," I snap at Wicksy and Kath.

Kath's sneaky smile makes it worse as I push through the glass doors. I haven't got a coat or my car keys.

I don't own Garett. We're not a couple. My anger only warms me for so long, and soon I'm shivering.

Voices herald that the women are leaving the cookery school. I sneak across the frost-covered ground to hide from them, and my shame combines with cold as the shivers become full-on shakes.

"How embarrassing was that woman?" one of the hens says. I recognise her voice from when she was chatting up Garett. "Who does that in the middle of a cookery class? I'm going to give them a low rating online."

My heart sinks. This was why I avoided letting my feelings spill over into the business.

The future bride, who wasn't flirting with Garett, replies, "They're obviously dating. I'd have done the same if you were flirting with my man, Caroline. Don't you dare give them a low rating. Honestly, it makes me want to give them a higher rating. I'm heading home to jump my man's bones and feed him cake."

The rest of the hens cackle. I release a quiet breath. Thank God for brides. Their cars disappear into the darkness, but I still hide. I can't go back in and face the team, especially not Garett. I lick my lips. I can still taste the orange cocktail. I still want him. It never stops. And I can't forget that he called me his good girl. Fuck, I felt that between my thighs.

"Rubes," Garett calls out in the darkness. There's a worry in his voice, and I flatten myself against the wall. If I'm stealthy, he'll give up. The light from a phone falls on my body. "Baby, if you're going to hide, maybe don't do it so close to the front door."

"You're teasing gets old quickly," I reply frostily, but it comes out jumbled as my teeth chatter.

"You're cold. Why are you out here? You'll get ill, and you can't get ill now." I don't know if he's referring to the busyness of the cookery school, the competition, or Christmas being nearly here. "Come here," he says softly, opening his coat.

I sigh as I slip inside and against his chest as he wraps it around me. He smells glorious as always, and the warmth instantly heats my body. "You brought a coat." My words are muffled against his chest, but he understands me.

"I didn't know how long I'd have to search for you."

That hits my chest like lightning. I hold my breath. He was willing to search for a while. This relationship will destroy me if I let it, yet I snuggle closer and breathe him in again. I get on my tiptoes, and he leans down and brushes my lips with his. "I'm sorry for the way I acted."

"It doesn't matter, Rubes. I'm sorry for being weird with you over the last weeks."

"I thought you didn't want to sleep with me again."

"It's all I've thought about. That night was the best I'd ever had, but I've had stuff going on in my head, and I wanted to give you the best version of me."

I can't tell if he's lying. I hate that Neil made it harder to trust. Garett kisses me again, stilling my fears. It's soft and gentle, but then, desire kicks in, and his hands are holding me close as he sucks my lip and takes control.

"Can we stay late and maybe use the hideaway?" I'm breathless and trembling from the kiss.

"Not tonight. I've got plans, but I must take you to the wine warehouse first. That okay?"

"Sure." Disappointment threads through my body like his hands thread through my hair as he kisses me again. I whimper into his mouth.

"Night, you two," Kath shouts as she leaves the cookery school. The door bangs. Wicksy can't be far behind her as his chuckles carry on the wind.

"I'm comforting her," Garett grunts.

"Of course you are. The best kind of comfort, mate," Wicksy replies with a snigger.

I bury my face against Garett's chest. He pulls my hair out of its elastic and plays with it. "Don't worry. I've told them not to say anything." He softens my fears even when I don't share them.

But the idea that my family might find out still terrifies me, and I pull back. "Cool. Thanks. Right, let's get to the warehouse, as I have a date with my bullet vibrator tonight."

My joke elicits a growl from his chest that makes me hornier.

Fucking Garett and his fucking plans.

Chapter Thirty-Eight – Ruby

"**R**uby, I need to do this before we go." He yawns again. Something is off, but I can't put my finger on it. He moves around the cookery school like a man on a mission, grabbing different things, but with his back to me, I can't see what.

"Sure," I reply, forcing an airy sound as if I couldn't care less, but I do, and that annoys me more. He grabs his demonstration cakes and pops them into a tin. He adds another cake tin to the pile. "Who are the cakes for, Garett?"

"No one."

A realisation has me gnashing my teeth behind his back. They're for Chantelle at the wine merchants. He wouldn't do that, but I fist my hands like I'm making dough anyway.

"Are we going, then?" I ask a couple of minutes later. All his jobs are done, and he's wearing his coat, but we're still in the cookery school. He checks his phone before sliding it into his pocket.

"In a minute." He drums his fingers against a countertop before reaching for his phone again.

He checks it before sliding it back into his pocket. "Right. Let's go," he replies casually but won't look at me.

"Okay."

Maybe he's ready to end our agreement that we never really started because of how difficult things are. It's all rules without sex. A flashback so heady that it makes my stomach roll over with arousal hits me. I glance at his lips and instantly regret it. He licks them slowly as if he knows what I'm thinking, and I have a vision of him lifting me onto the countertop. I want his hand in my hair and my legs wrapped around his waist and––

"Rubes?" I shake my head as if it's an Etch A Sketch where one shake will delete the sexy thoughts from it for good. "We should go."

He's standing by the door, tapping his foot repeatedly against the tiling.

He rechecks his phone, his face pales.

"You okay?"

"Yep," he stutters, but his eyes widen as he looks back at me. "We'd best go. Are you ready?"

"Yeah, sure." The sooner we're back and I can get home to my vibrator, the better.

As we drive to the merchants, the cakes resting in my lap, I consider asking him who they're for. He won't look at me. I flip down the visor, but it's too dark to check my make-up.

He signals left.

"This isn't the way to the wine merchants."

"I know," he replies.

He's guarded and keeps yawning. I grip the tins and squeeze my lips tight to stop shouting. The scent of chocolate orange buttercream fills the van.

I stare out the window. Garett's reflection looks at his

watch and then at me, but by the time I turn, his focus has returned to the road.

We cross roundabouts that signal we're nearing the small town where Amber and I live. "Are you taking me home?"

When we stop at traffic lights, the cake bangs in the tin. He glances over at me. The whites of his eyes glow in the semi-darkness of the van. The sudden terror that he wants to end what we nearly had because of my behaviour in class today makes bile rise in my throat.

That doesn't explain why he brought me home without my car. I turn towards him, my eyes tight in interrogation mode. "Do you need something from Amber? Are the cakes for her?"

"Huh?" He taps his hands against the steering wheel as we wait for the light to change. It's barely green before he takes off.

"We're nearly at my house."

He pauses too long. "Oh yeah." He brought the cake because I'm going to need comfort food after he dumps me, although we're not even dating. "I thought I'd give her cake and go over kitchen stuff. You know?"

"What sort of kitchen stuff?"

He mumbles incoherently as he pulls up to my sister's house. The top cake tin topples out of my hands when he breaks hard. It flips onto the floor. "Shit."

He rechecks his phone. Many cars are squeezed into my sister's driveway, but all the lights in the house are off.

My parents' car pulls up beside us. "What's going on, Garett? Is my sister okay?" She told me she was spending the day with my parents, buying things for the nursery.

"Come on, Ruby," Garett says. "And don't forget

the…" His words trail off when he sees the cake tin upside down on the floor. "…delicious mess."

We leave the van, and I find myself standing next to Amber, who's exited Mum and Dad's car.

"You okay?" I ask her under my breath.

"Yeah, but what's happening? Who do all these cars belong to, and why are you here with Garett and cake tins?"

I shrug. "I thought we were going to the wine merchants."

"Ladies," Mum says, "come with me."

We stumble behind her like two awkward teenagers heading to a posh restaurant.

"Close your eyes," Garett says.

We step through the front door with Amber leading the charge, wobbling with her huge pregnancy belly and hands over her eyes.

"Close your eyes," he repeats. I glare at him, and he stares back until I close them.

My body shakes as Garett grips my hips and helps me walk straight. I wet my lips and embrace his scent.

Suddenly, a crowd shouts, "Surprise!" and lights flash on. My eyes open wide. There's a giant green banner above the fireplace. *Amber's Baby Shower* is decorated in bright orange.

I recognise a couple of her friends who used to hang around before I left with Neil. Wicksy stands with Kath and a couple of strangers. In the corner, Flora beams. Jem stands to the side, looking like he's turned up at what he thought was a slash metal concert, only to find it's the Spice Girl reunion.

"This is amazing," I say, laughing. "You did this for Amber?"

He blushes. "It was your parents' idea. Flora helped a lot."

The space is decorated in every colour but pink and blue. My sister will love it. The room is filled with some of the fanciest food I've seen. A range of hors d'oeuvres, patisserie-style desserts, and gourmet pies and appetisers leave my mouth watering and my belly rumbling. My brows furrow as I stare at Garett.

"Did you?"

"Something little for you and to say thank you to Amber." His words are cut short by a scream that silences the crowd instantly.

Fear fills my heart like ice has been dropped down my back, but as I look back, Kalen, my brother-in-law, walks across the room and takes my sister in his arms. He holds her close as she weeps. He covers her with kisses, and she sobs between words. "You came home. Please tell me you're home now."

"I'm home, baby. Now let's get you looked after and rested because you deserve it."

The outpouring of love is so dazzling that we divert our eyes so they can have their reunion. My parents beckon everyone to the kitchen to get a plate, and Flora walks around the group, asking who needs a top-up of Cloudy mocktail.

Garett takes my hand and leads me to the garden.

"Why didn't you tell me? I could have helped."

I see the reason as he pushes open the door to my cabin: a *Welcome Home Ruby* banner drapes across my room. My cabin is full of candles and special toiletries. I walk around the space, gasping as I reach for icing nozzles that create shapes I've never seen before.

"Custom-made Ruby nozzles," he says, leaning against the wall with a beaming smile.

Sitting on the bed is a bowl that looks exactly like the one my cheating ex smashed.

"How?"

"I interrogated your sister and had one made. You've had a shit time, Rubes, and as much as this party is for Amber, I wanted to make sure you were treated, too. I was a dick when you joined the school, but you've made every day fun, and I wanted to say thank you. It's a thank you from all of us."

On the edge of the bed are my favourite cookery books and some clothes I didn't pack when I left Neil's. As if reading my mind, Garett fills me in. "Kath told me there were nice things back at your ex-boyfriend's that you wished you'd kept, so Jem got some back."

I whip around. "Was everything okay?"

He nods but doesn't add anything else. I start leafing through all the stuff in my cabin but freeze when out of my clothes falls the box where I kept my sex toys. If my brother saw my sex toys, they're going straight in the bin. "Did Jem go there alone?"

"I helped. He hasn't had anything to do with what's in that box," Garett says.

"Cool." I can't stop swallowing.

"Shall we get back to the party? I expect you'll want to eat one of those cakes I made you drop."

He leads me back to the party. Suddenly, he whispers in my ear, making my shivers less about the frosty atmosphere and more about his seductive growl, "And that purple vibrator in your box looks especially powerful. I've charged it because I hoped to watch you use it later."

My eyes are wide as I stare at a chuckling Garett

walking away. The sooner this party finishes, the better, because all I want is for him to instruct me and call me his good girl again as I put on a show for him.

CHAPTER THIRTY-NINE – GARETT

Rubes has talked to people for the last hour. The hugs she gave Jem and Kalen is another reminder of the family I've never had. But that's less important to me tonight because this family has welcomed me. Even Kalen hugged me. It hurt because the guy is like a brick shit house, but I loved it.

Every time Ruby smiles at me, a zip of happiness fills my belly.

"Hey, big bro. Stop making goo-goo eyes at Ruby, or everyone will know how much you like her," Flora says as she bounds up to me. She nudges me hard. "You did good, though. I'm really proud of all your hard work tonight. Any news from you-know-who?"

My phone burns a hole in my pocket. I was checking it for messages from Flora and Ruby's parents about when to arrive at the party, but as we were leaving, I received a message from Ciara.

"She's formally offered me the job."

"And?" Flora whispers.

Ruby looks over, and I grin at her.

"And I've got to tell her by Christmas Day if I'm going to take it."

"And?" Flora raises her voice, but no one is close enough to hear us.

"And," I whisper, "I will decide by then."

"I want what's best for you, and so will Ruby. But make sure you're doing it for the right reasons."

I don't know what the right reasons are anymore. Before I worked at the cookery school with Ruby, my decisions were always determined by what would make me the most successful.

"Okay," I reply before yawning so wide it hurts my face. I'm exhausted from going to Neil's house as backup for Jem. I briefly spoke to the jerk and told him to leave Ruby alone. Jem was okay with me during the trip, although he made it clear several times that I wasn't to date his sister. Thankfully, he's already left, because I'm unsure how long I can hide my "goo-goo eyes."

"I told her you made all the food for the party, by the way," Flora adds.

"For Amber's party."

"For Ruby's sister's party," she teases. That's the other reason I'm tired. I didn't go to bed last night because I wanted it to be a banquet.

"It's really kind of you to help plan this. Party planner, secret keeper. Is there anything you can't do?"

"Make you make the right decision," she says with a half-hearted laugh. "Besides, I owe this family. They gave you a job, helped us rescue Cookie, and Ruby's mum told me I could stop by their house whenever. They gave both of us a chance. Ruby thanked me for helping, too."

"You didn't mention Clive, though?" I ask sharply.

Flora shakes her head. "No, he's still a brilliant chef and competition organiser as far as she's concerned." I let out a sigh of relief. "She's mentioned a couple of times that it was your ex-girlfriend that kept your dog. Are you going to tell her the truth?"

Ruby looks over again and smiles. I hope she doesn't know we're talking about her. She's savvy as hell with an impressive sex toy collection that I haven't forgotten about all day.

"I will tell her about Clive once she's won the competition. She'll walk it based on the things we've baked together over the last couple of weeks. That win will give her money for her sister, raise her profile, enable her to start her business, and bring attention to the cookery school. It will be the future everyone deserves."

"But what if you're also her future?"

At that point, Iain, Liz, and Ruby join us. "Thank you again, Garett, for all you did for the party. The food is incredible." Iain pops one of my chicken, cranberry, and brie canapés into his mouth in one.

"Although I might send you a hospital bill if Iain eats anymore of these. He's going to have a stomach ache all night," Liz adds, winking.

I laugh with them.

"You're wasted at our cookery school. You should be running your own restaurant," Liz says.

Flora shifts awkwardly next to me.

"I love working there," I reply. Ruby stares at me, her head cocked.

"But if you could work in a restaurant again, would you?"

Is Liz a psychic?

"Sorry, this might be a sore subject after what happened," she adds when I fumble my words.

"What do you mean?" Ruby asks.

She can't find out about Clive, but I can't get my words out.

"Well, you know how Garett came to us."

Before I can jump in, Iain explains, "His old partner told every restaurant in the area not to employ him. He had no job. When they tried the same with us, your mum told him to go cook himself." Iain lowers his voice. "Only your badass mother didn't say cook."

"Mum!" Ruby exclaims.

Liz shrugs, although a smile tips the corners of her mouth up. "He had it coming. How dare C—"

"Aren't they cute?" Flora blasts, changing the subject as Liz is about to reveal Clive's name. I owe Ruby's parents more than I realised. I believed Clive hadn't bothered calling them. "I suspect the party will wind up soon."

Everyone looks to where Flora is staring. Kalen holds Amber close. He whispers in her ear and occasionally bends to talk to her belly.

"My daughter is very handsy with her husband," Liz says. To Ruby, she adds, "You may prefer to stay at ours tonight, honey. Give them their space."

"Mum, I'm all for sex positivity, but—" As if on cue, Amber's hand slips to Kalen's bum and squeezes it hard. "Okay, never mind. I'll stay with you."

"How about you stay at mine for a girl's night?" Flora offers. "Garett could give you a lift there while I tidy up. He needs an early night." She gives me and Rubes a wink when Iain and Liz aren't looking.

But one of the rules is no visiting each other's places. Although we've already broken the staying professional one.

"Good plan," Ruby replies. "I'll get my bag and pack everything I need." She elongates the word everything, fixing me with her stare and raising her eyebrows twice quickly. The purple vibrator is going on a trip. "Meet you in the car."

Before I can catch up and consider the problems with this plan, she's said her goodbyes to everyone and rushed from the room.

Thank God my place is Ruby ready. Flora popped around this morning while I was at the cookery school to tidy up as if she's planned this all along. Before going to Neil's, I stayed up all night cooking for the party. I should be exhausted, but the prospect of another night with Ruby has my nerves buzzing.

My conscience takes a stay of execution, too. After what I've learnt tonight, I should be doing everything I can to keep the Cloud family happy, especially Rubes, but the mixture of seeing her smile at me all evening, those kisses at the cookery school, and then the promise of watching her use her vibrator demands that I take her to mine and reward her with all she wants from me.

Ruby runs to my apartment's front door. My place isn't good enough for her. She deserves a beautiful space with fairy lights everywhere and plush furnishings, not a bedsit where damp covers the room's edges and a mysterious bad smell lingers in the bathroom.

Her energy is addictive, but I still take my time prowling towards her. We haven't got any bookings at the cookery school until tomorrow evening, and we tentatively discussed spending the whole day together. I lock eyes with her and stop a couple of metres away. Her stare rakes down my body. The temperature has dropped to zero, fitting for December, but my whole being burns with fire for her.

Christmas trees light up the houses and apartments around us, a reminder that our world will change in less than ten days.

"Are you going to take all night?" she says, her voice carrying on the bitter breeze.

"That's the plan," I growl. She sucks her bottom lip into her mouth. "Did you bring your toy with you?"

She nods slowly. "And I want to use it while you watch. I want you to guide me."

"Are you sure, Rubes?" I tease. "What if you can't control yourself? What if you beg me to be inside you?"

"I've had a fantasy where I'm on my knees begging you to do things to me," she replies raspily.

"Good girl." Her smile makes me hard. "You have a thing for men telling you what to do in the bedroom."

"Maybe I have a thing for you telling me what to do. All those times you've instructed me during our private classes make me needy for you."

My heart thuds in my chest. I'm not usually this alpha, but I will be anything she wants me to be, and I want to be the only person she desires. "Have you played with your toys while imagining me instructing you?"

"Yes," she gasps. "Many times."

"Then let's make *our* fantasies happen."

Her grin eclipses her face. It hits me like a lightning bolt. I need this woman on top of me, underneath me, against my wall.

But first, it's toy time.

CHAPTER FORTY – RUBY

He leads me to his bedroom. My chest rises and falls as I suck in deep breaths. It's a struggle to keep myself calm, especially when I face him and he tracks the way my breasts move with each of my gasps. I can't stop trembling under the stare of his desire. He's filled my heart. Right now, I want him and don't want to consider the repercussions or the future.

"Take your skirt off," Garett instructs, "slowly and turn around. I adore your bum wriggling around the cookery school, but tonight, I want to savour it."

I turn away from him and flip the button on the back of my skirt, unzipping it. A mirror stands in front of me.

"This way, I can see every part of you. Now pull it away from your waist and push it down." I do as he says, enamoured by his reflection. His eyes fix on my body like he wants to consume me.

"That's right. Bend over. And you can leave your heels on," he hisses. "You're going to look like my classy sex goddess when you play with yourself."

He's kind and feral, and I need every part of it. I bend slightly, and his growl fills the room. My leather skirt hits the carpet.

"You wore your hold ups today." Cinnamon fills my lungs. "Turn and face me, baby."

My breath sticks in my throat. I close my eyes under his inspection as I turn.

"Keep your eyes open. I want you to see what you do to me."

"Yes, Chef."

His eyes get impossibly darker. "Fuck. Say that again."

I lick my lips slowly. "Yes, Chef."

His eyes fix on mine as he slowly undoes his jeans, and his erection pushes its way out from his zipper. He runs his hand up and down his cock. Wetness gathers in my knickers as he fists himself. "Now undo your blouse, button by button. Don't take it off until I say."

My fingers tremble as I follow his orders. Slowly, I reveal inches of skin.

The depth of his voice thrums through my limbs. "You're so sexy, baby. I'm so hard for you. All I think about is being inside you." He pauses and growls, his face strained and his jaw hard. "Fuck. You're everything."

He drags a breath into his mouth, and his nostrils flare. "Shit, I've never been this turned on before."

He shakes his head, and my whole body flushes under the intensity of his dark-eyed stare and tight jaw.

"I haven't stopped wanting to touch you since we were last together. I fantasise about you every night until I might burst with need for you. Do you think of me?" He grinds his teeth for a second, and I sense a vulnerability.

Finally, I find my voice. "Every second. I need you inside me. Some days, it's all that fills my head. Working with you day after day destroys me because all I want is to fuck you."

A tentative smile turns up the corners of his mouth, but then he returns to his role of commanding me.

"That's my good girl. Now show me what's hiding beneath that blouse." I do as he says. My nipples press against the lace of my bra, and he licks his lips slowly as if he's readying himself to devour me. "Is your toy in your bag?"

I nod. "I've got lube, too," I whisper.

"Good girl. Get them and sit on the edge of the bed facing me. Lube your toy, but don't slide it inside until I say."

"Yes, Chef." Just saying that makes me pant with anticipation. "Should I keep my knickers on?"

He shakes his head. Every part of him focuses on me. I remove my knickers gradually, my bum facing him, but I watch him from the mirror again. I've learnt what he likes, and I'm rewarded with a groan that fills my entire body, building my arousal impossibly higher.

"Now give me those little lace things."

I pass them to him, and he takes the opportunity to run his fingers between my legs. "Wider," he grunts, and I obey. He rubs my clit and slides a finger inside me. I whimper but force my eyes to remain open. His stare is dark and filled with desire. "You're soaking wet for me. I want to be inside you, but you promised me toy play. Now go to the bed."

He continues to stroke his cock, his eyes wide with awe as I follow his demands. "Bra off."

I undo my bra, and it falls to the floor. "Your tits are fucking amazing. Or do you prefer it when I say breasts?"

"Tits are good," I say. The word is harsh on my lips, but I like it.

"Are you doing okay, baby? Am I too feral and coarse for you?"

I shake my head.

"Good, because you know there will be plenty of time for soft and slow later. I want to make love to you until dawn."

I hold in a gasp. He said make love! I can't linger on it, so instead, I cling to the lust blazing through me.

"Now work that toy into your pussy, gorgeous. It vibrates in two places, so I want you to press it against your clit at the same time." I whimper as soon as I touch myself. "You're so needy for it."

"Needy for you," I rasp as reason tries to leave me.

"Is that right?"

I nod, eliciting a smile so hungry from him that it makes my stomach roll repeatedly.

"I want you to work it faster inside you. Can you do that?"

I nod again.

"What do you say?"

"Yes, Chef."

"That's my good girl."

He's wrapped his dick with my knickers, and he's fisting them around his cock quickly. When I speed up, he does, too.

My pulse climbs, and I ache for his body against mine. My wetness covers the toy, and I moan as I press the toy deeper. Occasionally, my eyes flutter closed, but I force them open again. I don't want to miss how hard I make him. I pull my lip into my mouth and suck on it as his tongue pushes out of his mouth, and his dark eyes track my thrusts.

He stares at my breasts as they heave up and down, bouncing with each press of the toy as I start to ride it into me. He murmurs his praise and growls his arousal for me.

I've never felt so desired.

"You're so fucking sexy. Every day, your sexiness and beauty overwhelm me. I can barely think straight most of the time. All I want is to be around you, smelling that passion fruit scent that fills my dreams, touching you, and hearing you laugh." He's rebuilt everything others tried to demolish, and he's doing it with awareness of *my* needs. "And now you're in my bedroom, your scent on my blankets in those sexy heels and hold ups, doing what I ask. I don't deserve to be in your presence. You're the whole fucking package, beautiful, sexy, sassy, and painfully intelligent with a skill that blasts everyone else's out of the water. You're everything."

My whole body burns as if fuel has been poured directly onto my skin. "You're thrusting that vibrator in deeper and harder. Did I say you could do that?"

I shake my head. I didn't realise.

"I love how desperate you are to come." He's right, I am, but his words demand these actions. He's sped up, too. I don't know how, but I'm already on the edge. "Do you want to come as I watch, baby?"

I nod.

"Use your words."

I glare at him, and his laugh is strained. His need is as obvious as mine.

"Then be my good girl and come hard and just for me. Come for me, Rubes."

I whimper as my orgasm explodes. I can barely grip the vibrator as my body shakes like I'm in a violent storm. He walks over to me, holds the vibrator inside me, and kisses me hard on the mouth as the orgasm rolls again and again across my body. I'm gasping and writhing on the bed, sweat beading my skin, but he's with me every step. My pleasure is everything to him. My heart bangs in my chest. Sparks catapult around my head as I finally close my eyes and let everything he's offered me own my body.

"That's my good girl," he says, eventually easing the vibrator from inside me. He lifts me and eases me further up the bed, so I'm lying against his pillows. My heart starts to slow, and I can finally take a deep breath. His kisses cover my skin, and he lies beside me, stroking my hair. "Fucking hell, Rubes. I wasn't expecting that. I was trying to be a domineering fucker, but you took my breath away. You're so fucking sexy."

The vulnerability is back. It's obvious even through my blurred climax vision. "You were amazing," I rasp. "You know my body so well."

His smile makes every part of me that his words didn't ache. "Are you okay?"

I want to tell him that I'm scared because of our future. I won't find anyone who makes me feel like he does again. But instead, I say, "Yes, completely. It's your turn next."

"If I died right now and your climax was the last thing I saw, I'd die happy. I feel like I already had my turn. But I did promise slow and sensual. Let me know when you're ready for that."

"Ready," I say instantly.

He shakes his head before grinning back at me, and he slowly starts to undress.

CHAPTER FORTY-ONE – GARETT

The following week at the cookery school is like a perfect dream.

"We've had another query for something in the new year," Ruby calls out. Her smiles are infectious, and there's joy among the team. Maybe it's because Christmas is coming or that the business is doing well. We're working twelve-hour days with groups and then kept busy with the prep and cleaning for the subsequent sessions, and laughter fills the room all the time.

"That's brilliant. Amber's smashing it," Wicksy replies as he tidies up from the last session. It's nearly nine at night, and we've got another group coming in early for sunrise Christmas. It's for people with dementia who struggle with sleep and the people who care for them.

Kath winks. "The only thing Amber is smashing is her husban—"

"Kath," I gasp, but she only shrugs. Ruby giggles.

"Have you bought a lifetime supply of earplugs?" Wicksy asks as he dances to the first bars of Mariah Carey's "All I Want for Christmas." "How do you get any sleep?"

"That's not a problem for Ruby, is it, hun?" Kath says with a cheeky smile as she grabs Wicksy into something that resembles a clumsy waltz.

Ruby's smirk betrays her as she shakes her head. "I don't know what you mean." But she does because, since the surprise party, Ruby's spent every night in my bed. And every morning, she's at my breakfast table gorging on whatever she's demanded I prepare for her.

When we're at the cookery school, we act professionally, but at night, we explore and learn about each other's bodies and lives. I know so much about her past and dreams; she also knows mine. Wicksy has no idea what's going on after the debacle of Ruby getting jealous with the hen party, and we want to keep it that way.

"Of course you don't, Ruby. Now dance with your number one chef."

"Number two," I counter, "although Mary Berry is—"

"More of a baker," Wicksy, Kath and Ruby say in chorus.

"Have I mentioned that before?"

Ruby replies, "Only once."

"Twice!" Kath shouts.

"A billion times!" Wicksy hollers as Kath dips him before spinning him around the room.

"I don't know why I put up with you all," I grumble, but the corners of my mouth tug up into a smile, betraying me.

"Grab Ruby and dance. She's waiting."

I gaze at Ruby, who shrugs. She presses her lips together and taps her feet. My lady is indeed waiting to dance. I bow in front of her and hold out my hand. "Would you be kind enough to dance with this penniless, imbecilic, second-to-many chef?"

She holds her chin as if she's debating it.

"Rubes," I warn. Her cheeks flush.

"Of course I'd love to dance with the man whose skills pale compared to Mary Berry."

I roll my eyes as I grab her hand and twirl her. Her girlish laugh fills me with light. Her eyes dip, and her eyelashes flutter. This cookery school is my home, and Ruby has quickly become my world.

"All I want for Christmas is you," she sings along to the chorus while wrapping her arms around me. It's safe to say that Ruby is no singer, but as she wails, I long for her to sing those words for me alone.

My phone vibrates in my pocket. It's the scheduled call with Ciara. I haven't given her an answer, but she wanted to share her plans for next year. She said it's for my professional opinion, but I suspect she's using it to convince me to move.

Ruby radiates the scent of passion fruit mixed with brandy, ginger, and other Christmas spices. It's a bizarre concoction, but it smells like home. I breathe her in, ignoring the vibrations. I want to immerse myself in this fantasy future for a little longer.

"Is your phone buzzing in your pocket, or are you enjoying watching Kath and Wicksy dance a little too much?" Rubes teases me.

I can't answer it in front of her. "I'm sure they'll call back."

"It might be Flora. I called and invited her to our family Christmas meal in a couple of days. She sounded keen but nervous. You've spent all this time with me, and I worry she'll hate me for taking her big brother away." Ruby's concern for Flora and her desire for her to join the family makes hairline cracks in my heart. If I leave, which is more likely than not, unless Ruby tells me she wants to do the couple thing, then I'll hurt this family I've grown to love.

At least Flora will have them when I desert her. The phone stops, and I continue holding Ruby close, but then it starts again.

"Garett."

"Okay, I'll take it. Maybe you should meet me at home." I step away. "As much as there's been a lot of laughter today, we're all tired."

"I won't get any rest at yours." My blood burns with prospects of what we might get up to tonight.

We've continued to be fuck buddies, but I want to be the boyfriend that I pretended to be weeks ago and not just the man she wants for sex.

"Besides," she adds, "we need to do the next part of the baking. I need to get that last technique down for the competition. I'll be here when you're done. Now go answer that phone before Flora kicks off."

I force a smile. "Hey," I say to Ciara. I shake away the weird image of the hairline cracks in my heart, frothing with guilt. I lie to Ruby every day that I don't tell her the truth about Clive and this job offer, and I lie to her whenever I don't tell her I want more—a lie of omission but still a lie.

"You okay, mucker?" Ciara asks. "Is this still a good time?"

I stare warily at Ruby, who's dancing with Kath, her cheeks pink from laughing. In five days, it's Christmas, and my decision will be made.

"Yeah, all good," I say with a throat that's sandpaper dry and emotion welling up. "Tell me about these plans."

When I come off the call, my body sparkles with excitement. Ciara's dreams for the restaurant resonate with everything I want to do. I've tried to forget how much I love running a restaurant and making it my signature place, but that call with Ciara enthuses me.

"Fuck you, you floury dickhead," Rubes shouts at whatever she's working on at the demonstration counter.

"Floury dickhead?" I ask as I near her.

She slams down a crushed macaron.

"Whatever," she grumbles as she throws another onto the side. "How was Flora?"

"It wasn't Flora. It was a chef I know."

If she senses my awkwardness, she doesn't comment.

Ruby attempts to fill the macaron, but it disintegrates in her grip. "They're not working."

I stand behind her and attempt to massage her shoulders, but she shrugs me off. It's weird how much that hurts. I never hugged my parents because the couple of times I tried, they shoved me away, too busy smoking or playing on their phones. Has a fear of rejection stopped me from having relationships, too?

I take a breath. This moment isn't about me. "Rubes, why are you making macarons? They're bloody difficult and will be impossible to fit in with timing when it comes to the dessert you have planned for the competition."

Ruby rounds on me, and I swallow loudly. Her eyes blaze, and tears slip down her face. "Because I want to win. Amber mentioned money to Kalen when I popped in this morning. I was preparing to tell them I was still happy at Flora's when I overheard her say something about 'raising enough with all these new things happening.' I need to win for them."

I open my arms, and the fear of rejection grips my

heart. "Then we're going to win. But you're not in any state to try something new. You're hyper-focused, and it's destroying your creativity."

When she sighs, all the air goes out of her, and she presses herself against my chest. I hold her against me as she breathes slowly. "Cinnamon, something like fennel, and another scent."

How did she get fennel? She guessed two of the secret ingredients from my pasta dish that won Clive the best restaurant competition. He couldn't get one of them. I made her bread with them this morning. She shouldn't be able to smell it after all our Christmas cooking today, though. She's fucking incredible.

"You can't call macarons floury dickheads because they haven't got flour in them," I whisper as I brush kisses against her hair.

"I know that. Are you trying to make it worse? I'm so wound up that I can't even give them good angry nicknames."

I hold back my laughter. "Let's go for a walk while we devise other nicknames for them. I was considering bourgeois bastards." She chuckles against my chest. "Or baked bitches?"

"What about eggy twats?" she says before lifting her face to mine. I kiss her briefly on her lips, which are salty from her tears.

"Agreed," I reply before shouting at the macarons, "Now go cook yourself, you eggy twats. We're heading out."

CHAPTER FORTY-TWO – GARETT

Ruby has a twinkle in her eye as we sneak out of the cookery school. In the bitter cold of December, I'm shivering instantly. Maybe this walk was a bad idea, but that twinkle and beaming face could lead me to death, and I'd go willingly.

"Where are we going?" I ask as Ruby grips my hand and drags me to the road.

"Trust me." Frost is already on the ground. A car zooms past with Noddy Holder's voice screaming from the stereo. There's no denying Christmas is coming. In four days, it'll be Christmas Eve. I'll make my decision, and Ruby will be crowned Best Cotswolds Baker and earn a job at Clive's restaurant.

I don't think of it as my restaurant anymore. The cookery school healed me.

I follow her as she drags me through the pub car park. We pass the For Sale sign, which hasn't changed to sold since I joined the cookery school. I try not to linger on how soon I will leave the only family who's been there for me, but melancholy still fills my bones.

I haven't given Ciara a yes yet, but that's probably down to a ludicrous hope that Ruby wants to be my girlfriend.

Ruby pushes a side door open and winks at me.

"You can't go in there. It's trespassing."

"Don't be such a scaredy cat," she replies with a cheeky smile.

"I'm not a scaredy cat, I just—" Suddenly, a car coming along the road sounds, and I jump through the door.

She lights the space with her phone's torch. We're in a kitchen. I gasp louder than I intended, and it echoes throughout the room. Light bounces off the marble countertops. "It's bigger than my old place," I murmur.

And it's beautiful, too. Everything is laid out like it should be, with easy access to the ovens and enough space so that staff wouldn't trip over each other. That was the problem with Clive's place. He wanted to cram in older bulky, clunky equipment to save money, but that meant it was often breaking down, so we needed more mixers and even an extra oven just in case.

I brush my hand over one of the ovens. It's grimy, which is no surprise, as no one's cleaned it in a while, but it comes alive in my head as I envisage preparing millefeuille and tiramasu with it.

"This is state-of-the-art equipment. Why did the owners leave?" I whisper as if the ghosts of the building might find us.

"The owner had a heart attack, which isn't unusual in the chef business when people are overworked." Her comment reminds me of how I used to live. "His wife made him move to Spain with the whole family. His heart went out of the business a couple of years before. He cared about the place, though."

"But why hasn't anyone bought it?"

Next to me, she shrugs while shining her torch across the room. "I think he was looking for someone who wanted to make it a restaurant again, not a housing development or anything like that, and because it borders the cookery school, they can't expand."

"But it's beautiful. If I had the money, I'd…" My thoughts battle. If I had the money, I couldn't live next to Ruby, knowing we can't be together.

"I know, right? But wait until you see the restaurant part." She fumbles through the drawers, looking for goodness knows what. "There's the badger."

"Please tell me you've not found a badger in here."

Her chuckles don't fill me with confidence.

She slips through another door. Darkness surrounds me, and the chill that was missing due to my excitement permeates my coat.

A flash catches my eye, and suddenly, Ruby is bathed in candlelight. My arms bracket the doorframe as she lights candles, filling the room with a golden glow. Soon, the whole room is revealed. A fireplace in the corner brings to mind cosy winters and lights hanging from the ceiling. The tables need a good scrub and some love, but the wood is good quality, with a perfect dark-stained finish. The original bricks of the building aren't hidden. Instead, they add a feature to the room. I turn in circles, visualising ivy along the beams and bottles on the walls so people can choose the wine they want with their meal.

All the aspects I chose for the restaurant with Clive that he's since gotten rid of would make this place even more impressive. I'd combine all my wants with the beautiful things already here to make an Italian restaurant so unique that people would want to come here to sample the atmosphere and food. It'd be a cosy hideaway for delicious moments and family gatherings.

"You look like you've fallen in love," Ruby says,

drawing my attention to her.

I smile back at her. I have fallen in love, but I daren't tell her. Because the feature that makes this room more perfect is her. I'm honoured that she showed me this place, although it can't be mine. It's given me hope. She's gifted me hope. An intensity propels me to share this as I sweep her into my arms and kiss her. I prop her on one of the empty tables.

Her moan is instant, and suddenly, I need to act on this emotion before I lose it. My kisses are soft and frantic, which has as much to do with the cold as my need for her.

"Garett," she whimpers as I push her hair to the side and kiss her neck. She thrusts something into my hand. It's a condom. I don't need to ask why it's in her pocket. I love that I'm on the same page as this woman. "But be quick. I don't want to get frostbite."

My deep chuckle echoes as she tries to undo my belt, but I still her hand with mine. The glow from the candles shows her eyes pinched in confusion. "This first," I murmur as I shove up her skirt and push her knickers to one side. She's wearing hold ups again, which must be enough to make her shiver, but it's all heat against my fingers as I rub her clit. Her wetness quickly covers my thumb as I continue to brush her skin with my lips.

Her coat tries to thwart my access to her chest, and she giggles as my kisses find the zip rather than her cleavage. The giggle dies quickly when I suck her wetness off my fingers and slide them into her soaking sex. She grabs me by the back of the neck and fixes me with a stare so full of need and intensity that it takes my breath away. I thrust one finger, then a second, hard and fast inside her as she demands more with hungry kisses. Her tongue is in my mouth, ramping up the heat until I'm boiling, all while we shiver together.

She pulls back. Her lips are rosy red from the fervour of our kisses. "Fuck me, baby," she demands.

My breath catches in my throat, but not because of the animal in her—I've seen that many times when we're in my bed—but because the power she's harnessing pulls a pain from my heart.

I think I love her.

She challenges me, makes me laugh, and makes me feel things I didn't think possible. She's more than I deserve, yet she lets me share in her sunshine for precious moments. I didn't know this was what it was like to fall for someone. If I see something funny, I want to share it with her to hear her cheeky laugh. If I know she's sad, I'm desperate to be there for her in whatever way she needs.

Ruby is the most incredible woman who has existed.

She should be with someone who gives her every piece of joy she deserves. I try, but I can't change that staying with me will hurt her family. She promised her brother that she'd keep them happy, but being with me pulls her in two directions, and she needs someone who keeps her whole. She needs a guy who fills her entire heart and looks after it. That's the only way she can be truly happy. It's also why I have to leave. If I stay here, this thing between us won't stop. It's like a snowball that keeps tumbling down the hill, growing each day. If she's going to have the things she wants, then I need to remove myself from her life.

But I must make the most of our last days together, too.

"There's my Rubes," I reply as she undoes my jeans and shoves them and my boxers out of the way. I slide the condom down my erection quickly and penetrate her with one quick movement. Her leg wraps around me to pull me in deeper. She's ferocious with her fucking. Tonight, when we get home, I will cover her in kisses, but in this cold restaurant where my woman is bathed in candlelight, we fuck quickly and without thoughts other than how good it feels. All previous sexual experiences pale in comparison to when I'm inside her. She owns my body with loving, feral care. I didn't know it was possible to crave intimacy as much as sex, but with her, I feel that and everything more.

Her moans and whimpers echo around the room. My balls tingle with expectation. Everything is on fire, and my need to come is already closer than expected. She senses it, too, because she says the words I gave her the week before when she played with her vibrator under my instruction. "Come for me, baby." That gravelly whisper shoots arousal straight to my dick.

I shake my head. "Not before you. I want to make you happy."

"This makes me happy," she says, pulling me in deeper with her foot pressing against my bum. I don't know if it's the way her hands grip my shoulders like I'm her world, the abandoned desire across her face, or the commanding way she speaks, but the next time she says, "Come in me, baby. I want to watch you come," I do just that.

"Yes, Rubes, yes," I reply between gasps and grunts as I come hard. A cold sheen of sweat covers my skin as I shake against her. She holds me close as my body threatens to collapse from the intensity of my orgasm.

"We need to go," she demands as she brushes kisses to my lips and forehead, soothing me from the moment that still leaves me trembling.

"But you didn't come."

She smoothes my forehead lines away with her lips.

"Garett, it's like two degrees, and frost is already on the ground. If we do it like I want, my nipples will fall off with frostbite. Let's get home and do it somewhere warm. I'll let you make me come at least three times before you do again."

I chuckle as I bury my head in the crook of her neck. "Deal."

CHAPTER FORTY-THREE – RUBY

"You're ready," Garett says as he brackets my body with those beautiful forearms.

It's my last practice session before Christmas. Tomorrow will be our annual Christmas Cloud Burst, also known as the Cloud Family Christmas Meal at the cookery school, and the competition is the next day.

"Are you sure?" I ask, too scared to meet Garett's gaze. He turns my chin and sweeps a kiss across my lips.

"You will win the competition with this creation. You'll be pushed for time, but you'll do it. It's stunning."

We stare at my cannelés de Bordeaux lining my velvety spiced orange ganache layer cake. The spun sugar creates a protective dome over the top, and the tiny orange flowers peeking out around them make it ostentatious. I'm proud—no, more than that. I'm in love.

Garett beams. Shit. It's not just the cake giving me this weird, shaky reaction. It's him. But I can't say anything. I promised my family would remain the most important people in my life, and that hasn't changed.

I extract myself from Garett and his delicious forearms. "We'd best tidy up if we want to get home before ten tonight." It's the *Great British Bake Off* Christmas special, and we promised each other we'd watch it before we "sleep." We've had sex every night because that's what fuck buddies do. The night we stop doing this, I shouldn't stay over, because that means this is a relationship. I can't destroy my family and break Jem in the process.

I want Garett every second of the day. Even when I'm leading a class, which I did today with him acting as my kitchen assistant, I have flashbacks of what we've done before and consider what I still want. I love falling asleep in his arms, too.

"I've already tidied up."

"But there were so many bowls, and I used every piece of equipment in this place."

He shrugs in a way that makes me want to elbow and kiss him all at once. "I'm your kitchen assistant today."

"But that was just for class." Why is he so infuriatingly lovely?

"Which you were brilliant at, by the way. Soon, they won't need me to lead classes because you'll be able to do it all." There's an edge to the sentence.

I push his compliment away with the sweep of my hand. "Either way, you didn't have to tidy everything up."

He leans against the countertop in a way that makes me want to press my hands against his hard biceps. "I have plans for us tonight—that include Bake Off, of course," he adds before I argue. "And I wanted us to have a nice night and lots of time. I created a banquet for you while you were cooking."

I was so in my world that I didn't notice. This competition means everything to me. I look at him, my mouth squeezed tightly, and realise that the competition means *nearly* everything. "But not a date. It won't be a date."

"Obviously not because dates go against the fuck buddy rules." His voice is tight. Hearing him say that makes me bite the flesh inside my cheek, although they're as much my rules as they are his. "We're two friends hanging out."

"With sex because there has to be sex as per sex buddy etiquette."

He smiles, but his lips are tight, and it doesn't reach his beautiful brown eyes. "If you insist, Rubes. If I must have sex with you, then I will. My life is such a trial."

I laugh, but it's not genuine.

"I'll race you back to mine," he adds. We bring separate vehicles each morning so no one guesses that we're together every night, although, of course, Kath knows.

"Winner comes first."

But he's already running out the door. "Don't forget to lock up," he shouts.

"You're a cinnamon-smelling shithead." But he's already too far away to hear me. I'll still win because I love making him come.

He pops the last chocolate-covered strawberry in my mouth. He prepared a living room picnic for me. The low lighting, watching my favourite programme while eating my favourite foods, which he hand prepared, and soft Christmas music playing in the background make this a date. He's even wearing the lounge pants I love and a Christmas jumper I left on his bed as an early present.

294

But as long as we have sex tonight, I can pretend this is a prequel to fuck buddy times.

I kiss him hard on the mouth so that he gets the taste of my strawberry lips.

"Lush," he murmurs before I settle against his chest. "I want to say thank you again for showing me that restaurant, Rubes."

"Your face was amazing. It was worth it for the cold in my bones that took three scalding hot showers to get rid of," I say with a smile. "You were so happy—like a kid in his first candy store."

His chest rumbles against my back as he chuckles. I love sitting between his legs like this. It means he can play with my hair, kiss my neck, and hold me with those panty-wetting forearms.

"It gave me so many ideas. I'd love to make a place like that my own. When I tried to sleep last night, I came up with a menu and décor."

"I know. You kept mumbling while I was trying to sleep."

"As if," he says, squeezing me. "You were snoring."

"I was huffing in the hope that you'd shut up."

I kiss his knuckles as he tells me about the appetisers on his dream menu. "And then I'd have this big opening ceremony for everyone who's come to the cookery school over the last months. The day before, we'd have a soft launch where you and your family tried out the dishes. Kath would tell me that my bread was the best she'd ever eaten while trying to guess the ingredients, and Wicksy would chat up the waitress. Unsuccessfully, of course."

"Of course."

"Your parents would say the kindest things. Meanwhile, Flora would be beaming because she would

295

have planned a great opening. Your desserts would be front and centre because you're a baking goddess."

"So why don't you?"

"Put your desserts front and centre?"

"Why don't you get investors, buy the pub, and make your dream a reality?"

The sigh against my shoulder breaks my heart. I want what he wants and know he could create this dream place.

I swallow the lump in my throat and try again. "It's not just that you have the vision. You're the most hardworking person I know. You're always coming up with revolutionary ideas for the cookery school, and they work because you take people with you, and then you graft so hard. Why don't you make your dream for the pub a reality?"

"Because of my parents."

During the last week, he's shared stories of his childhood, how he found his love of cooking, and the trouble he got into when he was young and then later in the kitchens, but I'm still surprised. "How come?"

He pulls me closer. "I can't get credit. Over the years, my parents have stolen money from me in little ways, and then several years ago, I found out they'd taken out credit cards in my name but hadn't paid them back."

"Your own parents?"

He sighs long and loud. "My own parents. It was the final straw in our relationship. It's why I wasn't on the contract for the place I co-owned. So even if I were liked in this town and could find investors, which, based on your parents being the only ones who'd employ me, it seems unlikely that anyone would trust me financially. My credit rating makes me look reckless with money and worse than a risk."

"But it's not your fault."

"That doesn't matter."

"And you can't go into business with your old partner because they ruined you."

He's never really explained that. Over the last weeks, I've considered that person might be Clive. If it was, then why would Clive stop any restaurant from taking him on? And why would Flora still be so close to Garett?

His warmth gives me the hope that escapes him. "I wouldn't do anything with that guy." There's an unexpected bitterness in Garett's tone. "He double-crossed me and ruined my future as much as my parents did, maybe more. He was the one who took Cookie, and he was the one who stopped every restaurant in this town from employing me."

I turn. His mouth is downturned, and his eyes have sunk. "So that wasn't related to an ex-girlfriend then?"

"I've never had a girlfriend before..."

I turn one-eighty and straddle his legs. "Before what?"

I should be asking him about Clive, but this moment is significant for us.

Is he calling me his girlfriend? Emotions conflict, beating me with what he might mean, but he won't meet my eyes.

"Just before." He sighs again, and it breaks my heart. We both know there's no future in this, yet that little light of hope guiding my actions since we became friends refuses to be extinguished. "Ruby, I've got something to tell you. Please don't be mad at me."

He still can't meet my gaze. I tip my finger under his chin to lift his head. "I don't know who hurt you, baby, but don't be scared to tell me things."

What's between us is more than friendship and more

than lovers, and yet the sadness of Jem catching us together still stops me from suggesting more.

"I'm leaving the cookery school," Garett says. "On Christmas Day, I'll leave the country and move to Ireland to run a restaurant."

I pull my lower lip between my teeth, but overwhelm still fills my body.

"Is it because of me?" I hate how vulnerable I sound. I vowed not to let a man hurt me again. And yet, he's only doing what I asked.

"Partly. I can't be around you knowing we can't be together, but I respect the reasons why. If I had a family like yours, I'd do everything to ensure they were happy."

Tears spill out and roll down my cheeks.

Garett continues, "But it's not only that. I want a future. I need to work in a restaurant kitchen again. I've loved every second of working in the cookery school—"

"Even when you found me with a knife cut on my first day?"

"Even then." He chuckles as he thumbs my tears away like I did him in the hospital when we learnt he might get Cookie back. "I've especially loved every second I've spent with you, and I wouldn't change that for the world, but I need to work somewhere I can build a future, create menus, and design the interior to make a place great. Our trip to the pub helped me decide to go."

"I understand." And I do, which makes me hate myself. "I want that for you."

"And I won't be leaving your family in the lurch. I've spoken to some people who can do one-off sessions, but they don't need to. I know your sister originally mentioned you leaving the cookery school at Christmas, but with me gone, you could stay working there if you want to. Since your first week, you've proved that you could easily lead the cooking sessions. Watching you today was one of the highlights of my career."

Tears are slipping down his cheeks now, and I repeat the action he used on me.

"You've got it all sorted."

His body trembles. "Are you angry with me?"

"I'm not. I wish I were because that would make it easier to say goodbye. You'll be gone in three days, and one of those is the competition."

He nods his head, his eyes avoiding mine again.

"Can we just go to bed and cuddle tonight?" I ask. "I'm tired after some intense weeks and want to be held by you."

"But isn't that against the rules?" It's a slight tease, which slows my tears as I shrug.

"Maybe. It will mean that we're not just fuck buddies."

"Were we ever?" He brushes my lips with his before lifting me in his arms and carrying me to bed.

CHAPTER FORTY-FOUR – GARETT

Flora slips into my passenger seat. She wrings her hands as soon as she's clicked in the seatbelt.

"It's going to be okay. They want you there, Flora." My stomach bubbles with excitement and anxiety for the Christmas Cloud Burst.

"I know, but I'm not used to being welcomed by a family. Aside from you, I haven't had anyone in years." Her parents barely recognised her presence above their business adventures, and Clive is a chip off the old block. "I've never had a proper family Christmas celebration before."

"It will be great, and you've brought something."

"Who doesn't love Christmas biscuits?" She opens the tin, and I chuckle. Father Christmas is missing an eye, and the Christmas tree looks drunk. She explains each messy biscuit to me and retells all the incidents that brought them to their present state.

"They're awesome, Flo."

"You haven't called me that since Clive ruined you. So you're moving to Ireland, then."

Driving helps me because I can focus on the road and not her puppy dog face, which she'll make, though she doesn't want to. "Yes. I have to. I handed my resignation letter to Amber this morning. She asked me to stay, but she understood when I explained my new job." I tap the steering wheel and clear my throat. "As the cookery school isn't opening in January, and I've got the contacts for them, there shouldn't be much upheaval." I didn't give my Ruby-related reasons. I promised I wouldn't

"Does Ruby know she's one of the reasons why?"

A tractor pulls out in front of us, and I remember the day I met Ruby. I wanted her out of "my" cookery school, and yet she's the best person for it. As much as I want her to win Clive's competition for the money, I hope she doesn't. Although her skills are in baking, she's fantastic at the school and she should have her own baking business.

We crawl behind the tractor, and I glance at Flora. I owe her so much, and avoiding her pain isn't the action of the man I want to be. "She knows I'm going because we can't be together. She also knows it's because I want to work in a restaurant, and I can't do that here because of a former business partner."

"And does she know that business partner is my brother?" I grind my teeth. The tractor takes its time. "I'll take that as a no."

The chugging vehicle finally turns into a field, and I continue driving to the school.

We pass the pub. It looks like someone knocked the For Sale sign down. I pull into the school's car park. Candles lead to the doorway. Once darkness comes, they'll give the place a fantastic atmosphere. A giant inflatable penguin that's had half the air knocked out of it bounces, too. It wouldn't surprise me if that were done on purpose. I love this family.

Neither of us moves after I turn the van off. I make a mental note to hand over the keys to it tomorrow. Ruby has promised to care for Cookie until I can arrange to bring

301

him to Ireland.

"You're setting Ruby up to be used as brutally as Clive used you," Flora says, taking my trembling hands. "What if he steals her ideas?"

I stare out of the windscreen at the pub. Seeing that place was a catalyst for my decisions, but they're choices I wouldn't have to make if it wasn't for Clive's betrayal. But as much as I hate the guy, I wouldn't have met Ruby without him.

"I'm going to tell her after the competition and before I go so that she can make her mind up for herself. And don't forget that she has support. There are people around her ready to protect her at any point, and some of those people know about Clive even if she doesn't. I'll speak to her parents when I say goodbye to Cookie tomorrow, and then once she wins, which she will do because she's a baking revelation, I'll tell her."

"But—"

"She won't be alone," I reply firmer. "She has people. I didn't have anyone."

"You had me." Flora's voice wavers and tears brim her eyes.

"Shit. Of course I did, and I still have you, and you have me." I pull her into my arms and she cries against me. "You'll always have me, and I hope you feel the same. You can live with me in Ireland if you want. You're my family, and I love you, Flora."

"I love you, too," she replies her tears stilling. "No one knows me like you do."

I squeeze her tighter. "I wish lots of people knew the real you and saw how amazing you are." I don't know what it will take for Flora to fully let people in. Hopefully, one day, she'll be surrounded by friends and understand how incredible she is, if that's what she wants.

I sense movement outside the car. Ruby waits for me. The silver jewels on her navy blue jumpsuit sparkle in the sunlight. Her waves crowd her shoulders, the gold ribbons adding to her angelic look. She's a vision.

I love her.

I've thought it before, but I've never been more certain of anything. She steps back. She knows I'm needed at this moment.

"Go to her," Flora says.

"No. I need you to know I'm here for you no matter what. You're my family."

Flora hugs me. "I know, big bro. But it doesn't hurt to hear it once in a while." A hiccup bursts from her mouth. "I love you, Garett. You're my big brother, and without you, I'd be a mess. But right now, you need to go to her. I'm going to tidy myself up."

I stay for a couple of seconds, making sure she means it. Flora's always had my best interests at heart, but her firm stare tells me to go more than her words could.

I step out of the van.

Ruby stares at me with her big brown eyes. "Is she okay?"

"She will be."

"I'll look after her when you've gone. She'll be my favourite little sibling. I'll tell Jem he can go swivel."

She's holding it together. We're all holding it together. "No more talk about me leaving, okay? Not today."

"Promise."

"You're breathtaking. You're the most beautiful woman I've ever seen."

"And sexy?"

"If I weren't worried about ruining my trousers before the Christmas Cloud Burst, I'd be on my knees in this car park, declaring your sexiness for the world to hear."

She steps into my open arms. "Best not. Mum and Dad don't need to hear that, and I don't want Wicksy making suggestions about your dirty knees." Passion fruit fills my lungs, marking them with her scent and presence. She presses the squeaky reindeer nose on the Christmas jumper she bought for me. "Cute."

"Not sexy or breathtaking?"

"You're no Mary Berry."

I press my lips to hers. "I can't compare to that goddess."

The van door opens, and Flora shouts, "Come on, you two. We've got a dinner to attend."

I open my hand to her, and Ruby steps to my side. We agreed that we'd act like colleagues and friends at the party. My body chills at losing her touch. I'd better get used to it because I'll have a lifetime without her.

Cookie bounces from person to person as we set the table for the meal. Everyone sings Christmas songs, and Iain and Liz whip each other with any tea towel they can find.

Kalen clucks over Amber, who is nearly nine months and not far from being induced, and she keeps shoving him away and telling him, "I can do it. Stop mothering me." She then sits with her feet up while making him bring things to her.

Kath and I sit together, watching the spectacle of a

Cloud Christmas. Flora, Jem, and Wicksy perform Michael Bublé classics together when they're supposed to be place setting. I wouldn't be surprised if both men have crushes on her.

I'm so proud of my little sister. Knowing I won't be here to protect her from all that life throws at her causes another crack in my heart. But as Ruby says something to her and she giggles, I'm reminded that she won't be alone.

"You're leaving us, aren't you?" Kath asks as Amber throws something at Jem. I bet they were exhausting growing up, especially with Ruby's lively grandparents. It must have been a wonderful chaos.

"How did you know?" I shove up my sleeves. "Let me guess. Because you're a wise woman who knows when it will snow before weather forecasters?"

She chuckles and nudges me. Her elbows are like spikes. "Nah, I caught Ruby crying when I went to help her tidy the hideaway."

That hurts, but I shouldn't be surprised. "She'll cope okay without me."

"I know. She's strong."

Ruby tickles Jem. Then Kalen picks Jem up and carries him to Amber so she can help, too.

"Be aware that sometimes everything changes, and you must change with it."

I glance at Kath, who's chuckling at the tickling fight. "Is that one of your wise woman sayings?"

She shakes her head. "No. Let's say I know things you don't, and the next two days aren't going to go according to your plan."

Liz calls everyone to the table before I can ask what she means.

CHAPTER FORTY-FIVE – GARETT

This family know how to Christmas up a table. Fairy lights snake around the food bowls. The turkey glistens like it's salivating at the prospect of being carved, steam rises from roast potatoes, and the sprouts are the greenest I've ever seen. I hide my mouth with my hand for fear that the drool collecting in my cheeks might slip out and ruin the cool chef persona I've created.

Ruby nudges me. "You're not hiding anything. You're hungrier than a playboy at a nightclub."

It's true. My stomach growls as I scan the table again. The bread I baked, with the same secret ingredients as my famous pasta dish, sits between the bright orange carrots and the bacon-covered sausages.

"I should take my bread off the table. It's not Christmassy, and it doesn't belong," I hiss.

I reach for my bread, but Flora slaps my hand away. Ruby sneaks a bit off and pops it into her smug mouth. As soon as she chews, her brow furrows, and she stares at me even though we're sitting right next to each other. She recognises the taste, but her twisting mouth as she looks down and then back at me suggests she still doesn't know the secret ingredients.

I chuckle as Jem shouts, "This is why I love my family."

"When you say this is why you love your family, what are you referring to? It better not just be the food, Jem," Liz says, standing by the table. "You're cruising for an empty plate."

"I love you for lots of reasons, obviously," he says quickly while his dad titters.

"Liar," Amber says. I glance at Flora, who witnesses Amber, Liz, and Iain teasing Jem. Is she wondering if every family is like this, too?

"It's not always this chaotic," Ruby whispers. She perches her hand on my knee. Thankfully, it's hidden under the table. I don't want to be dragged into any family moments. I'm still not sure if everyone is fighting or bantering. "I blame Amber and the fact that she knows that for as long as she's this pregnant, she can get away with anything."

"Don't believe her," Kalen whispers from my other side. "It's always like this, but I've got you, Garett. You and me need to stick together, seeing as we're both with Cloud sisters."

My stare jumps around at the family, but no one's heard. "But Ruby and I are just—"

"Sure you are," he replies with a grin so big it nearly eclipses his face. "I always let my friends touch me under the table."

Ruby yanks her hand back as Iain announces it's time to carve the turkey. She reaches again for bread.

"Stop right there, Ruby. We all need some of Garett's special bread."

"But it doesn't fit the table," I stutter as smiles, smirks, and grins come at me.

"As if that matters, you grumpy sausage," Kath replies. "Have you seen Flora's biscuits?"

"They're ridiculous," Jem mutters.

"Hey," Flora and I say simultaneously.

"Hey, nothing. You're both part of the Cloud family now, and you're free game," Liz replies. "Do we all agree?"

As each family member nods their head, my heart crushes a little. Tomorrow, they'll know that I'm leaving and rejecting them. I catch Amber nodding at me, as well as Kath. They know I'm leaving, but for them, I'm still part of their family. Amber dead-eyes me and mouths, *You're family now, champ.*

"I guess it's unanimous then," Liz adds. Even Jem nods. "As Iain cuts the turkey because I'm too impatient, let's—"

Iain holds the carving knife aloft. "I'd like Ruby to do it. She's the real chef, after Garett, and this is her first Christmas with us in six years. I want to celebrate that."

A sob escapes Ruby's mouth as she stands and hugs her parents. I can't get in the way of Ruby and her family. If I ever needed a visual representation of why I'm going, I just had it.

"And as Ruby cuts, it's tradition time." Liz looks at Flora and then at me. "We must say something we're looking forward to next year. I start, and carver finishes. Are we ready?"

I grind my teeth.

"I'm looking forward to the surprise we have for all of you at the end of this meal," Liz says. "And before any of you argue that it's not next year, it has next year repercussions."

"You stole mine," Iain moans.

"Suck it, bitch," Liz replies.

"Mum!"

"Sorry, I may have drank too much mulled wine. Anyway, it's your turn, Flora. What are you looking forward to?"

"Finding out what I'm good at and then doing it as a career," Flora says. Her head dips, and she's vulnerable in a way that makes my heart stutter. She looks directly at me. "And don't say I'm good at everything, big bro. I want to know my thing, like cooking is yours."

She's got me there. "I look forward to seeing you do that, too."

She gives a tentative smile. A crack in my heart widens. I won't be here for that.

In turn, each person says the thing they're looking forward to. Jem talks about returning to university even though most of us know he's dropped out. Iain wants to try something new, at which point he winks at Liz, and everyone makes vomit noises.

"Grow up, all of you. It's not what you think," Liz snaps. "Besides, we've tried everything sex-based." She pretends to do a mic drop, but everyone misses it while fake vomiting.

Then Wicksy mentions getting his head shaved, which makes everyone gasp. Kath says she has two things left on her bucket list, so it will probably be skydiving, as she's not ready to fly to America yet. Amber responds loudly that she's most looking forward to eating soft cheese and drinking alcohol, which makes everyone laugh. Kalen blushes as he says he's looking forward to being a dad.

And then it's my turn. I swallow loudly and stare at everyone but Ruby. Cookie shifts in his sleep by my feet. "I'm looking forward to having Cookie live with me." I don't add that it won't be here.

Ruby's finished proving she isn't a turkey carver based

on the pieces she's hacked up, and the family tease her for her efforts.

"Oi, it's my turn, so shut up so we can eat because I'm famished and I haven't eaten much yet today," she shouts. Kalen elbows me, but I ignore his comment about how he'd bet she's more hungry for a particular chef's meat.

"The thing I'm most looking forward to is, hopefully—" Ruby pauses so long that I'm a mixture of terrified and hopeful that it relates to me. Instead, she says, "Working in Clive Macdonald's restaurant after I win his Christmas Eve competition."

"What?" Liz snaps.

"You're not working for that man after what he did," Iain hollers a lot louder than necessary, considering we're all at the same table.

Ruby drops the carving tools and shoves her hands on her hips. "What do you mean?"

"Mum, she doesn't know," Amber says.

But Liz pushes her chair back. "You can't work for that piece of—sorry, Flora—you can't work for that man after what he did to Garett, not to mention what he did to Cookie."

I should stop this, but it's like I'm watching it on double time and holding on for dear life.

"What do you mean?" Ruby stares at me. Her eyes are wider than the silver baubles on the tree behind her.

"Mum, stop," Amber says, but she's struggling to get to her feet. Cookie is restless beneath the table, and I try to settle him. "Garett didn't want her to know."

"You didn't want me to know what?" she snaps, baring her teeth. Flora shakes on the other side of the table, and I'm torn between protecting her and fighting a battle I shouldn't have hidden from.

I fumble for words, but it's too late. I'm no match for Cloud women.

"Clive Macdonald won the Best Cotswold Restaurant competition with Garett's dish, but he double-crossed Garett and took his restaurant from him. He told every restaurant, eatery, and cooking school in the area not to employ him and that if they did, he'd ruin them."

Flora pushes her chair away now, and it's all I can do not to run to her. She clears her throat and says, "Clive kept Cookie and wouldn't let Garett have him or visit him. And Clive wasn't nice to Cookie and tortured Garett with photos and videos of him." She takes a deep breath. "He is a piece of shit, Liz. I'm so ashamed of him. Garett is my big brother as far as I'm concerned."

Ruby walks up and jabs me in the chest with her finger. "You knew all of this and didn't tell me? I thought there was something about him, but I trusted you. I didn't believe you'd lie about something so important. How many other lies have you told me?"

"None. You said you needed to do that competition, and I didn't want to stop you from doing something important. I was going to tell you what he was like after the competition," I bluster.

"But what if that had been too late? He could have ruined my reputation by then or stolen my ideas," she hits back.

I hold my hands out. "I didn't think he'd treat you like he treated me." My voice loses power with every word I speak.

"Why?"

I can't find my words. I can't explain myself when I'm faced with all this emotion. This is the side of families I

311

can't do. "Because."

"You're no different than Neil," she snarls. "Garett, you lied to me daily and set me up for this. Is Clive the real reason you're leaving the cookery school? Now you've got your dog, you can leave and work at that restaurant in Ireland." There's a series of gasps, but my focus fixes on the woman I love, throwing every ounce of her anger at me. And I deserve it because I lied to her repeatedly.

"It's not like that. You know how I feel about you," I whisper, because even after everything, I don't want her family to know about us.

"I don't know anything anymore. You've been lying to me for weeks," she replies under her breath. "I thought we had something special."

"We did." I hold my hand out to her.

"You meant everything to…" Ruby looks at her family, who stare at us like we're a rowdy couple from reality television. They look around the room as if they hadn't been staring at us the whole time. She squeezes her eyes tightly shut and shakes her head. Her voice drops, and my heart breaks. "It doesn't matter. I was wrong. Please leave. I can't do this anymore."

I pull my hand back, and it hangs loose at my side.

"I'll never forget you," I whisper so quietly that I'm not even sure she hears.

No one looks at me. Ruby is right about everything. I don't deserve this family because I've lied to them, too. They welcomed me in, and now I'm ditching them, but more than that, I don't deserve Ruby. I thought I was protecting her, but I was taking away her chance to decide about Clive and the competition for herself.

When I turn, Cookie and Flora try to follow me. "You

two stay. This is your family, not mine."

"No, I'm coming with you, Garett. You're my family." Everyone else is speechless.

"Please stay. I can't take Cookie yet, and he needs to have you close when I'm gone." And Flora will need these people once I'm gone. As much as Ruby hates me, I'm certain that Amber and Kath don't hate me, and the others might not eventually.

"I'll bring the van back tomorrow," I say to Amber. "Thank you for everything."

And with that, I stumble to the van. A forlorn Flora stares at me from the door, Cookie in her arms, as I drive out of the car park. The rest of the family haven't come to wave me goodbye. I don't deserve it anyway.

It's time to pack because Ireland is the only place that will have me now.

CHAPTER FORTY-SIX – RUBY

The lump in my throat won't go away even as I swallow chunks of Christmas dinner. It probably tastes heavenly to everyone else at the table. I glance up and find everyone except Flora sending me daggers. She's too busy sliding little bits of food under the table for Cookie.

"What?" I say to the table. "Why are you all glaring at me? He was the one who lied, yet you're all on his side."

"Because you told him how important the competition was to you," Amber replies. "Because you made out that you needed to do this competition no matter what."

"And he's helped you by teaching you techniques every night when he should have earned more money, but he didn't." I'm taken aback by Kath, who delivers the explanation so softly that I question what I've heard. When I left the family for Neil and only came back briefly for my grandparents' funeral, she never told me I was wrong. "He knew that whatever he taught you could be stolen, but he did it because he wanted you to win."

"For Amber. Yes, I was doing it to start my own business one day, but Amber and Kalen need the money for the twins." I'm doubling down and not accepting responsibility like a petulant child.

"No, we don't," Kalen replies. He turns to Amber. "We

don't need it for the twins, do we? You know I've got enough, baby."

"Of course I know that. I'm the one who manages our finances. You've earned enough, and the cookery school is booming, thanks to Garett, Ruby, and Kath," she replies. Wicksy clears his throat noisily. "Sure, you too, Wicksy. We're good for money."

"But I heard you talking about needing money," I say.

"That's not what you think. That's—"

"Shit," Mum says.

Amber rounds on Mum. "Why are you swearing? This was my secret. You don't know—"

"You'd best tell them *our* secret, Liz," Dad says with the longest sigh ever.

I stand again. "Is everyone lying to me at the moment?"

"Such a drama queen," Jem murmurs.

I point my wobbling finger at him. My adrenaline spikes. "Do not mess with me, Jem. Garett is leaving because of you. Okay, because of me, but you didn't help."

"What did I do?"

"You told me I couldn't date him because I tore apart the family when I was with Neil. Fine. It's all my fault, but I'm still annoyed with you."

"Well, you did," Jem snaps back.

"But I didn't mean to. I was young and doing stupid shit—"

"Nothing new there, then," Jem replies, wagging his face.

Kalen helps Amber to her feet, and I'm pretty sure I can see Cookie's paws on the table near the turkey.

"Since when are you, Mr. Perfect?" My blood boils, and my jaw hurts from clenching it Garett-style.

CLANG. CLANG.

My mum bashes a saucepan with a wooden spoon as she marches around the table. Kath takes Flora and Cookie to the side of the room, and they watch us all like we're in a Greek tragedy.

"That's it!" Mum shouts. "Cloud children, sit your asses down. We're getting to the bottom of this right now." She hands her pan and spoon to Kalen. "Sailor, you bash that if any of them start arguing again. You've got your orders."

"Yes, ma'am," Kalen replies, saluting Mum using the wooden spoon.

"Hey, you're meant to be on my side," Amber whines.

Kalen bashes the pan until Amber stops whining and receives a nod from Mum.

"Good lad. Never mess with your wife's mum, especially as you'll need me for nappy changing and babysitting duties in the future."

"Yes, Mumma Cloud. Exactly," Kalen replies.

"Right." Mum stands and points at me. In that second, she displays precisely how she built a successful business, even with my grandparents arguing. I adore her. "Ruby, you first. Were you dating Garett?"

"No." She continues to eyeball me until I speak. "We were hooking up."

Kath raises her hand. My mum points at her. "Yes, Kath."

"He loves her."

"He does not!" I stand and splutter. My reward is Kalen bashing the pan near my ear until I sit down.

"That explains all those secret looks he gives her when he thinks she can't see. I know love when I see it," Mum replies with a wink at my dad. "And does she love him, Kath?"

I want to shout that I'm right here, but Kalen hovers over me with that damn pan. He's eyeballing me, desperate to use it. I fold my arms and glare at him.

"The jury is out," Kath replies. "I think she does, but she's not ready to fully admit it to herself yet."

I open my mouth, and Kalen bashes the pan. "Hey, I didn't say anything."

"You wanted to, though. Well done, Kalen," Mum says.

I scowl at Kalen first, then Mum with all the force I can muster. She smiles sassily. I really am like my mum and grandma.

"Now to Jem. Son, did you tell your sister she couldn't date the delectable and lovely Garett because she 'tore the family apart' when she was with Neil?"

Jem rolls his eyes, and Kalen walks over and bangs his pan. "Fine! Yes. I told her that because she did. When I was fifteen, all you two did was row."

"Because you were a punk-ass teenager causing them problems by bunking off school and being a lazy bastard," Amber says. Instead of a banged pan, Kalen kisses her cheek.

"Why does she get a kiss?" Jem moans.

"Do you want a kiss from your brother-in-law, Jem?" Mum asks with her hands in the air.

"No," he replies, sliding down in his chair. "Just saying it's not fair."

"Let's straighten this out. Your sister is in love with someone who foolishly lied, thinking he was protecting her, but couldn't date her because her ass of a brother said it would break up the family when some days we like him more than you, Jem."

"And now he's leaving," I say. Kalen steps closer, but Mum waves him off. "He's moving to Ireland to run a restaurant because he misses being in charge of a kitchen and using his creativity and skills that way. It's what he was born to do."

Flora's hand shoots up.

"Yes, Flora?"

"He's also leaving because he's in love with Ruby and can't be near her without being with her. And while we're telling secrets," Flora adds. Cookie sits patiently at her feet. "Jem dropped out of university several months ago."

Dad turns to Jem.

"Flora, seriously?" Jem shouts. "Why are you selling me out?"

"Because you called my cookies ridiculous."

Jem shakes his head and glares.

"But Jem is working in a café," Flora says before looking at Jem. "You should have told your mum sooner."

"We went there the other day, and he was a brilliant waiter," Kath comments, and she and Flora nod at each other.

That makes Jem sit up and smile until Mum turns back to him. "I'll deal with you later."

"He also needs somewhere to live, but I'm going to rent a house, and both he and Wicksy, as well as Wicksy's chickens, are moving in with me," Flora adds.

Everyone stares at Flora until my mum cuts in. "So let's establish some facts. Firstly, Jem was a difficult teenager, but hopefully, he'll be a better adult, and this family's survived a lot worse than Neil. You can date who you like, Ruby, as long as they make you happy. Secondly,

Garett and Ruby love each other and should be together."

I open my mouth to speak, but my mum holds up my hand. "I'm not done yet. Thirdly, your dad and I need to take some responsibility for the mess of this situation. Not the love bit, that's all on you. But we should have mentioned our surprise present for Ruby and Jem and what we're looking forward to next year."

Jem and I lock eyes and shrug.

"Right, everyone, follow your dad and me."

CHAPTER FORTY-SEVEN – RUBY

We all follow Mum and Dad as they walk through the cookery school and out the doors. Wicksy is at the front with Flora and Cookie, followed by Jem, who tries to help Amber, but she slaps his hand away, telling him she can walk perfectly fine by herself while also making him carry her bag. Meanwhile, Kalen bangs the pan like he's commanding his unit.

I'm bringing up the rear with my arm tucked in Kath's. It's not for her, though. I need support after the revelations of the last half hour.

"Do you know what all this is about?" I ask. She nods. "But you're not going to tell me?"

Her laugh eases some of my anxiety. Grandma and she must have gotten in trouble a lot when they were my age. Kath is trouble enough on her own now.

"Your head is spinning," she says as Mum and Dad lead us through the car park.

My head is all over the place for more reasons than whatever secret Mum and Dad are keeping. "Garett hurt me, and I can't hide from that. How much of our relationship—which wasn't supposed to be a relationship—was real if he could lie to me so easily about something so important?"

"All I'll say is," Kath replies, "if it was the other way around, if Garett needed the money and was going into a competition to win it, no matter the consequences, would you have lied to him?"

"I don't know. Probably. I helped him get Cookie even though it was dangerous."

"And he protected you then, too."

"I knew he was keeping something from me. How can I trust him? And it's messed up that he did that rather than let me decide for myself."

Kath nods. I wait for some of her wisdom, but it doesn't come.

I sink my face into my hands and add, "But he's never had a relationship. There was no ex-girlfriend. He's barely had a family, and most of those close to him have double-crossed him, like Clive and his own parents. Do you think he was not only scared of losing me but of letting me in, too?"

Kath chuckles. "I appear wise, but I barely know what's happening in my head most days. Maybe it's all that, or maybe he wanted you to have what you wanted. You had us, but when Clive did what he did, Garett had no one except Flora."

Mum and Dad lead us to the pub next to the cookery school.

"Mum, this is trespassing," Jem hisses as we approach the door where Garett and I sneaked in the week before.

"Oh shush, Jem, you're the worst badass ever," Mum replies with a grin. Dad holds the door open, and we step through.

"Do you love him, Ruby?" Kath asks.

I remember all those nights when he showed me how to cook, the looks he gave me when I achieved something new, and how he was there for me when I couldn't get out of my own head. He took me for a walk, and we ended up here. I consider all those times he didn't force a relationship even though a part of me suspected that's what he was hoping for. I lied to him, too, just not in the same way. I pretended we didn't have a future when I could have sat down and spoken to my parents rather than hide from the impact of my past. He was always about me, and I ignored him.

"Yes," I reply.

"Welcome to your Christmas present, kids," Mum announces from the restaurant part of the pub.

"What?" Jem bellows.

"This is our new venture," Dad says. Jem freezes, and I sit on the nearest chair I can find. Wicksy leans against the table Garett pinned me on. Awkward. "We should have said sooner. Your mum and I are bored in retirement. We miss running something. The old owner came to us months ago and asked if we would buy the place, but we pretended we were happy gardening and going on trips."

"We were lying to each other because we thought the other person was happy," Mum adds before Dad continues. The subtext isn't lost on me.

"Even couples in long-term relationships sometimes lie when they think they should. And we'll learn from that. When you're in a relationship, you're always learning, making mistakes, and trying not to make them again."

"Ruby gets it, Dad. Move on," Amber grumbles.

"Anyway, we decided to buy the pub with the help of some investors. Didn't we, Kath?"

Kath offers a wide smile. "I have a lot of savings, and I've always wanted to invest in something."

"We hoped Garett would run the restaurant and be one of the partners. We'd manage it for the first couple of years, and then it's up to Ruby and Jem. That's if you want it. Kath would also move from the cookery school to the restaurant, and Ruby, you'd lead the sessions at the cookery school, with Wicksy working as head kitchen assistant. Kalen and Amber would manage the school when they could, and me and your mum would step in when needed."

"And me?" Flora asks, although she does it so quietly that we'd have missed it if we hadn't been silent.

Kath takes Flora's hands. "Flora, honey, you can work in the cookery school or the restaurant. You believe you're not good at things, but you'd be brilliant as a party planner, project manager, or workshop leader."

"Don't forget dog napper," Jem adds, and Flora chuckles. It's like when Garett gives out prizes at the end of a children's cookery session and the shy child realises they have value. I wish Flora could see what we do.

Mum laughs, too. "How could any of us forget that?"

"I do have a plan for you, Flora, but first, I want to see what you do and enjoy. How would you feel shadowing me and Ruby at the cookery school and the restaurant?" Kath asks.

Flora smiles. "Yes, please. I'd love that." Tears brim my eyes. This side of Flora makes my heart break. She's not had anyone but Garett on her side for a long time. "And I'd like to pay the money needed for Garett to be a partner. I have a big trust fund."

"Garett doesn't need to pay anything," Dad replies. "We want him on the books from day one."

"I hate to be a dick," Jem pipes up.

"No, you don't," Amber and I reply together before

high-fiving. Jem gives us each a middle finger, and I'm reminded how much I adore my family.

Jem continues, "But Ruby kicked Garett out because she's a..."

Mum cuts him off with one raised eyebrowed look.

My punk-ass brother is always there to remind me how quickly you can go from loving your family to wanting to kill them.

"Anyway," he says, "he's also leaving because Mum and Dad took too long to tell him about the restaurant."

"Hey," Dad replies with his hands in the air. "We only signed the contract today."

"I wish I'd known. I'd have stopped him," Amber replies.

"He'd want to know. He had such a vision for this place," I murmur. "We came here the other night, and he was so alive after seeing it. He was hyped up."

"Did you do anything else while you were here?" Jem asks, his face pinched. Only he'd ask.

My face heats as I stare at where Wicksy leans against the table, and everyone looks at him, too.

"Ew," Wicksy cries before running to the other side of the room.

"Hold on," I say, desperately trying to distract everyone. "Amber didn't know about this, so why was she worrying about money?"

"I've been planning a Christmas present for you that would mean you wouldn't have to work with Clive. It wouldn't surprise me if Garett knew you'd be safe even when—"

"If," I cut in.

"Even *when* you win tomorrow," she continues. "I

want to give you money to start your own business. There'd be no business partners to betray you. This is just you, starting Ruby Cloud's Treats or whatever you want to call it. You could build it around doing sessions at the cookery school."

"And link it with the puddings at the restaurant," Mum cries, clapping her hands. "If Garett is happy with that."

I rush to cuddle my sister, although it's tricky getting my arms around her. Mum hugs us, too, and soon, it's a giant family group hug that even Cookie tries to get in on.

"You guys are ignoring key details. How you've ever run a cookery school is beyond me," Jem says, muffled against my back. "Garett is leaving, and he's not your biggest fan anymore, Ruby."

Everyone's grumbles become an orchestra of noise.

"I have a plan," I say, but it's drowned out because everyone speaks simultaneously.

Suddenly, Kalen bangs the pan, and everyone freezes, looking at Mum, who shrugs.

"Ruby has something important to say," Kalen says.

I give him a quick hug. "Thank you. I have a plan to get Garett back and get some retribution for him, too. But I'll need everyone's help, and it's a risk. It will take something big, and I might have hurt him too much, so it might not work. Are you in?"

For a second, I hold my breath. We're good at talking in my family, but are they willing to take a risk for Garett?

One by one, they put their hands out and shout, "I'm in," as if we were a basketball team preparing for a big game. But because it's my family and we're not in a circle, we look like a poorly organised kid's dodgeball team.

CHAPTER FORTY-EIGHT – GARETT

What is it about wearing sweats and eating cookie dough ice cream out of a cardboard tub that screams break-up?

But we weren't dating, so I can't call it a break-up.

I should be packing, but I'm watching *Love Actually* because a kitchen assistant I slept with and then didn't want to date once told me that I needed to watch this film at least ten times. She said that if I were to understand the level of heartbreak I cause in all the women I've never wanted a relationship with, then Alan Rickman and Emma Thompson would do it. So far, I've learnt that Martine McCutcheon is bloody gorgeous and that the early 2000s had offensive views on curvy women. Oh, and that Hugh Grant will always be the most attractive English man. After me, of course.

A sob builds in my chest as Colin Firth declares his love for a woman with whom he's never had a proper conversation. For all he knows, she could have a collection of dead men's toenails, but sure, she looks good when she jumps into a lake semi-nude to rescue his book, so of course, he wants to give up everything he knows.

Ruby would say it's love, and so, of course, he gives everything up. No, Ruby would say that she'd prefer Hugh Grant. She has good taste and likes her men funny.

I laugh as a tear springs free and runs down my face.

My ice cream–covered spoon slips out of my fingers and into my lap. I scoop the spilt ice cream up with my fingers and toss what hasn't melted into my mouth. I look like I'm wearing cum joggers.

Several bangs on my front door have me jumping up. Everyone should be at Clive's Christmas Eve competition watching Ruby smash it..

The door bangs again. It's like an entire police force is at my door.

I peek through the peephole.

"I know you're staring at me," Flora shouts. "Open the door. I need you, and Ruby needs you."

I yank open the door.

"What do—"

"Shit, Garett. Are you crying and wanking over *Love Actually*?" She looks between my ice cream–covered crotch and the television.

"No," I grunt with my hands in surrender, but she's winking at me. "What do you want, Flora? I'm packing."

She grabs my ice cream tub and inspects it. It's nearly empty. "Busy as a bee, aren't ya?"

I huff my response as I take the tub from her and finish it before tossing the spoon in the sink. At least I won't need to live in this awful bedsit. I'll earn money in Ireland and live above the restaurant.

Flora pokes me in the back. "Hey, Earth to Garett."

I round on her. "Whatever this is, hurry up. I've already walked and wept as I said goodbye to Cookie." I also left the house keys with a thank you card on the table of the empty house. There's been too many tears today. "But I still need to pack and then drop the van off at the cookery school before the family comes back from the competition. I don't want to see them."

"You don't want to see Ruby," she says as I pretend to pack. She follows me around the room. I don't have enough to fill two suitcases and a couple of extra bags. Before the Cloud family came along, I worked until I dropped, and that's precisely what I'll do when I get to Ireland. It's the only way to stop replaying every moment I spent with Ruby. "Admit it."

I pick up one of the wooden spoons Ruby gave me. Her grandad handcrafted it. It sits next to a present she left in the van when the family set up for the Cloudburst Christmas Meal. It says not to open until Ireland.

"Sure, whatever. It doesn't matter anyway. She doesn't want me near her because of my lies. I can't change that, so the sooner I'm out of here, the better." I turn the wrapped box over in my hand.

"She needs you right now."

I ignore Flora as I shake the box. I turn it over. The words "fragile" cover one side. Whoops. In the movie, a kid runs through an airport. Someone should be arresting him. I rip open the wrapping. I blame the kid for making me angry.

"What is it?" Flora asks, but I'm busy opening the box and pushing the tissue paper to the sides. Flora looks over my shoulder. "It's a bowl."

But it's not any bowl. It's nearly identical to the one I decorated and gave to Ruby at her sister's party. It has the Ruby artistic flare that mine didn't. There's a reason why she was always better at decorating cakes. A note sits inside the bowl. I gently place the bowl on the countertop, fearing it will explode like my never-happened relationship.

Garett, you weren't meant to open this until Ireland.

You cheated and did it early.

I chuckle. I'm a control freak like every chef, and I don't like surprises.

It was meant to be a Christmas present, but you can take it to Ireland now. I know we couldn't be together because of circumstances, including my need to protect my family—like Romeo and Juliet without the ridiculous and unnecessary deaths. I want you to have this so that wherever you are, you'll remember me every day that you eat breakfast and when you remember to put ice cream in a bowl rather than eat it from the tub.

I glance over my shoulder as if she's behind me, but it's Flora peeking at the note.

You gave me happiness I didn't know I deserved. You think you're grumpy and that no one wants to be around you, but every second I've spent with you, except the first day we met when you were a dick, has proved that you're a baked Alaska—hard on the outside and soft and squidgy on the inside, and everyone loves ice cream and meringue. I'm sorry we don't have a future, but don't forget we had a past. It was the best two and a half months of my life. Now don't break this bowl, or I'll come over to Ireland and kick your ass. You know I can.
Lots of love, your Rubes.
P.S. My grandparents would have loved you, and they were the best judges of character.

The note leaves me numb. I wanted her to tell me that she was in love with me. Even now, I'm trying to control her emotions. Isn't that what got us into this situation in the first place, me trying to control her? I shake my head.

"Don't you dare act like that message meant nothing," Flora says, poking me again.

I step back, knocking the bowl. It rocks and nearly falls off the countertop, but I grab it and hold it tight.

"That was close," I gasp, holding the bowl against my chest. "I thought it was a goner."

"The bowl is not Ruby," Flora says with a roll of her eyes.

"I know that."

"Good. Her note was lovely." I glare at Flora. She shouldn't have read it. "And she wants to be with you and loves you."

"It didn't say either of those things," I snap, walking to the other side of the room with the bowl still clutched against my chest.

"It said you're not grumpy, and I'm struggling to believe that right now."

"What are you doing here, Flora? I have to get on, and forcing me to confront my failures isn't helping."

She starts grabbing my keys and my jacket. "You need to come with me. I overheard Clive say he'd do something to Ruby and her family at the competition. They're livestreaming it. He said he's certain the family helped with Cookie and he was livid that they ignored him and employed you. He told someone on the phone that he'd destroy Ruby's reputation in the cookery world and steal her ideas. He aims to terminate the cookery school and take the whole family down. And before you argue, the family asked me to get you, so you're not really going against Ruby's wishes."

"Why didn't you say?"

I got her into this mess, and I'm the only one who can save her. Not that I know how. I shove my feet in my boots and grab my phone and wallet as I head for the door.

"You're not going in cum trousers," Flora says, riffling through my stuff and throwing a pair of jeans at me. "You can change in the car. I'm driving."

Credits roll on *Love Actually* as I turn the television off. I bet Hugh Grant's never changed in a car or been caught in cum trousers. Actually, if anyone has, then it's him. And he'd try and rescue his woman, too, even if it made her angry.

I will not let anything happen to Ruby or the cookery school.

No one hurts my family.

CHAPTER FORTY-NINE – RUBY

"**T**his is your ten-minute warning," Clive's lackey shouts. I glance at where my entire family, including Kath and Wicksy, sits. The only people missing are Flora and Garett. Maybe she couldn't convince him I needed him, or perhaps everything I said yesterday ruined anything he might have felt for me.

I'm still annoyed that he lied, and if we're to have a future, I need to talk with him about that, but I love him. I'm sure he wanted me to have the things I said I needed, although he went about it the wrong way.

But if he's not coming, all this deliberating is pointless because it means he doesn't want me.

"Don't lose focus, Ruby Cloud," Clive says over my shoulder. "We can't have daydreamers working in a kitchen."

He's inches away from me, breathing on my neck. He rests his hand on mine. Throughout the competition, he's perved on the younger women. I couldn't work for him even if I didn't know how he treated Garett and Cookie. He's proved he's a misogynistic pig over the last couple of hours. The men get different comments, but they're equally disparaging. When he's not creeping out the contestants, he's doing what he can to ramp up their anxiety while crushing their confidence. He's the polar opposite of Garett.

Maybe four months ago, when I was at my lowest with Neil and Viv, I'd have done anything to work for Clive, but I have self-worth and belief in my abilities now. He doesn't deserve me or my skills.

Suddenly, he snarls next to me. Flora slides into the row with my family, and she's not alone.

"What the hell is that joker doing here?" Anger radiates from him. Clive might act like nothing can harm him, but it's clear that Garett lives rent-free in his head. I hide my smirk.

"Five minutes," Clive roars right next to my ear, and I fake a flinch. He needs to underestimate me and think he's better than me.

Garett stares at me, but I pretend not to notice. Clive can't guess that there's something between Garett and me.

Clive joins Barry Barringer, a baking YouTuber with a massive following, in front of the camera. They're both leading the show today. Barry updates the viewers that there are two minutes to go before the timer is up.

Clive sneers. "Cooking fans at home, we have a former chef in our midst. This fool used to work for me."

I bite my tongue, although the voice in my head screams, *With. He worked with you. You're nothing compared to him.* Instead, I finish the flowers on my cake.

Clive instructs the cameraman to focus on where Garett sits. He's between my mum and Amber, as planned. Clive wouldn't humiliate a pregnant woman on screen. "Look at this guy, cookery fans, it's like he's got a bouncer on either side of him, although those aren't bouncers but the people who own the Cloud Cookery School here in the Cotswolds. The man you're looking at is Garett Kelsey. He'll have you believe he's a chef with great skill, but he's a fraud, which is why no one but these two will employ him."

I taste blood from biting my lip. He's publicly ridiculing my family. But instead of shying away, my mum and sister wave. My whole family are waving until the camera pans away. My mum sticks up her middle finger at Clive.

My dad tries to lower my mum's still high finger, but she slaps him away as Garett stares at them, wide-eyed. Kath chuckles.

"Time's up," Clive hollers, "all of you. We don't want any cheating here." He points at me. I duck my head as if embarrassed, but I don't really care because it means my mum has got to him.

One by one, the contestants go to the table where Barry stands next to Clive. The piece of shit sits on a goddamn throne. How does his giant head fit through any doorway?

Every contestant receives insults hidden behind faux recommendations for improvement. He flirts pitifully with the younger women and asks the better cooks what ingredients they used or techniques they employed. He'll steal their ideas like he stole Garett's.

We're on the last but one contestant. I'm last, which was carefully engineered by Jem. He used to date one of the staff members on the show, and they owed him a favour.

The contestant Clive judges dramatically throws her hands in the air before shimmying to the camera. I wouldn't have expected any less of Betty. Our friendship has come a long way since I stabbed myself in front of her in my first cookery class. Now, she and Kath meet fortnightly for coffee and to share baking ideas. Kath has primed her to lay the compliments on thick to lower Clive's guard. She'll be a great addition to the Cloud restaurant, cookery school, and treats businesses. I can't wait to offer her a job on the team.

Betty trips and "accidentally" drops her cake into Clive's lap. Barry laughs awkwardly as Clive jumps up, barely holding onto his anger in front of the camera. Amidst the commotion, Dad walks Garett down to wait in the wings with Jem and the floor manager, and I swap my apron for the one I've hidden in my ingredients basket. This whole thing is unnecessarily complicated, but I needed to ensure all my family had a role in the plan, or they'd try to get involved and mess it up. Wicksy's job was to smile throughout the whole thing, and he's doing brilliantly, bless him.

Based on my performance, Clive presumes I'm stupid and lacking confidence. I tiptoe to his throne in my special apron with Clive's branding on a Velcro patch. Later, I'll remove it to reveal the Cloud Cookery School logo emblazoned on the front. Kath stayed up all night to make me a special one.

"Right. Ruby Cloud, it's your turn to wow me, although, with your pedantry techniques, it's unlikely," Clive says. He creepily keeps using my full name, but I've never been more proud to be a Cloud, so although I drop my head in a fake demonstration of my shyness, my heart jumps.

I glance briefly in the wings. Garett grinds his teeth, and Dad chats to him like he's coaching a football team. I falter and nearly trip, which isn't part of the plan. Seeing him properly for the first time since I raged at him hits me hard. I love Garett. I actually love him. When I look at Garett, I want to run into his arms and tell him about the plans for today and the future. I want to make him smile and bring that joy he needs. I want to get that ice cream middle out of him. I want to hear how he says my name and all the faces he makes when he does. I want him to know I love him.

Get it together, Ruby. This isn't the time.

Clive cuts a massive slice of my tiered cake, and Barry commentates. Garett furrows his brow. This isn't what we agreed on me baking for the competition.

It's a simple cake with a basic frosting, although I've decorated the hell of it so that Clive doesn't clock that I'm deceiving him. He must eat the sponge.

He shoves his fork into the sponge. "I expected better from you, missy, although I'm not sure why, as you're from the Cloud Cookery School." He laughs to himself. My red face is from anger, not shame.

He lifts his fork closer to his mouth. *That's right, take a big fucking bite, you bastard.* He shoves the chunk of cake into his mouth.

Choke on it.

And then he does.

CHAPTER FIFTY – RUBY

Clive coughs, splutters, and shouts all at once. I cover my face as if I'm shocked, but it's to prevent me from revealing my smile.

"Oh my god, are you okay?" I squeal, my body trembling.

He gulps down water. His face is bright red, and his eyes bore into me, but he can't get under my flesh, although my petrified stare suggests otherwise. "What did you do to that cake?"

I know his reactions before he does. The first is shock about how gross the cake tastes, but I'm holding out for the second reaction.

He gags, and I shake violently as if I put my heart and soul into every crumb. Technically, I put my love for Garett into it.

"I made it to the recipe," I stutter. The exact recipe.

Now comes the aftertaste.

His eyes are wide, and he presses his lips together.

Boom.

"Is everything okay?" I ask as he takes another bite. The two cameras are fixed on this moment. Everyone in the audience is silent as the scene unfolds. Garett whispers to my dad. I can lip-read Dad's reply. *Just wait, champ.*

Clive's eyes pinch, and his tongue moves around his mouth, pressing his cheeks out occasionally. "Clive, I'm so sorry if I did something wrong," I say. Every pathetic moment in my relationship with Neil helped me create that confused, sad voice.

"What is in this cake? Specifically, what ingredients?" he snarls at me.

"Self-raising flour, milk, softened butter, eggs, a little baking powder, sugar—caster sugar." I reel off the ingredients while ticking the things off my fingers. I do it slowly as if I'm confused. It will annoy him further. I know what he wants, but he doesn't realise that yet. "I used muscovado sugar once. That was a big mistake."

I laugh, but he doesn't laugh with me. Betty and a couple of the other bakers do, though. They know what a mistake that would be.

He taps his fork hard and repeatedly against the countertop until the floor manager waves his arms. He sneers, "And what else?"

"Ummm." I tap my fingers against my chin. Clive's face gets redder. "Good question. Oh yes." He raises his eyebrows. "There's buttercream, too, and all the decorations. So we have softened butter. I've used so much of that when practising. Icing sugar, vanilla extract. Everyone in my family loved my preparation for this competition, including my boyfriend, who is a chef. He's called Garett. You might know him. He's outstanding. Anyway then, for the decoration we have—"

"Stop," he roars. The filming crew wave their arms and rush around behind the cameras. Clive is meant to be less nasty than Gordon Ramsay but fiercer than Martha Stewart. I gasp as if scared. I want to bring this man down.

Barry smiles awkwardly at the audience, but Clive hasn't finished ranting. "Your boyfriend is Garett Kelsey?"

I nod. I suck my lips into my mouth and make my eyes wide like I'm an innocent young woman. "He helped me with a few bits. I hope that's not cheating."

"Did he give you ingredient ideas? I meant the ingredients you haven't mentioned yet, the ones that have given your cake its... unique flavour." He presses me with his questions.

I smile broadly. "Yes, he did. He's so good to me. I don't deserve him."

Clive's jaw hardens. I laugh but cover it with a fake sneeze. "Sorry, Clive. Allergies." Allergies to massive shitheads.

"And what ingredients make your unique flavours?" He nears me, and I step back as if worried. Again, the filming crew shake their heads. He can't be seen bullying a lovely baking contestant.

"That's a good question." I tip my head to the side. "It's a really good question."

Time ticks by slowly. His body shakes beside me with increasing anger.

"Answer me, then!"

I hold my tongue as someone from the filming crew rushes to him and says in his ear loudly, "Maybe we should announce the winner."

He pushes the staff member hard enough to make the audience murmur.

"Not yet. I need to know what's in this cake."

And that's when I land my blow. "You should know. They're the same ingredients from 'your' famous pasta recipe," I counter, "the one you haven't made since you won that competition."

The crowd gasps, led by my mum, Kath, Amber, Wicksy, and Kalen. They're loud and attention-seeking, and everyone joins in.

Clive fists his hands. "I'm aware. You've stolen my secret ingredient."

"That's impossible, Clive. How would I know it? They're your secret ingredients"—I emphasise the plural—"that you famously said you never told anyone."

"But I—"

I turn from confusion to confrontation. "So what is in the cake? If you don't tell everyone, then I will. Why haven't you made any pasta since the competition?"

He stutters before snapping, "I haven't been able to source the ingredients. They're hard to get hold of."

"That's weird because I bought them from the local supermarket. Try again. Why haven't you made it since?"

He bashes his fist on the table. "Tell me what the ingredients are."

"Clive, why are you so angry? You must know," Barry Barringer replies. "Whisper them to me, and I'll get Ruby to whisper, too, and I'll tell you if they match."

"I can't," he snaps.

"Why not?" An unsuspecting Barry does my job for me.

Clive looks around. His eyes are wild. "Maybe we should cut to something else."

"That's not how livestreaming works, Clive."

"Tell them, Clive," I say slowly. "Tell them why you can't reveal the ingredients, or I will."

Clive looks set to run off, but that's when Dad and Garett walk on. They stand on either side of him.

My family in the audience start the chant, "Tell us. Tell

us. Tell us" Soon, the audience roars the words while the cameras film. A staff member whispers that the number of viewers are going up and up.

Barry silences the crowd with his raised hand. "Maybe you should tell us what this is all about," he says, turning to me.

I don't miss a beat. "For this year's Cotswold's Best Restaurant, Garett Kelsey made a special pasta dish with his secret ingredients." Barry tries to jump in, but I shake my head. "As soon as it went to judging, Clive Macdonald ditched Garett. They'd developed the restaurant together, but for reasons I won't share, Garett wasn't on the deeds. Once he'd ousted Garett from the restaurant, Clive threatened every restaurant, eatery, and cooking school in the area with ruin if they employed him. The Cloud Cookery School doesn't respond to the threats of bullies, so he's run sessions at our cookery school ever since. He's made pasta and bread using the secret ingredients at school. I used them in the cake today to show what a fraud Clive is. Clive can't distinguish what they are because he never knew."

Barry rounds on Clive. "Is this true?"

"Clive also stole Garett's dog, Cookie, the face of the restaurant, and sent cruel messages to Garett. He treated Cookie badly, but we rescued him," I add.

The audience shouts in disgust.

Clive bellows, "You took him?"

"We rescued him," a member of the audience hollers. Red hair flies as she runs down the stairs to stand in front of the camera.

Barry's eyelids flicker. "Who are you?"

"I'm Clive's sister. Everything Ruby said is true. My brother is a nasty piece of work. I've tried to give him the benefit of the doubt, but I can't anymore. Do you know that he now employs the prettiest inexperienced women in his restaurant and then tries it on with them even though he already has trained and experienced staff?"

The audience gasps.

My sister yells, "Oh my God. He's a dog-stealing misogynist."

"And he's stolen someone else's hard work. He's the worst. I'd hate to eat his food. I bet it tastes of lies," my mum shouts.

It's all I can do not to laugh. There's no one like a Cloud woman.

"Everyone, calm down. There's one key person we haven't heard from. Garett Kelsey, I recognise you," Barry says, turning to Garett, who works his jaw like he's trying to destroy his teeth. I slip a piece of gum out of my pocket and pass it to him. His stare is all knotted eyebrows and twisted lips. I'm not surprised. I angrily blasted him out of the cookery school the last time I spoke to him. "You're an amazing chef. I still remember the focaccia starter you made at a restaurant two years ago. I asked for extra to take home."

"You should taste this." I tip my head at Mum, who rushes down with a Tupperware box.

"I'm a big fan, Barry. Massive. If I weren't married, I'd want your number," Mum says with a wink.

"Mum, get back up the stairs," I hiss.

She winks at Barry. "I'll look you up if anything happens to my man."

Amber moans, "Mum." Kath chuckles, and Dad shrugs.

"Anyway, I'm afraid this is a day old, but we've tried to keep it fresh." I pass Barry some of the bread that Garett brought to our Christmas meal yesterday. "While you enjoy it, Garett can fill you in."

Barry pulls a bit off the remaining loaf and pops it into his mouth. His loud moan echoes around us. "That's bloody gorgeous."

I nudge Garett. "Tell him what happened."

As Barry stuffs more of the bread in his mouth, Garett tells him and the cameras everything that Clive did. It's honest and raw, and I want to pull him into my arms. To my surprise, he also explains why his credit was so low. The Garett who had more barriers than an army base is now so beautifully open that I find tears slipping down my cheeks. I push them away, shaking my head. He sees though. Of course he does.

"Every story needs a hero, and you're ours," Barry says, returning to the camera.

"The Cloud family are your real heroes. They were the only ones who gave me a chance, and they welcomed me like no one ever has. Clive's sister, Flora, is also an honorary Cloud family member."

"Then let's bring them all down."

CHAPTER FIFTY-ONE – RUBY

The streaming continues as Barry beckons my entire family, including Kath and Wicksy, down the stairs. It's all my mum can do not to dance.

I pull Garett to the side.

"I'm sorry—" we say to each other simultaneously.

"Why are you sorry? I lied to you," he says.

"Because I didn't let you explain properly. I didn't see things from your side and shouldn't have jumped down your throat. You shouldn't have lied to me, but it's all learning, right?" I explain.

His eyes are wide as he processes what I've said. I take his hands in mine as he stutters, "So what now?"

As my family jostle each other in front of the camera, Barry grabs the last bite of the bread. "Is this made using your secret ingredients, Garett?" Kalen and Jem are flanking Clive. Let him watch what he tried to destroy.

Garett nods. "I'll let you know them if you'd like."

Barry twists his lips as he considers. "Maybe one day. I like not knowing and trying to guess."

"It took me nearly three months, being around him most days and falling in love with him, to guess the ingredients," I whisper to Barry.

"We have a love story, too?" Barry says with a laugh.

"So tell me, how can I get more of this bread?"

He pops it into his mouth as Garett stutters, but before he can form a sentence, my mum jumps in, "Garett will be head chef, partner, and one of the developers of Every Cloud restaurant, which will be here in the Cotswolds next to the Cloud Cookery School. It opens this summer. A rustic Italian perfect for families, tourists, and those who love excellent food. Every Cloud has a silver lining. No matter what day, the silver lining in your life will be Garett's food."

Bloody hell. My mother, always the businesswoman, hasn't even asked him. His eyebrows reach his hairline. "If you want to," I whisper. "But no expectations. Ireland waits for you."

He doesn't answer, and I try not to let sadness touch the corners of my lips.

My mum still makes the most of Barry's full mouth and continues her plug for the businesses. "The puddings will be made by my daughter, Ruby, a baker whose cakes will leave you desperate for more, which you can have because she will also run a mail-order brownie and cookie business from our Cloud Cookery School and Restaurant. Her company, Cloud Nine, will fill needs that other things can't."

Did I agree to that name? I adore it but still glare at my mum for railroading me. She's too good.

"There's so much love and fun here," Barry says.

"It's impossible not to love this family," Garett murmurs, reaching for my hand. He brushes his lips across my knuckles. "Especially this one. I fell in love with Ruby around the same time I fell in love with her baking. I expect she'll be running sessions at the cookery school if she can find the time, although she'll never make what she made today again."

I shiver as he kisses my hands. "That was just to right some wrongs."

"How did you work out my secret ingredients?" Garett asks me.

"When you weren't with me, I thought about you. I even dreamt about you. That's what it took to learn what went in your pasta," I say.

He understands instantly. One of the key ingredients was cinnamon, but so were raisins soaked in a particular orange drink that he would give Flora when she was bullied and fennel roasted with a sauce that smells similar to his mum's microwave-burnt pasta. There was also something that he sneaked into our picnic when we watched *Bake Off*. No one will ever guess these unless they listen to his stories and fall in love with him as I did.

Jem and someone from the crew gives out glasses of prosecco. Clive doesn't get one, obviously.

"Well, there you have it," Barry says to the camera in his sign-off. "We have a cancelled restauranteur, a love story, intrigue, passion, and secret ingredients, but at the heart of all this is a love of cooking and baking, which I can't resist. Have a lovely Christmas from me and the Cloud family." He holds up his glass, and all my family hold theirs up, too. "Cheers."

"And we're out," Jem's friend says and whispers something to Barry.

Barry turns to us with a beaming smile. "Thank you, everyone. We got more hits on that than anything we've ever done. Once the New Year is over, you'll hear from me. I'd love to feature your cookery school, Every Cloud restaurant, and Ruby's Cloud Nine in several videos. Maybe we can come to classes and film the opening. Thank you for everything." He points at Clive. "Clive, a word."

"I need to speak to Garett," I say to my family as Garett and I walk to the corner of the room. I turn at the footsteps behind us. Their faces, a mixture of wide eyes, smiles, and furrowed brows, look back at me. "Alone."

They all grumble as they walk to the seats in the audience.

I pull Garett around a corner. "I need to know, are you still moving to Ireland? I'll understand if you are, and whether you stay or go, we don't have to be together if you don't want and—" Garett presses his finger to my lips.

"Rubes, did you hear me say I fell in love with you earlier?" I nod. "Your dad told me that he knows about us, and nearly nothing would make him happier than us dating except the safe birth of his two imminent grandchildren."

I grin.

Garett continues, "If you'll have me, I want to try the boyfriend and girlfriend thing. I want to be an annoying couple who make out in public and laugh at the weirdness of strangers. I'll be grumpy, and you'll be more sunshiney than a freaking Barbados holiday, but I want to try what this relationship thing is. I used to fear relationships and thought that work would always come first, but you come first for me, Rubes." I giggle, and he huffs. "That was not meant to be an innuendo."

I push my tongue out of my mouth—his finger tastes of cinnamon, orange, and other secret ingredients.

"When did you touch my cake?" I say, my words muffled behind his finger.

"I needed to taste what was so awful. It was hideous," he grumbles. "I'm annoyed at all the hours I wasted on your baking."

I lick his finger and wince. He's got a point.

"Stop distracting me. I'm trying to tell you that I love you and want to be with you," he says as he chews the gum I gave him.

"I love you, Garett. You're everything I've always needed and so much more. I thought I knew what love was, but then I met you, the grumpiest chef of all time, and I learnt what it is to be respected, valued, and wanted. You make me laugh, you make me cry, and you make me come like I didn't know was possible. And you like my family."

"I love your family."

"Stop distracting me. I'm trying to tell you that I love you and want to be with you," I reply, using his words while grinning.

Garett picks me up and spins me while laughing. "I love you, Ruby Cloud." He presses his lips to mine.

"I love you, too, my number one chef," I say. His lips are soft, and he tastes like those special ingredients.

"I won't tell Mary Berry if you won't."

"Deal," I manage before his tongue presses my lips apart. I wrap my legs around him.

A round of applause stalls our kisses.

"Rubes, your family is giving us a standing ovation," he whispers against my lips.

I peek over his shoulder to find my entire family, including Flora, Kath, and Wicksy, cheering us on and clapping. Kath winks and grins. It wouldn't surprise me if she engineered the snow that brought us together in the first place.

"Could you guys not?" I shout as Garett lowers me to the ground.

"Champ is our family now, too," Dad says.

There's a weird moaning. We all stare at Kalen and Amber. "I hate to break this beautiful moment up, but Amber is, um, needing a hospital."

Everyone freezes.

Amber holds out her hands. "The excitement and the love story—"

"And the curry you ate for breakfast," Kalen adds.

"I told you not to say," she hisses and Kalen blushes. "The love story inspired the babies. We need to get to the hospital."

Suddenly, Jem runs around shouting that he needs a phone while Flora points at the one in his hand. Wicksy screams that he doesn't want to see a birth while Mum asks the sound man for hot towels, and Dad tells Barry what names he wants to give the twins. Meanwhile, Kath and Kalen are helping Amber out of the side door that leads to the car park.

Garett turns to me. "Your family—"

"Shouldn't be allowed out in public?" I offer with a shrug.

"Your family and Flora are the third best things to happen in my life after you and Cookie." He kisses me on the cheek and takes my hand as we slip out the side door, following my sister. It looks like it will be a hospital Cloud Christmas this year. Those poor nurses.

EPILOGUE – GARETT

"Are you ready for the soft opening?" Ruby asks. She's wearing a sky blue cowl neck dress that cinches at the waist with a knot before dropping to her knees. It lifts up and off with just a pull of a knot. We worked that out when she tried it on last night. Her skin is bronzed from the fake tan she said she needed for opening day confidence. It makes her blond waves glow even more ethereal than usual, especially when naked.

Focus, Garett .

"Rubes, I've told you before that it's called a soft launch," I reply as I run through the jobs I need to finish before friends and family come for our trial night. The big opening night is tomorrow.

Ruby sidles up to me and pulls me down to her mouth by my blue tie. "But doesn't a soft opening sound sexier? I bet you'd love to touch my—"

"Put the poor man down," Amber says as she enters the dining area. Kalen and Iain follow behind, each with a six-month-old baby strapped to them. Amber officially takes over the cookery school tomorrow, at which point Ruby will permanently run her Cloud Nine business and oversee puddings here at the restaurant while doing the occasional class.

Jem ensures all the menus are at the front desk.

"This restaurant was the making of him, wasn't it?" I whisper.

Ruby smiles, her eyes shining with pride.

"Don't start crying again," Jem hollers. "Every time you see me working hard, you and Mum cry."

"Maybe Mum is still dealing with the trauma of finding out you dropped out of university and spent all the tuition money when you didn't go to lectures," Amber retorts.

Luckily, I grew up in noisy, angry kitchens, because the Cloud family resemble a Gordon Ramsay cookery show.

"Whatever. Now, one of you sort out the lights up there. Some of us are too busy working to chat and kiss." Jem glares at Ruby, and she winks back at him.

"Sorry, no one wants to kiss you, baby brother."

He glares as he continues sorting things. Jem is so quiet about his love life that none of us know what's going on. I thought he might date Flora, but nothing is happening with them.

"Leave your brother alone," Liz calls as she bustles around the room, trying to change our agreed-upon layout.

"Liz," I warn. "Put the cutlery down."

She side-eyes me and slowly lowers the fork. I continue to watch her until she steps away from the table.

Iain must sense she's going to continue to change things as he hands her one of Amber and Kalen's twins, saying, "You take Iris while I help with the lights." She was named after Ruby's grandma. You can imagine the tears in the family when that was announced. The other baby was called Holly because it was the first thing Kalen saw after the babies were born. That will happen on Christmas Day. I bit my tongue and whispered later to Ruby that it was lucky there was no mistletoe or baubles on the ceiling, as they could have named their daughters Toe and Balls. I got a punch and a laugh for that. Totally worth it.

"We're nearly ready," Kath announces, bringing in Chrissy from Clive's former restaurant. All the staff who worked with me there are now part of Every Cloud.

All the wishes I didn't let myself have when I was kicked out and extra ones I never imagined have come to fruition. Ruby pretends to put her hair in a bun but then lets it drop like ribbons of gold. She winks at me. The woman is non-stop teasing, and I can't get enough of it.

"Stop flirting," Jem shouts again. I can't do anything without this entire family seeing. Well, nearly nothing. I'm on a promise for a soft launch celebration with Ruby in the hideaway later. We've sneaked there several times since the snowy night and always with a cheese board. She brings her own cakes for pudding.

"Can I come in? I've got Cookie," Flora says, pushing through the main door. He runs between me and Ruby before settling down next to Flora. We're allowing him to be part of the soft launch. He's been part of the journey, although he's not the face of a restaurant now. He's just Cookie. "Barry is setting up his camera to film a piece outside. He mentioned Clive."

"Have you heard from him?" Liz asks.

As much as she couldn't stand the guy and told him to "go 'cook' himself," she told me during one Cloud Burst that she wanted him to change his ways rather than suffer forever. Then Iain called her a liar and it ended in a jovial argument. That's how most Cloud Bursts end. I love them.

"Yeah," Flora replies, bending down to stroke Cookie. "He's travelling. He messaged me before he left for a monastery in Thailand. He's trying to find himself and work on not being the bad guy in every story. We'll see. He said he was proud of me. He knows I was shadowing Ruby and that I'll run the children's parties and cookery school with Amber."

Liz hugs Flora. "As he should be. We're all proud of you. You've made such a difference already, and there's so much potential for other things, too."

Flora's grin reminds me of the day I first complimented her. She didn't have enough positive role models until this last year. She's doing great things, although she confessed to me privately that she's still not found her passion.

I glance around the room. The family and workers surround me. Now's the moment.

"Ready?" Kalen asks. I nod at him and tip my head to Jem, who points at Iain and nods. All the Cloud men have helped me with this.

Iain hits the fairy lights, and Jem turns off the main ones. Flora passes me the dessert I prepared that morning.

Ruby catches the movement. Her brows are low in a glare.

"Rubes," I say, getting on one knee. Everyone turns to stare. There are gasps and smiles, but all I see is the beauty in front of me. "From the moment I first saw your bleeding hand and nearly lost my shit—"

"Nearly?" Ruby cuts in.

"Shush, Ruby," Liz says. "Let him do this."

"You shush," Iain says.

I raise my hand before it descends into another family tussle.

"From that moment, I had to know more about you. Every second I've spent with you since has shown me that I was missing significant light from my life. You brought this cheeky sunshine that I needed and wanted. No matter

353

what happens, whether we're a success or if I end up in another God-awful bedsit, I want you with me. Every cloud does have a silver lining, and you were mine at a time in my life when I thought I'd never see sunshine again."

Liz bends and stares at me. "I think you'll find we were all that silver lining, Garett."

"Mum, let him finish," Jem crows.

"Your whole family changed my life. This means that there is no chance for me to get rid of them. But I love them nearly as much as I love and adore you."

Iain makes a happy sigh.

"I'm saying, Rubes, will you eat my pudding? I made this crème brûlée just for you. It's called the Ruby Red." She eyes me suspiciously as she takes the teaspoon I offer her. "It's raspberry and white chocolate, but with one special secret ingredient."

"I'll never say no to one of your desserts, although can you not say 'eat my pudding' in front of my family because it gives me filthy ideas?"

"Ruby," Iain warns, and Amber laughs.

She cracks the sugar topping in one go—the spoon clinks against something.

"What did you do, Garett?" she asks, but she's struggling not to turn those beautiful lips into a smile. Using the end of the spoon, she hooks a silver ring that sparkles with rubies. "My grandma's?"

I nod. "She'll always be with us, and I'm sorry I didn't get to meet her, but this family is as much a part of our future as they are your past. I'm saying, Ruby, will you marry me?"

"I feel we should have given some sort of blessing," Liz comments.

"I already gave it," Iain replied.

"But he didn't ask me."

"Or me," Amber adds.

"I'm sorry, Liz and everyone," I say, although my focus is on Ruby, who still hasn't answered. Not that her family give her space to. "Can I have everyone's blessing as I know I'm never getting away from you?"

Liz grumbles.

"Not that I'd want to," I add with a smile.

"Yes," everyone says with a cheer.

"Now, everyone, quiet. The man is proposing," Kalen calls out, pointing at Amber, who closes her mouth instantly.

"Back to Ruby," I reply, staring at her as she worries her lip. Oh shit. She wishes I hadn't asked. "I'm sorry, Rubes. Shouldn't I have done it in front of your family? I know it's quick, but I—"

She kneels beside me, and Cookie crawls over to sit with us. She plants a kiss on my lips. "It's a yes. It's a billion yesses. Of course I love you and I will marry you, and you did everything right." She kisses me again, and everyone cheers once more. "But did you have to ruin a dessert to do it?"

I scoop a finger of crème brûlée as I remember all the times she's let me lick the bowl when she's finished icing cakes. "Open wide, baby," I say.

"Aren't we saving that for when we're in the hideaway?" she replies, making me blush and chuckle all at once.

"Enough of that, you two," Kath says. "Right, everyone. The soft launch is in thirty minutes for all our favourite cookery school clientele, so we need a meeting in the kitchen and then the last checks. Flora, take Cookie to

Garett's flat upstairs. Jem, do one last visual of the place settings. Liz, step away from the restaurant. I see you changing things. Staff will be in the kitchen in two minutes, and the rest of you get lost so we can welcome you all properly with an opening to remember. Tonight is about making mistakes and learning from them to improve the launch. And if anyone is good at learning from mistakes, it's you lot."

I kiss my future wife once more. "Good luck, Rubes."

"Good luck, you sexy, grumpy bastard."

And then a voice carries through the doorway. "Where is the famous Garett Kelsey?" Surely, it's not Mary Berry? It can't be.

THERE'S MORE...

I hope you enjoyed the first novel in my Cloud Family Series featuring the chaotic Cloud family and friends.

Sign up to my newsletter to get updates on my book releases, as well as access to giveaways and exclusive bonus content including a bonus scene between Garett and Ruby, which is free to everyone who signs up.

You can sign up via: https://tinyurl.com/Rebecca-Chase

Or via my website: www.rebeccahchase.com

In the meantime, keep reading for the Go Cook Yourself playlist and information x`about my previous books. There are also hints about the books I'm releasing in the next two years. And here's a peek of Regally Binding, an enemies-to-lovers bodyguard romance and the first book in my Closest Protection Series.

If you like spicy, humorous British romance with a bad boy book boyfriend then you need to give Bear a try.

REGALLY BINDING

CHAPTER ONE

Liss checked her mobile from under the bar as she wiped down the worn wood. Still no message from her latest Tinder match, although there was a breaking news notification about the Royal family. Liss swiped the notification away without reading it. She just wanted a response to the underwear picture it took all her courage to send. She shouldn't have done it, but she wanted to feel attractive and carefree and like her best friend, Isla, who wouldn't hesitate to send something like that.

"Have you heard from Hugo today? He's checking in a lot," Greg, the pub's regular, whose ear hair was longer than his eyelashes, said through a yawn before supping the head of his pint. His dog, Joyce, was propped on his knees, eyeballing Liss.

"Not yet," Liss replied with a shrug. Hugo, the pub's owner, used to be happy with Liss running the place, but now, there were rumours that he was selling the pub to a chain, which would leave Liss without a job.

"You could do better than this place, you know," Greg added, tipping his head in the direction of the two university students who were sucking face. "You could run a bar where your boss doesn't take credit for your ideas."

"A smile from you is worth the stuff I have to put up with," Liss said, her gaze flicking to her phone, where another breaking news notification flashed up. She swiped it away without reading it as Greg grunted. It was probably about the royal wedding happening later in the year.

Steve, one of Liss's closest friends and the pub's deputy manager, was making the most of the late morning lull, reading a newspaper while occasionally glancing at Liss above it. "Liss won't leave us. She always says this place is her family."

He had a point. It had been like her family since her mum died.

"We all know why you stay, Steve, even though you spend too much time judging the people who drink here," Greg grumbled as he fed Joyce bits of sausage. "Especially when your middle-class parents with upper-class judgements visit."

"I don't know what you mean," Steve retorted with a huff. But he did. Liss and Isla had spoken to him about it before. He grumbled that he could work in any city job.

Liss stared at her phone, willing the guy she'd sent an underwear pic to respond as she rejoined the conversation. "Why do you stay he—"

"No phones while working," Steve mumbled, cutting off Liss.

Liss dropped her grubby cloth onto the bar and glared. "I'm well aware. I was the one who came up with the rule."

"Who are you waiting to hear from?" Steve replied, dropping the paper and collecting glasses.

The one thing Liss refused to talk to Steve about was her dating life or, rather, lack thereof. He always got weird about it but never explained why. And besides, it was humiliating telling anyone that she'd messaged a sexy picture to a man she'd not yet met, and he hadn't replied. She tucked her phone in her pocket. "Oh, it's nothing—"

"BBC1! BBC1! Give me the remote, Liss!" Isla ran into the pub, saving Liss from the awkward conversation.

"Isla, chill." Liss paused at the till, pushing back strands of her brown hair before surrendering to the frizz and tying it into a ponytail. The humidity wasn't helping the frizz, nor were the hoodie and jeans she'd thrown on that morning.

Isla dived onto the bar and fumbled for the remote they kept near the tills.

"Isla, no." Liss slapped Isla's hand away and popped the remote into the back pocket of her jeans. This pub was her kingdom; not even her best friend controlled the television. "You have no say on the channel the pub is watching."

Isla did a dramatic look behind her. "You're the only one of the five people here who cares."

"We're fifteen minutes from the lunch crowd coming in, and they'll want to watch horse racing," Liss countered, hands on the curve of her hips. "Tell me what's so important, and I'll consider changing the channel."

Isla huffed before throwing her arms in the air.

Liss stood on the step behind the bar she used when she needed to meet customers' stares, which was tricky at her five-foot height. She eyeballed her bestie.

"Liss has more attitude than the King's corgi," Greg said with a chuckle.

He was kind of right. If you put her in front of anyone but her friends and punters, she turned into her latest date, running for the door with no intention of returning. But in the bar, she controlled her anxiety.

"The King, the actual King, is doing a live broadcast in two minutes," Isla ranted.

"And that's important because?" Liss wiped the bar with the damp and oddly smelling cloth. Maybe she should consider moving on, but this was the only place she'd worked since dropping out of university five years ago. And her only skills were pulling pints and cleaning toilets.

Joyce walked around the bar and sniffed the spilt beer on Liss's dirty Doc Martens. Even the scents from her mango moisturiser and vanilla and strawberry shower gel weren't strong enough to overwhelm the beer smell. Liss's raised eyebrows were enough to send the pup back to its owner, though not before Liss sneaked her a biscuit from her pocket.

"This never happens." Isla's leg bounced.

Liss moved around the bar and started moving chairs to prepare for the lunchtime rush. Isla followed her around the pub.

"Kings don't do live broadcasts," Isla continued. "Every year, he makes a Christmas speech that's filmed weeks before and has a carefully managed script. He doesn't do anything like this because it's not allowed. My media colleagues have messaged our networks for the last hour, and it's all over Instagram."

"So I'm asking again, why is this important?" Liss's voice echoed around the pub.

Steve collapsed into a chair and propped his feet up on a table, commentating, "The big fight resumes, Liss Granger in one corner and Isla Redding in the other."

Liss raised her eyebrow, and he dropped his feet to the floor.

"You don't have social media, so you don't get it. But this is massive. No one talks about the royals on social unless they're in court, doing something controversial, or getting married. The royal media team is streaming his announcement everywhere. This is epic. Please, Liss. I'll come to yours and do your washing up for a week," Isla begged.

The teenagers watched the action from their worn wooden chairs before resuming their kissing. Oh, to be that desperate for someone else that you didn't care about the shitty décor and bad furnishings. This pub needed work. If her mum were still around, she'd have helped Liss improve the place herself with little touches. But she wasn't and never would be again.

Liss shook her head and stepped closer to Isla, crossing her arms over her chest. "You don't do your own washing up."

"Fine. I'll cook for you for a week." This broadcast must have been significant. Isla's career, and climbing the ladder in the PR firm she'd joined out of university, were everything to her. Although they were best friends, they were painfully different. While Isla was conquering the PR world, Liss was still trying to find her purpose.

"A month," Steve called out.

"Shut up, you," Isla called back, swatting his presence away with her hand. "Please, Liss, I need to see this. It might help my career."

"And you can't watch it on your phone because...?" Liss stared at Isla, who was looking anywhere but at her.

Steve jumped in, "She's run out of data watching all those dodgy videos her Tinder dates send her.

"There's nothing dodgy about sexy videos, Steve. Stop being judgemental."

Liss winced. This wasn't the first time they'd had this argument. At least Isla was getting videos. No one sent Liss videos of what they'd want to do with her. But then again, she'd probably freak if they did. She had to focus on finding a good guy; that was what being around her lonely mum as a teenager had taught her.

"Fine." Liss switched to BBC1 and stood with Isla to get a good view of the television—anything to stop Steve and Isla from arguing. Isla hugged her tightly.

Her phone buzzed with a call as the announcer appeared. Surely, the guy she messaged wouldn't call. Still, she glanced at the phone screen with hope.

"I bet it's Nana Bets," Steve said, sidling up to Liss. Only Liss's two friends, work and her grandma called her, although her grandma only called when she wanted something. "Tell her I won employee of the month again."

Liss glared at him as she answered the phone. Hugo awarded Steve that honour every month. Hugo went to school with Steve's parents, although he denied that had anything to do with his choice.

"Hi, Nana. Is everything okay? I can't talk right now. The King is doing a live broadcast, and we're all watching," Liss whispered as Isla snatched the remote and increased the volume with exaggerated presses of the remote control.

"You can't watch that broadcast until you see me. Come outside," her grandma ordered. She had a lot of audacity for a woman who was usually swanning around the world visiting her former dancer friends. "I'm waiting in a Bentley."

"But—"

"No buts. Right now, Felicity," she snapped.

Liss winced before mumbling, "Everyone's so bloody demanding today. I don't like stressy people."

"And yet you're friends with us." Steve chuckled. His skin turned pink when she shot him a look.

Isla grabbed her hand giddily. Liss liked to see her pseudo family happy. They were the only family she had aside from her nana.

"Hello. I am sure this is a surprise for you all." The King stared into the camera, his chin raised in pride. There was that charisma the country loved.

"He looks a bit off. He should be wearing a tie," Steve mumbled.

Isla shushed him.

The way the King slouched slightly in a grey woolly jumper ticked the "break from protocol" boxes.

The King continued, "It's unprecedented for a monarch to speak to his country like this, and I realise you are all waiting to hear what I have to share. But first…"

"Felicity, you'd better not still be listening to the King. My only grandchild is usually so obedient when her poor grandma needs her," Nana Bets whined down the phone. Liss ground her teeth. Her nana's guilt-tripping tactics were legendary.

"Don't worry about the lunchtime rush," Greg said, understanding her reluctance. "Mr. Employee of the Month can cover it."

"I'm not doing toilets," Steve grumbled. Liss stared at the two of them. She always cleaned the toilets. Her job used to make her feel valued, but not recently.

Isla gasped. "The King is talking about abdicating in the future because he's unwell."

"And I have something further," the King continued. "I believed this would remain private my entire life, but I'm nearing death due to a complicated illness, and I must share something personal because it has implications for the country."

That one statement stopped the teenagers from kissing. They stared at the screen as people drifted through the doors, instantly drawn to the news.

"Felicity," her nana pressured.

"Fine," Liss grumbled, hanging up and sauntering around the bar, locating her bag and keys.

Liss tiptoed to the door, stalling to catch the King's announcement. Since Liss's mum died four years earlier, she always responded to her demanding grandma when she called, but Isla's enthusiasm about the announcement and her grandma's command she not watch it had piqued her curiosity.

Liss grabbed the edge of the door as the King said, "Nearly forty-five years ago, while I was a prince and learning about my country, I met a woman studying dance at a nearby college, and we fell in love. Our secret relationship was brief, but it broke my heart when I had to choose between her and the throne."

Everyone gawked at the television.

"After lengthy discussions," he continued, "we agreed that royal life wasn't for her and that my calling took precedence for me. However, this week, I learned that she gave birth to my child after we split. Elizabeth Mead, the woman I once loved, later became Guinevere Granger."

Isla and Steve gasped in Liss's direction as she speed-dialled her grandma, still gawking in the direction of the King.

He slowly sipped water before continuing, although his voice remained gruff, and his eyes appeared glassy. "She was my sweet Bets."

"Nana, we really have to talk!" Liss shouted down the phone as she bolted through the door.

CHAPTER TWO

A black Bentley sat outside the pub on double yellow lines. It was a joke between Isla and Liss that her grandma had friends in high places, but the King's revelation thrust that into a new light. The spring sunshine glinted off the paintwork, straining Liss's eyes, but she made out the personal number plate that shouted luxury. It was totally out of place in her dog-eared neighbourhood.

One of the back passenger windows lowered, and her nana's pinched face popped out of it. Her make-up was immaculate, as always. The years spent performing in ballet shows enabled her to draw attention to her doll-like eyes and cute button nose. She'd tried to impart her make-up skills to Liss several times, but the information never stuck. The flawless make-up and coiffured hair were the last straw. Her grandma must have spent hours perfecting her look when she should have shared crucial information.

"You have so much explaining to do. What the actual hell, Nana?" Liss cried out.

Her grandma glared at her from the open window.

"We don't have time for one of your tantrums. Get in the car, Felicity," she snapped. Liss learned her brusque manners from her grandma, although she saved them for critical pub situations to avoid offending others.

The passenger door flew open. Liss folded her arms with a humph to avoid stamping her foot. Her grandma always brought out the teenager in her. It was lucky they had so little to do with each other. Liss let her nana get away with her behaviour to keep her only family happy in case she was left with no one. The door wasn't closing anytime soon, and arguing with her grandma, who won every battle, was pointless, but Liss took her time climbing into the car.

She pushed up the sleeves of her hoodie as she sat in the backseat. "This is fu–"

Three pairs of eyes whipped her way.

"Get in the middle," her nana demanded with flaring nostrils. "Bear, get out and go around. I don't want to be sandwiched between you two."

The dark-haired stranger with big brown eyes and impressive broad shoulders grunted before getting out and walking around to her side. Liss barely resisted the temptation to touch his arms to check his body wasn't just padding as he climbed in beside her.

Nana Bets smoothed her classically tailored skirt, took a deep breath, and waved to an empty pavement as if she were the queen while the car pulled away from the curb.

Liss's blood boiled. "Who are these guys, and where the bloody hell did you get a Bentley?"

Bear's body pressed against hers. He widened his thighs, forcing hers to close. There wasn't enough space for his hulking body and certainly not enough to mansplay— the audacity of the guy.

Her grandma hissed, "Less attitude from you, young lady. I will explain all later, but for now, be quiet."

Nana Bets lifted her chin and waved again. She curved her hand and smiled demurely at strangers. Liss's phone buzzed with a message from Isla.

Isla: What is going on? Did Nana Bets fuck the King? That makes you a princess or something, right?

Liss: I've no idea. She won't tell me anything. I don't know where we're going, and I've got some hot-suited man next to me.

Isla: Tell me more. Which celeb does he look like?

Typical Isla. There wasn't enough space in the tiny car to hide the phone from him and her nana, but he wasn't paying attention to her anyway. She took a surreptitious look at him from beneath her lashes.

Liss: Maybe Tom Hardy, but when he was younger and without a full beard. He's kinda hot if you like that sort of thing.

Which Liss secretly did even though both her exes were like preppy perfection with button-down shirts and smart jeans. Bear's thighs widened further.

Isla: Would you fuck him?

Liss looked again. The stranger was more likely to feature in her unshareable fantasies than he was to get a right swipe from her. He stared straight ahead, oblivious to what she was typing.

> Liss: God, no. And he's a dickhead. He keeps mansplaying. He probably has a small dick, but he's trying to pretend he has a footlong.

"I'll take that." Bear snatched her phone. His voice was so low it thrummed through the car.

"The hell you will! Give me my phone back." Liss tried to grab it, but Bear slid it into his inside pocket. Had he seen what she'd typed?

"Nana," she implored, "tell the man with a stupid name to give me my phone."

"No, Felicity," her nana said sharply before resuming her wave.

Liss opened her mouth, but Nana silenced her with a pointy finger. Instead, Liss studied Bear with a glare. He was big, the sort of man that little guys wanted to fight to prove something. His suit fitted his body perfectly, gripping every muscle pressing against her. The tailored outfit that displayed a subtle nod to wealth highlighted his biceps and trunk-like thighs. Liss sensed he wasn't comfortable in it but couldn't put her finger on why.

"I want my phone back." She needed to keep Isla updated with her destination. She fixed him with a scowl, but he stared straight ahead. Adrenaline rushed through her limbs, and her fingers tingled. Although she'd never had a sibling, much to her disappointment, she'd learnt via Isla and Steve how to annoy those close to you. "Are you a naturist, Bear? Is that why they call you Bear, Bear? Is it actually spelt B-A-R-E?"

But her digs hit his vast muscles and pinged off. She was still in fight-or-flight from the stress of the morning. Her nana's attitude and unanswered questions made her jittery, and she poked his thigh with her fingers. Her chipped blue nail varnish was bright against his dark suit. Each prod met resistance. Not only did he have thick muscles, but his mansplaying thighs were taut as if he was tensing. She swallowed the saliva building up in her mouth.

Liss gritted her teeth against a sigh. She was supposed to be getting to him and not vice versa. Was it his muscles, the deep voice that climbed into her body, or her existing annoyance? Damn Isla for making her consider if she'd fuck him. The attraction freaked her out. Her hands were clammy, for goodness sake. She sighed dramatically, making the wisps of her hair falling from her ponytail jump in the air. She'd always crushed on big men with strapping bodies that could throw a woman around a bedroom. Not that she'd experienced it herself, but it was on her fantasy list. Aches pulsed in her belly, and sweat beaded the back of her neck. The guy was pissing her off, and she wanted a reaction from him.

"Is the naturist thing why you're uncomfortable in a suit, Bear?"

Still nothing.

"So that's a yes then, Bear. Do you know where we're going? Give me my phone back, Bear." Every time she said his name, she overemphasised it. The B was like a poke.

371

Bear's only movement was widening his legs as if hinting at the package in his trousers while squishing her limbs tightly. With broad thighs and taut trousers, she couldn't stop staring, even as he disregarded her space. It turned out her message to Isla was wrong. He did look bigger than she'd suggested. But the size of his package was irrelevant. She shouldn't be attracted to this knobhead. She licked her lips and fisted her hands. Her body was intent on embarrassing her.

She side-eyed her nana, who was busy staring out the window while speaking on her mobile. In her faux upper-class accent, she was giddily telling someone called Sergio about the King's announcement. She was so involved in her conversation that she was unaware of the drama next to her. Why was she allowed her phone?

Liss needed to get her phone back and control her growing lust. If asked, she'd explain her next tactic was because, once, her mum told her after a detention, "You catch more flies with honey than vinegar." But in truth, Bear's widening thighs pressing against hers were doing things to her. She desired a reaction from him and couldn't stop herself.

"Look, Bear. Maybe we can come to a deal." She slid her hand down his thigh. His leg shuddered so subtly that she would have missed it if she hadn't touched it. Liss fought the temptation to squeeze it to get a bigger response. She was supposed to get her phone back, not seduce a stranger.

He cleared his throat, and there was a teeny twitch to his right eye as he picked up her hand and popped it back on her lap. His hand was hot and coarse, like she fantasised a night with him would be.

Liss leaned into his ear. He smelt of aftershave, something with notes of wood and citrus. She was tempted to breathe him in and imagine his scent on her skin after a night of decadence. Fuck. It was too long since she had sex. Maybe that was why she was acting so out of character.

"Okay, so I need my phone. I don't want my grandma to know why." Liss sneaked a look at her nana, but she was still engrossed in her phone call, cackling loudly.

"I'm listening," Bear grunted.

"The thing is, I sent this guy a picture of me in underwear an hour ago, and he hasn't replied," she confessed in a rush of words to the brooding stranger. She wasn't this confident with strangers, yet his impenetrable persona made her want to poke the bear.

"Does the photo include your face?" His voice was gruff, and it made her skin tingle. She added his voice to fantasies she didn't need to be embracing. Her throat dried at the idea of sharing the image with him.

"No," she replied quietly. "I never include my face, and I don't normally send underwear pics, but my potential date asked, and he's really hot, and he probably hasn't replied because—"

"I don't care how hot he is. I was asking for security reasons." He refused to make eye contact, as if she wasn't worth his attention. Seeds of anger threaded through her desire.

"Rude much?" Liss folded her arms and stared at a spot on the windscreen. Her skin heated, and she ran through everything she should say. Usually, with strangers and out of her comfort zone, she'd sink into the seat and hide away.

"And for the record," he whispered in her ear before slowly looking her up and down. Liss clenched her thighs under his inspection. "If he hasn't replied to an underwear picture within five minutes, he doesn't fancy you."

Again, she was reminded that he was too big for the back seat when the driver took a corner too quickly and his entire body pressed into hers. She avoided the need to release the moan tickling her tongue. Liss shifted, which made his thigh slide against hers. She stilled suddenly, processing his words. How dare he suggest the guy didn't fancy her. But the statement gripped her fears about her Tinder match, who hadn't appeared as keen as she hoped and bruised her further. Bear had no right to say that to her. She hissed, "He's busy, and he's working—"

"I don't care what he's doing." Bear's voice was like thick, sweet honey, and his breath as he leaned in close made the hairs on her skin rise. "Once, my fuck buddy sent me a photo of her in a couple of dresses. They weren't fancy, but she wanted help to decide what to wear before seeing me. I excused myself from a meeting, feigning that it was an urgent work issue. Then I called her immediately and told her what I would do to her in my favourite of her dresses while she played with herself in the changing room. I only returned to my meeting when she came from my words. Her moaning climax made me hard as a rock. And I have a big rock."

Oh shit. He'd seen her messages to Isla.

His dick juddered as if remembering, and Liss fisted her hands, sinking her nails into her palms. The pain from her nails in her skin and the silver ring that dug into her flesh was almost satisfying. Anger and arousal blistered as she imagined his thick London accent telling her to touch him while he stroked between her thighs. Liss shifted awkwardly in her seat. *Don't let him in your head.*

Bear leaned in again, and his scent filled her once more. Her whole body quivered. Her fantasies were suddenly more vivid, filling with colour as she memorised every aspect of him. His full lips parted. "If your date hasn't replied by now, then bin him off, because he doesn't want you. And buy better underwear, because that must have been a shit photo for him not to respond even now."

Anger won, and she snapped back, "Fuck off. I looked great. I'll show you."

"No, thanks and you're not getting your phone back. Besides, the last thing I want is to see you like that."

Liss reared away from him, but there wasn't enough space. Her lips were tight, and her face burned.

"I've got to go, Sergio. My granddaughter is being a drama queen." She hung up the phone and handed it to Bear. "Stop wriggling, Felicity," her nana reprimanded, making the fire in Liss's cheeks from Bear's insult grow further. Her nana reached up to touch Liss's hair. "And do something about your hair. You look like you work in a pub."

Liss batted her hands away as her insides flamed. "I do work in a pub."

"Yes, but not as a cleaner."

Bear chuckled, and Liss glowered, but he smirked before mumbling something towards the window.

Liss rallied at Bear. "Is it 'have a go at Liss' day? And you still haven't answered my questions. I don't know where we're going or why you're talking to yourself, Mr. Meathead."

"We're here," the suited stranger in the front passenger seat announced. Camera flashes penetrated the windows from outside the car as they slid through a set of gates, and the driver spoke to someone from his open window.

"Where's h—" But she was cut off by the front passenger getting out and opening the door for her nana. Bear had said earlier that he needed her phone for security reasons, but she'd been too distracted by his body to ask what he meant.

Bear dived out his door before holding it for Liss. She huffed as she slid across the seat and climbed out. He offered her his hand, but she ignored it, instead sticking up her middle finger at him. At his chuckle, she barely resisted the temptation to claw out his eyes.

"The ladies are out of the car. We're coming in now," he said with a quiet grunt.

"Who are you talking to?" she snarled. Bear pointed to his earpiece with a roll of his eyes.

Everyone was rushing around the car, noises coming from all angles. Strangers walked out of what appeared to be an old building into the courtyard before them.

Questions about the past and present flooded her consciousness. Her ears pounded, and she planted her feet firmly on the ground. "I refuse to go anywhere until someone tells me what's happening. I've had enough of being forced here and there. Someone tell me something, or I'm going back to my pub. And you"—Liss jabbed a digit at Bear—"you give me my bloody phone, or I'm coming for it myself."

She reached into his jacket, but he wrapped his hands around her wrists with lightning-quick reflexes and pinned them mid-air. Her legs quaked, and her skin blistered as arousal filled her veins. *Why does that do it for me?*

"I will pick you up if I have to," he grunted. "There's very little stopping me from throwing you over my shoulder and taking you to the—"

"I can't apologise enough," a male voice called out in the classiest accent she'd ever heard. Even that couldn't stop the heat burning between her thighs at the idea of being popped over Bear's shoulder. It was so caveman, and yet fuck, it was hot. None of the preppy guys from her past would have considered it, let alone dared to do it. "The secrecy is all my fault, darling Felicity."

Liss spun and gasped loudly. She was in the presence of King Archibald.

The King opened his arms, and a measured smile covered his face. "Please come in and have coffee with my family, Miss Granger, and I will explain everything. And security, unhand her. Felicity Granger is a princess now."

GO COOK YOURSELF PLAYLIST

Ego – The Saturdays

Choose Your Fighter – Ava Max

Sweet Like Chocolate – Shanks & Bigfoot

Christmas Tree Farm – Taylor Swift

The Only Exception – Paramore

Sunshine – Gabrielle

In Your Car – Kenickie

Ready to Go – Republica

She's Electric – Oasis

Golden Hour – Kacey Musgraves

Free – Calvin Harris, Ellie Goulding

Starving – Hailee Steinfeld, Grey, Zedd

Kite – Benjamin Ingrosso

Cut to the Feeling – Carly Rae Jepsen

All I Want for Christmas Is You – Mariah Carey

Running – Norah Jones

Someone Out There – Rae Morris

L-O-V-E – Nat King Cole

ACKNOWLEDGEMENTS

I want to give a special mention to my dog Charlie, who inspired Cookie. He is a bundle of floof who sits with me when I edit and always brings joy, even on the darkest days.

To my husband, who checks a lot of my work, listens to me talk endlessly about writing and content, and never gets frustrated, even when I say, "Five more minutes" when we both know it will be thirty.

Elizabeth Holland, Kathryn Kincaid, and Sarah Smith are the most insightful, patient and understanding beta readers I know. I'm the luckiest person, and I'm grateful to them for all that they do to help me. All three of them have fantastic romance books that you need to read.

An extra thanks to Kathryn Kincaid, who is an excellent beta reader, my biggest cheerleader, and sounding board. Without her, I'd still be stuck on my third book, unsure how to improve, market or understand the whole process.

Thank you to Joanne Machin, a world-class editor whose comments transform my writing into something perfect for readers. Her messages also make me smile.

I can't begin to explain how lucky I am to have the readers I do. To those just discovering me, I hope one day I will write your favourite book boyfriend. And to those who have been with me since the beginning, a billion thank yous. I can't believe where we are now after all these years.

To irdeinfierno and AveryDaisyBookDesign, who designed my book cover, I am grateful for your skills, patience and kindness. And Cookie, the dog, is perfect.

And a huge thank you to friends and family whose support, cheerleading and love have got me this far. I don't know what I'd be doing if it wasn't writing, but I'm so glad all of you are making this possible.

ALSO BY REBECCA CHASE

Head Over Feels: An enemies to lovers steamy sports romance (The Bulls Rugby Series Book 1)

Stalling in Love: A steamy opposites attract romance (The Bulls Rugby Series Book 2)

Regally Binding: An enemies to lovers bodyguard romance (Closest Protection Series Book 1)

Occupational Hazard: An Anthology of Spicy Workplace Stories

Keep in Touch: A sweet coming-of-age love story

Rebecca Chase is featured in the following anthologies

Best Women's Erotica of the Year, Volume 4

Erotic Teasers: a Cleis anthology

COMING SOON

Start Your Engines: A spicy brother's best friend enemies to lovers sports romance (Coulter Formula One Racing Team Series Book 1) – dual POV, 1st person. **Out 14th March 2025.**

Once a promising racing driver, Senna Coulter must revive her family's failing racing team, but her past is haunted by a crash caused by Connor Dane—her first crush, nemesis and brother's best friend.

Connor was a playboy racing driver with the world at his feet, but now he's forced to join Coulter Racing Team. No one knows that Connor is scared to drive. How can he work under the woman who hates him, especially as he used to have secret feelings for her?

With Senna's family desperate to protect her, Connor fighting with his teammate, and loneliness overwhelming her, Senna loses hope. On top of that, it seems her crush on Connor never went away.

As months pass and the team starts to implode, Senna learns what really happened on the day of her crash and how Connor needs her. But can the dangerous racing driver and her have more than a friendship, and what happens when the man she refused to have anything to do with becomes the man she can't live without?

Fake A Chance On Me: A fake dating sports romance (The Bulls Rugby Series Book 3)

Closest Protection Series Book 2: Strike's and Millie (Title TBC): A second chance, friends to enemies to lovers bodyguard romance

Cloud Family Series Book 2: Flora and…

About Rebecca Chase

Rebecca Chase is an English rose and a pocket rocket with a taste for drama, romance, spice and love. She adores writing, whether it's a short story with unexpected passion or a novel that takes you through the ups and downs of a blossoming relationship. She's always looking for everyone's next book boyfriend. When it comes to her stories, you can guarantee there will be romance, there will be mind-blowing sex, and, most of all, there will be love that lasts a lifetime. You'll be desperate for more while aching for a happy ever after.

CONNECT WITH REBECCA

Website - www.rebeccahchase.com

Twitter - twitter.com/rebeccahchase

Facebook - www.facebook.com/RebeccaHChaseAuthor

Tiktok - @rebeccachaseauthor

Instagram and Threads – rebeccahchase

Goodreads - 15019280.Rebecca_Chase

Printed in Dunstable, United Kingdom